REDEEMING LIBERTY

A NOVEL

REDEEMING LIBERTY

DIANE / DAVID
MUNSON

MicahHouse
media

Grand Rapids, Michigan

ISBN-13: 978-0-982535-547

ISBN-10: 0-982535-546

Scripture quotations, unless otherwise indicated, are taken from the HOLY BIBLE, NEW INTERNATIONAL VERSION®. NIV®. Copyright ©1973, 1978, 1984 by International Bible Society. Used by permission of Zondervan. All rights reserved.

This is a work of fiction. Names, characters, places, and incidents either are the product of the authors' imaginations or are used fictitiously. The authors and publishers intend that all persons, organizations, events and locales portrayed in the work be considered as fictitious.

Printed in the United States of America
16 15 14 13 12 11   7 6 5 4 3 2 1

DEDICATION

To the countless men, women, and children of Sudan, who were taken by invaders and sold into slavery. To the many children who fled in advance of invading armies in Sudan and struggled to survive in refugee camps prior to arriving in the United States. To Debora, Deng, Jiech and Rebecca who assimilated into American culture, completed their education, then entered seminary training with the commitment to share their love of Jesus by returning to Sudan.

ACKNOWLEDGMENTS

It is one thing to write a novel. It's quite another to see that novel take the form of a book to hold and enjoy. We thank Micah House Media and those supporting them for assembling *Redeeming Liberty* into the book we delight in promoting and think you will enjoy reading. Thank you, Pamela Guerrieri, for your editorial adjustments to what we created, and to Ginny McFadden for creatively making our story fit between the covers. Once again, Randy Groft has exceeded our expectations with a beautiful cover design. We are grateful to M.D. Van De Mae, M.D., for her expert opinions regarding medical issues.

ABOUT THE AUTHORS

ExFeds, Diane and David Munson write High Velocity Suspense novels that reviewers compare to John Grisham. The Munsons call their novels "factional fiction" because they write books based on their exciting and dangerous careers.

Diane Munson has been an attorney for more than twenty years. She was a Federal Prosecutor in Washington, D.C., and also served the Reagan Administration, appointed by Attorney General Edwin Meese, as Deputy Administrator of the Office of Juvenile Justice and Delinquency Prevention. She worked with the Justice Department, the U.S. Congress, and the White House on policy and legal issues. More recently she has been in a general law practice.

David Munson served as a Special Agent with the Naval Investigative Service (now NCIS), and U.S. Drug Enforcement Administration over a 27-year career, where as an undercover agent he infiltrated international drug smuggling organizations. In that role he traveled with drug dealers, met their suppliers in foreign countries, helped fly their drugs to the U.S., then feigned surprise when shipments were seized by law enforcement. Later his true identity was revealed when he testified against the group members in court. While assigned to DEA headquarters in Washington, D.C., David served two years as a Congressional Fellow with the Senate Permanent Subcommittee on Investigations.

As they travel to research and cloister to write, they thank the Lord for the blessings of faith and family. David and Diane Munson are collaborating on their next novel.

www.DianeAndDavidMunson.com

GLOSSARY

Agency   Slang for Central Intelligence Agency

CIA   Central Intelligence Agency of the U.S.

Company   Slang for Central Intelligence Agency

DIA   Defense Intelligence Agency of the U.S.

DST   Directorate of Science and Technology—Division within CIA

FBI   Federal Bureau of Investigation

ICE   Immigration Customs Enforcement

IED   Improvised Explosive Device

Institute   Slang name for Israel's Intelligence agency—Mossad

MiG   Russian fighter jet

Mossad   Hebrew word meaning "Institute" for Israeli Institute for Intelligence and Special Operations

NCS   National Clandestine Services (CIA's foreign spying activities)

NIH   National Institutes of Health

PCR   Polymerase Chain Reactor—Laboratory method for analyzing disease

Skip Pierce Alias used by CIA agent Bo Rider

S300   Russian Surface to Air Missiles

TOPOL–M   Russian Intercontinental Ballistic Missile

WMD   Weapons of Mass Destruction

1

Dawn Ahern couldn't have dreamed of a more picturesque afternoon for a May wedding. Lofty breezes played Cupid with her warm cheeks, ruffling her hair. Surely a master painter had dipped the Potomac River gold and crimson for the occasion. But neither the shimmering water nor gently rolling green hills meant anything to her.

Everyone was inside, but not the most important man. Dawn fought back fear something terrible had happened to him. She hurried on her silver pumps toward the glass doors of Grace Church, stopping to gaze down Lyon Street, expecting to see his car come roaring up any moment. Her emotions spiked—he was nowhere to be seen.

She shielded her eyes against the bright sun, straining to see beyond the corner. Fingering the white rose that adorned her long black hair, Dawn didn't know what to do. Sounds of quiet music from inside the sanctuary drifted past. She must go in!

Dawn yanked open the door, and in spite of apprehension bubbling inside her, she glided into the narthex where the sweet smell of roses was overpowering. Red and violet light streamed through stained glass windows, showcasing the altar at the end of a carpeted aisle. Everything was beautiful, yet nothing was right. Where was Griff Topping?

Family and close friends jostled in narrow wooden pews, trading whispers, and Dawn caught a snippet: "The groom's not here." Then a powerful hand seized her shoulder. "You do look stunning."

Her heart quickening, Dawn whirled to face Griff, the man she loved.

"Why are you so late?" she asked, no joy lifting her smile.

Did he have second thoughts about being here?

"A bank robbery kept me up all night," Griff grumbled, blowing out an uneven sigh. "I'm beat, but glad I made it. Where do you want me?"

He leaned over, planting a welcome kiss on her cheek. To quiet her beating heart, she playfully nudged him away.

"It's bad luck to see the bride before the wedding. That also goes for bridesmaids."

The glass door behind them swished open. In waltzed the bride, holding up her snow-white gown. Dawn's friend from the office, Stephanie Huddleston, seemed to float on air. Alert to her duty, Dawn bent down, adjusting the designer gown's satin train.

When she straightened, Stephanie snatched her brother's arm. CJ Huddleston lingered next to his sister, his furrowed brow a curious mix of worry and doubt. But his peculiar reaction didn't surprise Dawn; Stephanie had confided at the bridal shower that CJ opposed her marrying Leonard, a man she'd dated for only two months.

Dawn snatched Griff's hand, seeking to brighten the gloom surrounding the bridal party. "Stephanie, this is Griff, who I've told you so much about."

A shadow darted across CJ's face. As Griff stepped aside to make room for the bride, he banged his leg against a table. He grimaced, but managed to shake Stephanie's hand. "It's an honor to see Dawn's friend get married."

Stephanie's eyes sparkled with delight, but her brother flashed Griff a defiant stare, sputtering, "Dawn mentioned you. We don't appreciate FBI agents around here."

Dawn swallowed a terse retort. The Commonwealth attorney for Elizabeth County seemed only too happy to show off his famous temper, a perfect match to his flaming copper hair. CJ also nurtured a consuming desire to occupy the Governor's mansion—no secret to those in the know in northern Virginia.

CJ's probing green eyes locked onto hers. Despising the heat of his gaze, Dawn lowered her eyes, elbowing Griff in the side. "You should take your seat. Where's Wally?"

"Tying his shoes in the hotel room when I left." Griff intertwined her fingers in his, lowering his voice. "Wally's started calling me Dad."

Dawn held his eyes, knowing this must be important to him. Griff had no children of his own. She longed to spend precious time alone with him, but with CJ looming, she revealed none of those dreams simmering in her heart.

Instead, she said, "Since both his parents were killed in Sudan, I'm glad Wally has you."

"I ran ahead to be alone with you. I wonder if later—"

The pianist began playing *Pachelbel's Canon.*

"I need to start down the aisle. We'll talk later," Dawn whispered, her fingers resting on Griff's arm.

"Topping," CJ said, clearing his throat, "do you mind getting out of the way?"

Griff stalked off, selecting the pew in the very last row. Dawn smoothed her nerves and stepped down the carpeted aisle in perfect timing to the music. She passed Griff, her heart reaching out to him. She beamed, hoping he'd treat her to a smile in return. When he did, her heart went wild.

Though his lips were partially hidden by his moustache, she knew the wide grin was meant for her. She made it the rest of the way down the aisle, walking carefully in her pointed high heels, until she found herself standing by a wooden altar carved to resemble a cross.

Dawn's eyes traveled to Griff, but he failed to meet her gaze. Her spirits sank. She'd so looked forward to enjoying this special day with him; now he seemed mired in his own world, probably thinking about that case he'd spoken of. Would he ever leave work behind and spend carefree time with her? Not likely, she thought, eying the tips of her shoes.

When she'd transferred to the Federal Probation Office in Alexandria, Virginia, she couldn't wait to live closer not only to her son Brian, a cadet at Virginia Military Institute, but also to Griff. Only life hadn't worked out according to her plan. She and Griff rarely saw each other because of his constant travels for the FBI.

The pastor's wife, Laurie Nebo, struck triumphant chords on the piano, providing a melodious accompaniment to Stephanie's march down the aisle. But then, Dawn watched, perplexed, as the bride stopped suddenly, halfway to the altar.

What was going on? Had CJ forbidden her to marry? Although Laurie kept playing *Here Comes the Bride*, the bride was not coming.

WALLY SCOOTED FROM THE ROOM at the Patriot's Inn, almost closing the door behind him but not latching it. Where was his room card? He felt in his trouser pockets, but came up empty. Concern thudded against his chest.

When Griff had left, he'd yelled for Wally to get a move on. He should have gone with Griff. His large hands flew to his suit jacket pocket. Yes! There was the thin card, right where he'd put it.

His mind was so forgetful on this trip. All he could think of was Liberty, his girlfriend back in Sudan. He tugged the door tightly and rushed down the steps, his lanky legs enjoying the expensive fabric rubbing against his skin. He had never worn a suit before. And he owed it all to Griff, who had driven him to J.C. Penney's the day before, wanting Wally to look spiffy for his talk at Dawn's church.

He practically ran through the lobby, which was decorated with small American flags and paintings of former presidents, shoving his fingers between his neck and the collar. How would he make it for hours with a tie nearly strangling him?

His hand hit the door just as a woman called from behind the desk, her yellow hair fluffed over her eyes. "You look suited up for church. How come? Today's Saturday."

"I'm late for a wedding," Wally said, checking his watch.

"Are you the groom?"

She smiled as if she were happy for him. Wally pushed open the shiny glass door to the street, saying over his shoulder, "They are friends of my Dad."

Just calling Griff by that name warmed Wally inside. Griff had befriended Wally at work—Rob's deli near Washington, D.C. Now Griff was his family. Both Wally's mother and father had died in Walu during Sudan's civil war. Once he married Liberty, she, too, would be part of his family.

A whistle flying from Wally's lips—life was good and soon would be better—he picked up the pace, afraid he would not reach the church on time. A police car screeched to a stop by the curb. Wally slowed his pace, but felt confident that, in his business attire, the police could want nothing from him.

"Hey, you! Stop!"

The voice held such force that Wally spun to see who had yelled. A uniformed policeman marched toward him, waving both hands fiercely. Wally was already late and had no time to talk, so he kept going.

"I said stop!"

Maybe Griff had arranged for the officer to drive him to the church, he thought. So Wally strode over to the officer saying, "You must know my dad."

Unlike the clerk at the hotel, the police officer acted stiff and unfriendly.

"Get your hands on top of your head."

"What did I do wrong?"

"I said get 'em up!" He glared up at Wally, looking angry in his black uniform with his cheeks growing red and puffing out like a poisoned fish.

At six foot, four inches, Wally towered over the officer, who barely reached Wally's shoulders. He raised his arms above his head, but the officer pushed Wally's elbows.

"Keep those arms high."

He grabbed Wally's suit coat, pulling open one side and then the other.

"What's your name, Stretch?"

Wally respected the law, although his college friend's had complained about a police officer's sour attitude toward black men.

"I am Wally Manja, sir."

"Let me see your driver's license."

Wally reached for his back pocket, but the officer barked, "Not so fast. Turn around and show me your backside."

Getting scared, Wally pressed both hands on his head, turning halfway around. The officer lifted his suit coat and Wally wondered what he was looking for in his back pockets.

"Okay, I see you ditched your gun. Get out your driver's license and face me."

Wally did as the officer demanded and quickly handed over his license.

"You lied about being Wally," the officer scowled. "Says here your name is Rumbek Manja."

Sweat beaded on Wally's forehead. He needed Griff!

"I was born in Sudan, but came to this country as an orphan when I turned sixteen. The relief agency had me choose an American-sounding name. I picked Wally because my village is Walu. My real name is still Rumbek Manja."

The officer glared at the photo on the license, then into Wally's eyes.

"Where you goin' all slicked up?"

"A wedding. The church is two blocks that way."

Wally pointed down the street, but the officer's eyes didn't follow. Instead, he tilted his head, looking Wally over from head to toe.

"There's no black church nearby. I bet you ran from the Night Owl to this inn and got dressed up, nice like." He nodded toward Wally's pockets. "Where's your gun?"

"I don't have one."

"Pull out your pockets. Let's see what you've got on you."

Wally's knees started wobbling. Maybe this was why his friend did not like the police. Though he had done nothing wrong, Wally pulled out the pockets. His room card fell to the pavement along with a wad of bills—single dollars plus fives and tens. The officer snatched these up, stuffing the money in his own front pocket. He clapped Wally on the shoulder, nodding toward the roof.

"Assume the position."

Confused, Wally just stood there.

"Don't play dumb with me." The officer wrenched Wally's hand to the roof of the car. "Put your other hand up there and spread your feet apart."

The officer's way of running his hands around Wally's back and inside his suit jacket shook him and he was unprepared for the policeman roughing up his legs.

"Night Owl clerk says you stole her cash. We're finding out at the station."

Wally's heart banged fast, like a drum. What a terrible mistake! The officer must think he was someone else, someone who stole money. Wally never took anything that did not belong to him, not even when he was starving in the refugee camp.

"Please, I must get to the church."

"Shut your mouth."

The policeman pushed him toward the cruiser. Wally fell, banging his chest against the roof. Pain collided with his breastbone. Before he regained his footing, the officer yanked Wally's other hand behind his back. He tugged Wally's arms backwards and slammed metal handcuffs around his wrists so hard that intense pain shot to his brain. Wally's head throbbed.

The officer shoved Wally and his head struck the car's roof. Bright lights flashed. His body went limp and he collapsed to the curb, where the officer kicked him again and again. Wally knew if he cried out, it would make the officer angrier.

The policeman forced Wally into the back seat—lifting his long legs and stuffing them in a small area where they didn't fit. Terrible pains cramped in his body as he half-lay, half-crouched in that seat. The car door slammed behind him. Wally flinched, feeling all alone in the world.

2

Back at Grace Church, Dawn shifted on her flimsy sandals, uncomfortable hearing Stephanie's fever-pitch voice as she debated with CJ, halfway down the aisle. Why couldn't the bride's brother act civilly at his sister's wedding?

Griff fidgeted in the last pew, clutching something in his hands. Stephanie tugged her brother's arm, practically pulling him down to the altar. Dawn's heart ached for her. Pastor Nebo adjusted his tie, looking bewildered next to the best man, whose hands were thrust in his pockets. Dawn realized why CJ had stopped Stephanie. The groom, Leonard Twining, was nowhere in sight.

The best man glanced around awkwardly, questions written all over his face. Murmurs spread through the guests like smoke in a wildfire. Dawn lunged at CJ.

"What've you done with Leonard?"

"He must've gotten cold feet."

"How can that be? Leonard loves Stephanie."

"I warned my sister not to marry him," CJ snapped, anger flashing in his green eyes. "He's a slacker who won't amount to anything."

Stephanie's bottom lip trembled and she fought back tears. Dawn seized CJ's arm.

"Call Leonard. Something is terribly—"

Loud thumps interrupted Dawn's plea and she glimpsed a man dashing past the choir loft, windswept hair dangling in his eyes. Leonard's torn white jacket was stained with mud. He was full of apologies.

"My truck broke down. I punctured a tire. Spare's flat. I ran all the way here. Forgive me?"

Dawn drew in a breath, wondering what Stephanie would do in her expensive gown before one hundred guests. Would she say her vows? If only Leonard could wipe the smudge off his face. Dawn carried only white roses; she wished she had a tissue for the groom. With one loving stroke, Stephanie rubbed the grime away from Leonard's cheek with her fingers.

"It's all right, Lenny. I'm marrying you, not your truck."

As if she'd knighted her man with a sword, he squared his shoulders and took his place beside her. Dawn cherished a smile in her heart. *Good for you, Stephanie. You've won him for life.* She vowed her wedding wouldn't be marred by such antics—if she ever remarried.

The white-haired pastor finally began with a prayer, which lasted only moments. When Dawn opened her eyes, she saw that Stephanie smiled through tears cascading down her pale cheeks. Leonard's grin reached across his sunburned face.

"Who has the honor of presenting this bride to her groom?"

Stephanie's only sibling—both of their parents having passed from the earth—hung his head.

"Guess I do," CJ muttered.

With a flurry of moving arms, he released his sister into a future life with a man he obviously didn't approve of. Dawn suspected CJ would try to bend her will to his as he did with judges and juries. He had even attempted his tyrannical ways on Dawn, and though she'd refused to go out with him, the Commonwealth's attorney kept pestering her to change her mind.

Stephanie handed Dawn her bouquet and grabbed Leonard's hand. Pastor Nebo opened a Bible.

"The Apostle Paul says love is patient and kind. Pure love, the kind we find in Jesus, is not easily angered and keeps *no* record of wrongs."

Snickers rippled through the audience. Stephanie smiled at her soon-to-be husband, her face glowing. Dawn wondered if Wally had slipped in. Not daring to turn and look, she concentrated on the ceremony.

"Love always perseveres." Pastor Nebo's voice grew serious. "Stephanie and Leonard, you had a momentary trial this afternoon, but take this important truth into all the days of your marriage: Love *never* fails."

Tears sprang to Dawn's eyes. Though it seemed like another lifetime, she and her late husband, Bert, had shared a forever love with each other. Could she ever love Griff as completely when he didn't share her faith? It might be kinder to let him find another relationship where he'd be more comfortable, but her heart cried no, she couldn't. Not yet.

Dawn suspected Griff worked so hard as an FBI agent because he still pined for Sue, his late wife, who had died young after battling cancer. A ragged sigh escaped her lips. Pastor Nebo must have heard, because his kind eyes flitted to hers and he spoke more rapidly. Dawn ventured a look at Griff, whose tie hung loose around his shirt collar. His muscles were contracting in his handsome face.

He seemed tense. When Dawn didn't see Wally, her fingers coiled around the rose.

As Laurie Nebo softly played *Amazing Grace*, Police Chief Dalton banged the doors open. Like a great gust of wind, he vaulted down the aisle, his huge gun belt shaking at his side. He bounded straight for CJ Huddleston's seat. Dawn froze. Would the chief haul Leonard away to stop the wedding?

CJ scowled fiercely at Chief Dalton, gesturing toward the back. Dawn's instincts as a federal probation officer put her on high alert and she expected sudden disaster. Griff, too, seemed poised to act.

Pastor Nebo signaled his wife, and Laurie began singing in a beautiful contralto voice, "I once was lost, but now am found, was blind but now I see."

CJ strutted up the aisle alongside Dalton, whose black uniform brought a sinister oppression to the flower-decked church, smothering the joy of Stephanie's wedding. Dawn watched, transfixed, as CJ and Dalton stopped next to Griff. When his face blanched in horror, fear seized her. She gripped the rose, fighting to keep her hands from shaking.

Laurie ended her hymn. Letting nothing hinder their union, Stephanie and Leonard each touched separate candles to one unity flame. Griff lurched from the pew and, without glancing Dawn's way, fled the church with CJ and Chief Dalton hot on his heels. Dawn desperately wanted to follow, but wouldn't injure her friend, who'd survived enough heartache during this ceremony.

Knees trembling and heart fluttering, Dawn kept her place, silently beseeching the One who sustained life and moved mountains.

3

Wally groped along the dimly lit cell, stumbling over something. He caught himself on the wall.

"Ouch!" he cried, wrenching his wrist.

"Quit yer whining," yelled the man he'd tripped over.

Wally steadied his body. Sliding a hand down the wall, he tried sitting down, which only worsened the shooting pains in his lower back. His head felt like it had been smashed by a hammer. He dropped his face into his hands. All his dreams of graduating from college and earning the bride price were shattered.

Griff would disown him when he learned of the arrest. Liberty would not come to America as his wife. His mind scrambled for comfort, but found only sorrow colliding with his hurting places. Tears pressed from his eyes. Wally swiped them away, not wanting the angry man to see him cry.

A terrifying thought tormented him. He would be forced back to Sudan, where militants had already killed his entire family. Wally shifted his legs, trying to ease the pain on the hard cement. He saw no way out, but maybe God did.

The only cellmate kicked Wally's legs and he keeled over.

"God, help me!"

"Shut up!" The man leapt to his feet, raising a fist to Wally's face. "Quit talking, or I'll bust yer mouth."

Wally shuddered, stuffing words inside. At a refugee camp in Ethiopia, a crazed man had killed another man with a long knife outside Wally's tent. Images of the dead man's blood-stained shirt rose in horror before him. He slammed his eyes shut, his heart pounding in his chest. All grew quiet. Finally, the man angled his body an inch away.

"If you mention religious crap again, you'll be sorry."

Wally peered through one eye, saying nothing.

"I warn you, it ain't pretty."

The man's jeans and baggy shirt were covered with holes. He stalked off and from a corner, trained an evil eye on Wally. Surely if Wally closed his eyes, the man would take his life.

Born to loving parents in Sudan, Rumbek Manja had fled the terrors of war and evil men. Here in the cell, Wally Manja thought only of his dad, Griff, coming to save him. What if Griff did not find him for a long time?

Wally prayed like never before, not just for himself, but also for the man wearing the ragged clothes. His prayers were the silent kind. Wally did not want to heap any more trouble on his hurting head.

HIS INSIDES WERE BOILING. Blistering anger propelled Griff beside Chief Dalton, who was a few inches shorter and labored to keep pace with Griff's long strides.

"The clerk called 911," Dalton huffed in short bursts. "Listen to the tape yourself. A black man wearing a gray hoodie stole every buck in her drawer."

"I bet Wally didn't have on a hoodie when your officer stopped him."

"Course not. He'd already changed."

"What time did the clerk call 911?"

"I'm not exactly sure. It'll be on the tape."

Was there even a tape? Had a clerk really made any call? Griff mentally punched holes in the paper-thin evidence, finding it difficult to hear the chief imply Wally was a criminal. He pressed his lips closed to avoid aggravating the chief. If Griff came off as a "know-it-all" FBI agent, the locals would dig in their heels all the more. A wiser course would be to squeeze every bit of info from Dalton before pulverizing the guy.

"My officer caught the robber, a lanky black guy, running from the Patriot's Inn. He's a smart one, alright."

"Your officer is experienced, then?"

"Ryan? Nah, he's still learning," Dalton snickered. "I mean the robber we caught. By the time Ryan stopped him on the street, he'd put on an expensive suit and tie."

"Yes, the one I bought him for the wedding. Don't you think it makes sense for Wally to wear a suit and tie?"

"So he claims. Listen, Mr. Topping, Summit Ridge is a quiet place. Last year, we had one fatal car accident. Otherwise, we rout out all characters prone to violence. No murders, no robberies, and I mean to keep it that way."

Griff could almost read Dalton's mind. Being different, Wally was an interloper, so he must be blamed for the recent crime wave. Griff clenched his fists, figuring Ryan had arrested Wally for being the first black man to appear on the street.

They'd almost reached the police station and Griff still hadn't found out what these officers had on Wally.

"Besides telling Ryan about the wedding, what else did Wally say?"

"That's a good one." Dalton smacked his lips, his right hand resting on a pistol sticking out of his holster.

"When the robber told us to find his dad at the church, I sped over there, looking for a black man who's supposed to be an FBI agent." He threw Griff a knowing look. "I figured I had a con man behind bars when I found no such agent."

"You found me. I'm an FBI agent." Griff hauled out his credentials, thrusting them under Dalton's nose.

The chief bristled. "CJ already told me you were an agent."

Without breaking stride, Griff stuffed his badge and creds back in his pocket, tasting bile rising in his throat.

"What I can't figure," Dalton said as his blue eyes shifted, "is how the black guy *knew* you were here. As I said, he's smart. Probably staked out your room."

"Wally is with me. I am that young man's dad."

"You are?" Dalton slowed. "You adopted him? I mean ... uh, is his mother your wife?"

"Ever hear of the Lost Boys from Sudan?"

Dalton stopped in his tracks.

"You mean that young boy is from Africa? I know all about 'em. My sister moved to Pennsylvania. One of your *lost* boys got drunk and smashed into her house. Drove right through her living room window and nearly killed her."

"Wally is nothing like that. He will graduate from my alma mater, where he earned a scholarship. He studies hard and has a 4.0."

Griff grabbed Dalton's arm. "I consider him my adopted son. He doesn't drink alcohol or smoke. He's speaking at Grace Church before their mission trip to Sudan."

"Save your glowing story for Judge Fox, FBI man. You've got no jurisdiction here."

Dalton twisted away from Griff's grasp, launching up the steps to the police station next to the jail. Griff followed him up the concrete steps, racking his mind over how best to help Wally, whose future rested in Dalton's hands.

Did Dalton run rough shod over the town folks, throwing his weight around, chasing arrest stats to impress town council members? Or was he a naïve guy, interested in finding truth and justice more than promoting his career? Griff sure hoped he fit the latter description.

When the chief held open the station door for him, Griff accepted the gesture as a positive sign. He entered the nerve center of police headquarters—a square room fitted with two desks. A younger officer sat behind a console.

"Any new calls, Ryan?" Dalton asked, leaning against the high counter.

"No, but I picked up Elmer Callaway for fighting again." Ryan jerked a thumb over his shoulder. "He's in the cell with the robber."

"My son isn't your robber."

Griff folded his arms across his chest, ready to battle with this know-nothing officer, who looked like he'd just graduated from high school. Ryan slammed down a notebook; he held a pen at an odd angle and seemed as if he might throw the sharp end at Griff.

"Chief, I'd like to see Wally. He must be upset at being wrongfully accused."

"Wrongfully accused? The clerk identified him as the one who robbed her. It's a slam dunk case and I made it."

Ryan's deep-set eyes dared Griff to challenge him, but Griff held his tongue. Identification by the only witness might be difficult to break. He turned to Dalton.

"You promised I could talk to him."

"There's no urgency. He's not leaving my lockup anytime soon."

Dalton dug his beefy hand into a bowl of candy on the counter.

"Have a Tootsie Roll. They help me think on the sweeter things in life."

"After I visit my son."

Griff's nerves were getting the better of him in the cramped space. He swallowed his claustrophobia before it could rear up. As Dalton unrolled another piece of candy, Griff doubted Wally was even here. A ringing phone provided another delay.

Ryan snapped it up and Dalton quickly motioned Griff through a half-door separating the public from the inner workings of the station.

"Don't let him go in there," Ryan fumed.

"He's FBI. It's professional courtesy."

Griff stormed past Ryan's obnoxious glare. Okay, so the kid was upset because Griff had the guts to interfere with his well-orchestrated case. Most likely it was his first arrest. All the way around, trouble was building like a pressure cooker, which seemed ready to blow off its top.

4

Griff's heart was ripped into pieces when he saw Wally hunched on the cell floor, his jacket lapel torn and lower lip bleeding. Griff pressed himself against the bars, shocked to see blood staining Wally's white shirt collar.

"Wally, Dad's here."

"Oh!" He rose slowly to his feet, crying out as he got to his knees, but then clamped a hand over his mouth.

"I told you to shut up!"

Wally's black eyes darted to a man leaning against the bars. Dalton ignored the outburst, just folded his arms across his ample chest. As Wally shuffled toward the bars, Griff was surprised to see his shoes had no laces.

"Topping, you have five minutes."

"Alone?"

"No. I'm staying."

"You told Ryan you'd allow me to see Wally as a professional courtesy. Why not show the young officer what that really means?"

Their eyes locked for the briefest moment and Dalton's humanity shone through. A small Virginia town might be the chief's fiefdom, but Griff believed he and Dalton shared a common interest in the truth.

"Okay. I'll go review Ryan's report."

When Dalton eased out the door, returning to the station, Griff reached through the bars, trying to give Wally the best hug he could. Wally clung to him.

"Dad, I knew you would come!"

Griff dashed away tears, pulling a handkerchief from his back pocket and passing it through the bars.

"Son, how come your lip's bleeding?"

Griff now realized he considered Wally as his son, even though he hadn't formally adopted him. Wally wiped his lip, staring at the red blood on the hankie.

"Wally, we have only a few minutes. Tell me how you were hurt."

"I never told you about the boy ahead of me in the river." Wally gripped the cotton square in his large hands. "I ran for days, eating nothing. Before my eyes, a crocodile dove from the bank. Just when I thought it was going to eat me—"

His eyes pooled with tears and his voice fell to a whisper. "Dad, what the young officer did to me was not as terrible as what the crocodile did to my best friend."

Horror, mixed with rage, ravaged Griff's gut. He steadied himself against the steel bars. He'd be crazy to get arrested for assaulting a stupid twenty-something police rookie. Besides, more violence wouldn't free Wally.

"Say no more. Of course you didn't rob that store."

Wally seemed to stand straighter, gaining strength from Griff's words of support.

"Did Ryan or Chief Dalton try to make you confess?" Griff asked, shielding his lips in case a video camera was trained on them.

"He insisted I hid my sweatshirt. I told him I did not have one. He shoved me into the car, kicking me."

"Shhh!" Griff dove at the bars. "The chief's coming back. I think he's a good man. I'll ask him to protect you."

"Just before you came—" Wally looked toward his cellmate, and then shook his head. "I want to believe God will protect me, but it is hard."

God? Hadn't Ryan beaten Wally while on his way to church? What kind of God allowed that? Griff sensed, rather than heard, Dalton walk up behind him. Griff squeezed Wally's hands through the bars and took the handkerchief from Wally, showing the blood to the chief.

"Your officer was out of line. You'd better scrutinize his report carefully."

"What does that mean?"

"Ryan roughed up Wally using his foot. I'm heading to the church to talk with CJ Huddleston about setting bond. Will you ensure Wally's safety in here?"

"Do you think I wouldn't?" Dalton's hands flew to the pistol lodged on his hips. "Give me a break." But then he flinched under Griff's rock steady glare and strode to the bars.

"Show me your lip."

After looking at it, he asked Wally if he needed a bandage.

"Doesn't anyone care about me?" the unshaven inmate shouted from the corner. "I've been in this dump since before breakfast and ain't had no food."

"I do not appreciate false claims against my officer," Dalton said, blinking rapidly, as if he was dodging dust, "but I see something happened. I doubt you, an FBI agent, punched him in the face behind my back. CJ phoned and won't agree to bond until Wally's arraignment Monday morning."

"Will he let Wally go in my custody?"

"I can ask, but I've learned the hard way that CJ takes pride in being his own man. Mr. Manja, I'll get water for that lip. Follow me, Agent Topping."

"Wally, stay strong. Meanwhile, I'll try to get you released."

A sad smile flashed across Wally's battered face, haunting Griff on the way out front. He needed to rely less on his FBI instincts—his badge counted for zip here. Dalton had admitted as much.

Leaning on the counter, Griff cooled his agitation, turning his mind to how to start acting like a defense investigator. An idea came to him when Ryan said into the phone, "I'm coming right over to take your statement. Don't you dare leave the motel."

Griff snatched something from his pocket, holding it up to Ryan's skeptical eyes.

"When you searched Wally, did he have a room card? It looks like mine."

Dalton glanced over at Ryan. The lanky officer pushed his four-wheeled chair back from his desk, deftly swiveling it to face Griff and the chief.

"He did, and I insisted the manager void the key. When Mr. Huddleston is available and done giving his sister away at the church, I'm getting a search warrant for the room. Until then, it's sealed."

So Ryan had cancelled Griff's room key. Most likely, a judge would sign a warrant. Meanwhile, Griff was barred from his room. He'd forged a plan, but would it work? He leaned across the counter, determined to find out.

"How'd you like to search our room without waiting for CJ? I give my consent."

Surprise hit Ryan's squared-off face. He squinted as though Griff were trying to trick him.

"Why would you do that?"

"Simple. Searching our room is the fastest way to prove you've arrested the wrong man. Then Wally goes free."

"I dunno."

"Chief, if you assist, it won't take long."

"Let's do it." Dalton seized a wad of keys from a desk drawer. "You both go ahead and I'll call Officer Carlyle. He's working on his car engine, but he can cover things while we're at the inn."

Dalton seemed like an upfront guy. His comments reminded Griff that real folks lived and worked in this small town, which was teeming with its own problems. If only Griff could convince the chief of Wally's innocence.

GRIFF RAN TO THE CHURCH, taking long strides over the curb. The clerk had refused to let them in the room without the manager, who was still at Stephanie Huddleston's wedding. His lungs gasping for air, Griff arrived at Grace Church in time to see the bride and groom climb into a white limo. Dodging a shower of rice, he spotted Dawn alone near the steps. He raced over.

"I'm locked out of my room and need Harold Kurchner. Can you point him out?"

"Is everything all right?"

"Don't worry." Griff tenderly touched her bare arm. "I'll meet you at the reception in a bit."

"Where's Wally?" Dawn gazed beyond Griff, down the street.

"Please, I need Kurchner. He's the manager of the inn."

"Why do I sense you're keeping something from me?"

Her intense gaze never wavered. An excellent federal probation officer, Dawn rarely missed much as she tracked convicted offenders released from prison. Griff had admired the tenacity she'd shown when they'd worked on a case together—but not at this moment. He didn't want her worrying about Wally yet.

"Dawn, do you trust me?"

Her eyes met his and she nodded, gesturing toward a dour-looking man who was chatting with two women wearing hats.

"Kurchner's the guy in the bright blue shirt."

"No tie, right?"

"Right. Promise not to stand me up at the reception." Dawn arched her brows.

"I'll be there."

Griff dashed off to corner Kurchner. "I'm agent Griff Topping and need to get into my room. Chief Dalton asked me to fetch you."

"Since the chief asked," Kurchner grumbled, hitching up his pants, "but I'm giving the toast for Leonard. He's my nephew, you know."

Griff didn't know. But, it was becoming clear everyone in Summit Ridge knew each another. Maybe Kurchner also was related to the chief. When Griff mentioned Dalton's name, the manager had stiffened. Or was it his imagination?

Griff tossed aside misgivings about leaving Dawn, hustling with Kurchner back to the inn. He totally ignored the older man's nonsensical banter about Leonard's trusty old truck making him late for his own wedding.

As soon as Kurchner let Griff, along with Dalton and Ryan, into the room, he hitched up his pants. "I'm off to the reception. The yacht club's all decked out, you know."

Wally had left the room pretty neat, with their clothes hanging on metal racks and towels drying over the shower rod. Wally's Bible lay open to a passage he'd been reading. Their suitcases were zipped shut on luggage stands. Griff hauled these off, setting each on a separate queen bed.

"Chief, I'm going to the lobby while you help Ryan with the search."

Griff set off to grill the clerk, confident they'd find nothing incriminating in the room. He stepped from the elevator, sizing up a middle-aged woman behind the counter. Strands of yellow hair sagged into her eyes. Had she already made a statement to Ryan?

"Hello, ma'am. How's your day going?"

"I've stood behind this counter since six and don't get off until six."

Griff glanced at the wall clock beyond her head. Another hour. He selected a newspaper from a stack. "Heard the police made an arrest out front this morning."

"He was a nice young man and one of our guests." She turned bloodshot eyes from a computer screen, scowling.

"That must've surprised you. Know what he was arrested for?"

"He was in here for breakfast, carrying his Bible, and asking how I was, like you. Later, he walked through dressed up for a wedding. I watched him go out front, but a police car came and blocked the young man's path."

"I'm FBI." Griff flipped open his official credentials. "What else did you see?"

"Oh!" She stepped backwards, looking rattled. "I thought you were a guest."

"I'd still like to know what happened."

"It really disturbs me how that officer roughed him up like."

"Wally. His name's Wally."

"Okay. Sudden like, I saw Wally thrust his hands on top of the cruiser. That officer started searching him. I wondered if some crime occurred here at the inn."

"Miss, I'm sorry, what's your name?"

"My name tag—" She jumped, snatching her rumpled vest off the back of her stool. "Gloria Little."

"What else did you see, Gloria?"

"That officer—he's new around here and I don't know his name—handcuffed Wally's hands behind his back. He opened the rear door, pushing him in the back."

Gloria winced as if in pain.

"Are you okay?"

"Don't worry about me. It's Wally I feel for."

"I'd like to know why."

"Because when the officer pushed him, Wally's face smashed into the car." She rubbed the side of her face, showing Griff where Wally had bashed it. "It must've knocked him out, because his whole body went limp." As if on stage, her body drooped just like her hair. "Wally slumped right down on the curb."

Griff felt sick, but didn't want Gloria to guess his close relationship with Wally. He braced himself to sound like an impartial FBI man.

"Did the police officer help him get up?"

"Help him?" Gloria's arms flew above her head. "No, sir. He kicked Wally in the stomach. There's no cause for him to be so mean. Like I said, he's new around here."

Griff clenched his fists. If he'd known what Ryan had done, he never would have allowed the search. Griff could hardly contain himself, wanting to bolt upstairs and confront Ryan. He forced himself to think. Perhaps Gloria herself had a run-in with Ryan, and Wally's arrest was a chance for revenge. Then Griff remembered she said she'd never met Ryan.

"What did the officer look like?"

The phone rang, and Gloria grabbed it right away.

"Just a moment," she chimed, putting the call on hold. She lifted one hand over her head. "About an inch taller than me, but way shorter and heavier than Wally."

That sounded like Ryan.

"What did the officer do next?"

Gloria reached for the phone then stopped. "Oh! He's the same officer who came in here earlier demanding a master passkey for Wally's room. I told him he'd have to get one from Kurchner. Let me get this call. I hate leaving people hanging in dead air."

She concluded her business while Griff scratched notes on a travel brochure. Gloria hung up, getting back to what she'd seen. "Anyways, the officer pushed Wally into the back seat and drove off."

"What else?"

"The whole thing makes me sick. I need some sweet tea." She licked her lips.

Ready to tear Ryan apart, Griff folded the Summit Ridge brochure into his pocket. He leaned toward Gloria.

"Would you write down everything you told me?"

"I can do that. It's not too busy."

"But don't tell the chief we talked—at least, not yet."

Her tired eyes rounding with new life, she actually smiled. "Count on me, agent. There's plenty goes on around here I never tell anyone, not even my hairdresser."

5

When Griff knocked on his room door and Dalton swung it open, Griff did a double take. He'd executed hundreds of search warrants as an FBI agent that left homes completely disheveled, but he was totally unprepared to be on the receiving end. The bed mattress and box spring stood on edge. Bedding was crumpled and piled on the floor.

"You jailing me, too," Griff said as he pushed past Dalton, "for not keeping a tidy room?"

Ryan was making a mess of the bathroom, unfolding and tossing towels as though searching for something hidden in the folds.

"Things don't look good for your ... ah, son." Dalton gave Griff a serious look.

"You imply you found evidence of a robbery. I let you search thinking that, with you here, nothing would be planted to phony up a case against Wally."

"We found lots of singles, fives and tens, I'm afraid," Dalton said.

"Look here," Ryan said as he strutted to Wally's suitcase. "The robber stole singles, fives and ten, as well as twenties and some fifties. We've searched the whole room, but your Wally must have ditched the twenties and the fifties where we can't find 'em."

Relief filled Griff's troubled heart. The money, he could explain.

"Wally's a college kid who owns no credit card. Uses cash for everything."

"He's got three hundred dollars here in singles, fives, and tens." Dalton lifted his square jaw, pride seeping out the edges of his curled lips. "It's solid evidence. The cashier had five hundred in the cash register."

"Wally isn't your man," Griff insisted, folding his arms.

"Oh, he's our guy alright." Ryan bounced into Griff's comfort zone. "We just don't have a clue where he hid the twenties and fifties he stole."

Griff was losing the last shred of respect for Dalton and his crummy department. He palmed his moustache, searching for a way to make these locals believe the truth.

"Wally is a waiter at Rob's Deli outside Washington, D.C., and lives on tips. He doesn't have twenties and fifties because the folks leave smaller tips using ones and fives. You don't have a case. You need to let him go."

"Think so?" Ryan tossed open Griff's suitcase and, with one wild sweep, yanked out a gray hooded sweatshirt with *Redskins* emblazoned on the front.

"You're so smart, explain this."

"I don't need to explain my sweatshirt—unless maybe you think I'm the robber?"

"The clerk said the robber wore a gray hooded sweatshirt, just like this one." Dalton stuck out his lower lip and pointed at Griff's sweatshirt.

Griff's temper flared and he went eyeball to eyeball with Ryan until Dalton wedged in between the two of them. Griff slammed his suitcase shut.

"Let me save you from being embarrassed before a jury. Examine the in-store surveillance video. I'm sure it won't show a picture of Wally or a Redskins sweatshirt."

Ryan's eyes danced furtively toward Dalton. In that instant, Griff knew he'd stumbled onto something. But would the chief see reason?

"You didn't mention any video of Wally, so I suspect there isn't one. Right?"

"Ryan took a mug shot of Wally to the store clerk," Dalton spat back, "and guess what? She ID'd him faster than you can tie your shoe."

So that's how she fingered Wally.

Griff confronted Ryan. "How many other black males were in your photo spread?"

"What difference does that make?"

"Surely you know appellate courts have ruled that a witness must choose a suspect from a group of photos that are similar in age, race, and gender."

Shifting his weight from one foot to the other, Ryan dropped his defiant stare. "I didn't have any other mug shots."

Griff's anger waned as his confidence surged. He had them now.

"Before you rush to trial, tell CJ that I, the FBI agent staying with Wally, will testify that's *my* hoodie. Tell him that you have no video, and that the identifying witness saw only one photo—that of Wally Manja. I bet CJ will release Wally pronto."

He pocketed his hands. "On second thought, I suspect he'll make him stay in jail until Monday, to protect *you* from a false arrest charge."

"Not so fast." Ryan stood on his toes. "I figure Wally took your sweatshirt, robbed the store and returned the hoodie to your suitcase. I'm taking the hoodie and money as evidence."

Griff tried to slow the adrenaline pumping through his veins like lightning. If he made another wrong move, Wally's life would plunge downhill. Maybe he should hire a defense attorney. The brutal truth made his blood run cold.

"I hope CJ has more sense than you both. If you're done, maybe Chief Dalton will help me hoist the bed back onto the frame."

As they rearranged the bed, Ryan thrust his evidence into a glassine bag and prepared to leave.

"Not so fast, pardner." Griff lifted his six-foot-one inch frame. "You owe me a receipt for evidence you're taking without a warrant. I'll even sign it, since you failed to have me sign a consent search form. Otherwise, CJ will think you dropped the ball."

Ryan stalked by Griff, uttering a few choice words, the bag of evidence under his arm. It seemed the rookie cop didn't appreciate Griff's criticism of his work ethic.

Dalton grabbed the box springs. "Agent, how about a hand here— or are you too busy looking for ways to make things worse for Wally?"

Those words hit Griff in the middle of his chest. Why was he trying to prove he was the better man? That was a given.

"Chief, Wally's innocent. After what he's lived through, for this to happen—"

Griff stopped talking, setting the springs onto the frame. He lifted the mattress by himself, plunking it down with a loud thump. "It's just dead wrong."

"We'll see." Dalton tossed the blanket onto the bed in a tight ball. "Summit Ridge was a fine place until you two showed up."

Griff made an instant decision. Besides saying nothing more to these two locals, he'd find a hotel in neighboring Fredericksburg, *outside* Dalton's jurisdiction. He let the officers leave before stowing his shaving kit in his suitcase. He tucked Wally's Bible in the other case and locked their luggage in the trunk of his car. It galled him that Wally had to spend another minute behind bars.

GRIFF LEFT THE PATRIOT'S INN convinced the last thing he wanted to do was celebrate a wedding he'd barely attended. He drove down to the yacht club, careful not to press the accelerator too hard—he didn't need a speeding ticket—intending to corner the infamous CJ Huddleston. Griff tromped into the club, relieved to see Dawn dart over as if she'd been waiting for him.

She placed a hand on his shoulder. "Get into your room?"

"I got in all right."

"Where's Wally?" Looking past him, her hand didn't move. "You left him at the motel alone?"

Griff took her by the elbow, ushering her outside to the roomy deck. Her dark eyes shining in the setting sun made him forget his angst about Wally. His bottled feelings for her threatened to spill over as he stood beside her. Griff wrapped his hands around hers.

"Dawn, do you know—"

A pesky blue jay buzzed overhead and Griff ducked, the bird's chaotic call bursting their special moment. He swiped at his rumpled hair and sweating forehead.

"You're acting weird. Tell me what's going on," Dawn implored.

"The local police ... " Griff's voice broke and it was all he could do to retrieve it. "They stupidly arrested Wally, claiming he robbed a local store. I've pleaded for him," he said, searching her eyes, ready for condemnation, "but I only made things worse."

She flinched as if wounded, but her eyes held his gaze. "What can I do?"

"Reason with your friend, CJ Huddleston."

"I'm his sister's friend," Dawn shot back, tilting her head.

"You're unwilling to pave the way?"

"Don't be unfair. It's just that," Dawn eyed the railing, refusing to meet his eyes. "You don't know CJ like I do. He's a troubled man."

When she lifted her eyes, Griff spotted something he had to delve into.

"What's he done to you?"

"I should've mentioned it before. He constantly asks me out, only I'm not interested. He won't quit."

"The man's a cad."

"CJ already knows I prefer you."

Griff absorbed her words. Here on the deck, with the magnificent sunset backdrop, he longed to tell Dawn how much he cared for her. But the words wouldn't come—not with Wally bloodied and alone in jail. A shattering revelation exploded in Griff's mind.

CJ was behind this scheme. He was trying to get even with Griff for loving Dawn. CJ couldn't wrongfully accuse an FBI agent—that would derail his ambition to be governor—but a young black man made an easy target. Griff's tortured mind heaped blame onto Dawn.

"You look like a thundercloud about to let loose," she said.

"Never mind. I'll talk to CJ myself."

Griff rotated on his heels, an icy stare frozen on his face. He shut Dawn out of his turmoil, leaving her on the deck. Whatever he'd hoped for in their relationship was crushed by an intense hurt. Dawn's relationship with CJ—one she'd only admitted to under pressure—was the impetus for Wally's predicament.

Griff bore upon the hapless CJ, having no clue the attorney was well into his sixth whiskey sour. They met by the bar, which was shaped like an old schooner, and Griff let him have it with the force of an M60 tank.

"You say I've no jurisdiction. What Wally describes is a Federal civil rights violation. Unless you want Summit Ridge crawling with FBI agents by Monday morning, you'd best talk to Dalton. Will Ryan's arrest withstand scrutiny by a Federal grand jury?"

CJ lurched forward, jabbing a finger in Griff's chest. "Know thish, I never lost a case. Never. And I mean never."

His words were slurred and his pale blue eyes bloodshot, but CJ exuded the aura of a man who wouldn't run from a fight. Well, Griff wouldn't either. He reared back and was about to let loose another blast when a hand reached around his upper arm.

"Griff means there are more facts than what the police told you."

Dawn's lilting voice dissolved all tension between the two men. CJ's frown eased, but probably not for long. All might be calm in the eye of a hurricane, but great and devastating forces crouched on the other side.

CJ arched his back, gaining his full height and a few inches on Griff. *So what?* Griff thought. *He's a puny man in a giant's body.* Griff would bring the entire U.S. Justice Department down on CJ to free Wally.

"What if we talk things over tomorrow—say, after the Sudan trip meeting at Grace Church?" Dawn kept a steady hand on Griff's arm.

Her wavering smile and liquid black eyes stole Griff's heart. Here she was, running interference with CJ, just as Griff asked. What a blockhead he'd been to think she'd caused CJ to target Wally. Griff pivoted his mind from the settling of scores to that Sudan trip. He'd totally forgotten she was going.

"Fine. Shee you then." CJ jangled his car keys.

"You're not driving."

Dawn swung her head toward Griff's as if he should prevent it.

"Try and shtop me."

"That's not a good idea, is it, Griff?" Dawn asked.

This whole line of conversation got on Griff's nerves; no way he'd climb into a car with the prosecutor and risk blowing the case for Wally. But CJ had other plans. He thrust his keys into Dawn's hands.

"Fine. You take me home."

Her somber eyes appealed to Griff. Hadn't she just complained about how the guy wouldn't leave her alone? Here was his proof. Griff slid the keys from her hands.

"Tell you what. CJ, I'll drive your car, and Dawn can follow us in hers. After that, she and I are taking flowers from the church to the hospital waiting room."

Dawn looked so pleased at his impromptu idea that Griff began to believe things would turn out okay. A guy could hope, couldn't he?

"I'll wish Stephanie and Leonard a joyous honeymoon in Hawaii," Dawn said, "and meet you both outside."

Griff trailed behind CJ, watching in amusement as he threw an awkward salute to his new brother-in-law and nearly collided with a couple dancing. Griff considered dropping the drunken lawyer on the far side of town and letting him walk home.

But he fought down his warrior instincts and eased behind the wheel of CJ's Cadillac. He wondered if Dawn would admit anything else about CJ when he finally got her alone.

6

When Dawn's alarm blared at seven the next morning, she tossed off a handmade quilt, her shoulders and neck aching from stress. Sleep had come in mere snippets. Worry over Wally huddling in jail while she slept comfortably had kept her eyes open most of the night. She pushed her legs to the floor, her mind pondering a new concern.

Griff had made things worse last night when he'd dropped an intoxicated CJ at home, choosing that moment to argue about Wally's arrest. She'd driven Griff back to the reception to get his car, but he hadn't said much. When she'd told him it hadn't been smart confronting the attorney who held Wally's future in his hands, Griff's nostrils had flared and his eyes had flashed. Dawn took the hint and said nothing more about CJ.

Griff had hopped out of her car and she'd added softly, "Come for breakfast."

"See you about nine?" Griff had hovered by her car door, peering in.

"Sounds great. We'll put together a strategy."

"But I'm not going to church," he'd said, before walking off.

She brought her mind to the present, deciding she should shower, although the cool water did nothing to calm her. The future seemed uncertain. Did Griff have any place in it? As she hauled a yellow dress out of her closet and slipped on a pair of sandals, loneliness invaded her heart. She and Griff were facing trouble, but all he wanted to do was push her away, building walls.

Dawn laced her damp hair into a braid and snapped a ribbon around the end with nimble fingers, not caring what she looked like. Wally sat in jail because she'd invited him to tell her mission team about Sudan. He had reaped trouble—not of his making—all while intending to do something noble. It made no sense.

After she threw open the kitchen window, instead of the breeze refreshing her, heavy, humid air reminded her that the holding cell had no air conditioning. While coffee brewed—Kona, Griff's favorite—she forced herself to consider Griff's strengths. His positive qualities were many—courage, loyalty, devotion—but this raw stubbornness she'd not witnessed before. She sipped coffee, her ear tuned to the front door.

The strong brew upset her stomach, so she poured the rest down the drain. Her ranch house seemed quiet, eerily so, as she pulled open the refrigerator, looking at nothing in particular. Her mind felt mired in wet mud. Finally, she opted for a simple meal—bagels with cream cheese and fresh strawberries.

Dawn sliced berries, waiting to toast the bagels, her eyes drifting to the digital clock on the oven. Nine thirty. If Griff didn't come soon, she'd be late for the eleven o'clock service. She'd found Grace Church a few months earlier and her spiritual life was blossoming under Pastor Nebo's deep love for God. He had lived a wild life as a young man, even spending days in jail before finding God's purpose in his life.

She perched on a chair, thumbing through her Bible, unable to get Griff from her mind. He needed her more than ever, but how could she reach him? She spotted a parable Jesus had taught his disciples about a widow and she read with interest until a car door slammed. Dawn peeked out the front window.

Griff's pressed lips and haunted eyes squeezed her heart. She flew to let him inside, heat and swirling wind blowing in with him.

"How's everything going?" She lightly touched his arm.

Griff didn't exactly cringe beneath her hand, but anger seemed to vibrate on his skin.

"I threatened CJ with a civil rights violation," he said, his knuckles white. "But he won't budge."

She tossed her braid over her shoulder, not knowing what to do or say. Unease settled into her bones. "I am sorry for everything. Want coffee while we talk it over?"

Griff's shrug gave her pause, yet she ushered him to the dining room anyway. Food might smooth his ruffled temper. She quickly toasted the bagels and then they sat around her cherry wood dining room table, Griff's large frame looking none too comfortable on the small chair. His face seemed haggard.

"You also had a sleepless night, I think," she said.

"The Lamplighter motel is so quiet, I should've nodded off, but Wally's swollen face revolved in my mind until about five. Guess I slept an hour."

"Coffee and a bagel might set you right."

"Coffee sounds okay, but I couldn't eat. I stopped to see Wally and Ryan, Mr. Gatekeeper, gave me a hard time. Dalton happened by and let me in."

"The chief has a fine reputation. He came to D.C. once, testifying in my case against a woman who housed a meth lab near here."

"Good for you—but doesn't that put him on the wrong side for Wally? I should never have asked Wally along to this wedding."

"I woke up this morning blaming myself."

Griff thumped his elbows on the table, looking away. Dawn fixed a plate and pushed the bagel toward him.

"After all," she sighed, "I suggested Wally meet the mission team."

"Look at us, battling over who's at fault. Throwing stones won't help Wally."

"Precisely. I've prayed for direction, asking how we can turn his dilemma to the good."

"Last night as I was tossing on the hard bed, I figured you would be praying." Griff downed his coffee. "Thanks. Your Kona always hits the spot."

Tightness in Dawn's neck relaxed and she nibbled her bagel. Griff speared a red berry, seeming to savor its sweetness.

"This is good. Dalton told me he eats Tootsie Rolls to remember life's better things. I thought he was nuts."

Dawn smiled. Before divulging the plan she'd concocted, she let him finish his fruit. He caught on.

"What's up?" He set down his fork.

"You're uncanny. I need your support at church."

"Not a chance. Manipulating me won't work."

"I agree. You're too smart to be manipulated."

"Tell that to Officer Ryan," Griff groaned. "I kick myself for allowing the pipsqueak to search our hotel room. He's convinced he's made the case of the century against Wally."

"Join me and think of something besides Wally's predicament. Is that so wrong?"

A fleeting smile revealed his pain. "I figured with Wally in jail, you'd cancel the event."

"I've been reading some Bible passages where Jesus told his disciples about a widow who kept pleading with a judge for justice against her adversary."

Griff bolted from his chair to study a photo of Dawn's eighteen-year-old son. Dawn took a deep breath. Was he even listening?

"I'm a widow, Griff."

He turned from the hutch. "What happened in your story?"

"The judge refused to act until one day he became so worn down from her pleas that he finally gave her justice."

"And that helps us how?"

Dawn opened her Bible. "Jesus tells it better than I can. 'And will not God bring about justice for his chosen ones, who cry out to him day and night? Will he keep putting them off? I tell you, he will see that they get justice, and quickly.'"

Griff sat down, his expression quizzical. Dawn slowly closed her Bible.

"I believe in my heart God will ensure Wally is *not* wrongfully convicted. I wish you believed it too."

"If God was interested in justice, he wouldn't have allowed Wally to be wrongfully arrested in the first place," Griff replied, his face twisted.

Dawn eased off. "You were looking at Brian's photo. He likes VMI well enough."

"I'm sure he fits right in."

His voice buoyed, but Dawn hardly felt like talking about her son, who grew more distant by the week.

"He doesn't call much, except on Sundays," Dawn said, sadness washing over her. "I'd like to be back in time from our appointment with CJ to get his call."

Griff reached out for her hand.

"I need to ask … Do you know how much I've missed you with all my travel?"

Her heart fluttering, Dawn saw in his expressive gray eyes a gentle gaze drawing her into his inner thoughts, something that rarely happened with Griff. She savored this time alone.

"Griff, I'd love to know—"

The ringing phone interrupted the tender moment. She was tempted to ignore it, but only for a moment. "Maybe it's Brian calling early." She dashed to the kitchen, grabbing the call.

"Hello?"

"It's Rick Nebo. I just heard Wally Manja is in jail. What about our luncheon where he's scheduled to speak?"

She returned to the dining room with the portable, letting Griff hear her part of the conversation. "Pastor, Wally's being held for a crime he didn't commit. Griff and I are sorting through it, trying to get him released. We'll both be at the luncheon to tell what we can about Wally's time fleeing the war in Sudan."

She sought Griff's eyes, seeking permission for what she'd just said, and he nodded in agreement.

"I trust the misunderstanding will be sorted out soon. You should know," Pastor Nebo said, clearing his throat, "CJ called about our noon mission meeting and claims the case against our friend is airtight."

"Years as a federal probation officer has taught me Solomon's proverb is true. The first to present his case seems right until someone questions him."

"I agree."

"You and Wally spoke many times about his hopes for the future. You'd carry weight with Judge Fox to release him. Can you come to the bond hearing?"

Pastor Nebo didn't reply and she heard someone talking in the background. Though he'd referred to Wally as "our friend," she became concerned about CJ's pressure. The guy was a menace in her life and now in Wally's. When would he stop?

She whispered to Griff, "He hasn't said if he'll come to the hearing."

"Dawn, the service will be starting. I have to run."

"We were about to leave when you called." She hung up, facing Griff's smirk.

"You are wily, I give you that." Griff treated her to a smile. "Am I dressed okay for church?"

She eyeballed his khaki slacks and blue shirt. "You look great to me."

"Your pastor can probably do more than I can to convince the judge to set bond." Griff thrust his hands into his pockets. "I'm FBI, but dead in the water here."

Dawn snagged her purse and a small box in the back hall. "I printed handouts about the Lost Boys of Sudan. Sounds like CJ may come to our mission meeting."

"He'd better stay out of my way. I'm not the forgiving type, even if I am sitting in church for a second day." Griff took her box, walked over to the front door, and swung it open for her.

Dawn's shoulders sagged. She wanted to tell him forgiveness was a gift to the forgiver. Instead, figuring it was wiser to let him air his feelings without a lecture, she locked the front door.

In his car, a brand new Camaro, a deep chasm seemed to separate them. She watched Griff shift into reverse. His manly face touched with pain seared her heart. It took enormous willpower, but she tore her eyes away, making up her mind. While she sat next to him on the pew, she'd be praying for Griff's soul.

7

Griff heard no more than a few words from the minister. His mind was consumed with how to beat the locals at their dangerous game. The police were so sure Wally was their culprit that they weren't searching for the real one. Then, apparently church was over, because Dawn and everyone else stood up. Griff went straight for the door.

"Excuse me, are you Griff Topping?"

Griff swiveled his head around to see who dared accost him and looked into the cordial eyes of the white-haired minister who'd married Stephanie and Leonard. He offered a firm hand and Griff gladly clasped it.

"Glad you joined us in worship."

"Me too," Griff replied, though he'd been lost in thought the entire time.

Dawn greeted her pastor and Rick Nebo introduced his wife, Laurie, a petite woman with graying hair who wore a friendly smile. She and Rick were whisked away by an elderly woman needing help with the buffet luncheon.

"Isn't it amazing how the blind African man found sight after dreaming of God?" Dawn asked as she slid the box of handouts under her arm.

Too bad Griff had missed that. If Dawn learned of his mental wanderings, she'd be disappointed again. He skated on razor-thin ice with her after his run-in with CJ.

"Rick makes everyone feel important," was all he said.

She accepted his observation with a smile. "The village where the man received his sight is near where the medical team is going in Sudan. Ready for lunch? We're having crab salad."

Griff's stomach rumbled a complaint at the word salad. He reached for the box of handouts she held.

"Should I hand these out during your presentation? I'm no good at church stuff."

"Relax. These folks aren't any different from you or me. You'll know what to do when the time comes. It's just like when you testify before the jury."

"Okay, I get it," he grinned. "You want me to tell the truth."

"Maybe you won't have to say anything. Let's see what the questions are."

She led him downstairs to the fellowship hall, a large but simple room set with round tables and plenty of chairs. Sandwiches on platters and salads in big bowls covered two long tables at the far end. Dawn set her purse on one of the tables and when she went to go help in the kitchen, Griff worried someone might steal it. Then he remembered—he was in a church. Boy, had he spent too much time around criminals.

Tables quickly filled with twenty or so men and women dressed in their Sunday best. Dawn and Griff eased into seats next to each other and Rick opened with prayer before introducing the mission team going to Sudan. Dawn stood with the rest of the group, making Griff uneasy. Sudan was a dangerous place and she was no doctor. What was she going for?

He joined her at the buffet, scooping food on his plate. He pushed aside lettuce, but enjoyed the tangy crab salad. Warm slices of corn bread slathered with butter filled him up and he turned an ear to the doctor leading the team. He was a surgeon named Ralph Kidd, and his specialty was complicated operations for children. Griff snickered, hardly believing Doc Kidd treated kids. Had he selected his medical specialty to match his last name? Griff watched Dawn as she prayed aloud.

"Father, protect us as we head out to care for your people. Bring to us any Sudanese who've lost their legs and need hand-propelled scooters. We seek courage for the unknown and boldness to share the good news of Jesus."

She said it well, but Griff didn't believe God heard his prayers, though Dawn truly believed God answered hers. A door slammed and Griff jerked his head to see. In swaggered CJ Huddleston, who dropped into an empty spot at another table.

Dawn saw him too and gave CJ a friendly wave. Her denials notwithstanding, *something* existed between those two—and that something Griff didn't like. He tilted his head closer to hers.

"He attends this church?"

"No," she said, looking concerned. "I don't know why he's here."

Griff cast a sideways glance at her and she caught his eyes.

She leaned over, confiding in a whisper, "My Granny always said, 'Dawn, love, face the enemy with a smile. They'll never know what hit 'em.' She lived through the devastation of Pearl Harbor."

So Dawn considered CJ the enemy. Useful information. Satisfying, too. Her little wave troubled him, yet she had a point. Griff's own grandmother once told him something similar. She and Grandfather

Topping had survived the European side of World War II. But she lived in Cornwall, England and offered Griff her advice in a crisp, British accent.

Okay, how to get CJ on their side? Griff downed the final drop of weak coffee, an idea slipping into his overworked mind. Before he could explain it to Dawn, Doc Kidd turned things over to her. Griff grabbed her hand as she rose.

"I need to talk with you when you're done."

"This won't take me long."

She sent the handouts around the room before addressing the group.

"You expected Wally Manja; however, he couldn't be here due to circumstances beyond his or our control."

Griff turned and CJ's sinister eyes glared back. Ready for battle, was he? Okay, Griff would try a new tact, right here in the church fellowship hall. The next thing he knew, Dawn was introducing him as her friend, the FBI agent who'd come with Wally.

"So let's give Griff a hearty Grace family welcome."

Applause lit up the room. Without looking, Griff knew CJ was sitting on his hands, counting the days before he added another notch to his conviction belt. Griff eased out of the flimsy chair, gripping the back of it.

"When I use my courtroom voice, everyone usually hears me. Am I right?"

"You are, Agent Topping," Rick shouted.

"Close your eyes for a moment. A thin boy is running, trying to catch his breath as he flees from his enemies."

Every person in his line of sight followed his instructions. So his FBI status counted for something with these church folks. He didn't check to see if CJ had closed his; he figured the jerk was stabbing him in the back with his laser eyes. Griff lowered his voice an octave, striking the mood he wanted to achieve.

"Rumbek Manja was chased away from his tukul in Walu by the militants who killed both of his parents. On bare feet, he ran for days, which became months, which turned into terror-filled years. Rumbek lived in the desert. He faced swollen rivers and dodged hungry lions on the prowl."

Eyes flew open, some wide with disbelief. Griff had their attention. As with a jury, Griff sought the eyes of every person in the room, but he refused to glance at CJ.

"Rumbek fled Sudan for Ethiopia, only to have an uprising chase him from there. Militants invaded the refugee camp and Rumbek, along with hundreds of boys and a handful of girls, grabbed their meager possessions, only to run again."

Griff gestured at his wristwatch. "I'm ashamed to say I find waiting in line at the gas station inconvenient. What if your son ran thousands of miles back through Sudan and into Kenya, evading warriors, guns, and lions? What if he was a skinny boy of seven years old? That was when Rumbek saw many boys drop dead in the desert."

A loud gasp punctured the room. Tears glistened in several pairs of eyes, including Dawn's.

"Exactly. I'll fast forward to five years ago, when I met Rumbek. He served my meals at a restaurant, and we became friends. At the refugee camp, he had taken the name Wally after his village, Walu. He told me he worked two jobs, saving for college, and that he wouldn't stop until he found God's plan for his life."

A ripple of applause. From the corner of his eye, Griff glimpsed Dawn's sparkling smile. Griff had them in his hands, but he couldn't stop until he got what *he* wanted.

"I'll admit, I don't share Wally's strong beliefs. After years of pursuing criminals, I'm more cynical. Yet after all he's endured, Wally's heart remains pure. Because I admire his deeply held faith, I helped Wally apply for a scholarship to my alma mater. Based on his hard work and effort, he received a full-ride. He graduates after one more year."

Griff sipped water from a glass at his place setting. Nearly done with his story, he wanted to ensure this group of do-gooders really felt Wally's pain. He set down the glass.

"Imagine if you were a widower with no children and Wally called you up one day, asking a favor."

Rick Nebo nodded, anxious for the punch line.

"Do you need money for textbooks, Wally? Help on your term paper? But it was none of those things. On the phone, he asked me—"

Griff had trouble continuing. He wiped his eyes, quickly telling them, "He asked if I'd attend Parent's Day at the college with him, because both his parents had been killed in the war."

His voice thick with emotion, Griff didn't linger on his involvement. "I feel honored that Wally thinks of me as his dad. He needs my help and *your* help today. I never planned on sharing this, but you need to know what your police chief and the Commonwealth attorney have done to him."

"What have they done?" Doc Kidd demanded, rising to his feet.

This was it. Griff spun on his heels, glaring at CJ, who looked dumbfounded.

Before his nemesis seized control of the meeting, Griff added, "Your town's least-experienced police officer accosted Wally, claiming he was the black man who robbed the Night Owl. He went peacefully, but Wally's lip and face were cut. He is innocent. If you want to hear me explain all this to Judge Fox tomorrow at nine a.m., I'd appreciate your help in assuring his release."

Griff sat down and Dawn grabbed his hand, saying, "You were fabulous."

She stood and said, "The tragedy Wally faced in Sudan continues for those who remain. Please pray for Pastor as he leads us to the town of Bor, where we hope to change lives with the help we bring. Thanks for coming."

In a flash, Doc Kidd knelt by Griff's side, pledging his prayer support. Griff observed CJ's stare, an eagle spotting its prey, before the attorney stormed out the back.

"I wonder if our meeting with him is still on or if he's canceling that," Dawn wondered aloud.

"Forget him," Griff replied. "He has bigger mountains to climb."

Rick handed Griff a note with a phone number written on it. "Jeffrey Truhart is an attorney in our congregation. He'll do a fine job representing Wally."

Griff pulled out his cell phone, touched by Rick's concern. "I'll step outside and call him right away. Wally needs the help. And Rick, if you're not busy at nine, I wish you'd come to the court hearing in the morning."

"I will try."

LATE THAT SAME NIGHT, Wally was surprised and comforted by Griff's soft voice at the metal bars.

"You all right?"

"Better now you are here, Dad. How did you get in?"

"Chief Dalton. He didn't rough you up, did he?" Griff leaned in closer.

"He took my photograph and fingerprints, that's all."

"Good. Everything went smoothly at church, but you were missed."

"I wanted to be there."

Wally's eyes flooded with tears, but he knew he had to stay strong for Griff, who did not believe God cared. Wally knew He did.

"I had to see for myself that you were okay before I could sleep," Griff said, his voice hushed. "I'm in another hotel."

"Did I let down the church people?"

"Don't worry about that. In the morning, I'll come back with your lawyer."

Then the door creaked open and the chief stood in the light, looking like a tribal enemy. *God help me,* Wally cried inside.

"Agent Topping, time for lights out."

"I'll see you before your bond hearing. Get some rest."

Griff squeezed Wally's hand before disappearing out the door. A few minutes later, Officer Ryan came in, yanking Wally's hands behind him and pulling on plastic handcuffs.

"Where are you taking me?"

"Move it, buddy. You're leaving our nice lockup. The jail should be real fun."

Wally ducked his head, shuffling behind the officer. The transfer of cells happened swiftly. In the new one, instead of a hard metal bunk, Wally rested on a thin padded mattress.

Another man lounged on another bunk. He had long greasy hair dangling below his shoulders and his clothes were full of holes. Wally instantly recognized the angry man from before. His heart began beating faster. He lay down on the little bunk, his legs and feet hanging off the edge. He curled on his side, determined not to offend his cellmate, who was the size of an oak tree.

Sometime later, a man in a gray uniform brought food. It was tasteless, but Wally ate it anyway. Then a friendly jail chaplain stopped by and said, "If you need peace, read this."

"Leave me alone, parson," the other man yelled.

Wally jumped from the bunk, gladly receiving a Bible the chaplain handed him. Stamped in gold letters on front were the words, "Gideon." God had not forgotten him. The lights were on in the cell, so Wally sat on the bunk, his legs crossed, searching for passages to help him survive in this strange place. When he found one about blessings crowning the heads of the righteous, Wally began to count his blessings.

His lip had started to scab over, which was good. Officer Ryan had not come to bother him in jail. The proud policeman walked a dangerous road, and Wally did not trust him. The man Griff called

'Chief' seemed concerned about doing what was right. Wally thought of another good thing—Griff had gone to church.

He had never gone before, not even when Wally had asked him. Maybe Griff went because he was more interested in Dawn. As Wally closed his Bible, he puzzled over how, instead of him telling the church people about Sudan, Griff had to. It was all so strange.

Then in the morning, he had to face the judge. Should he be afraid?

8

For breakfast the following morning, Wally ate toast and a slim piece of cheese on a tray. A television that hung from the ceiling outside the cell boomed loudly with a news program. Other inmates in other cells shouted down the corridor.

His anxiety grew as he thought the judge would make him stay in jail. Then what he told Griff came into his mind—what Officer Ryan did to him was *not* worse than what the giant crocodile had done to his friend in Sudan. Memories of Wally's homeland crashed into his mind like the muddy waters of the dreadful river he had crossed.

"What are ya doing over there? Yer awful quiet."

The gruff man who had pestered Wally in the lockup dropped down from his bunk and scurried over.

"What's the problem? Cat got yer tongue?"

The man stared, but Wally gripped his Bible. What would the man say if Wally told him he had just been thinking of swimming away from crocodiles? It did not matter. What did was that he was no longer a scared boy in the wilderness, but a twenty-two-year old man sitting in jail. This moment was real and he had to make it count for God.

"I am reading my Bible." Wally peered up at him.

"That stuff's all rot."

"Not to me sir," was all Wally could think to say.

"My dad was religious," the man muttered through clenched teeth. "Every day he found reasons to smack me around. I wasn't smart enough for him. At fifteen, I left home and haven't talked to my old man or darkened the door of a church since."

Wally cringed inside. With his long hair pulled tightly behind his head and puffy eyes, the man looked dangerous. He had already threatened Wally once with his fist. Then Wally thought how much the man suffered by walking away from God. Rather than argue, he should share the truth.

"Jesus cares about you. I know. Hateful men killed my father and mother. I was seven years old when I ran from my village because those men wanted to kill me, too."

Wally's heart filled with sorrow, and in this forlorn place, he grieved for his dead parents. Islamic men had killed them with powerful guns because they were Christians. He had seen the blood covering their bodies as he hid behind a tree.

"Talking with you makes me realize I need to forgive those men. Jesus is more powerful than anyone's wicked schemes over me or my family."

The man grunted and walked away. Wally turned some pages in his Bible, wanting to stand before the judge clothed in God's words. He started reading Genesis 39 about Joseph, the son of Jacob, who was sold into slavery by his jealous brothers. Eventually, Joseph went to work for Potiphar, whose wife falsely accused Joseph of trying to seduce her. Potiphar locked Joseph in prison.

Wally cradled his Bible on the rock-hard bunk. The clerk had falsely accused him. He never went in that store, never saw the woman. Maybe she was robbed by another man who looked like him.

He continued reading. Joseph gained the trust of everyone in jail and was freed. When Pharaoh placed him in charge of all of Egypt, Joseph rescued his family during a terrible famine and forgave his brothers for selling him. It was God's wonderful plan, and one that Joseph probably never could have dreamed up himself. Verses of freedom calmed Wally's nerves, but he had to do something before he could feel peace.

"God, you are watching me," he whispered. "I forgive the bad men in Sudan."

"Hey," a voice yelled, "why'd ya call me 'sir'? I'm no one."

"You are someone to me."

At this, the man lunged at Wally's bunk, towering over him. But Wally was no longer afraid.

"When yer out, would you call my mother? I haven't talked with her in years."

"I'll try."

He told Wally her phone number, which Wally tried to memorize.

"Will you do me a favor?" Wally asked.

"There's always a catch."

Wally held out the Bible. "Jesus changed my life. It tells about Him in here. A boy taught me about God in the refugee camp before I came to America."

"Refugee camp? I don't read much." Still, he took the Bible.

"I am Wally Manja. What is your name?"

"Elmer Callaway. Friends call me Cal."

"Hello, Cal."

Wally shook the man's hand with a vague hope that his case would turn out like Joseph's and he could phone Cal's mother. An officer approached the door.

"Manja?"

"I knew yer release would come soon."

"That's me." Wally jumped up, careful not to step on Cal's feet.

The officer inserted a key and opened the door. "Your lawyer is here."

Wally's heart crashed with a thud. He was not really getting out. He gave Cal a tepid wave. "Don't forget to read the place I marked about Jesus. He can save you from whatever brought you here."

The cell bars clanged behind Wally and Cal leapt at the bars.

"Call my mother!"

The officer took Wally down a hall and unlocked the door. He let Wally inside the narrow room, which had one table and three chairs squeezed together. Griff was talking to a man in a shirt and tie. Dizziness overpowered Wally as he collapsed on a chair.

"Wally, do you hear me?"

He focused his eyes on Griff's face and the dizziness went away.

"My body is empty of food. It would be good to eat."

"I'm trying to get you out of here." Griff folded Wally's hands into his.

"Thank you, Dad. Do I talk in court?"

"Meet your attorney," Griff said, draping an arm around Wally's shoulder. "Mr. Jeffrey Truhart goes to Dawn's church. I trust he'll prove your innocence and convince the judge to let you out on bond."

Mr. Truhart stood, shaking Wally's hand in a secure grip. Shorter than Griff, the attorney wore crooked rectangle glasses. His thinning brown hair grew from a high point on his head. He looked serious, but his face had no wrinkles. This man lived easily while trouble swirled around him.

"Sorry to meet under trying circumstances. Let's get busy." He sat down. "Griff told me how you came to the U.S. and you now work as a waiter. How much do you make?"

Why did Wally's mind feel so blank? The only words he thought of were Dinka words, and he felt certain Mr. Truhart had never been to Sudan. Wally shut his eyes, asking God to help his brain work in English. When he opened his eyes, Mr. Truhart was staring at him.

"Because of Dad," Wally answered as he nodded at Griff. "I attend his college."

It didn't take long for Wally to tell of the scholarship, his business studies and work schedule at Rob's Deli in Virginia. The lawyer wrote on blue-lined, yellow paper.

"I am supposed to graduate next spring."

Wally didn't dare look at Griff, not wanting to see disappointment on his face.

"You had small bills on you. How much were you carrying?"

Wally knew. "I had three hundred dollars in my suitcase for Liberty. I wanted Miss Dawn to take some to her. The policeman also took money from my pockets."

"Who is Liberty?" Mr. Truhart's head snapped up from the notes.

"She is to be my wife. We were born in Walu, the same village in Sudan. When we fled the rebels, Atong ran too. She and I lived for years in refugee camps."

"And who is Atong?"

"I mean Liberty. Atong is her Dinka name."

A tear plunged down Wally's cheek. He might never see her again. But God's love for him was everywhere. God had saved Wally from wild animals, found him a job, and provided the scholarship.

"When we had to run again, we became separated. The refugee agency said she died. But then, two years ago, a missionary visited my church. He said he was going to Walu, so Griff bought me a video camera. The missionary took it with a message for anyone who remembered me. It got mailed back to me by Jeremy Bonds—"

"Who is Jeremy Bonds?"

"A missionary pilot who flies into Walu. The memory card contained a video of Liberty. On it she said she survived rebel attacks and moved back to our village with her uncle."

"Wally was thrilled Liberty was alive," Griff added.

"I sent the camera again to Jeremy, asking on a new video if Liberty would marry me. Jeremy mailed the camera back to me and Liberty said yes."

"I'm glad you found A—" Mr. Truhart quit writing. "How do you spell her name?"

"Atong means 'a girl born during war.' Call her Liberty, the name she took in the refugee camp. It was the name she wanted to use when she came to America." Wally's gaze fell to the floor. "Only she never made it."

"But she will someday," Griff promised.

"About the money—the police claim you stole it from the clerk."

"Never. Pastor Nebo and I talked many times on the phone. His mission team will fly medical supplies to Walu. I asked Miss Dawn to take my money to Sudan and buy a SIM card for a cell phone for Liberty. I kept fives and ones customers left me at the deli."

"A cell phone for a Sudan village?" The lawyer tapped his pen on his palm.

"They work there," Wally insisted.

"In court, Griff will post whatever bond is set by the judge. I speak for you. Any questions?"

"Dad," Wally reached for Griff's arm. "When does the clerk tell the judge I robbed her? I *know* she never saw me."

"Not until the preliminary exam, which we'll discuss later." Mr. Truhart picked up his pad, rising from his chair. "She won't be in court this morning."

Wally sighed. The legal case might go on forever. One more thing worried him.

"The police took my money." Wally rubbed his sweaty hands together. "I have an account in Pennsylvania, but I forget how much is in it."

Griff put an arm around Wally's shoulders again. "I wrote Mr. Truhart a check to cover his work for a while."

"I will pay you back, Dad. This is my trouble, not yours."

"The main thing is to get you freed," Mr. Truhart said, pressing the buzzer. "God has never left me broke or hungry yet."

Wally hugged Griff. What the lawyer said reminded Wally of God's promise in the Bible never to leave or forsake him.

9

Although he routinely testified in Federal court, Griff had no official role at this arraignment, so he let Wally's lawyer take over. Still, he didn't appreciate being relegated to the audience. In the cracker box of a room, he turned in his front row seat, looking for Dawn. It was close to nine o'clock. Wasn't she coming?

Rick and Laurie Nebo streamed in, their faces pensive as they snuck past him to the end of his row. Disappointment rolled over Griff—apparently his pleas at the church hadn't moved other folks to come. Just then, someone breathed close to his ear. Dawn leaned over, her eyes filled with concern.

"How was your meeting with Jeffrey?"

"Wally confirmed a few things that may help secure his release."

"I've been hard at prayer."

Griff's retort got lost in a flurry of court personnel hustling into the courtroom. CJ Huddleston sauntered in; his arrogant face was a dramatic contrast to Pastor Rick's humble one. Something akin to hate buffeted Griff's mind, but he had no business desiring to pummel the guy. Jeffrey would beat the lawyer in his own arena, fair and square.

The back door burst open and in full police regalia, Officer Ryan strode through the courtroom, carrying a bulging file. Griff snickered under his breath. That punk couldn't have amassed so much evidence against Wally; it was a gimmick to fool the judge. Defense attorneys often employed such sneaky tactics.

Huddleston tossed a sinister glance over his shoulder at Griff, who merely nodded, his lips pressed together, conveying no sign of weakness. He knew Huddleston's egotistical type and refused to allow him or Ryan to ruin Wally's life.

Having Dawn beside him, as she chatted quietly with Rick, helped Griff refocus his thoughts. Why had he blamed her for Huddleston's persecution of Wally? That was absurd. But he knew it was still possible that Huddleston had flexed his legal power to triumph over him.

A metal door at the far side of the courtroom clanged open. Wally sidled in, a chain dangling between his ankles and his flip flops dragging along the floor. He wore a bright orange jumpsuit and his hands were cuffed at his waist. Blood roared in Griff's ears. He leaned forward so Wally couldn't miss seeing him. Their eyes caught for a fleeting second, but then Jeffrey Truhart took his seat beside Wally.

The bailiff called, "The court of Honorable Judge Roman T. Fox is in session."

Griff turned at sounds of voices. In marched Doc Kidd and a group Griff recognized from Dawn's church. They silently filled the empty rows. Griff quickly revised his harsh opinion of churchgoers: these people kept their word. He brushed Dawn's arm with his elbow.

"I hope Jeffrey is convincing. I can't bear Wally spending one more night in jail."

Dawn shut her eyes briefly. When she opened them, tears clung to her lashes. Judge Fox stormed in, a thundercloud blown by ferocious winds, his shirt collar sticking up over the top of his black robe. He swept into his seat behind the bench. One look at Huddleston and Ryan's heads huddled together was enough to make Griff grind his teeth. These guys were all wet.

The bailiff announced, "Commonwealth of Virginia versus Wally Baca Manja."

Good. The judge would hear Wally's case before his mind became contaminated by hardened felon types.

"The prosecutor will read the charges against Mr. Manja."

Judge Fox turned sunken eyes to Huddleston, who was still whispering to Ryan. Griff plunked his elbows on his knees, scrutinizing the judge. Fox didn't move a single face muscle when he talked; his razor-thin lips only moved a fraction. Yet his southern accent reminded Griff of greens and ham biscuits. Elizabeth County might be an hour from D.C., but he'd been dropped into the Deep South overnight.

"Your Honor," Jeffrey called as he popped to his feet. "The defense waives the reading of the charges. Mr. Manja is prepared to enter a not guilty plea."

"Morning, Mr. Truhart. We haven't seen you in our court since last week. Glad you're keeping busy in your practice. I'm sure you don't want these nice folks from Grace Church hearing what your client's accused of, but I run my court formal-like, as you should know."

The judge snatched up a sheet of paper and waved a hand toward the prosecutor, who seemed to be in better shape than he'd been at the wedding reception. Huddleston rose, not a wobble in sight. Griff bored his eyes into the back of the man's swelled head, just willing him to dismiss the case. That didn't happen.

Huddleston cleared his throat and, with a flair for the dramatic, raised his voice only to lower it. "The defendant is accused of robbing the Night Owl convenience store on Saturday afternoon. We will prove Mr. Rumble Manja put the clerk in fear of harm as he robbed the Night Owl of all its money, five hundred and forty-six dollars. The second degree felony carries a maximum sentence of fifteen years in prison."

"Your Honor, my client's name is *Rumbek* Manja, but he goes by Wally."

"Sit down, Mr. Truhart. We favor swift justice in cases like these."

Swift justice? Cases like these? Griff tried to calculate the judge's meaning. He needled Dawn's arm with his elbow. As he rolled his eyes, Fox happened to survey his courtroom, his eyes landing on Griff.

Go ahead, find me out of order. I'll bring the whole Department of Justice down on your disgusting town. Sinister thoughts raced through Griff's mind, but he smiled at the judge, folding his arms.

When Judge Fox lowered his eyes, Griff felt he had scored a small point. If he told Dawn, she'd say he was making Wally's dilemma worse. She might be right; however, it was impossible to stay cool while the legal system was grinding to pieces someone he loved.

"Mr. Truhart, how does your client plead?"

Fox turned those hollow eyes toward Wally's lawyer the way a fox might survey its prey.

Jeffrey stepped behind Wally, gripping his shoulders with both hands. "Not guilty. My client is innocent."

That got people talking behind Griff, so much so that Fox rapped his gavel.

"Juries appreciate theatrics, but I spurn them in my courtroom. Mr. Huddleston, what is your bond recommendation?"

Still on his feet, Huddleston adjusted his tie and, after looking back at Dawn, pivoted his head toward the judge. "No bail, Your Honor."

Dawn gasped. She seized Griff's hand, which kept him from jumping into the well of the court and doing something he might regret.

"Mr. Manja has no ties to Summit Ridge," the prosecutor intoned. "He's a drifter passing through. He claims to live in Pennsylvania, but he's really from Africa."

Fox cast a watery eye upon Wally as if he were the worst offender the judge had ever seen. Wally conferred with his lawyer while Huddleston pranced around the well of the courtroom as though it were his personal arena.

"That's right, Africa. Not only does he use an alias, but Mr. Runningbek Manja was born in *Sudan*—one of the premier countries harboring terrorists who attack our country."

"This is no terrorism case," Jeffrey said, leaping to his feet. "Wally entered the country legally and became a U.S. citizen two years ago. And Mr. Huddleston knows his name is *Rumbek*, not Runningbek."

"Your untimely interruption is overruled." Judge Fox frowned. "I want to know why the prosecutor argues for no bail. You'll get your turn to swat flies."

Jeffrey sat back down, whispering something to Wally. Griff's insides churned. A volatile war raged in his stomach knowing that a Summit Ridge jury might be only too happy to convict Wally of wrongdoing.

"He may be a citizen," Huddleston said as he raised his voice, puffing out his chest, "but he might return to his tribe and slide out from Your Honor's court of justice."

"Excellent point, Mr. Huddleston." Judge Fox pointed a bony finger straight at Wally. "It's my experience, when one deer crosses the road, others are sure to follow."

An absurd comparison. Wally was no wild animal, following instincts of the woods. He was a young man with bright prospects. Griff flexed his right hand, eager to take the stand and counter Huddleston's lies. The courtroom seemed to be the prosecutor's stage and Wally had been cast in the role of antagonist. In an instant, Griff saw it all clearly.

This had nothing to do with him or Dawn. Huddleston meant to build his career on the back of a lost boy from Sudan. Griff vowed to defeat him with every trick he'd ever learned.

If a bank had been robbed, Griff could've gotten the nearest FBI office involved. But because the case involved a local store, Chief Dalton had authority to investigate and Huddleston to prosecute. So be it. Griff would use all his vacation and stay in this backwater town until Wally was exonerated.

Jeffrey Truhart was talking to the judge and motioning toward Pastor Nebo. Griff forced his internal battle to cease.

"Wally is no drifter. The pastor of Grace Church will testify Wally accepted the church's invitation to help their medical mission team to Sudan."

As Jeffrey explained about Rick's contacts with Wally, Judge Fox acted bored, flipping through a stack of papers. Griff was grateful for one thing—the judge's cavalier attitude didn't diminish Jeffrey's fervor to get Wally released.

"Besides being connected with Ms. Dawn Ahern, a federal probation officer in Alexandria, Wally is mentored by FBI Agent Griffin Topping."

Fox picked that moment to lock eyes with Griff. CJ must have clued the judge that an FBI agent was in his court. Griff flashed a toothy smile, but Fox pursed his lips, not swayed by the friendly gesture.

Jeffrey again rested his hands on Wally's shoulders. "My client gives his word to return for whatever hearings are necessary."

The judge cut in, "Mr. Truhart, I appreciate your client's promises and those of his well-connected friends. But they've not convinced me that he won't flee the country."

Griff could stand the judge's prejudice against Wally no longer. He leapt to his feet. "Your Honor, he can live with me while he finishes school. I will make sure he gets to court. We'll surrender his passport."

Fox aimed a cold stare at Griff. "Who are you?"

Griff edged to the gate separating the well of the court from the audience, taking out his credentials and flashing them open. "FBI agent Griff Topping. I'm Wally's dad."

"You say you are this young man's *father*?" Fox looked rattled.

"Not legally, but in life. He looks to me for guidance and I consider him my son."

"Seems your guidance went haywire." Fox toyed with his gavel. "Sit down."

"Your honor, Wally has a 4.0 grade average. If he isn't allowed on bail, he'll—"

Down came the gavel. "I said sit down."

Folks from Grace Church who'd come to support Wally all began talking at once, with Rick Nebo trying to garner Jeffrey's attention. The lawyer finally saw his hand and dashed over to speak to him while Fox banged his gavel more forcefully.

"Pipe down or I'll clear my court. Mr. Truhart, do you have more evidence in support of setting bond before I issue my ruling?"

Griff couldn't hear what Rick was telling Jeffrey and all he could see of Wally was the back of his head.

"Mr. Truhart, step to it. My docket's full."

Wally's lawyer sped to counsel table. "I call Rick Nebo, pastor of Grace Family Church."

Fox lifted his pointed chin, darting a glance at the prosecutor who, surprisingly, made no objection. *Jeffrey must have something amazing up his sleeve or he'd never risk putting the pastor on the stand*, Griff thought. He slid his clammy hands down his knees, shooting a glance at Dawn. She was on the verge of tears, her lower lip trembling. Griff suppressed a powerful urge to hold her in his arms.

Rick raised his right hand, recited the oath to tell the truth, and took the witness chair. Dawn slipped her cold hand into Griff's warm one. He despised the bitter feelings that stole into his heart. Her friend Huddleston was a real loser.

Griff let Dawn's hand slip away, purposely folding his arms across his chest, his emotions bouncing like a racquetball. Why did he feel so hardhearted toward her all of a sudden? He forced himself to listen to Jeffrey's questions.

"How long have you been pastor at the church?"

"Thirty-one years."

"You've lived in Summit Ridge that long?"

"Yes," Rick said, nodding his full head of white hair.

Jeffrey snatched up his legal pad. "Is your address 540 High Tower Lane?"

"That's right."

"You own your home free and clear?"

"My wife Laurie and I own it together."

Rick's eyes drifted to his wife, who sat beside Dawn twisting a tissue between her fingers. "We paid off our mortgage five years ago. She and I have talked it over, and we pledge our home for Wally's bond."

Huddleston jumped up as if his suit were on fire. "I object!"

"Excuse me, judge," Rick said, turning in his seat to face Judge Fox, "but this young man has been through hell on earth. After surviving rebels, hunger and war, he discovered God himself was his source of strength. The prosecutor can say he robbed the store, but I know differently. He would *never* turn his back on God and break one of the Ten Commandments: Thou Shall Not Steal. So, Laurie and I pledge our home. That's how much we believe in his innocence."

Jeffrey nodded as if he agreed with every kind word the pastor uttered and then said quietly, "No more questions."

"What's your home worth?" Huddleston shouted, stalking up to the witness.

"About three hundred thousand dollars or so."

"You're prepared to lose your house if Mr. Runningbek Manja runs away and proves you wrong?"

In spite of Huddleston mispronouncing Wally's name again, Rick kept his voice steady. "Yes, and so is Laurie. God is our help and salvation."

Huddleston shoved his hands in his pockets, shaking his head side to side as if the pastor had lost his good sense. Judge Fox, his fingers stroking his chin, ordered Rick to return to his seat. It was probably a good thing Jeffrey hadn't called Griff. He might have let it slip Wally hoped to marry a Sudanese girl from his village.

Griff turned to Dawn and, not surprisingly, tears flowed down her cheeks. He handed her a clean handkerchief. She blotted her eyes and tried to hand it back, but he held up his hand.

"You might need it."

The judge stared at Wally and whispers floated behind Griff. This time, Fox didn't pound anything. Instead, he lifted a pen and began writing. If Griff was a praying man, he'd ask God for help. But he wasn't, so he steeled himself for the worst. Besides, he was pretty sure Dawn, Rick, and the other church folk had the prayer aspect covered. If Dawn's God let Wally sit another night in jail, that would convince Griff he wasn't real.

Finally, Fox laid down his pen, surveying his courtroom as if it were a kingdom he ruled. Then he spoke.

"Bond is two hundred thousand dollars. Make sure Pastor Nebo gets the proper paperwork. Preliminary hearing will be held in two weeks. Court adjourned."

Why hadn't Griff put up his house? He'd been too emotionally involved to think clearly. Before he could rebuke himself further, Judge Fox burst from the bench and Griff heard him blowing his nose. Griff zoomed to the gate before Ryan hauled Wally away.

"Son, we'll have you out by noon."

Wally shrugged as he was led away. Griff felt stricken. Didn't he want to be freed? What went on in his head? He was probably overwhelmed by being handcuffed in court.

Griff found the pastor's hand and shook it. "I never saw anyone show so much love to a stranger."

Rick deflected any praise. "Everything Laurie and I own belongs to God. We want our house not only to help Wally, but also to encourage others."

10

Dawn folded the hankie and, as she placed it in her purse, smiled at Griff.

"I'm inviting you and Wally for dinner. How's seven o'clock?"

"Great. Spending an evening with you is exactly what he and I both need."

"I won't have time to cook, but I can pick up barbeque."

Hurt vanished from his eyes. Dawn carried that hopeful sign with her during the long trek to Alexandria and hectic meetings with parolees. Her mind inevitably traveled to Wally's dilemma and her pastor's sacrifice for a young man he'd never met.

At four thirty, she shut down her office computer to tackle her inbox. She signed a bunch of reports, scrawling her name without thinking. As she twisted her pen closed, her phone rang and Dawn plucked up the receiver.

"May I help you?"

"Why are you supporting a criminal's release? Your duty is to keep our communities free from crime."

The coldness of the voice shook her.

"Who is this?" she demanded.

A muffled pause, then, "Don't do anything you'll be sorry for. Just know I'm watching your every move."

Dawn banged down the phone, angered over the anonymous threat.

Punching in an extension, she asked the receptionist, "Who was that caller?"

"Ms. Ahern, I received no call on the main line. In fact, by my watch, it's five minutes after five. So any call should have connected to our answering device."

"Heather, it was a crank call."

"Sorry."

Dawn had been so deep in thought she'd failed to realize the caller used her direct number. That narrowed the field of suspects considerably. Her parolees were *never* given her private line to call—only the main number.

The warning rattled her to the core, dissolving any happiness over Wally's release. She locked her desk and drove to the market, keeping an eye behind her as she shopped for pulled pork, kettle chips, and fresh fruit. Her unease escalated as she inched home in rush hour traffic, which didn't let up until she reached her neighborhood.

She'd lived among the sprawling oaks for almost a year and her neighbors on either side seemed friendly. But tonight, she couldn't help checking for strangers passing by. After a click of the remote, she pulled safely into the garage. She turned the double locks and stored the groceries in the fridge before changing into slacks and a pink blouse.

Dawn let her long hair hang loose past her shoulders, giving it a few flicks with the brush. Light music on the radio failed to lift her flagging spirits. She wanted Wally to find peace in her home, but how could he if she didn't? There was only one thing to do.

"Oh Lord," she whispered, "change the heart of whoever called me. Show him your love."

She washed her hands in the sink, hoping the crud in her heart would swirl down the drain, too. Her eyes fell upon the one plant she'd brought from Florida—an aloe growing on the ledge above her sink. Just as aloe could be a healing balm to burned skin, she had to trust her prayer would be a balm to her hurting spirit.

Dawn warmed barbeque in a pan and, as she cut into sesame-seed rolls, the doorbell pealed. Her heart contracted. She'd neglected to reset the security alarm. What if the strange caller found out where she lived?

Her knees trembled as she crept to the living room and peeked out a side window. The sight of her dearest friend replaced all fear. Griff stood beside Wally, who carried a colorful bouquet. She opened the door and Wally handed her flowers.

"Miss Dawn, thank you for coming to court. It helped knowing you were there."

"It's wonderful to see you."

Griff stayed on the porch, acting restless. She wanted to tell him about the hateful call, but thought better of it. This was supposed to be a celebration. Dawn fixed a welcoming smile on her face.

"Come on in. We'll all enjoy dinner together."

"Thanks for asking us over."

Griff touched her cheek lightly with his lips. She longed to throw a hug around his neck, but he'd already gone to the kitchen. She grabbed Wally's hand.

"You must be tired. Let's put these in water while you get comfortable."

She showed Wally to the family room, where he flopped down on her sofa, thrusting out his thin legs. His face looked rugged, a scab marring his lip.

"This feels like home."

"Great. Dinner will be ready in a jiffy."

Dawn turned to the kitchen and nearly bumped into Griff, who hovered in the doorway. What could possibly be eating him?

"Dad, are we leaving tomorrow? I am working." Wally called. His head rested against the sofa.

"That's the plan."

"Want some lemonade?" Dawn slid her arm around Griff.

"Okay." With his free hand, Griff palmed his moustache. He looked nervous, as if he'd had several pots of coffee and nothing to eat. She patted his shoulder and darted to pour three glasses of lemonade. When she returned with the drinks, Wally pointed to a photo of a young man in uniform.

"Is he your son?"

"Yes. I hope you and Brian will meet. He attends the Virginia Military Institute."

She checked for Griff's reaction, but he was staring off into space. Maybe that was what he needed, space. After chatting a few moments about Brian's second year at VMI, she left Griff and Wally to talk alone.

Haunting questions followed her like a shadow as she spooned meat onto rolls, popping them into the hot oven. Why had she encouraged Wally to speak at church? Was it her opposition to CJ's attentions that made him persecute Wally? She leaned against the counter of her compact kitchen realizing that her dream of growing closer to Griff had become a nightmare, and it was all because of CJ—a man in whom she had zero interest. Griff seemed hurt and she ached to comfort him. But that would have to wait.

Instead, she assembled their meal, ladling strawberries and melon into fat, round bowls. Her ringing phone made her flinch, which sent the spoon clattering to the floor. Dawn looked at the number on the LED screen; when she didn't recognize it, she let the answering machine take the call.

"Dawn, we need to talk. I saw you in court."

She flew at the machine, fumbling with the volume button, but couldn't turn it down. CJ's demanding voice filled the house.

"Why should you back some kid from Africa? The club's shindig is next week and you promised to go with me. You'd better not back out."

An earsplitting buzz and he was gone. His malevolence shook her. Dawn bent to retrieve her spoon and, when she straightened, she saw Griff leaning against the counter. He glared at her, his face a portrait of confusion.

"Did Wally hear that?" she whispered.

"Yes," he replied, pressing his hands on his eyelids. "But I don't think he realized CJ aimed the barb at him. Are you dating that clown?"

"Forget him already. I've told you, he's not my type."

"Why take his calls or wave at him in church? You welcome his attentions."

"Just the opposite." Dawn touched his arm. "I received another call—"

Unpleasant smells of charred bread reached her nostrils. "Ooh, dinner is burning!"

"Here." Griff tossed her a towel, which she deftly caught. She pulled open the oven and whipped out the sizzling tray. Several rolls were charred beyond recognition.

"At least there's enough for you and Wally." Her voice trembled. "I'll eat fruit."

Ever so slowly, Griff pulled the towel from her hands. He enfolded her into his arms, pressing her to his chest. How safe, how heavenly it felt to be this close! Wonder echoed in her heart. Dawn rested her head against him, drawing in the scent of him, hoping it would last until they saw each other again. His hand fingered her long hair.

That was how Wally found them.

"Sorry." He twirled around, leaving quickly.

"I don't want Wally thinking he's in the way," Dawn explained as she untangled herself from Griff's arms. "Put these plates on the trays and I'll serve dinner."

She split the unburned sandwiches between Griff and Wally, placing a small portion on her plate. In the cozy family room, she asked a blessing for the food. Then she told how Doc Kidd helped children. Wally didn't seem to appreciate the irony, but his face took on a look of surprise.

"Oh, I nearly forgot! I see a reason I stayed in the jail."

"How can that be?" Griff scowled, holding a sandwich near his lips.

Wally first bit into his sandwich, chewing it carefully. "This is delicious. I am thankful for each morsel I eat."

They ate in silence until Wally picked up his earlier thread. "The man in my cell had not talked to his mother in years. He asked me to call her. Miss Dawn, may I use your phone later?"

"There's one on the table, and it is okay to call me Dawn. We are family, you know."

She wanted to see Griff's reaction to being family, but he seemed not to have heard.

"I don't like you mixing with criminals," he said, a scowl etched on his face.

"Let Dawn call the man's mother and pass along the information."

"I promised." Wally tilted his head. "And I think God wants me to."

"And I think you're wrong, but who am I to get between you and God? If you're set on calling, dial star six seven first so she doesn't get Dawn's number."

Griff tossed a chip on his plate. Dawn cringed at Griff's harsh words, deciding to change the subject.

"Wally, I leave for Sudan in a few weeks. When you get a cell phone for Liberty, I'll take your photo with it. She'll have your face for her wallpaper."

"You're definitely going?" Griff sounded worried.

"My visas came through. I didn't have a chance to tell you."

"Miss Dawn, you are very kind to help me and Liberty. She will always live inside me, even if we do not see each other soon."

"How did you and Liberty meet? I've never heard," she said.

Wally swallowed the last of his meal and began simply—telling how he had followed older boys along treacherous paths caught between two dangerous countries.

"We were heading back to Sudan from Ethiopia because rebels were coming after us. Militias had already killed most adults in my village. With the other boys, I ran from first light until my lungs could burst. We spent nights in trees, listening for soldiers and snarling lions. I remember one night …"

"Wally," Dawn said as she edged her chair closer, "you don't have to talk about it."

"In jail, I thought of nothing else. Dad, you haven't heard some of this, either."

"Only if you're sure." Griff took a seat next to Wally.

"The moon was bright. In my tree, roars came closer. I was afraid and shook on the limb. With its giant claws, a lion could reach into the flimsy trees and rip me down. Somehow they missed me, because in the morning, I climbed down and saw blood. My friend had disappeared."

"How awful." Dawn shuddered.

"I stared at the blood, and so did Nuban, an older boy. Then we ran, thinking every second we would not reach Sudan before Ethiopian rebels killed us."

"You must have been so scared. How old were you?" Griff set his tray on the floor.

"Maybe eight." Wally shrugged. "As I passed some bushes, I heard a whimper. Not like an animal, but I was about to run away. The whimper came again. I sank to my knees and saw tangled blue cloth. A young girl stared at me with big eyes."

Wally wiped his eyes with his napkin. Dawn cleared away the trays and half-eaten sandwiches. When she returned with cookies, Griff and Wally spoke in such low tones that she took a step back.

"No, please, Miss Dawn." Wally beckoned her to sit. "It is when I knew God's hand protected me."

"That, I'd like to hear."

She set the cookies on a side table before perching on a chair.

"I yanked the crying child to her feet. Then I recognized Atong from my village."

"Atong?" Dawn folded her hands over her knees.

"You can't guess?" Wally's face glowed. "She is Liberty! That is the free name she took later in camp. She and I ran until the line of African boys ahead of us stopped. We spread along the river's edge. Whispers reached our ears. A giant crocodile waited for us on the other side!"

Facing such dangers, no wonder Wally's faith was so strong, Dawn thought. She understood more fully why Griff cared for Wally and his anger at what had gone so wrong in Summit Ridge.

"But you and Liberty made it together, right?" she asked.

"What happened next, I will never forget. Fear of the Croc kept me from running down the bank. Shouts came: Rebels are coming. Cross now!"

"Nuban blew air in my plastic bag, the one with all I had. He urged me to float on it. I helped Liberty in the water, lowered the knotted bag and jumped on my bag. I kicked, trying not to make waves and pulled her hand, my eyes watching the Croc. Nuban swam ahead, yelling, 'Swim fast, he's not hungry.' When we reached the middle, the beast splashed into the river. Terror twisted inside me and Liberty's hand slipped from mine."

Wally's voice broke and tears glistened on his cheeks.

"The Croc swam close to Nuban. I stopped in the water. So did Liberty. A loud scream and Nuban sank below the water. The Croc's giant tail slapped the water. I never saw my friend again. I got Liberty to the other side and we ran for days to another refugee camp. There we learned English, read the Bible, and got baptized together."

"I see why you both want to marry." Dawn leapt from her seat to kiss the top of Wally's head. "I can't wait to meet her in Walu."

Griff, too, sprang from the couch and began pacing the living room. "I wish I could believe Wally was safe with me, but that's not the case—thanks to CJ Huddleston."

"Don't waste your anger on him," Dawn said. "It's meaningless. I have to believe this will be resolved soon and Wally will be exonerated."

She passed the cookies and Wally selected a lopsided peanut butter one.

"It's my mother's recipe. Griff?"

"Why not?" He snatched up a cookie while turning to Wally. "We should get to bed soon and make an early start in the morning."

"What about your phone call to the man's mother?" She handed Wally the phone. "Besides teaching me to bake, my mother always urged me to do what God placed on my heart."

She went to the kitchen, hoping Griff would follow, but he didn't. Choosing not to listen in—Griff was fulfilling his expanding role as Wally's Dad—she rinsed dishes. A thought popped into her mind. Maybe she should let God inspire Griff through Wally.

Her trip to Sudan couldn't be happening at a more perfect time. Sounds of voices drew her back to the present and her heart quickened to see Griff peer around the corner.

"I'd like to stay, but Wally is tired."

With that, he whisked Wally to the car. Dawn pressed her face to the window, watching them drive off.

Later, in bed, she tossed and turned, wondering if her pride wasn't stung by Griff's distant attitude. If only he'd share what bothered him. Maybe living closer to each other would bring the end for them. Dawn threw her pillow to the floor, pushing that awful thought from her mind. Maybe when she flew to Sudan, he'd miss her.

Hadn't her mother always said absence made the heart grow fonder? Dawn wished it would be true for him—because she was beginning to desire Griff in her life for always.

11

Tuesday morning, when the alarm buzzed at six, Griff dressed quietly. He grabbed his laptop computer and tiptoed from the room with a lighter step than the day before. Wally was still snoring, which Griff hoped meant he wasn't as anxious about the future. By seven, Griff had already downed a dry muffin, guzzled several cups of tepid coffee, and checked his e-mails in the Lamplighter's lobby.

Griff refilled his cup, stretching comfortably in an overstuffed chair. His eyes focused on a flat-screen TV, but his mind was stuck on Dawn's upcoming Sudanese trip. He'd finally done some online research and was surprised to find that the State Department warned Americans to avoid Sudan. Yet talking Dawn out of the trip didn't seem likely.

His eyes wandered to weather radar flickering on the TV. A storm was blowing across the Blue Ridge. He and Wally better get a move on. Wally even returning to work was due to Rick and Laurie Nebo's generosity.

Griff finished his coffee, regretting how little time he and Dawn had spent together over the weekend—or ever since she'd moved to Virginia. Things kept happening to prevent their special time.

He headed for the elevator, the computer bag slung over his shoulder, when the glass front doors swished open. A stunningly beautiful woman waltzed in. Griff turned to stare, thinking his imagination must be running wild. She strolled straight for him, her midnight-black eyes shining with the light of a new day.

"I couldn't let you leave without seeing you again."

Griff grabbed Dawn's hands, the soft touch of her fine-boned fingers sending his pulse racing.

"How's Wally?" she wanted to know.

Griff released her hands. She'd come for Wally, not him. That spoke volumes. Their relationship wasn't just off to a slow start—it had completely derailed.

"Griff, what's wrong? You look ill."

"I didn't get much sleep."

"Me either. I wanted to call you about one, but I figured you'd be sleeping."

The lilt in her voice touched a nerve and he knew he was off-base again. Dawn cared for him—otherwise, why would she be here?

"I wasn't. That's why I'm awash in coffee."

"Where's Wally? You didn't leave him alone again, did you?"

"Ah, he's still asleep."

Just then, Griff's cell rang. It was Wally, who was ready to leave.

"Okay, buddy. I'll be right up. Dawn came to say good-bye."

Griff folded the phone.

"Is he okay?" Dawn's face was a picture of tenderness.

"He's nervous. I warned him not to leave the room or let anyone in. Dawn, before I hit the road, are you set on going with Rick and his team?"

"I've got lots of unused vacation time. Helping Wally stay connected to Liberty seems a perfect way to use it."

"Having flown with you a few times, I know you're one gutsy lady." Griff looked deep in her eyes, seeing determination and courage. "But there's renewed fighting in Southern Sudan near Bor, where you'll be staying."

"I'm not deciding to go, so much as God is sending me."

The elevator door creaked opened. A woman holding the hand of a crying child got off. Griff motioned Dawn down the hall toward the indoor pool.

"Listen," he said, lowering his voice. "When I should've been sleeping, I logged onto my computer. The State Department has issued a travel advisory. Sensible Americans are leaving Sudan, not trying to get into the war-torn country."

"I intend to make up to him for what happened here," Dawn said, her eyes flashing. "I will bring Liberty that cell phone and get her the SIM card so Wally has something to look forward to."

Griff ran his hand over his moustache, knowing further appeals would be futile. "You can't blame me for being concerned for your safety," he said with a shrug.

She shot Griff a penetrating look. "Most of the trouble is in western Sudan, not the south. The people there need our help."

Griff touched her arm, trying to dial back his anxiety. The last thing he wanted was harsh words with her in a hotel hallway.

"The trip isn't for three weeks yet. Perhaps things will simmer down." When the tension in her face didn't disappear, he added, "Want to stick around and say good-bye to Wally?"

Her eyes were misty. He wanted to tell her how much he'd like to spend the day together. But she was on her way to work and he had to get in his car and take Wally to Rob's Deli.

"Dawn, I'm sorry to order you around. I have no right."

This brought a long-awaited smile. "You have more right than any man I know."

"More than CJ Huddleston?"

Dawn thumped his shoulder. "Quit it. He means nothing to me, except as Wally's nemesis."

"That's not the impression he gives. He phoned you again last night."

"Forget CJ. When will I see you again?"

Griff leaned down, touching her lips with his. Remembering that Wally waited upstairs, he made it a speedy kiss.

"Not soon enough. You mentioned you might go to Parent's Weekend next Saturday at VMI. Want company?"

Sadness flickered in her eyes. "Brian never called yesterday."

Griff playfully took hold of her hand. "We could leave early and enjoy the trip together with no CJ Huddleston to interfere."

"You should get Wally. I have to leave in a few minutes."

"Dawn, why continue dealing with a guy who seeks to further his own career by sending Wally to the slammer?"

Dawn said nothing, her face turning cloudy.

"You're ignoring my question."

"It deserves no answer, but I'm thinking about changing my phone number."

Griff lobbed back, "How about just telling CJ to leave you alone? Period. Better yet, if he's truly a bother, why not get a protection order against him?"

"You've got to be kidding! I'm sure the impartial Judge Fox would sign an order against him, aren't you?"

"He let Wally out on bond."

"Wally's arrest is precisely why I'm trying to ignore CJ. Otherwise, he might make things worse, like appealing his release to another judge."

Dawn bolted toward the door, but Griff caught her arm. "Can I call when I get home tonight?"

She nodded and, in another second, disappeared out a side door. He wanted to kick himself. Why did he bring up CJ again? Was it just because Griff found the guy a menace to justice? Well, that and his nonstop harassment of Dawn.

As he shot toward the stairs, his mind reverberated with Dawn's suggestion. It would be smarter to forget CJ's power grabs and focus on getting Wally acquitted. He'd blown it by ramming another guy down Dawn's throat. With no answers to his personal life, Griff hiked the stairs two at a time. Wally stood in the room holding his suitcase.

"Sorry, Dawn had to race to work," Griff explained.

"Is everything all right?"

"I'm just anxious to get you to Rob's ahead of a storm."

Griff grabbed their suitcases and paid the bill. At least Wally was riding along on the trip back, instead of being stuck in a jail cell. But minutes later, as Griff eased the car onto the highway, he knew one thing was certain: nothing good had come from this wedding trip.

His anger at God for allowing a true innocent like Wally to be bullied twisted like a hot knife in Griff's heart, but he'd never admit such harsh feelings to Wally or Dawn. Their faith in God was too simple. They believed He solved every problem, while Griff's logical mind kept him from surrendering to a power he would never see or touch.

LIGHT FROM A FULL moon streamed in through Dawn's bedroom window, piercing the lace curtain. She'd chosen not to pull down the room-darkening shade, finding the moon wonderful company. The clock on her nightstand proclaimed it was nearly ten. If she didn't close her eyes soon, she wouldn't be able to get up in the morning.

Dawn plumped the pillows behind her back, finding it hard to concentrate on a particular verse in Jeremiah. For a third time she read: "For I know the plans I have for you, declares the Lord, plans to give you hope and a future."

The future. Brian seemed settled at military school, wanting to follow in his father's footsteps with a career in the Air Force. He didn't need her as much as he had when he was younger. Wonderful family memories of the three of them played in her mind—Bert and Brian flaunting their surfing skills along the Banzai Pipeline, splashing in the waves off the northern shore of Oahu, and picnics on the beach.

But Bert had died, leaving her to raise Brian on her own. She'd moved to Virginia to be closer to her son, but she rarely saw him. And now her hopes for a relationship with Griff seemed to dwindle by the day. Sadness threatened to overpower her. Dawn stared at the ceiling, searching for a hopeful thought, but none of them reached her empty places.

She was being silly. She slid her Bible next to the clock and snapped off the light, feeling wide awake. Her mind conjured up images of climbing a mountain. On worn-out shoes, she could get no traction, and she slid down a slippery slope.

"Jesus," she called softly, "I'm lonely. Please fill my life with your purposes, not my own. Am I right in going to Sudan? Show me what I should do. Amen."

With her head on the pillow, her mind drifted to her son, who still hadn't phoned. How could she fall asleep without knowing if he was completely well? She turned onto her left side and was striving to find a comfortable position when the phone rang. Brian! She snatched the phone without turning on the light.

"Brian?"

"Did I wake you?"

"No, Griff. You couldn't have called at a better time."

"Wally reached work on time and I'm finally home. You busy?"

"Not really," she said, watching moonbeams straggle in through the lace. "You caught me feeling sorry for myself. Brian still hasn't called."

"When I was his age, I rarely talked with my parents or wrote letters. I knew they were there for me if I needed them."

He sounded buoyant, so different than he had that morning.

"What's keeping you up late?" she asked.

"On the way home, I started marveling at how your church and Rick rallied behind Wally."

"They are the best, aren't they?"

"Dawn, they don't even know him. It would be one thing for me to put up my house for bond, but I never even thought of it." Griff yawned into the phone. "Sorry. I'm way past tired. I appreciate their concern and yours. Do you think they just were overwhelmed by what Wally's endured?"

A smile found its way to her face. "It's more than sympathy. Rick and Laurie love God and are loved by God. When Jesus lived on earth, he said to new Christians 'whatever you do for the least of these, you did for me.'"

"So they look for people to help?"

"In a way. We Christians should help the poor and those who suffer. Rick, Laurie and Doc Kidd would help you or me, too. They're living a life modeled by Jesus."

Griff stayed silent, but then said, "Wow! I was surprised to hear Rick say his house is paid for. He must get a pretty healthy salary."

"No. He really doesn't. In fact, he probably makes less than me or you."

"You think so?"

"He leads a modest lifestyle," Dawn said, wondering what was on Griff's mind. He didn't keep her waiting long.

"I'm embarrassed that Rick put up his house before I did. Do you think there's any way I could show my thanks? Does he need something I could provide?"

Dawn sat up in bed and snapped on the light, thinking that maybe she and Griff should talk about this in person.

"You're kind to offer. But it might deny Rick the blessing he'll get from God."

"Let me know if you hear anything. No one would do something like that for me. Well, Eva might. You should cherish your friends."

"I do, and I count you among them."

Griff chuckled. "If work cooperates, I'll take you to dinner soon, someplace nice."

"I have a full week, too. Saturday's a possibility." Dawn covered her yawn, but Griff must have heard.

"Good night. I'll be calling you."

She hung up the phone and reached for the light, when the phone rang again.

"Miss me already?" she said with a laugh.

"Sure I do. Listen, Dawn, I wanted to ask you about today."

The man's oily voice penetrated her nerves and she shuddered. Speaking to CJ Huddleston seemed like a nightmare, yet she had answered his late-night call.

"Oh?" Dawn kept her voice monotone, hoping to discourage him.

"Do you know Wally well?"

Was this some kind of trap? Anything she said, CJ could use against him. "It's late. Let's talk another time." She didn't want to mislead CJ and didn't want to annoy Griff.

"Great. What time do I pick you up Saturday night? Dinner starts at six."

Dawn stared at the receiver in disbelief. Would this guy never give up? Did she have to move back to Florida to get rid of him?

"Hello, Dawn. Did I lose your connection?"

For a split second, she fought the urge to press the button, ending the call. But that would be dishonest and against her core beliefs. She drew in a long breath.

"I never said I'd go to the gala. This is Parent's Weekend at VMI and I'm going to see my son. Good night."

Dawn set down the receiver, wondering if CJ had put someone up to making that crank call she'd received earlier at her office. She decided that, in the morning, she would change her home number.

Unsettled, she climbed out of bed and heated a glass of milk, needing something to take off the edge. Once she had rechecked all the doorknobs and was satisfied the house was snug, Dawn wandered off to bed, but not to sleep. Adrenaline kept pounding against her ears.

Finally, her feet hit the floor again. This time she sent a long e-mail to Brian, asking him flat out if he wanted her to come for Parent's Weekend.

12

For Bo Rider, a seasoned CIA agent, the Artic Circle was close by. Problem was, so were the Russians. Though he'd come to expect the unexpected, this sudden mission had him seriously on edge. He sat crammed in the jump seat of an Air Force B-1 bomber dressed in a tight, olive-green flight suit, tension rippling beneath his skin. Sweat stung his eyes. Would he make it back in one piece or get blown out of the sky?

The previous Wednesday, his clandestine source inside Russia had warned Bo not to get too close—yet here he was, a guinea pig flying straight toward disaster. The illuminated hand of his watch clicked to three a.m. He deserved to be in bed at such an early hour.

Bo tried swiping his forehead, but the sturdy helmet didn't allow him to wiggle in a finger let alone his whole hand. He desperately needed a shower and shave, but such luxuries would have to wait until he landed back on earth.

"Cap'n Pierce, we're heading over the Bering Sea."

Bo keyed his microphone to talk to the bomber pilot. "Captain Maloney, any sign of Russian MiGs?"

"Not yet."

Ace Maloney knew Bo as Captain Skip Pierce. While he posed as a Defense Intelligence Agency (DIA) officer, in reality, Bo was a former Army Ranger traveling for the CIA, putting out hotspots around the world. He'd logged thousands of miles in sophisticated military aircraft and had bent his six-foot frame into countless coach seats on 777's. Yet in all his travels, Bo had never revealed his true identity.

"We're in Alaskan airspace," Maloney declared, as if it were no big deal.

Bo wasn't so sure. "You got us here pretty fast."

"That's why I love flying the B-1. Won't be long now."

Seconds ticked by. The wait seemed an eternity. Bo's words of warning to the crew during a classified briefing a little before midnight came soaring back: "We haven't sent multiple bombers this close to Russia in years. Stay alert. Anything could happen."

Then they'd loaded into the B-1 Lancer and Ace Maloney had roared the bomber out of Ellsworth Air Force Base, which was a stone's throw from Rapid City, South Dakota. Two other Lancers flew behind them, somewhere in the pitch-dark night. Their mission was simple, but dangerous: to see how close they could fly to Russia's borders before being detected.

"Cap'n, we're passing over the Fox Islands in the Aleutian chain."

"How long before Russia reacts?"

"Wait," hissed Maloney. "Russian radar is painting us."

"Already?" Bo flexed his hands, excitement colliding with apprehension.

"Nope. It can't be." Maloney shook his head. "Our onboard detector must be malfunctioning."

Did Maloney know his stuff? "Are you certain it's a malfunction?"

"Yup, we're too far from Russia for their radar to paint us."

"If you say so."

Bo squirmed, longing to see out a window. Stuffed in the miniscule jump seat behind four other crew members, he was anything but comfortable.

While Maloney flew the plane, Bo took to cracking his knuckles on his left hand. His nerves were afire like a hot electrical current. What if the worst happened out here at the top of the world? Who'd look after his family?

A sad thought plagued him—his wife, Julia, and the kids wouldn't even miss him. He'd already been gone shy of a month. He had missed all of Glenna's dance recitals and Gregg's tee-ball games. Glenna had quit sending texts a week ago. Bo vowed to do better by them in the weeks ahead.

His mind snapped to attention when Chen, the defensive systems officer, suddenly leaned into his instruments.

"Sir, we've got company. Fighters heading straight for us, probably from Russia. I don't believe this." Chen's finger trembled as he pointed. "There's maybe eight—no, ten of them!"

"Could they be ours?" Maloney barked.

"There's no IFF signal saying so."

Bo's pulse skyrocketed. He watched, transfixed, as Chen manipulated his computers, calling out, "They're closing quickly!"

These words had barely left his mouth when there was a tremendous roar and the plane shuttered.

"Wow!!" shouted Maloney. "A MiG cut across our nose, missing us by yards."

Adrenaline pumped through Bo's veins. He gripped the flimsy edge of the jump seat, desperate to act. Could this be it—the final seconds of his life? He hated to think so. He hung on.

His voice cool as ice, Maloney ordered, "We're turning back. That's what the Russian pilots are warning us to do. Our other two bombers are reporting near collisions with MiGs. I'm not risking our lives."

"Glad to hear it." Bo blew out a tortured breath.

Of course, the aim all along had been to edge the B-1 as close as possible to Russia before being challenged. Still, Bo hadn't expected the MiGs to meet them in the air so quickly or aggressively. The plane banked and they reversed direction, upsetting Bo's empty stomach.

He heard Maloney say, "Captain Pierce, we just proved Russia must have something new. And whatever it is can detect us farther from their shores than ever before. We're heading home."

"You've got my vote."

Bo relaxed in the jump seat, one thought revolving in his mind. If Maloney had acted as the aggressor or if he'd waited a fraction of a second before turning back, Bo and the rest of the crew might have been wiped out by the Russians.

Somehow. he'd survived to live another day and to fight another mission. All he wanted now was to get home, kiss his wife, and hug his kids.

13

Safe on the ground at Ellsworth, Bo raced to the Com Center, anxious to tell his CIA boss about the near-miss. But the grizzled spy veteran couldn't be found. Bo left a hasty message for Director Wilt Kangas and then punched in Julia's cell number, which clicked right over to her voice mail.

"Honey, set an extra plate for supper," he quipped. "I'm coming home."

That should give her a bounce. Bo folded the cell, his stomach growling. He'd had no food since late the previous day. Though it was early, maybe he could eat breakfast before catching a flight home. Hadn't Maloney assured him there'd be hot grub?

Bo battled fatigue as he hiked to the mess hall; stepping inside, his mouth watered at tantalizing smells of frying bacon and sausage. He asked for extra helpings of scrambled eggs, grabbed a couple packets of hot sauce, and poured hot coffee to the rim.

At a table for one—bone-tired, he didn't feel like talking to anyone—he'd just sliced off a piece of sausage when his cell whirled against his thigh. He snatched it from his flight suit pocket, thinking it was Julia. Wrong. It was the duty officer at Com Center.

"Director Kangas is on the line for you."

Bo dashed down the hall and flung open the door, finding a secure line in a remote office.

"Captain Pierce here."

"Rider, do those people at the base believe you're Defense Intelligence?"

"Um, yes, they seem to, sir." Bo fought for breath. "We had quite a scare. A MiG-35 nearly collided with us."

"Isn't that what we wanted? Russia's interception of you so far from their shore corroborates your newest asset."

"I agree. My source warned that Russia's latest secret radar would detect U.S. aircraft quicker than in the past."

"He was dead-on," Kangas grunted. "Last night's exercise tested the radar and the truthfulness of your asset. What do you call him?"

"The Bear, sir. Bear for short."

"Rider, a recon report came to me minutes ago. An AWAC plane, flying high above you, detected Russian radar all the way from Nagomy, Russia painting your B-1. As Bear predicted, such long-reaching radar has never been detected before."

"Sir, I'm glad you have confidence in Bear, as I do."

Kangas sure sounded pleased. Pride swelling in his chest, Bo couldn't wipe the grin off his face. He hadn't been targeted by the Russians for nothing.

"I assume you're taking good care of Bear."

"There is one thing." Bo cleared his throat.

How much to divulge to Kangas? Should Bo admit how bothersome Bear acted on their last meet, demanding enough money for a Mercedes? Bo decided to probe the waters before plunging in.

"He hit me up for more cash. That had me worried until the MiG zoomed out to meet us. Seems his intel isn't bogus." Bo sank into a nearby chair but refused to succumb to jet lag—at least not until he had flopped into his own bed back in Virginia.

"Rider, I'll see if I can sweeten the deal with Bear. Meanwhile, delve into Russia's intentions with Iran in particular."

"Bear's been vague about Russia's support of Iran, though I confronted him during our last meet in Vienna."

"Stay on him."

"Count on it, sir."

Bo was about to end the call when Kangas slipped in, "Hate to do this."

Whatever Kangas had in mind did *not* sound pleasant.

"It's imperative you leave ASAP."

"Yes, sir, I'm flying home after breakfast."

Though his eggs were probably cold, what was food when you had the nation's security in your crosshairs?

"Not Virginia. I've got another assignment for you across the pond."

Was Kangas posing some bizarre test of Bo's sanity? "You're joking right?"

"This mission is more critical than the one you just completed."

Another trip? It couldn't be happening. His grueling schedule flashed through his mind in seconds as he struggled to make sense of what Kangas wanted him to do.

A month earlier, Bo had boarded a redeye to Vienna, Austria, where he'd camped for weeks, casing out cafés and train stations while waiting for Bear. When he'd finally shown up, Bear had hinted Russia had new, longer-reaching radar that some unidentified nation hoped to buy.

Bo had passed on the intel before rushing to Hong Kong to develop another source. Then things heated up with the Russian radar.

He'd left Hong Kong seventy-two hours earlier, stopping at Ellsworth to climb into the B-1, tangle with the Russians over Alaska, and fly back to the base—all while watching for Russian MiGs on his tail.

"Rider, within the hour, the Air Force will fly you from Ellsworth to Minneapolis, where you'll catch an early morning flight to London, arriving at Heathrow tonight."

Bo's heart started pounding erratically. He'd just made Julia another promise he couldn't keep. When he had left Austria, he'd boasted he'd be home in two days. She had sighed, telling him how much trouble the kids were getting into.

His life was spinning out of control and Bo felt compelled to salvage the remnants of his family. "Sir, isn't there somebody else? My wife—"

"Only *you* can fulfill this," Kangas interjected. "You'll take Hal Odessa's place at the conference for the International Association of Microbiologists. His wife nearly lost twins she's expecting and can't leave her bed."

"Did Odessa have his sights on anyone in particular?"

"I told him to recruit assets, using your methods. Did he ask you for a primer?"

"Nope."

"That's why I chose you to replace him. You wrote the manual on these capers."

Bo tried once more. "But, sir—"

"No buts, Rider. I've had Frank Deming change all reservations to Skip Pierce. Just report to the Hotel Excelsior and do an encore."

The line clicked dead, ripping from Bo any hope of convincing Julia that he still loved her. Foisted off onto Kangas' assistant, Bo stared in disbelief at the clock. Time held no meaning. His job kept pushing him to squelch one fire after another.

Truth hit hard. He wasn't going home. He suppressed an urge to fling the stupid phone against the wall. Instead, he stalked out of the Com Center and returned to the mess hall, where he tossed the congealed breakfast into the trash.

Two Air Force officers who looked like they'd just crawled out of bed approached him. The short guy asked, "You Captain Pierce?"

Bo nodded, but could spit out no words.

"I'm Captain Jordan Fitzpatrick," he said, gesturing to his sidekick. "He's Major Harold Sopko. We have orders to fly you to Minneapolis on the double."

"I heard that, too." Bo shook their hands, amazed by the Agency's superb orchestration.

"Join us at the flight line," Fitzpatrick snapped before walking away.

As the real Air Force Officers strode off, Bo grabbed his gear, angry at having to cross the pond. His all hadn't been enough. Bo shoved aside thoughts of duty, deciding that after the London meet, he'd get home somehow, no matter what new crisis Kangas dreamed up. Then he'd burst into Kangas's swanky office and quit.

Out on the tarmac, the sun perched above the horizon, giving the sky an eerie haze. Reality seeped into Bo's foggy brain—he'd have to resign through channels, like any other CIA agent. Only the success of his last few missions even allowed him direct access to Kangas.

Bo halted by the plane, an Air Force executive-sized Lear jet, and struggled to get hold of things. Out here in the wilds of South Dakota, he felt his life disintegrating. But maybe he should avoid rash decisions that could mess up his whole career.

TWO HOURS LATER IN MINNEAPOLIS, Bo thanked Captain Fitzpatrick for a smooth ride and hurried to find his gate. His plane was ready to depart, so he boarded the 777, grinding his teeth. A grueling flight to London lay ahead. He stuffed thoughts of home into a far corner of his mind.

The only comforting idea he could find was a sketchy plan for switching to the private sector, capitalizing on dozens of connections he'd made in high-powered security firms. He snagged an aisle seat in business class, wiping sweat from his brow and closing his eyes, exhaustion seeping into every particle of his being.

Did he doze off? His mind reeling, Bo couldn't be sure of that or anything.

"Orange juice or coffee?"

Bo jolted from his misery to gaze up at a bean pole of a flight attendant, the man's eyes glowing bright red against a white shirt buttoned around his neck. Bo wasn't the only guy in need of sleep.

"Sorry, what did you say?"

"Would you like something to drink?"

"When do we land?"

"In about an hour."

That soon? He must've slept through most of the flight. "Hot coffee, buddy. I need something to wake me up."

Bo wrapped his hands around the cup, dog-weary. He had just locked in a fresh Chinese asset—using promises of secret cash and existing for days on mouthfuls of rice and even less sleep—when Kangas ordered him from Hong Kong to act on the Russian threat.

In Bo's last conversation with Julia, she'd said Gregg opened the neighbor's gate, letting their dog escape. Bo blinked his dry eyes. By now, his kids had totally forgotten what he even looked like. He guzzled his coffee, asking for a refill and then raising his seat for landing in time to hear the pilot make a stunning announcement.

"This flight is being re-routed from Heathrow to Gatwick."

Bo bolted upright. He looked around the plane, trying to figure what had gone wrong. Other passengers appeared startled, but the flight attendant calmly carried his tray. Bo flicked on his call light when the pilot explained what happened.

"A baby white rhino escaped its crate and is being chased on a runway. We'll arrive in Gatwick soon."

Bo slumped in his seat, laughing. A wild animal had caused havoc in his already messed-up life. Some passengers turned to stare and Bo clamped his mouth shut. He might be going loony, but drawing scrutiny would turn stupid into plain dumb.

As soon as the jet landed, he jumped from his seat, hitched his bag from the overhead bin, and shot out of the plane as though he had another plane to catch. At least sitting in business class allowed him to exit first. In the busy terminal, he selected a quiet seat by a window to call home.

But Julia's cell just rang. The bleak sound gave him a hollow feeling. He entered their unlisted home number and a computer chirped, "The number you've dialed has been disconnected."

He'd probably misdialed. Bo tried again, getting the same blasted recording. His fingers flying, he sent Glenna a text, asking to have Julia call him right away. His daughter loved to text, didn't she? Bo ran to the taxi stand, not knowing what part of his life was real anymore.

The harrowing ride to London was sheer torture, the cabbie dodging double-decker buses and roaming tourists in the traffic-clogged streets. Bo usually found the city exciting, but tonight, the pomp meant nothing. He checked into the Excelsior, an upscale hotel in the heart of London, using his undercover name.

He found his second-floor room and dropped his bag to the floor with a thud. The place was cramped, a huge desk dwarfing the single bed. He could hardly turn around. And he hadn't heard from Julia or his daughter, which made him anxious.

Bo settled into a firm and unyielding chair, yet another disappointment in this swanky hotel. He phoned his neighbor, Carver Washington, who hadn't lived next door for long. The accountant worked from home consulting with government agencies. He answered right away.

"Carver, it's Bo. I can't reach Julia. Would you walk over and ask her to call?"

"Phones went out after the storm. Did you try recently?"

"Sure. It seems my home line is disconnected."

"Where are you?" Carver asked, and then quickly covered up his mistake. "Forget I asked. I know the State Department sends you all over."

"I really need to speak with Julia."

"Okay. I'll pop over and see if she's home."

"Thanks, Carver."

Bo hung up, picturing the tall, lanky, African-American neighbor "popping" through the manicured shrubs that separated their homes and giving Julia his urgent message. He'd passed Carver jogging more than once. The man seemed in good shape for an older guy.

But Julia's call didn't come. When minutes passed, Bo's eyelids drooped as if made of cement. When would life return to normal? He accepted that it wouldn't be any time soon and trudged off to the shower, letting the warm water make him drowsy.

He crashed on the bed and, in spite of his ragged mind, he drifted off to sleep, still unconvinced he had to be the one for this assignment.

14

Bo woke early Friday morning to sounds of honking horns, a far cry from his quiet suburban home in northern Virginia. He took a tepid shower but was still yawning as he flipped through the conference schedule, curious about which sessions might yield tantalizing results. He wouldn't listen to the speakers—his true goal was to spot foreign scientists working in civilian and warfare technologies. He really had no idea whom to target.

He'd had no chance to talk with Odessa, the CIA colleague who had dropped out of sight to care for his wife and about-to-be-born twins—or so Kangas claimed. In Bo's career with the CIA, and with the Army Rangers before his recruitment into the clandestine Agency, he had always reacted to changing circumstances with gusto. Why did he feel so different this time?

The sooner he found a scientist from an enemy nation willing to provide him with intelligence, the sooner Bo could jet home. He donned his last pair of clean slacks and a crisp, blue-striped shirt. He hung conference credentials around his neck and checked his reflection, rubbing a hand over his face.

He needed a shave. Still, the dark stubble gave him a rugged look, which suited Skip Pierce, the persona he'd adopted—either by genius or chance—as an international corporate recruiter. Bo pocketed his cell, wanting to sense the whirl against his leg when Julia phoned. He snatched a portfolio from his carry-on bag, steeling himself to prowl brightly-lit halls and stuffy meeting rooms looking for that one special "cooperative" scientist.

The elevator carried him to the first floor and he reached the exhibit hall, taking in the massive corridors of booths. Yikes! He wasn't ready for this. Less assured than usual, he gulped a cup of coffee and ate a cinnamon scone before searching for a stooge to turn.

Men in gray suits, poring through catalogues and talking in pairs, concealed their faces. Their eyes—he must see their eyes. That way, he'd know if it was safe to engage them. Bo circled the front of the hall where a woman registrar with reams of curly hair sat behind a table piled high with pamphlets, her violet eyes catching his.

"May I help you?"

"Nah." Bo reached into a corner of his mind, stumbling onto a name. "I'm off to hear Dr. Rani."

"Excellent choice." She stood, tottering on pointy heels, and whispered, "I'm off to get coffee. It is going to be a very long day."

She pulled on her suit jacket and wobbled off. Bo took a chance. Staring down at papers spread across her table, he could hardly believe his good fortune. A furtive glance over his shoulder. No one watched him.

In a split second, he swiped a stack from the table, casually sliding the list of conferees into his leather portfolio. He stepped toward the exhibits, adrenaline spiking, and paused by a booth displaying machines that analyzed DNA using Polymerase Chain Reaction (PCR).

"I can tell you how PCR analyzes diseases," piped the exhibitor.

"Sure, why not?" Bo said, shrugging.

Because he'd never heard of the gadgets, he grabbed a brochure, pretending to listen.

"Using three cycles of heating and cooling, our automatic cycling machines find bacteria and viruses. They further the study of genetic diseases. PCR also can determine DNA fingerprinting for paternity. One of our sales reps will visit your firm, sir."

The pudgy fellow looked so hopeful that Bo hated letting him down, so he opted for a soft landing. "I have your brochure and will look it over. Thanks."

Bo veered to another aisle and, rather than being proud of his actions, he felt deflated. So he'd copped a useless brochure along with a list of attendees. What did he know about chemistry and biology? He was all about defense—targeting aerospace engineers steeped in their countries' weapons systems to spy for the CIA.

Still, he had himself to thank for this gig—he'd so impressed his boss by co-opting Chinese aerospace engineers that Kangas had ordered other CIA agents to copy Bo's technique in other disciplines. As a result of his past success—and with Odessa out in the cold somewhere—Bo had to work his magic among scientists in London.

He rallied his nerve. Weren't all scientists alike, eager to spread knowledge to help the world? The fields of expertise were different. He turned over the brochure that extolled the wonders of the PCR cycling machine, feigning interest. When no one approached him, Bo sauntered to the lobby and dashed into the first elevator.

Minutes later, in the secrecy of his hotel room, he perused the attendee list, trying to focus his beyond-tired eyes on tiny letters spelling the names of Indian, Chinese, Russian, and Iranian conferees. His finger ran down the American names: Anita Crum, Ingeborg Sorenson, and Sylvester Teatree. Nothing clicked, so his finger roamed the rest of the names. Only a handful of scientists had the credentials fitting the profile he searched for.

A quick glance at his cell revealed that he'd missed no calls. He shoved the phone back into his pocket, slid the roster into his portfolio, and took off for Dr. Rani's session. He entered the glitzy lecture hall in time to hear the audience applaud. It seemed he'd missed that lecture. Oh well.

He turned, ready to find another session, when a dark-haired scientist grabbed the microphone and began speaking in heavily-accented English.

"I am Dr. Cyrus Tabriz from Tehran. I hope to challenge your thinking about my country's contribution to the world's new order."

Now that sounded worthwhile. Cyrus Tabriz might offer some political clues about Iran's closed society. Lights dimmed and Tabriz started his presentation of slides on a large, overhead screen. Bo snagged a seat at the end of an empty back row, nearly sitting on a valise whose owner was obviously missing.

Bo perched on the edge, half-listening to Tabriz urging attendees to lobby the United Nations to lift sanctions that were causing hardships for the Iranian people. Blah, blah. Whose seat had he taken?

He found the name tag, but didn't want to get caught staring at it. In the low light, he couldn't read the Farsi script. This could be a profitable find. He promptly left the lecture hall, grasping the valise as though it belonged to him.

What he lacked in knowledge about biology, Bo more than made up for in curiosity. He couldn't risk taking the leather case to his room, so he scooted into the nearest men's room, relieved to see no feet beneath the doors. He snuck into a stall, locked the door behind him and, resting one foot on the commode, balanced the valise on his knee.

The name on the tag was indeed in Farsi. Bo flipped it over. There he read the owner's name in English: Dr. Cyrus Tabriz, Director, Institute for Scientific Advances, Tehran, Iran. So the valise belonged to the scientist who was in there talking about lifting sanctions.

Bo rifled through the contents—pens, small pads of paper, an extra green and red tie—but found nothing scintillating. Then he grasped the doctor's passport. Thumbing through it, Bo couldn't imagine how or why the valise had been left on a chair.

Entry stamps heralded the doctor's travels to China, North Korea, and Russia—but never to the U. S. Bo carefully fetched his cell and, aiming it at the passport, snapped a picture of the first page with the doctor's name and photo—which proved to be a real juggling act. Just as he nearly tipped the valise into the commode, the phone vibrated in Bo's hand.

He scrambled to thrust the passport into the case while answering the phone at the same time.

"Hello," he huffed.

"Hello back," Julia said, her voice pinched.

"Julia! When I didn't hear from you, I got worried."

"Carver stopped by a little while ago. Guess you've been trying to call me."

"At least five times."

Bo gripped the valise under one arm, pressing the phone to his ear with the other hand.

"If you called, I never heard the phone ring. Carver nearly yakked my head off."

"Oh, I called. Why did you change our number?"

She ignored his question. She just talked on as if she hadn't heard. "When does your flight land?"

"What's going on? A recording said our phone was disconnected."

"A storm raged through last night. The kids were scared and I got no sleep. Wind knocked over the maple tree by the garage. Guess I should call the phone company."

Bigger problems than the phone loomed around the next sentence. He leaned against the stall door, gearing up for Julia's blast when he told her.

"I'm not sure when I'll be home. Kangas sent me on another mission." A dreadful silence met his ears. "Julia, I'm sorry."

Bo wanted to add "honestly," but she knew he meant it—didn't she?

"Say this isn't happening, Bo."

"If only I could get home. This isn't my doing."

"Guess you don't care Gregg got all D's on his tests," she sighed.

"Of course I care about him and Glenna."

"And me? I'm doing the job of two parents. I feel like I'm losing my mind."

"Me too. I mean . . . ." Bo's voice drifted away. What could he say? Of course she wouldn't take his news with a smile. "Julia?"

Silence. Had she hung up on him? She hadn't.

"Carver said he'd help find a tree removal company, so you don't have to worry about the hole in the roof." Her voice wavered. "He's a godsend with you gone."

Hole in the roof? Uncertainty rattled his brain. Bo felt the valise dragging down his arms, but he refused to sit in the stall.

"Let me know what's with the phone. I hate being unable to connect with you."

"Do you mean that, Bo?"

"I'd be home if Hal Odessa's wife wasn't expecting twins. The doctor ordered bed rest, so Hal's home taking care of her. The Company's not all bad."

"You're telling me that? My brain is so far gone, it's past the moon, Bo." Her voice broke, sobs catching in her throat. "I miss you."

Compassion for what his wife was coping with in his absence made him shudder. "Me too," he said, juggling the valise under his arm. "Kiss the kids for me. And Julia—I'll work like crazy to get out of here."

His life had become crazed alright. Bo ended the call. Why hadn't he told Julia that he loved her? Romantic words didn't come easily while he was holed up in a toilet stall.

Bo ripped through the valise, frantic to find something, anything, he could use. At the very bottom, he found some tiny notations. These he eased out with the tips of his fingers. Shock billowed through his mind. Before him were plans and formulas—for what, Bo didn't know.

He forced his mind to absorb every detail. What Iranian scientist would bring sensitive documents to an international conference? Unless …

He knew the drawings should be photographed, but such a sensitive operation would have to wait until he got to his room. He'd better get up there before Tabriz discovered his valise missing. Bo hustled by the concierge desk, passing a woman in a gray, western-style suit and black head scarf who was gesturing wildly in the face of a stoic security guard.

Bo angled toward a stairwell to avoid her, but it was too late. She had spotted him. With a startled look of recognition, she lunged at him, her face a storm in the making.

"There it is! Arrest that man!"

Bo tore through the front lobby, not waiting for the guard's response.

"Stop! I am Dr. Lili Tabriz, Director of Epidemiology for Iran's Health Ministry. That case belongs to my husband."

Before the smooth-faced guard could react, Lili Tabriz rushed toward Bo, a hostile gaze fixed on her face. She snatched the valise from beneath Bo's arm.

"This is my husband's. That man stole it. I insist you arrest him."

"Ma'am, I can take a report," the uniformed guard offered, shuffling his feet.

Bo might luck out after all. The security guard was about nineteen, maybe twenty, and seemed to have no experience enforcing any laws. A half-smile stole its way onto Bo's face.

An outraged Mrs. Tabriz shook the valise close to the guard's face, continuing to barrage him with reasons to take Bo into custody. But the more she talked, the more something seemed amiss about the middle-aged, Iranian doctor.

She had hidden her light blue eyes behind black-framed glasses and she wore a headscarf. Yet, she spoke perfect English. Her accent was definitely American—New York, possibly Brooklyn.

"I don't know what this woman's problem is," Bo said, keeping a level eye on Lili Tabriz, whose face was growing redder by the second.

"Does that case belong to you, sir?" asked the guard.

"I found it abandoned in the lecture hall. I'm on my way to the lost and found."

Bo's eyes flickered to Lili Tabriz. Her finely chiseled nose and light eyebrows gave her an appearance of Swedish or Norwegian descent. Though she spoke American-English, she had passed herself off as Iranian. Well, he wouldn't be drawn into her intrigue.

He edged away, striving to deflect unwanted scrutiny. Certainly Bo wouldn't approach either Cyrus or Lili Tabriz to work for the U.S. But then again, maybe Lili's outrage was a ruse.

"You are not coming from the direction of the lecture hall." Pure hatred spewed from her icy-blue eyes.

"If this were New York, you'd be explaining to the police how the case was abandoned on an auditorium seat."

"Don't speak of New York. That city is a rat hole and always will be. Besides, I was watching my husband's property, but I left to use the restroom."

Bo glared at her, defying her to crumble and make an admission. When the guard answered a call on his hand-held phone, Bo thought it best to skedaddle. This conflict held only danger.

He walked away, ignoring her tirade and searching for a way to recover his momentum. With his cover nearly blown, maybe he should catch a cab and fly back home. The thought of surprising Julia and the kids gave his heart a jolt. Yes—he'd do it.

15

In his tiny hotel room, Bo changed socks, tossed the old pair with the worn spot on one heel into his carry-on bag, and splashed water on his face. He was on hold with the airlines when another call came in. The number was blocked, which meant the Agency was reaching out to him—again. Bo suppressed an urge to ignore the call and answered.

"Mr. Pierce, Mr. K. wants you on a secure connection for a message."

"What else can you tell me?"

"Just get to one ASAP."

Bo's heart lurched in his chest. It must be urgent if the duty agent wouldn't even give him a clue over the phone.

"Tell Mr. K. I'm off to find one."

"Roger that."

If Kangas had another mission for him—no, it couldn't be! Maybe his boss wanted to find out what Bo had accomplished here. If so, he had zero to brag about.

On impulse, he grabbed his bag, the same one he'd hauled from Vienna around the world to London. Rather than wait for the elevator, he bolted down the steps two at a time, exercising caution while waiting in line at the reception area. He didn't want another confrontation with the Iranian doctor. With the crush of folks in front of him, how long would it take to get out of here?

At last, he signed out as Skip Pierce, using the credit card assigned to United Search Associates, the undercover company created for him by the Agency. Bo fidgeted with the pen, waiting for the clerk to finalize the bill. What did Kangas want, anyway?

Maybe he already knew of Bo's run-in with Lili Tabriz. If Kangas had someone keeping an eye on Bo, that stung. Had Kangas planted an Agency watcher to watch him?

Bo jostled his credit card into his wallet, making for the glass door on the far right. He let his body weight push open the door handle. Muggy London air enveloped him as a group of conferees angled past and herded into the lobby. Before he reached the step, he felt a sharp jab on his neck. Someone had yanked on his collar backward, nearly strangling Bo. He struggled to get free.

"Hold on chap. You gotta answer a few questions."

"Who are you?" Bo ground his teeth, desperate to see who held him prisoner.

The tightness of his shirt collar suddenly eased from his neck, allowing him to breathe. He spun around, looking into the sly eyes of a London policeman. The bobby, decked in full regalia, black hat and all, smiled.

"They calls me Officer Oliver. If you please, this lady says you lifted property belonging to her."

"She is wrong."

Lili Tabriz waltzed out from behind Oliver, staring at Bo from behind those hideous spectacles, her cheeks flaming red and her bony hands clutching the infamous leather briefcase.

"I know you're doing your duty," Bo said, smiling with his eyes, "but did she admit that I *found* the case abandoned when I attended a lecture?"

"No," Oliver declared, shaking his enormous head.

"I bet she didn't tell you the case belongs to her husband, Dr. Cyrus Tabriz, an Iranian scientist. Being a law-abiding citizen, I was taking it to lost and found when she corralled a security guard into accosting me. I wonder why she pesters a Good Samaritan."

"Ma'am?"

As Officer Oliver turned a penetrating gaze upon Lili Tabriz, Bo slid one foot toward the door, ready to disappear in the crowd mingling outside the hotel.

"He's an American spy, I am sure."

"Officer," Bo laughed, "take a look at us. Me—I work for American companies looking to hire. In fact, I'm on my way home to Chicago. This woman, with her blue eyes hidden behind thick glasses and speaking in an American accent, is wearing Middle Eastern head garb. Who looks like a spy to you?"

That got Oliver agitated. Bo gave a little wave.

"Happy to help London keep law and order. Good day."

He stormed outside, surprised by the sudden cold rain. Bo eyed an empty taxi. Shivering, he sprinted to the back door and leapt inside.

"Piccadilly Circle and step on it."

"Watch me."

The taxi driver, smelling suspiciously of fish and chips, banged his meter to start and roared away, leaving Lili Tabriz and Officer Oliver behind. Bo's mouth began to water—how long ago had he eaten that stale scone?

"Where to in the Circle, chap?"

Giving an approximate address, Bo stayed in the shadows of the backseat, saying no more. His driver didn't take the hint.

"Nice, high-end financial district," he whistled. Then he launched into tourist jargon. "How's if I swing past Buckingham Palace? Give you a look-see at our royals. They might even be greeting folks by the front gate. You'll see the Palace Guards, as most Americans want to do."

Bo grunted, "Not this time," wishing he'd given the American Embassy's address. That facility boasted high-tech communications where Bo could easily pick up his message. Nope, he couldn't endanger his cover any more—America's Embassies were watched by host governments and any number of enemy government agents. Being seen entering the Embassy, even as an international corporate recruiter, would blow his cover sky high.

"Rain's over. How about stopping for fish n' chips? Me mum runs a place that serves the darkest ale this side of the Thames. I've not had me lunch."

"I'd love to, but sorry—it's all work and no play for me."

Bo folded his arms, blanking out the guy's endless banter and creating scenarios about the urgent message Kangas had waiting for him. At the corner with Barclays' bank on one side and Riley's pub on the other, Bo reached over, lightly tapping the driver's shoulder.

"Let me out here. How much?"

"A tenner, if you please."

Bo handed over a ten-pound note plus a quid for a tip. The cabbie wheeled to the curb and Bo hopped out, a block from the safe house. He ambled down the sidewalk, keeping an eye over his shoulder. Was that shadow moving over by a tree? Or was Bo's mind playing tricks on him?

He wandered into Riley's and ordered black coffee with steak pie. He inhaled his lunch in a far booth, waiting to see who might come in behind him. The end of a narrow passage held a possible escape route—a back door. He sipped the dark java while watching the front door. A burly man staggered in; the large jagged scar under one eye gave him a shady appearance. Bo got ready to flee.

Suddenly, the bartender waved, calling to the man, "Clyde, this one's on me. You played quite a match."

Bo stayed long enough for Clyde to sink his face into a glass of ale, weaving a tale of woe about how he smashed his leg in the last cricket match. Then Bo left and stepped around the corner, reaching the safe house. It was a three-story, brown brick affair that looked like an ordinary commercial building—only it wasn't.

Inside, the CIA staffed offices on each floor. Bo gazed down both sides of the street, spotting men and women in business attire sweeping along the sidewalk. None stood out as a threat.

A couple of young women in short skirts with cell phones plastered to their ears surged past. It seemed safe to enter. He pulled the heavy wooden door, walking into the export-import company run by the CIA, all a plausible front. Bo cleared an extensive security ritual before striding into the Com Center and logging onto the secure system.

His eyes rapidly scanned Kangas' missive: *Rider, Bear sent you a message, recovered by one of our agents in Moscow. It's extremely urgent you meet Bear on Monday. Call for details. WK—DCO*

Bo's heart utterly failed him. Moscow! Another trip taking him farther from home. He yanked the secure phone, hitting in the numbers for Kangas' private line.

"Sir, I have your secure message. If I leave, we risk losing a potential source inside Iran. Three of their scientists are here and I've met one, who is *not* a possibility."

Kangas held firm. "And I'm acting on live intel. Bear says Iran is red-hot. Meet him Monday at the Jefferson Memorial, six o'clock. Squeeze from him every last drop."

"Director Kangas, wait."

"I'm on my way to the Pentagon."

"Do you mean the Jefferson Memorial, as in D.C.?"

Kangas barked into the phone, "Get home and be quick about it. What Bear has is more crucial than anything you'll chance picking up in London."

Had Kangas just ordered him to America's capital and *not* Russia's? Before Bo could ask for more details, his boss was gone. Whatever Kangas intended, Bo knew one thing—Bear had been right about Russia's new long-reaching radar, and that meant whatever he had on Iran would be spot-on.

A sudden thought kept Bo from leaving the Com Center. He must have had a weird sense he'd be leaving London. Why else did he take his carry-on when he left the Excelsior? The duty officer handed Bo a sealed envelope.

"Sir, this arrived for you."

Not expecting to even be at the safe house, Bo stared at the envelope, which was marked High Priority. "You're sure this is for me, Skip Pierce?"

"You are Bo Rider, correct?" The officer stared at him through gold-rimmed glasses.

"Yeah," Bo dipped his head.

"Thought so," the officer smirked. "It came for you thirty minutes ago."

It was Bo's turn to flash a crooked grin. "Oh yeah. I forgot where I was."

"Printing out the directive, I saw your past travel. No wonder you don't know where you are."

Bo thanked the officer and walked out of the glass cubicle. He slid a single sheet of paper from the envelope. Kangas had pulled out all the stops. Bo was booked on a flight from Heathrow, arriving in Virginia at midnight. The typed message told Bo to catch shut-eye at home before meeting Kangas at his office at three o'clock. He'd even arranged for Bo to catch a ride to Heathrow with an officer from the safe house.

Well, the old boss still had it in him to smooth Bo's ruffled mind. At Heathrow, Bo stopped at a café and pounded down a pie and coffee. He called Julia, giving her the good news.

"Leave a light on, honey. I'll be home about one."

She could only cry.

On the flight, Bo yawned. He could hardly believe he was going home. He fell into a disturbed sleep, the kind with wild dreams. When he woke, he didn't know where he was. Engines hummed out his window. Oh—he was flying above the earth, heading for Dulles, his armpits dripping wet. Bo longed for a hot shower and a full night's sleep.

He had to wonder: did Kangas have an inkling how he'd nearly blown it in London? Maybe he would never find out, but the fiasco with Dr. Lili Tabriz felt like total failure to Bo, a terrible new experience. This might be one trip he let slip into his sub-conscious, never to be remembered again.

16

Bo darted into his office at CIA headquarters in Langley, actually feeling human for the first time in a week. He'd arrived home from London late Saturday night. After Julia had cried on his shoulder, her emotions had leveled out. He'd made a dent in her to-do list—adjusting the master bathroom john so it didn't constantly run.

The previous morning, she'd fixed homemade waffles with sausage. Bo laughed with the kids, offering to toss a football with them. Julia told him about a new study group she was attending at a local church. Everything had seemed wonderful until he'd made the mistake of telling her over coffee this morning that he would miss dinner. It struck a nerve. She had stalked off to take the kids to school without saying a single word.

Bo turned his mind to immediate concerns, punching on his computer and trying not to get steamed about Bear dictating a meeting with no regard for Bo's family. So that his Russian asset wouldn't see him driving his classic Austin-Healy or know anything of his private life, Bo ordered a rental car.

After typing memos about his efforts in Alaska and London—the latter provided little fodder for boasting—he downloaded Dr. Cyrus Tabriz's passport photo and identification page from his camera into his computer. If only he could have photographed other items from the doctor's valise.

But Bo swung into action rather than staying stuck in the past. A CIA intelligence analyst answered on the first ring. He asked how Nanette Bing's ailing mother fared in Norfolk, and then launched into why he called.

"Delve into Doctors Cyrus and Lili Tabriz, both scientists in Tehran."

"Agent Rider, hold please."

Even mentioning the name of Lili Tabriz brought his battle with her at the Excelsior gushing forth, her icy blue eyes searing his mind. Maybe there was something—

"Sorry, I'm back."

Nanette repeated the names, spelling them to make sure she entered these into her system correctly.

"It would help to know precisely what you're looking for."

"Omit nothing. Even the smallest tidbit might be important," Bo insisted.

"Cyrus is a Persian name. I assume they are both Iranians."

"Lili Tabriz might be Norwegian or Swedish. What concerns me is how she speaks like an American. She and her husband attended a conference in London—the International Association of Microbiologists. She's a real corker."

"Do you need this expedited? My boss just dumped a new assignment on me."

"I hear your pain. Fit me in. This is partly a hunch, one of those gut things."

"So much for driving down to visit my mom for a long weekend," she sighed.

"Thanks Nanette. I owe you one."

"If you ever get by this way, dark chocolate keeps my fingers searching."

TEN MINUTES BEFORE SIX, Bo eased the rental sedan along Basin Drive, parking a hair west of the Jefferson Memorial. He figured that, because the cherry blossoms had finished blooming, the park wouldn't be crowded. A tour bus in the adjacent space alerted him to expect plenty of gawkers.

On the lookout for Bear, Bo edged along the north side of the memorial, a giant white marble dome that rose magnificently above the nineteen-foot-tall, bronze statue of Thomas Jefferson. He hopped out to join throngs of camera toting people—all wearing caps and vibrant tee-shirts—from Iowa, Texas, and Japan.

Too bad he hadn't thought to bring a camera so he'd blend in. Hold it—he formed a plan. Aiming his cell phone toward the columns as a tourist might, he ascended the marble steps, trepidation bearing down on him. What were Bear's true designs in requesting to meet? In the U.S., no less.

He casually peered at his watch. Five minutes past six and still no Bear. His Russian source had better not stand him up—not after the grief this late rendezvous had caused at home. Bo pocketed his hands, stopping to admire Jefferson's quotes engraved on the walls.

One about liberty caught his eye—*God who gave us life gave us liberty. Can the liberties of a nation be secure when we have removed a conviction that these liberties are the gift of God?*

It seemed an anomaly that the Russian military officer had asked to meet under those very words. While Russia had regained some freedoms after the fall of the Soviet Union, personal liberties were eroding under the present regime. Bo turned toward another panel; then a gruff voice in his ear startled him.

"We meet again so soon."

Recognizing Bear's nearly-accent free English, Bo faced Colonel Yuri Egorov, staring past him as if he didn't recognize him. Still being cautious, Bo gazed upward as if reading Jefferson's quotes.

"Follow me to my car. We'll talk there," he muttered to Yuri.

"Can't. I'm being tailed."

"How do you know?"

"A man from my flight is here," Yuri hissed.

Bo couldn't help glancing over his shoulder at a few tourists speaking in pairs. He hoped any observers would believe he and Yuri weren't talking or even acquainted as they both looked at the engravings, hands behind their backs. Bo slowly turned, pointing his phone at Jefferson's majestic statue.

He'd previously spotted what he thought were tails when he'd been spying in foreign countries. One time in China … No! He must forget about that and solve this dilemma with Yuri. Bo pointed his cell phone at Jefferson's head.

"Maybe he's a sightseer." He said talking from the side of his mouth. "Clean your tail, then join me in my car."

"I will do so."

Bo strolled from Yuri, going around Jefferson's statue before wandering down the steps, anxious to spot any followers. Near his rental car, he stopped and perused a sign. Yuri lingered behind him. Knowing Yuri could see the car, Bo walked over and climbed in. He jostled in the seat, adjusting the back when two tourists emerged from a taxi and Yuri slid in, gazing out the rear window as it drove off. Bo tuned the radio to soft rock, his eyes continually roaming to his mirrors and glancing out the windows.

No one acted unduly alarmed by a casually-dressed Russian spy leaving the area. Had Yuri invented a ruse simply to ditch Bo? That was nonsense. Why even suggest meeting? Bo chalked up Yuri's concerns to paranoia flowing from the colonel's seditious acts.

Bo had lucked out when he'd stumbled onto Yuri in Thailand a couple months back, where Bo had been ostensibly recruiting aerospace engineers to work for American companies. He'd offered the space engineer an eye-popping salary to stay in Russia's military. Yuri had correctly guessed Bo represented the CIA.

Yuri professed no qualms in handing over secret intelligence about Russia's military aims, so long as Bo kept the gargantuan salary coming. The Agency had good reason to pay such sums: the colonel had a perfect perch as liaison officer to the Moscow company developing missiles for Russia's military. Thus, Yuri could monitor Russia's newest secret weapons and whatever countries were negotiating with Russia to buy their obsolete systems.

His mind veering back to the present, Bo blocked out a guitar solo blaring over the radio, his eyes and brain alert to any strange behaviors. On a hot summer evening in the Tidal Basin, all seemed normal. Then a young man bicycling past his car for a second time struck Bo as peculiar.

He imagined the worst. Surely the guy on the bike had spotted Yuri, which meant the Russian would not return. Bo's shoulders caved. He'd missed his family's dinner for nothing. Since his bizarre trip to London, everything seemed off-kilter.

He was about to speed away when he checked the driver's side mirror, spotting Yuri in baggy jeans and sneakers bolt from a tram and head straight for the Memorial. He stopped on Bo's side of the street to light a cigarette, taking a long puff before snuffing it out on the side of a trash can.

Yuri walked for a second time to the Memorial, and Bo approved of his evasive actions. A few minutes passed before Bo's passenger door opened and Bo's Russian asset eased into the seat, extending his hand.

"Good seeing you again."

"Likewise." Bo jammed the car in gear, pulling from his parking spot. "We're outta here. Why choose such a public place?"

"Your President Jefferson believed in freedom." Yuri thumped his chest. "I also do."

"The message you dropped in Moscow got my attention, but I never expected you'd travel to D.C."

"What I have to tell can only be said in person."

"I'm listening."

Bo cranked the wheel through sporadic traffic along the tidal basin and Yuri pulled a small flask from his side pocket. He drew a long sip, wiping his mouth with the back of his hand.

"Ah, good vodka. You are driving or I would offer you some."

"Okay, spill what you've got," Bo said as he parked near the Vietnam War memorial.

"Elginski Technology, the company I am assigned to, sold a missile system to Venezuela. The company president is in Virginia trying to get component radar parts."

"Why did you have to come along?"

"I convinced my commanding officer I should accompany him so he doesn't give away any secrets." Yuri tipped back his head, laughing with gusto at the irony. "Besides, I ensure my Swiss account continues to grow."

So Yuri wanted something from Bo in exchange. No big surprise there.

"Know this. Your account will grow so long as you keep me well informed."

Yuri took a long swig from his flask. "First, I congratulate you for your successful test of our new radar near Nagomy."

Bo stared at Yuri, not seeming to understand.

"I heard about it from my contacts at military headquarters. They had been ordered *not* to respond to any U.S. incursion of Russian air space. They did not want you knowing of their improved system."

But they had responded. Bo simply nodded, which kept Yuri talking.

"They were supposed to wait until you flew close enough for the old S300 system to detect your presence. Your American government tested that radar many times before. But the new system lit up with three U.S. bombers en route. The officers were spooked and sent up interceptors prematurely."

Yuri passed the flask to Bo.

"No thanks," Bo said as he held up a hand. "I've got another meeting after this."

"Deny knowing about your radar test if you like. But I am sure your knowledge of our new radar happened because of information I gave you about the new system. I told you the old S300 system from Nagomy is being sent to Iran."

Bo narrowed his eyes, studying Yuri's placid face and shifting eyes.

"Hasn't Iran been trying to get Russia's S300 defensive missiles for a while?"

Rather than answer, Yuri asked, "Did you hear about the *Arctic Sea* being hijacked after its last contact in the English Channel?"

"Yes," Bo nodded. "A Russian ship destined for Algeria left Finland with a load of timber that mysteriously disappeared. I've heard the *Artic Sea* carried Russian weapons for Iran."

"Exactly." Bear spit out this word as he might a piece of gravel. He tapped his empty flask.

"Drive to a store. I need more vodka."

"We can't risk being seen together in a public place."

Yuri angrily shoved the empty flask into his pocket.

"Iran sent for our S300 missiles. I was in Tehran waiting to install and train the Iranians how to operate them. These missiles are far superior to your surface-to-air missiles. Only your F-22 can escape them."

Bo's jaw muscles contracted. The White House just killed funding for the F-22! He made mental notes to get this intel to Kangas right away.

"Israel's Mossad. It was their fault."

So Israel's intelligence service was connected to this enigma. "Russia's favorite game, always accuse Mossad," Bo said, tenting his fingers.

"This time it is real. My superior says Mossad discovered the missiles concealed in the timber and arranged for thieves to hijack the *Arctic Sea*. We launched a rescue, but by then the whole world watched. So the missiles meant for Iran were returned to Russia."

"What is Moscow going to do with those S300s?"

Bo sought to disguise how little insight he had into Iran's missile procurement. What Yuri just revealed held many implications. The question was, what did Kangas know? Because everything was compartmentalized in the world of intelligence for security reasons, the right hand rarely knew what the left hand was doing.

Yuri just stared out the window, looking thirsty.

Bo snapped, "Quit dancing around. Did Iran ever get the S300 missiles?"

"The 300s removed from Nagomy were the last to be shipped to Iran." Yuri wet his lips with his tongue.

"With such powerful missiles in the hands of the Iranians, has Russia put safeguards in place to prevent Iran's destabilizing the region?" Bo leaned back with his hands on the steering wheel, believing he glimpsed a hint of concern in Yuri's eyes.

"Only our Russian technicians have the codes to launch the 300s."

"Fine, but won't the Guardians of the Islamic Revolutionary eventually man them?"

"I do not know each agreement Moscow has with Iran." A lopsided grin erupted on Yuri's face. "But when I know, I tell you."

For the next several minutes, Bo listened to Yuri's gloomy details of the heavy arms trading between Russian and Iran, confident that much of what he heard would startle even his boss, Wilt Kangas, director of the CIA's National Clandestine Service.

Sitting curbside at the Vietnam Memorial wasn't an ideal spot for a classified meeting. Bo was anxious to split to his office and make copious notes. Though Yuri had emptied his flask, surprisingly, none of his words were slurred. Just when Bo thought he'd learned all he needed, Yuri the Bear dropped a bomb.

"Now I tell you why I wanted to meet."

"You'd better, if you expect me to keep funding your retirement account."

Yuri pulled a folded piece of paper from his pocket and handed it to Bo. "This lists the products Elginski is buying in Virginia, allegedly for South Africa and Liberia. Your laws permit those items to be exported there."

"That loophole will cost lives," Bo complained.

Yuri clapped Bo on the shoulder. "Da. You and I know these components have dual uses in the manufacturer of weapons of mass destruction."

"You expect we'll let you buy them?" Bo watched for any twitch of Yuri's eyes.

"If you permit the shipment, they will be repackaged by companies in South Africa and Liberia before being shipped to Iran. It is all a ruse to avoid U.S. sanctions. I assume you know what to do."

Bo tore a piece of paper from bottom of the list and wrote on it.

"Here's my phone number. Call before you leave the area, letting me know what transpires. I suggest you catch a cab back to your hotel."

"You will hear from me soon."

Yuri folded the note, jamming it into his sock. The large Russian man lumbered from the front seat, closed the door, and disappeared down the sidewalk into a sea of mingling tourists. Realizing it was too late to get home for dinner, Bo delivered the car to the rental company before roaring back to Langley in his Austin-Healy.

What he'd just learned about Iran couldn't wait until morning.

17

Morning arrived for Bo as if there'd been no night. He had slept for less than three hours; he was grateful Julia didn't awaken when he came home or when he left. He sped along the Parkway back to Langley, where he logged onto his office computer, eager to find out if his boss, Robert Shank, or Kangas had opened his memo with Bear's new intel.

No surprise—Kangas had, and Shank wasn't even in the office yet. Bo hunched over his desk, reviewing his encrypted messages that had arrived overnight. He expected to hear any second from Nanette Bing, the analyst searching for background on the Iranian doctors. As if on cue, the phone rang and he snatched up the receiver.

"What've you learned of Lili and Cyrus Tabriz?"

"Nothing. Was I supposed to?"

"Um … " Bo swallowed. "I thought you were someone else. What can I do for you?" he asked, not recognizing the voice.

"It's FBI agent Griff Topping, reaching out after months of no contact."

"I'm so glad it's you," Bo grunted. "Forget the names you heard."

Griff chuckled. "Still up to your usual shenanigans at the State Department?"

"Only you or Eva could find me here."

"Bo, the three of us should get together soon."

Bo realized that Griff got the connection to Eva Montanna. She was the Special Agent with Immigration Customs Enforcement who had introduced Griff when she and Bo were assigned to the Senate Intelligence Committee. Though she'd told Griff that Bo worked for the State Department, Griff never believed it and told Bo so. Bo trusted Griff—having worked with the seasoned FBI agent on a recent case of mutual interest—but he had never admitted he was CIA.

"How soon do you want to have lunch?" Bo asked. "I'm quite busy keeping our diplomats happy."

"Better you than me. You know how I feel about the slippery types at State."

"Try working with them day in and day out."

"Remember how, after our last venture together, I told you that I slept better knowing you and your colleagues were protecting us around the world?"

"I don't recall you saying so, but why?"

"Because FBI and ICE agents work around the clock protecting you and your family inside our borders, that's why."

"Have room on your office wall for a 'job well done' plaque?" Bo quipped, uncertain of the strange turn this conversation was taking.

"I'll tell you something and you can decide if you want to send one over."

"Okay."

Bo ran a hand through his hair. What kind of game was Griff playing?

"Late yesterday, we saw a Russian military officer meet with you at the Jefferson Memorial."

Dumbfounded, Bo couldn't muster one word.

"I understand you might be upset, but I'm giving you a head's up. We were concerned you were getting scammed and didn't know his real identity."

Bo leapt from his chair. He'd lost his special touch for this job. The Tabriz run-in had been a fluke. But now the FBI was following him, a CIA agent, around town? He inhaled, ready to blast Griff, when he reconsidered his suspicions. Maybe Griff had been following Yuri and not Bo.

"You're right. We need to talk," Bo agreed. "How's tomorrow sometime?"

"Meet me at Rob's deli today, say twelve thirty."

"I'll be there. That's the place with sandwiches named after golf, right?"

"You got it."

Bo hung up, wiping beads of sweat off his forehead. After this meeting with Griff, he'd probably be forced to turn in his walking papers. He'd seriously blown it—being compromised with his Russian asset in public.

And why hadn't Nanette gotten back to him about Tabriz? Bo grabbed the phone, but before he dialed, he wondered. Yuri had asked to meet at the Jefferson, with Kangas ordering Bo from London to get there. To discover that FBI and ICE agents had swarmed all over the rendezvous without tipping their hand made him think. He'd noticed the guy riding on the bike, but what more didn't he know that Griff could tell him?

A FEW HOURS LATER, Bo kicked his long legs out of his Austin-Healy, hair bristling on the back of his neck. He couldn't help gazing around, suspicious of which FBI agent might be watching him.

Blinding sun glinted off a car hood, drawing Bo's eyes across the busy street. He used a hand to shade his eyes, certain he saw no one.

He headed inside Rob's Deli, shaking off recurring doubts. At the far end of the deli, Bo saw Griff standing by a table. Over six feet with curly, brown hair, Griff looked every bit the FBI agent, in spite of being dressed in a collared knit shirt and khaki slacks. A broad smile spread beneath his trim moustache. Griff welcomed him to his favorite restaurant with a firm handshake. Neither his calm demeanor nor what he said next gave any clue of the dilemma he'd caused for Bo.

"I'm having the Duffer—beef patty on grilled rye bread, sautéed onions, Swiss cheese, and homemade dressing."

"I'm not hungry. I'll have coffee."

Bo shoved aside the menu. While his mouth screamed for the crab cake sandwich he'd once eaten here with Griff, his mind resented the idea of food. That other time, Bo had needed a favor from the FBI, and Griff's help had surpassed Bo's expectation.

This time, Griff knew too much about Bo's activities for friendly chat. Bo looked up at a very tall server whom he recognized. The young man smiled, his white teeth silhouetted against skin the color of purple grapes. Bo figured he must be over six foot, four inches.

"Hi, I am Wally and will take care of you today. I brought Griff a hot coffee. Sir, I remember you from before, but don't recall what you drink."

"Okay, bring me an Arnie Palmer."

"And what to eat?"

"I'll have my usual and my friend wants the Birdie." Griff ordered, ignoring Bo's grumpy attitude. "Make them both baskets."

As Wally left to put in their orders, Griff sipped his coffee before saying, "I like it here. Other than Rob and Wally, people don't know me."

"How did you and Wally meet?"

"Right here, in fact. Wally came to the U.S. from Sudan as a refugee. He fled thousands of miles, escaping civil war. His parents and most of his friends were killed by rebel troops. Those who moved to the States came with only the clothes on their back."

"It's coming back to me. You helped him get into a college in Pennsylvania."

"My alma mater. He's studying business and graduates next year. He's taken to calling me Dad."

Wally set down Bo's glass of lemonade and iced tea, and then hurried away. Bo fidgeted on his seat, troubled by Griff's having seen him with Yuri.

"I need to know what's going on."

"Where do I begin?" Griff plunked down his cup and rubbed his neck. "You know I've worked with Eva on an ICE task force, which she supervised."

"She's an excellent agent," was all Bo said. Where was Griff going with this?

"Since my wife died, Eva asks for my help with surveillance and stuff like that. Sometimes, I think she's just trying to keep me busy."

Bo listened to Griff with a boiling sense of betrayal. He worked in utmost secrecy. It had unsettled him to get this summons. He crossed his arms, and was fully loaded to blast Griff when Wally delivered their platters.

Griff munched some hot fries before adding, "ICE monitors international businesses, to keep American companies from supplying foreign governments with technology for use in weapon systems."

"And?" Bo's desire to eat had melted like hot ice.

"Yesterday afternoon, Eva called, needing my help on surveillance. I learned her well-placed source had divulged a Russian military officer was aiding a Russian company to buy U.S. dual-use technology for Iran." Griff glanced at Bo. "Any of this making sense to you?"

Bo stared back, his jaw locked shut.

"Imagine our shock when, at the Jefferson, we saw the Russian colonel slide into a car with rental plates. Eva burst on the radio, demanding that I drive by the car because she recognized the driver."

Bo heaved a sigh, turning his thumbs toward his chest. "Moi?"

"Bingo. We didn't reveal we knew you to the rest of the team. Later, when Eva and I talked, we figured we'd stumbled onto your operation."

"But she chose not to scold me to my face?"

"She's on a field trip with her daughter, so I'm the dreaded emissary."

"I don't like being spied on," Bo grumbled, his jaw tightening and his chin protruding. "My whole op's compromised."

"Sorry you feel that way. Should we have let you walk into a trap or get embarrassed after we arrested your source?"

Bo glared, his mind darting from one caustic comeback to another. None fit, so he stuffed a fry into his mouth and downed his cold drink. It would be insane to create a scene in a restaurant. Griff ate his sandwich in silence. Bo did the same, and the delicious food tamped down his anger.

"Same thing happened to me once," Griff shrugged. "Different agencies stumble into each other, but it rarely happens with *the* Agency. Guess that's because you mostly work overseas."

Bo wiped his mouth, tossing the napkin on his empty plate. "That Birdie was just as tasty as the last one. Glad my appetite came back."

"I'd hate to see you pass up a great meal because of me."

"You still flying to Florida and seeing the lady probation officer you told me about?"

"I met Dawn some years back when I investigated a guy. Can you believe she was his parole officer?"

"You're a pilot, but Florida's a long flight from Virginia."

"The good news is, she moved here after her son enrolled at Virginia Military Institute," Griff said, smiling broadly. "I'm happy we're seeing more of each other and—"

Wally walked up, refilling Griff's coffee cup. "Any dessert?"

"Warm some apple cobbler and throw on ice cream."

"Make it two," Bo said.

Griff touched Wally's arm. "Last time my friend was here, you showed him your fiancée's photo. There's been new trouble in Sudan. Have you heard from her recently?"

"She left Bor and returned to our village where she helps her aged Uncle, her only living relative." Wally knelt down on one knee. "I hope to visit her in Walu and marry her someday."

"After you finish college. Have any recent pictures?"

Wally removed a small photo from his pocket, setting it on the table. "Jeremy Bonds took that with his cell phone and e-mailed it to me."

"She looks happy."

"I am saving money for the bride price and to send her to Nairobi for some college classes. Her Uncle has returned to Walu. As for when we might marry," Wally's dark eyes twinkled as he clambered to his full height, "I think it must be after you and Dawn are wed."

Bo threw Griff a surprised look and Wally hustled off to get their pie. Before he probed into Griff's personal life, Bo had something else to tell him.

"It's top-secret," he said, dropping his voice, "but I developed the Russian officer while in Europe. Yesterday, he told me that Russia is purchasing dual-use technology and will divert the equipment to Iran."

"You see," Griff pounded the table, "Eva's source corroborates yours and vice versa. She'll be glad to know her source is reliable."

"My asset handed me a list of items Iran seeks to buy and detailed their methods in circumventing our government's sanctions."

"Then I've done my part." Griff lifted the cup, drinking his coffee.

Bo held out his hand to Griff. "Your knowing about my meet had me worried."

"You and Eva talk. I don't need and don't *want* to know any more."

"I'll see how Eva and I can help each other."

From Bo's former dealings with her on the Senate Intelligence Committee and other cases, he trusted that Eva wouldn't create an international incident. But Bo also was confident that Yuri would feed him much more intel than Eva could get from her source.

18

Far from Virginia, in the outskirts of Tehran, Lili Tabriz filled her mind day and night with warfare. This day was no exception. She huddled in her laboratory, a large, specially constructed room behind the kitchen of her house. As she reviewed the results of her experiment using Polymerase Chain Reaction (PCR), her blood pressure skyrocketed, but her taut face loosened.

She was a breath away from making a crucial breakthrough for her country. The Iranian government had warned her to keep the results of her vaccine secret, even from her husband. That should not be a problem. Since she returned from London, Cyrus went on an extended trip for the University of Technology, conducting research that was also a secret. She did not know where he was or when he would be home.

Lili blinked again, analyzing the results. Were they real?

A loud clanging noise outside the door assaulted her ears. Someone was close to her laboratory! Burning with rage, she wondered, who dared to get so close? She rushed from her chair, leaving the PCR machine cycling.

She yanked open the door, disgust building at the sight of the simple-minded Mabel crouched on the floor gathering nuts with her hands.

"What is the meaning of this?"

When Mabel said nothing, Lili stomped on her foot. Tears flowed down Mabel's black cheeks.

"Will you obey me?"

Mabel cowered beneath her on the tile floor. The slave woman had been in Lili's home for years, caring for their eight-year-old son, Farvad. She must have forgotten Lili's command. Mabel spoke English, but not very well.

"I told you never to disturb me!"

Spit worked its way out of the corners of her mouth as she ground the leather sole farther into the thin bones of Mabel's toes.

"Sorry. Will not happen again."

Mabel's high-pitched voice reminded Lili of a frightened puppy, and something in her tortured and well-guarded heart relented.

"Do not approach this door again when I am working, unless I ask you to. Return upstairs."

Lili lifted her foot. The African housemaid started to slink away, dragging her foot and gathering nuts into a fold of her long flowing dress.

"Wait."

Mabel crouched on the expensive Persian tile, which had been made especially for Lili by trained craftsmen.

"Is Farvad better today?"

"He is hot all over. I bring him fresh nuts to make him well."

"Tell my son I will come soon to check on him."

Lili made sure Mabel reached the top of the stairs. The slave would pose no more problems on this day. Her son might have a trifling cold, but Lili had important matters to finish. She returned to her machine, recording her advances.

Her heart soaring with pride, she carefully removed the test tubes from the cycling machine, concealing the vials in the hidden compartment of her refrigerator. The thrill of victory was so near that Lili forgot about her ailing son and left the house, making sure the door to her laboratory was double-locked.

She started her white BMW, a gift from the regime's president, and pointed the remote, which opened wide the electric gates. Her mind was busy scheming ahead to the next deadly step. She drove down back streets into the heart of the city, not even glancing at a woman wearing a black burqa and pushing a baby stroller.

Lili motored on until reaching her destination—a secure compound of the elite Revolutionary Guard. She gave her name and the security guard straightened, allowing her through the gate. Lili wheeled into the underground area, certain the weapon she had discovered would bring her a most treasured reward—war against America and Israel.

BO SILENTLY STEWED at a table in the rear of Rob's Deli, just inside Virginia from D.C. The night before, Yuri had phoned demanding an urgent meeting before going back to Moscow. So here he sat on Friday afternoon, irked that Yuri hadn't yet arrived.

It was well past the lunch-time crush with only a few stragglers staying to finish pie and coffee. Before long, Bo could claim the restaurant to himself. He had to wonder, was Yuri taking him for a ride? Bo drummed his fingers on the table, not interested in eating.

Since Griff preferred this out-of-the way spot, Bo figured no Russian embassy types or intelligence officers would show up. So far, that had panned out, but the waiting was getting on his nerves.

Thankfully, Griff's buddy Wally kept up a steady refill of Bo's diet cola.

Bo leapt from his chair and looked out a side window. Perhaps Yuri was being followed again, maybe even by Griff or Eva. Well, so be it. At least Griff knew this place. Bo checked his cell phone. No messages.

He eyed the clock, a garish monstrosity shaped like a huge golf ball. Yuri should have been here forty minutes ago. By the look of things, Bo had been stood up. So this was a first-hand example of inferior Russian spy craft. Bo could travel to the opposite side of the world and make a rendezvous right on time. Yuri couldn't meet on time when he only had to travel across town. Bo had just waved Wally over for his tab when Yuri straggled in the doorway, wearing the same scruffy jeans and sneakers.

Bo lifted a hand and soon the two adversaries huddled at the corner table, with Bo keeping a clear view of the door.

"Had a late night, did you?"

Yuri rubbed his temples. "Elginski's president wanted me to take him to Georgetown. How could I refuse?"

Wally appeared for their lunch orders.

"What have you got in a stout beer?" Yuri growled.

Wally's bright white smile flashed against his ebony face. "Closest is root beer. We do not serve any liquor. Rob has great sandwiches to go with whatever you drink."

"Did you know that when you picked this place?" Yuri flashed Bo a snide look.

"Like Wally said, a good sandwich is worth missing a beer. Bring me an Arnie Palmer and a Birdie sandwich. My friend wants unsweetened iced tea and the Duffer."

Wally wrote nothing down, just disappeared quietly, giving Bo time to quiz his hung-over guest.

"Did you clean your tail before coming in here?"

"My government trains us in counter-surveillance. I changed directions several times. Nobody followed me here."

Bo wondered if Eva's crew had the day off.

"What did you accomplish in our country?"

"I could enjoy living here," Yuri smiled, "once I retire, of course."

"Do you think the Russian military will deposit your retirement check in an American bank? Or maybe you'll provide me with such good information that I'll pay for your retirement?"

Bo wanted to keep pressure on Yuri to produce truthful and reliable intel.

"Because I do not approve of my country's dealings with Iran, I put myself in this visible place meeting with you." The Russian colonel returned Bo's intense stare.

"Let's get something straight. You already told me Elginski Technology was looking to buy dual-use components for Iran. But you're still here."

"Look at this and see what you think." Yuri deftly handed him a folded piece of paper. "Yesterday, Elginski arranged for a Chicago company to ship oscilloscopes to a hospital in South Africa. The specifics are on that paper."

Bo unfolded and read the detailed note. "It says here Elginski ordered vacuum pumps to be shipped from another Chicago company to South Africa."

"Da," Yuri said, lapsing into Russian.

"I take that as a yes. What are the pumps for?"

"Sorry. I will stick to English. The vacuum parts will help Iran enrich their uranium," Yuri spread wide his hands. "What else?"

"Such vague info will not guarantee your U.S. pension."

"The oscilloscopes and vacuum pumps will be repackaged in South Africa and then shipped to Iran. The oscilloscopes monitor the nuclear reaction leading to an atomic bomb."

"Are you certain?" Bo looked out the corner of his eye at a couple who laughed as they headed for the door. He lowered his voice a few decibels.

"Are these parts both to be used for a nuclear program?"

"I am not sure. Iran could also use oscilloscopes for guidance systems on their rockets. They do not tell me everything."

"You want a pension someday, right?"

"Skip, I will give you more of this good information when I get it. But with what is on that paper, you should be able to intercept the shipment, arrest some people, and discover Iran's intentions."

"Why would I go to all that trouble?" A smirk on his face, Bo slid the paper into his side pocket. "I have you to tell me about Iran's intentions."

Yuri opened his mouth, shutting it when Wally put down their sandwiches. Bo's crab sandwich hit the spot, but he couldn't help wondering how much more Yuri wasn't telling.

"Hmm, you were right," Yuri said, consuming the burger in a few bites. "This is pretty good, but would taste better with a beer."

Bo finished his sandwich and then leaned toward Yuri.

"To make your pension permanent, I need spectacular, verifiable intelligence about what Russia's military is doing for Iran."

"Elginski could buy oscilloscopes at home, but you know Russia signed the non-proliferation agreement. I assist Iran this way, but you intercept the shipment. That way my help is not discovered and you stop Iran from launching a nuke."

Bo's mind whirled and he thought of a scenario where Yuri's superiors had ordered Yuri to inform the U.S., all to secretly frustrate Iran's efforts, allowing Russia to maintain supposedly friendly relations with Iran.

Then again, Yuri might be telling Bo just enough so he'd arrange for Yuri to defect to the U.S. and retire with his financial needs met in spades. Before Bo could solve that puzzle, Yuri pushed his chair back from the table.

"I catch my flight at five. I will stay in touch as usual."

Bo let Yuri walk out ahead of him; no one seemed to be following. He paid the bill, leaving a generous tip for Wally. Bo had been in college once, before joining the Army Rangers, but being all military, his father had refused to pay one dime toward Bo's schooling. While Bo had been upset at the time, he thought of doing the same for his son. Still, Wally was an orphan who worked hard and could use the help.

As Bo sauntered back to his rental, the intel that Yuri had shared was pumping adrenaline through him. On the ride to switch cars, Bo vowed to strike at the heart of those shipments and expose whatever Iran was up to.

19

Bo returned to his windowless CIA office in record time and got busy typing up what he'd just learned from Yuri, but thoughts crept in of his aborted London visit. The mouthy woman, Dr. Lili Tabriz, made him think. She claimed to live in Iran, but Bo had a nagging suspicion she hailed from New York City.

Nanette Bing hadn't called to brief him about Cyrus Tabriz and his wife, and he grew tired of constant delays. He reread the report he'd written upon his return; then, wheeling to his keyboard, he typed in the name Cyrus Tabriz. The screen filled with so many entries, it startled him.

He hit the jackpot—his trip hadn't been for naught after all! Such a detailed list of file references would take all afternoon to finish. Bo grabbed a pen, ready to take notes—but to his horror, before he could open a single electronic file, his screen blanked out.

Bo tried repeatedly to get the files back, but nothing popped up. Had his computer died? After calling IT support, he logged off the Agency's computer and locked his office, heading to the cafeteria for a giant cola he hoped would satisfy his sudden craving for caffeine.

At the end of the hallway, he passed Kangas' administrative assistant, Frank Deming. Deming's brow was furrowed and his lips were puckered in a tight grimace.

"Hey Frank, something wrong?"

"I was going to phone you as soon as I reached my office."

That got Bo's dander up. "Not another assignment overseas. No way. My wife will go ballistic."

"You need to come to Mr. Kangas' office," Frank said, crossing his arms across his sizeable chest. "You've some explaining to do."

"I do?" Bo took a step back. Frank was acting more strange than usual.

"Not here in the hallway. It's classified. Just stop up when you're done here."

Bo turned, forgetting about his caffeine fix, and walked in tandem with Frank.

"Thanks. I'll go see Director Kangas. I've got something new for him."

As soon as they entered the reception area outside Kangas' office, Frank pointed to an empty chair beside his desk.

"Have a seat."

"Nope." Bo gestured toward Kangas' office. "You said he's waiting for me."

"Rider, sit down."

Bo decided to give Frank the respect due his position as Kangas' right-hand guy, but Bo's backside barely touched the chair when Frank hissed, "Why are you searching files on Cyrus Tabriz?"

"I'm not sure that's any of your business, Frank."

"It most certainly is. The system denied you access."

So that was why his screen had gone blank. In his years at the Agency, that had never happened before. He'd stepped into something odd, but this was no time for mind games.

"I'm preparing a memo about my recent trip, where I heard Tabriz speak and met his wife."

"That's it? You're looking for background stuff?"

"Frank, when you were a kid, did your family have one of the big, old TV sets?"

"I guess so. What does that have to do with anything?"

Bo laughed. "My dad is retired military right? So when the set went on the blink in the middle of Lawrence Welk, he'd bang on the side of the thing and it would start working again."

"Who cares? Rider, have you lost your mind? You've been gone too long."

"My point is this. As haywire as that old TV was, so is Mrs. Tabriz. She's a real loon, and she almost blew my cover. Don't you dare tell Kangas. I'm making a nice file on her, if she or her husband ever surfaces. I have a bad feeling about her."

"Okay, I'll grant you access for background info only."

"What do you mean *you'll* grant me access? I thought Kangas wanted to see me."

"Bo, I said I wanted you to come up to his office, but it was to see me. I don't sit outside his office just making him look important. He actually delegates stuff to me."

"Why restrict my looking into Tabriz?"

"Things here in NCS are compartmentalized." Frank said, leaning back in his chair. "When you queried Tabriz, the system denied you access. That alerted Director Kangas that some unauthorized person was trying to see that file. I'm notified to resolve the matter. It happens daily. Mr. Kangas can't be bothered with each one of these."

"I need to see the Director about something else. You never got back to me the other day."

"Yeah, I know. He's on the Hill, but I'll call when he's available."

Bo stood, hoping that would be soon. "And the Tabriz files?"

"I'm granting you limited access right now to his bio and summary data only." Frank turned to his computer.

"Want to catch lunch tomorrow?"

"Sure."

Before Frank even looked up from his computer, Bo dashed to the elevator. He took no chances that Frank might change his mind. The entire episode bordered on the bizarre. But then, Bo had found other secret dealings within the CIA perplexing. Back in his office, he started his computer. True to Frank's word, Bo reentered the Tabriz name, and poof! Two pages of sanitized data appeared on his monitor.

His eyes had consumed the first line when the IT whiz phoned, wanting to know what was wrong with his computer. Oops. Bo should've warned him off. He didn't want some computer geek messing up his access.

"I'm okay after turning it off and back on again."

"Next time, let me know, okay?"

"Sure will."

Bo hung up, eager to unravel the puzzle of Lili and Cyrus Tabriz. He read with interest an interview of the Harvard grad student who'd applied for a job at the State Department and had woven a colorful tale of what transpired when he'd had a few beers with an Iranian student named Cyrus Tabriz, then an undergraduate student at Harvard.

The second page offered curious insights into Lili Tabriz and her husband, two scientists working for the Iranian regime. Bo's printer had begun spitting out copies when his phone rang.

"Bo, Kangas has five empty minutes. Can you get up here?"

"Ah, I'm in the middle of printing. I'll be there in a flash."

His pulse raced. The second sheet finally landed in the tray. The pages still warm in his hands, Bo literally ran down the hall, pushing the elevator button three or four times before it finally arrived. He jumped in, quickly scanning the info. Kangas usually wanted him to get to the heart of the matter in seconds, not minutes.

Frank motioned for Bo to go right in. Kangas faced the window, but once Bo's foot landed on the carpet, the door swished shut behind him.

"Sir, let me brief you on my meet with Bear at the Jefferson. There is a new development."

"Get to it Rider. I have a National Security meeting here in twenty minutes and I won't keep them waiting."

Bo didn't even sit. He minced no words, telling Kangas how Russia was selling components to African nations, all of which were destined to end up in Iran. He also confessed he'd been seen by federal agents who'd been tipped to Bear.

"Sticky. What are your plans?" Kangas remained seated, tenting his hands.

"Both agents are trustworthy. As it turns out, Agent Montanna's source corroborated Bear. She and I will coordinate."

"Glad you got this to me. Keep me informed."

"Sir, about my London trip—though you called me back early, I met one Iranian scientist. It wasn't under ideal circumstances. Do you have time?"

"Iran is the very subject of my next meeting. Let's have it all."

Kangas turned to his computer, ready to enter any pertinent intel. Bo outlined the State Department applicant's allegations about the night he'd consumed drinks with Cyrus Tabriz.

"Back in 1979, Cyrus knew Bruce Laingen, State's *charge d'affaires* who was held hostage by Iranian revolutionary students. The applicant suspected Tabriz must have played a role in the hostage tragedy."

"Is he the scientist you met?" Kangas arched his brows. "He must be highly connected in the regime."

"I heard part of his lecture. Here's his passport photo."

Bo quickly explained how he'd stumbled onto Cyrus' briefcase, omitting the worst of his run-in with Cyrus' wife, Lili.

"I think he's got his wife so submissive, she feared injury by him because she'd left his briefcase and I found it. Unfortunately, I didn't get a chance to photograph several diagrams in his case."

"That's it?" Kangas sounded disappointed.

"Your belief that Cyrus is highly placed is accurate. He's also a radical."

For the next few minutes, Bo highlighted a report written by an FBI agent who'd been assigned to learn more about the identity of Cyrus Tabriz. Armed with a surveillance photo taken of Tabriz on campus at Harvard, the FBI agent talked to former State Department employees who'd been held hostage in 1979 by a group known as Muslim Student Followers.

"Sir, each one identified Tabriz as a militant student who had participated in the takeover at the American Embassy in Tehran. He later helped guard the hostages. These former hostages knew Tabriz by the name Ahmad, but they admitted the guards used aliases."

"So Lili Tabriz is married to a man who attacked and held Americans hostage. No wonder she's afraid of him."

"She acted hysterical—apparently, with good reason. One more item about her husband. In the midst of the FBI's investigation of him, Cyrus Tabriz graduated from Harvard and returned to Iran. A note was entered in his file to deny him a visa so he couldn't return to the U.S."

"Is he working on Iran's nuclear program?"

Bo shrugged. "I'll try to learn more. I'd just printed these when Frank called me up to see you. An analyst is running the systems, but I haven't gotten results yet."

"Stay on this husband and wife duo. They could provide the break we need. I'll authorize any travel necessary."

"Okay—I mean, yes, sir."

Bo stumbled out of the executive suite and past Frank's desk, deciding not to mention possible travel to Julia until it really materialized. Let his wife think he was home to stay and achieve some happiness in their lives. After all, as Kangas always bragged, intel was as fluid as a raging river.

20

Bo had been settled into his office for all of five minutes when his phone rang.

"Bo?"

The woman's voice sounded like Nanette Bing's, so he barked, "It's about time. What do you have for me?"

A laugh. "Nothing I can admit over the phone. It's Eva Montanna."

"Funny you should call. I've been thinking about your case."

"That is funny," she chuckled. "Let's meet for lunch. I'd pick Rob's Deli, but I doubt you'd want to eat there two days in a row—am I right?"

Great. Today's meeting, just like the one at the Jefferson Memorial, hadn't gone unnoticed by her.

"Name where and when, Eva. It's been a rough day."

"Sorry to hear it. Café at the National History museum, tomorrow at one."

"On Saturday?"

"Yup, then I'm going out of town."

"Alright," he sighed. "Now I've gotta run."

As Bo slammed down the phone, he couldn't help but smile. Yuri had been so sure he'd cleaned his tail, but Eva's team had stuck with him. His mind a cauldron, Bo secured Yuri's note in his safe and then decided to pay Nanette Bing a little visit. He needed to sink his teeth into something that didn't involve Eva.

It turned out that Nanette had gone to Norfolk. Her mother had taken a turn for the worse and she'd be gone all next week. Bo hightailed it back to his office, spending the rest of the afternoon writing reports to justify recurring stipends to his other assets.

At quarter to five, his cell rang. When he answered, a woman sobbed in his ear, sounding as if someone had the wrong number.

"Can I help you?" he asked.

"Bo, it's terrible."

"Julia, what's happened?"

"Gregg fell!" she cried. "He was riding his bike down the hill, flew over the curb and crashed in the road. Carver called an ambulance. We're at Northpoint's emergency room."

"Is he all right? I mean did he hurt his head?"

"He hasn't said a word. Oh, they want us to go for an x-ray."

"I'm leaving my office this second."

Bo darted to the door, remembering to lock up. Things probably weren't as bad as Julia made it sound. Her emotions usually soared pretty high in a crisis. Hadn't Bo banged himself up countless times at Gregg's age?

He reached Northpoint Hospital within twenty minutes, not even recalling the route he'd taken; his mind was so focused on Gregg. Bo had spent little quality time with his young son during these last months, so Gregg's crash weighed heavily on his conscience.

After parking his Austin-Healey, he ran to the emergency room, promising himself he'd be more involved with both of his kids as soon as work slacked off. He quickly scanned folks in the waiting room, but didn't see Julia. Off in a corner, looking more mature than her ten years, Glenna sat leafing through a book about oceans. Bo did a double take. At a glimpse, with her hair pulled back and her feathery bangs, she looked so much like Julia that, for an instant, he forgot the urgency of his mission. Where were the years going? She'd be getting her high school diploma before he ever really knew her.

He sped over to his daughter and tapped the magazine cover. She raised her eyes confidently as if she had no worries about her brother.

"Hi, pumpkin. Where's your mom?"

"Through those double doors," Glenna said, pointing with a slim finger, "in a tiny room with Gregg."

"Won't they let you in?"

"Dad, is he going to be okay?"

"Let's find out."

She shook her head. "I was in there, but I got scared by a woman moaning across the hall. Mom told me to wait out here so I wouldn't upset Gregg."

"You'll have me to protect you." Bo held out his hand. "Besides, I don't like you waiting out here alone."

Glenna rose to her feet, suddenly clutching Bo's hand.

"Daddy, I'm glad you came."

Bo's heart skipped a beat. For the first time in months, he felt like a father to his daughter. He dearly hoped Gregg was all right. In no time, he cleared through intake and a friendly clerk buzzed them into emergency care. He spotted Julia's dark hair through a partially open door and hurried into the exam room with Glenna still holding onto his hand.

Gregg's young face looked pale, but when he saw Bo, he tried to smile. Bo strode over to his wife, wrapping an arm around her shoulder. Julia looked worried, so he tried a lighthearted approach.

"So what's all this about your bike? The x-rays come back yet?"

"His left arm is broken," Julia announced, biting at her nails. "But he's been so brave. You'd be proud of our boy."

"I sure am, of both of you kids. Glenna filled me in so I wouldn't feel left out. Where's the cast?"

"I'm getting a blue one, Dad."

Bo gently ruffled Gregg's hair. "When I busted my arm in junior high, all they had was white. How's your bike?"

"Front tire's a goner," Gregg croaked, his lower lip trembling.

"Not to worry, we'll fix—"

A doctor wearing a white coat, a stethoscope around her neck, and a genuine smile on her face floated in on rubber shoes.

"I'm Doctor Van De Mae. If you will please step back, I am going to give this young man the bluest arm he's ever had."

Bo approved of the doctor's professionalism and kind ways. She kept up a running dialogue about baby rabbits living in her yard, asking Gregg about his favorite sports team and even coaxing Glenna to talk about her dance recital, which Bo knew nothing about.

When Gregg's arm was wrapped and in a sling, Dr. Van De Mae told him, "Your friends may want to write on your cast, but give it a few days. Here's what I want your son to take if he's in pain."

Dr. Van De Mae handed Julia a folded note and Bo's mind jerked back to the one Yuri had given him at Rob's Deli. The meet with his Russian asset seemed eons ago instead of mere hours.

He thanked the doctor for her help and followed Julia and the kids out to the parking lot. He'd almost reached home when he veered off to an ice cream parlor, buying a couple gallons of ice cream—strawberry cheesecake for the kids and chocolate fudge for Julia.

Back in his car with the ice cream stowed on the front seat, Bo flipped on the radio. He was shocked to hear the latest news. The Israeli Knesset had issued a warning to Iran not to go nuclear. The foreign minister of Russia had just landed in Tehran to finalize a shipment of nuclear fuel. A female news anchor reminded listeners that Tehran had previously threatened to wipe Israel from the face of the earth.

What Bo wouldn't give to be Israel's intelligence service at Mossad headquarters. He had met and trained a few of their agents at a CIA training school a few years back. Bo shook those thoughts from his mind and pulled into the garage, wanting a few minutes of fun with his family before the demands of work pressured him to leave again.

21

Life swirled by for Bo. After he and his family had come home from the hospital and enjoyed bowls of ice cream, Bo had stayed up late with Julia brainstorming ideas for summer vacation. She showed him pamphlets of places she wanted to take the kids, including Williamsburg. Julia mentioned a book she was reading by some religious guy. Bo listened without hearing. He was stymied by Yuri's schemes and what Eva knew of them.

The next day, at one o'clock, Bo found himself passing through the metal detector at the National Museum of American History, hoping to obtain a firmer grasp of the labyrinth that was Yuri's Russian mind.

After Bo made his way down to the Stars and Stripes Café in the lower level, despite hordes of people zooming by carrying trays, he managed to spot the attractive blonde responsible for his being on Constitution Avenue—Eva Montanna, the hard working and tenacious ICE agent.

It was just like Eva to arrive early and snag a table in the rear. He wound his way through a maze of crooked tables, feeling slightly intimidated because she had stumbled onto his asset. Anyway, things with Yuri were spinning out of control. Perhaps what Eva had to say could help Bo set things back on track. She jumped up, grabbing his hand.

"Bo, won't it be great collaborating again? I had a conflict and couldn't meet with you and Griff on Tuesday. Hopefully, he brought you up to date on what's happening."

"He did and you've probably figured there's more. I intended to contact you or Griff once I wrote my intelligence memo."

"Let's get our food and then talk business. Although Griff helped out at the Jefferson, he's not aware of all the details."

Bo shadowed Eva in line. Having never before set foot in this café, he copied her example, selecting a Cobb salad, heavy on meat and cheese. Back at their table, when Eva bowed her head, Bo felt awkward, so he slathered blue cheese dressing on his salad.

When she lifted her head, he asked, "So is your husband Scott still Press Secretary at the Pentagon?"

"Yes, but not for long. Some international conglomerate wants to lure him away, but Scott has another idea."

They avoided small talk, content to dive into their salads. Bo speared a green olive, trying to fathom what it would be like if Julia had a career. He couldn't imagine it—not with the intense demands of his CIA job. His wife brought stability to their family, even if her moods took a downturn at times.

"How are your kids? You have two, right?" Eva's blue eyes lit up.

"My eight-year-old son gave me a scare with a trip to the ER yesterday, but his arm will mend."

"My youngest two are all boy. Marty and Andy really keep me and Scott hopping. Kaley's entered her teen years, which provides lots of comic relief."

The personal chit-chat simply added weight to what bothered Bo.

"Eva, I'm used to working off shore and eluding foreign agents, but not other U.S. agencies. I need to know what you know about our mutual friend. Imagine if you were working in Berlin and I watched your every move."

"Bo, listen," Eva said, cracking a warm smile. "We had no idea we were following someone you were working."

"I should've known something was up—my contact thought he was being followed."

"Hmm. Yuri picked up our tail. That intrigues me."

Okay, Eva emphasized Yuri's name, letting Bo know how much she already knew.

"Mind calling him Bear?"

"Sure." She eased closer to him, lowering her voice. "Don't be uncomfortable. Our missions have collided, but we're on the same side."

"That's one way of looking at it. I'm telling you things I never thought I'd admit to anyone outside the Agency. It's disconcerting."

"I understand you're used to being a loner, but I can put you at ease."

"I'm all ears."

"My source is in the import and export business. These guys are at great risk because so many items being shipped around the globe are dual-use products also used for weapons of mass destruction. These brokers keep ICE informed of *anything* that might cause them to be arrested or sanctioned."

"That's why you were tailing Bear?"

"Exactly." Eva bobbed her head.

"Just between us, and *not* for documentation, he's a colonel in Russia's military, assigned as liaison to a Russian defense contractor," Bo explained. "Russia is selling permissible weapon systems to Iran and other countries. He shares with me how the contractor helps Iran acquire sanctioned or quarantined items."

"Oscilloscopes and vacuum pumps, right?" Eva asked. She stared at Bo. "Parts to be shipped to South Africa and then redirected to Iran, in violation of existing treaties."

Unbelievable! She knew everything. Bo might as well walk out. Why work for the CIA and put his life on the line day after day, week after week, being gone from his family for a month at time? It was ridiculous. The next thing he knew, his meetings with Yuri would show up on the front page of the *Washington Star.*

He said none of this to Eva, simply asking, "Can you tell me what I don't know?"

"I think you know more than I do," Eva laughed. "In fact, I'm sure of it. Did Bear give you a list of items Iran is seeking?"

Bo felt steam erupting in his chest. In a public place, he wasn't about to divulge the stuff on Yuri's list. He folded his arms, staring back.

"How about triggered spark gaps? Did he mention them?" Eva pointed her fork toward his eye.

She acted so confident. But how did Eva know those were on the list?

"He mentioned Iran wants those."

"That's what my source told me. Triggered spark gaps can be used in the medical field to break up kidney stones but they can also be used to detonate a nuclear weapon. Talk about a slippery slope. Did Bear find a source to supply them?"

Eva sounded like some college professor lecturing Bo, the neophyte freshman. He hesitated, thinking how best to reply. Eva gave him no chance, plunging forward.

"You realize we should compare notes. Otherwise, we'll undermine each other's efforts."

"Bear never said anything else about spark gaps."

Eva's hands flew to her face. "That's why you and I need to talk. Bear is deceiving you. He arranged to get them from a firm in Cleveland. They're being shipped to Monrovia, Liberia. From there they'll be repackaged and shipped to Iran."

Bo felt her sucker punch right in his solar plexus. Eva seemed to enjoy taunting him. Maybe she was getting back at him for what Bo kept from her last year—but hadn't they moved past that?

"I thought he told me everything."

"Bo, this isn't unusual. I've been deceived by many informants. Think of it this way. We don't often have the benefit of different sources telling us about Iran's efforts. We just might squelch their nuclear designs."

"I have some rethinking to do."

"Go ahead and write your memo, as you would normally." Eva shoved away her half-eaten salad. "ICE will intercept the shipment and it will be good for Bear to wonder if the Agency discovered the spark gaps. He'll have greater respect for you."

"Yeah," Bo said, grinning broadly. "And I'll reflect his shenanigans by adjusting his compensation. No more Mr. Nice Guy."

"Then we'll stay in touch?"

"It works both ways. You hear something, give me a head's up."

The two agents shook hands and Bo left first, pondering how to break the news to Kangas, who vigorously sought to stay one step ahead of other federal agencies.

22

After three days in Sudan, Dawn Ahern couldn't believe it was already Friday evening. Time had flown so swiftly! She stepped into a small tent outside the Bor hospital, extreme heat smothering her breath. The Grace Church team had painted the orphanage walls a sunny yellow—which she wrote about to Brian, filling page after page with a solar lamp as her only light.

Her pen had moved quickly, telling her son how Doc Kidd held a clinic treating sick mothers and children. Many villagers, even the elderly, waited in long lines to be treated for malaria and dysentery. She'd helped by organizing bandages, washing digital thermometers, and passing out aspirin.

She ended with a few personal thoughts:

I've gotten little sleep, but that means nothing, the needs are so immense. Don't worry about me and keep up your studies. Much love, Mom

Dawn folded the letter and then dug around the tent in the dim light, searching for something that had disappeared. It wasn't under the cot. She patted down the pockets of her cargo pants. Nothing. Her backpack had fallen over and she yanked it up.

There it was—the cell phone had slipped to the very bottom. It had been purchased for her by Jeremy Bonds, the sinewy Australian pilot. Dawn liked Jeremy and his wife Kathy, who had lived in Nairobi for the past five years. Jeremy, in his mid-fifties, flew all over Africa for the same relief agency that had invited Dawn's church to Bor. He even sent Wally a video of Liberty, helping them become reacquainted over thousands of miles.

Before she turned out the light, she made a phone call, her heart leaping at Griff's familiar voice. "Hi there. Can you believe I'm in a tent outside the hospital?"

"Can you talk louder?"

"Where are you?" she shouted back.

"I was out walking a trail along Penzance, but a storm blasted the southern coast of England. Now I'm resting by a blazing fire with Grandma Topping in Cornwall."

"You're in England? I don't understand."

He laughed. "That's because when you left for your trip, I had no idea I'd be flying here. Wally is doing okay. His lawyer is preparing for the preliminary examination."

"I hope he uncovers some exculpatory evidence."

"When Grandma asked me to attend the ceremony on Sunday to honor my Grandfather's involvement on D-Day, I said yes."

"Please give her my best regards. You make me homesick for your company."

She hoped she sounded lighthearted, yet his surprise stung. When she'd left for Dulles, Griff had called that morning saying he was steeped in solving a complex case. Well, it was his life, even if he chose not to share all his travels with her.

"I will. And Dawn, she sends her greetings to you."

"Is your grandmother well enough to enjoy your visit?"

"She's a rare breed. She gardens, rides a moped, and is fixing dinner for us and a few of her friends. Her neighbor's granddaughter, Claire, who is my age, taught me how to play croquet."

Dawn's mouth tightened. Griff was having fun with another woman. Perhaps that was how Griff felt about her relationship with CJ, even though there was nothing to it.

She couldn't help asking, "Do you and her husband play on the opposing team?"

"Oh, she's a single like me," Griff chuckled. "Grandma is a regular matchmaker and thinks it's high time I remarried. Not to worry, though. I've told Grandma about the pretty probation officer I'm seeing. "

There was a few second delay, so Dawn stretched out on a cot, the lamp casting weird shadows against the tent. She noticed Griff didn't say he had told Claire that he and Dawn were dating. Mindful of Pastor Nebo and Doc in the adjacent tent, she lowered her voice.

"I wish you were here. The wild animals we fly over are spectacular."

Another long delay before Griff said, "I forgot how much I missed this island."

That was certainly *not* the reply she'd hoped for. He sounded as if he didn't care at all about not being with her.

"Sudan is hot, yet so different from the way I thought it would be. I can't wait to get airborne and watch an African sunrise over Wally's homeland."

"You're going to Walu in the morning?"

"Yes, but when you speak to Wally, don't mention it. The weather could prevent our going."

"Sounds beautiful. Oh, wait a minute ... Sure, Claire, I'm almost finished. Dawn, Grandma needs logs for the fire. It's unusually cold here."

She heard an echo and then mumbling. "Griff, are you there?"

More voices in the background, but no one talked to Dawn. Then Griff said, "I'm losing the connection."

"Griff, I'm still here."

"Hello, Dawn?"

The next thing she knew Griff was gone, seemingly severing her ties with him. Jeremy had warned of fuzzy connections, even though cell towers dotted much of rural Sudan. Dawn lay on her cot, trying to be content with the awkward call she'd had with Griff. He knew she was thinking of him, though he'd been engaged in other activities. That she'd phoned from Sudan must count for something.

She dimmed the lamp and pulled mosquito netting over her cot, hardly believing the wonderful sights and sounds of Africa. She was here to share the love of Jesus. Clothed in cargo pants and shirt, Dawn stretched her legs, finding the canvas cot uncomfortable.

Goats bawled in the distance, the cacophony mirroring the state of her heart. Who was Claire? Why did Griff's voice have to sound so merry as he called out her name? Dawn pictured a golden-haired, blue-eyed beauty mesmerizing Griff in a high-toned British accent. Hadn't he practically bragged that he was single, all for Claire's benefit?

Dawn's bottom lip trembled. Maybe God was helping her to see it was time for her to make a fresh start, without constantly thinking of a future with Griff, a man who didn't cherish her beliefs. Tears filled her eyes. She turned over to sleep, willing her mind to quit working overtime.

At least she'd gotten to visit Brian on Parents Day, at his invitation. Griff had been busy with a case, so she'd driven to Lexington by herself, enjoying the day with Brian. He'd even introduced her to his buddies and acted glad for her visit.

She had some serious thinking to do, now that her son was maturing and her relationship with Griff seemed to be sputtering—but such deep thoughts were interrupted by a mosquito biting her leg. She turned on the lamp and spent the next ten minutes trying to kill the pest. Success came at last, but not before she'd knocked over her backpack and the cot as well.

"Dawn, is everything all right in there?"

It was Jeremy, right outside the flap of her tent.

"I'm battling mosquitoes. Sorry if I woke you."

"Nah, Kathy and I were out for a moonlit stroll and saw your light. Don't stay up too late. We'll be up early for our flight to Walu."

"Are they still predicting rain?"

"Yes, but it's a clear night. Sleep well."

So Jeremy and his wife were out enjoying the moon together. If only Griff—nope. Dawn had come here alone and would enjoy Sudan without him. Far too wide awake and riled to sleep, Dawn set the lamp on the crate, remembering the computer in the makeshift office, which also served as the communications hub. Maybe she should send Brian an e-mail instead of a letter.

She ducked out of her tent and strode through the hospital entrance. Things seemed pretty quiet, so she shouldn't be in anyone's way. Jeremy had shown her how to sign on to the computer a few days earlier. She'd sent Griff an e-mail, but because he'd never replied, an hour ago she'd made the call—only to find him on a lark in Cornwall.

Something Brian had said accentuated Dawn's somber mood. She turned on the computer to find out if he meant it. Dawn signed on to her internet service provider, typing in Brian's address.

I'm writing from the arid region of Sudan. Herders and farmers need encouragement because they have so little food. Longstanding drought hurts the children, who eat once a day, if that. They're poor by our standards, yet seem less anxious than we American's with all our advantages.

Brian, email back and tell me if you're staying at VMI this summer. Will you work with matriculating students arriving from high school? You enjoyed the program the summer before your freshman year. I'm so proud of you. You've gone from being a cadet to wanting to be an instructor—or is it helper? Your dad would be proud of you, too. If only he could see you as I do.

Tomorrow, I fly to a rural village to meet a young Sudanese woman who grew up with a young man I know back in Virginia. We hope to surprise Liberty with a cell phone and supplies. It's time for sleep. Let me know about your summer plans. Loving you, Mom.

Dawn hit the button, sending the missive to Brian with all the love she nurtured for him in her heart. Acknowledging in her e-mail that Brian probably wouldn't come home for the summer set her free to make other plans—whatever those might be.

23

The predicted rains didn't arrive. In the rising heat of early morning, Dawn and Jeremy readied the Cessna 208 Caravan for its flight to Walu. Pastor Rick climbed into the back of the plane, the sole passenger among boxes of relief supplies, with Dawn serving as Jeremy's co-pilot.

It didn't take long for them to approach Walu, a small village of the Dinka tribe, a proud people who'd lived hundreds of years in Southern Sudan tending scruffy goats and bony cattle. Dawn pulled off her headset, giving her an unobstructed view of the flat landscape below. She had never realized there were so many shades of brown. The Nile was a ribbon of fast-moving mud.

"G'day mates," Jeremy said, grinning. "It's a bonza day for flying."

"What's bonza?" Dawn wondered aloud. "Should we be worried?"

"You'd say 'super' across the pond."

Pastor Rick tapped her shoulder, pointing out the window at the swirling water.

"Look below and witness part of Cush, the land King David tells of in the Bible. Sudan and Ethiopia make up ancient Cush. It's amazing to be here and think of long-ago empires, but the passage of time hasn't dimmed the fight for this land or its people."

"Hostilities are resurging in Darfur, aren't they?"

"A disturbing report arrived this morning," Jeremy replied. "Tribes near Darfur are waging war and causing hundreds of injuries."

With that, Jeremy lowered the flap and configured the plane for landing.

"Aren't we quite a ways southeast of there?" Dawn's heart fluttered at the thought of facing possible fighting.

"We might as well be in Woop Woop."

Dawn glanced over at her pilot, struck by the comic look on his face.

"Hey Jeremy, I didn't bring my Aussie dictionary. Care to translate?"

"Think of us way in the bush out here. We should be plenty safe from Darfur's many conflicts."

Dawn watched the plane's shadow keeping pace with them along the river bank below. Then they veered west, where the earth looked even more barren, with only an occasional tree providing a circle of shade. No human could survive there for long. The air speed fell off and dry land rose up to meet them. Suddenly, they touched down on hard-packed earth that felt like no runway she'd ever been on.

As Jeremy brought the Cessna to a stop, a cloud of dust enveloped the plane. He switched off the engine and waited for the prop to quit turning before pushing open his door to slide out. Dawn stepped down, feeling the sweltering air surround her. She pulled out a hand-kerchief to wipe sweat from her hairline.

"I can't believe how you threaded the plane." Dawn nervously eyed two large trees growing on either side of a bumpy patch of earth she couldn't call a landing strip.

Jeremy's grin was enormous.

She smiled back. "For a split second, I thought we'd lose a wing. That's one for my record book."

An annoying fly buzzed around Jeremy's shiny balding head. He jammed on a baseball cap and then joined Dawn to heave wooden blocks under the wheels. The plane secure, Jeremy straightened, laughing good-naturedly.

"Do me a favor—tell my wife how safe you feel in my care. Kathy refuses to fly with me after I ditched last year on the upper White Nile with her aboard."

Dawn extended a hand to help Pastor Rick and he let loose a moan as he jumped down the big step.

"My knees aren't what they once were. Would you look at the vil-lage?" He gestured toward a jagged grouping of small huts made of sticks. "The people have to rebuild their tukuls each year because of the ferocious termites."

"It must be hard work putting the thatch up on those roofs," Dawn said, swatting a bug that crawled up her leg.

"What a rich blessing it is to have arrived safely," the pastor re-plied.

This was the Sudan, which Wally had so colorfully described. In the intense sunshine, she tried to imagine him waking as a boy to a horrible reality—unmerciful Islamic militants slaughtering his whole family. And then to be wrongfully accused back home! Though Dawn longed to make up for Wally's suffering, she knew Griff's love and concern were helping Wally to trust people again.

Instead of dwelling on such sorrows, Dawn looked around, trying to spot Liberty. There were no people in her line of sight. Only stark desolation lingered in the dusty spaces between the tiny dwellings. The tukul huts were perched a good distance from the strip behind a waist-high fence of twigs bound together with twine.

She'd hoped Griff might have come along, yet all her gentle hints had gone unnoticed. She wiggled the damp hanky into her back pocket, purposely shoving aside images of him looking out to sea with a fair-haired maiden at his side. Sounds of laughter grabbed her attention.

Walu villagers swept toward the landing strip, waving their arms. A small boy wearing a red shirt and cropped jeans pounded on a drum. A tall man with a scar running through his close-cropped, black hair stepped from the crowd. At well over six-feet-five inches tall, he looked like a movie character in a billowing, light blue shirt and neat, gray slacks.

He pumped Pastor Rick's hand as if it would gush forth water.

"I am Reverend Lowery," the man said in lilting English. "My bishop told me you were to visit a few days ago. But we are happy to greet you whenever you come. Please join us for tea after our Sunday service."

In this parched land, Dawn had already begun feeling dehydrated. Tea would be welcome, but they had to attend to more pressing business and unload the supplies. Pastor Rick introduced Dawn and Jeremy, telling Reverend Lowery about their work at the Bor hospital, which had delayed their trip. "Sick babies and mothers needed care. We bring you many supplies."

Whip-thin, Reverend Lowery's full lips spread into a gracious smile. "In the name of Jesus, we thank you for such gifts."

"Want to lend a hand, mate?"

Jeremy gestured toward the plane, which was crammed with cardboard boxes. Lowery shouted to three boys tending goats, who dropped their gnarled sticks and came running over. The two ministers worked in tandem, unloading bandages, medicine, soap, and sacks of dried beans. The young boys carried these off to be stored at the village church. There were also several bags of seed for the men to plant corn in a community garden.

Dawn smiled at the women and older men, who'd lost most family members. The adults murmured as they watched her.

"Hello," she waved, placing a hand over her heart. "I am Dawn Ahern."

Immediately, the women crowded around her, shyly touching her hands and arms. Was Liberty among them? Because Rick had cautioned Dawn to go slowly, she avoided asking any questions. A pretty, young woman, wearing vibrant green cloth the color of limes tied at her shoulder, pointed to the aircraft and then up at the cloudless sky.

"You flew the airplane?"

"Not me." Dawn nodded toward Jeremy who was still hauling out boxes. "But I flew very high in the sky."

"To be so close to God," the woman said as her face broke into a gentle smile, "would be like my dream when Jesus came to me."

Her eyes shifted to a woman standing next to her. "My friend saw the airplane bring corn to the refugee camp."

Dawn nodded to a slender woman, who shrank back. Taller than the other women, she wore a blue, sleeveless dress. Glass beads adorned her neck and her skin shone in the sun. She carried a regal look, even in her flip flops. Dawn recognized this graceful woman from the photo Wally had shown her.

No wonder he'd pined for Liberty all these years and wanted to be her husband! If only Dawn could speak to her alone. She didn't want the entire village seeing the gift Wally had sent her. But first, she needed to make sure she had the right woman.

"I am Baca Manja's friend."

The woman in blue tilted her head just a fraction. Maybe Liberty also sought to keep her relationship secret from the other women. An idea sprouted in Dawn's mind.

"Would you like to see inside the airplane?"

Another terse nod of her head and the woman in blue spoke in her native language to her friend, the woman in green, who was now retreating behind the fence. Soon, other Walu women disappeared back inside their tukuls. Pastor Rick and Reverend Lowery removed the last box of provisions, making room for Dawn to open the Cessna's side door.

"Do you speak English?"

"I learned in the refugee camp. Also I speak Dinka and Arabic."

"Are you Atong?"

"Yes, Wally calls me Liberty and says I am no longer girl from war." Her high cheeks beamed above a toothy grin. "Wally sent a message you might come. But, I think you do not come. Reverend Lowery says all things happen in God's time."

Dawn leaned under the right seat of the plane, removing a linen handkerchief, which she gave to Liberty.

"There is something inside the cloth. Wally wants you to have it."

"How is Baca?" Liberty took his gift without opening it.

"He studies hard and wishes he was here with you," Dawn answered, purposely avoiding any mention of his arrest.

Dawn stored in her memory bank that Liberty preferred Wally's African name even though, strangely, Wally viewed Atong as Liberty. Would the two of them be able to live as man and wife with their many cultural differences? Perhaps surviving the Sudanese war and several refugee camps together would bind their married future.

Liberty pressed the gift between her hands, fingering the material that came from Wally as if it were his flesh. Dawn's mind turned to Griff. She didn't always agree with him, especially on matters related to faith, but time seemed to be giving them more in common—she had a son, Brian, and recently Griff had informally adopted Wally. Maybe Griff would come to appreciate her same values—if he didn't fall in love with Claire first.

Liberty stared hard at Dawn, her large black eyes filling with questions.

"But is Baca safe?"

The question disturbed Dawn. Wally hadn't told Liberty of the criminal charges.

"I believe he is. Please open his present."

A hint of a smile adorned Liberty's lips as she unfolded the hankie and lifted up the phone. "It is for talking to Wally," she said.

"Yes," Dawn laughed. "And these go with his gift."

She eased from her cargo pants pocket an extra phone battery and a leather pouch to wear around her neck. Displaying them in her open palm, Dawn told Liberty, "Do not use the phone often. The battery will run down. Understand?"

Liberty touched the battery with her finger. To make her point, Dawn hunched her shoulders toward the ground as if she was a wilting plant.

"The batteries are like corn plants when they have no water."

"My people know about the talking tower near the next village. I will take the battery to Bor when it quits working."

Liberty knew plenty and was every bit as intelligent as Wally had said. Technology would bring Wally's world in America closer to Liberty's life in the African wilds. No doubt, the cell phone also would change Liberty's simple village life. Dawn showed her how to find Wally's number in the address book.

"This is his phone number. And this one," Dawn said, pointing to the green connect button, "you push to talk to Baca."

A questioning look passed over Liberty's face, but then she nodded, implying she understood.

"Press this button to find my number." Dawn carefully set Liberty's finger on the down button until Dawn's name appeared in the display. "Push this one to call me."

"Yes," Liberty cradled the cell phone, "but not many times."

Liberty comprehended her instructions. Should she let her try calling? Dawn looked at her watch. It was two o'clock in the afternoon, making it about seven in the morning East Coast time.

"Would you like to call Baca?"

Liberty gripped the phone, unsure what to do. Sweat seeped under Dawn's cotton shirt and clung to her back; a humid Virginia summer day felt cool compared to this hundred plus morning. Dawn licked her lips, craving ice cold water. Such things were dreams made of.

"It is as easy as grinding corn," Dawn said, lightly touching Liberty's finger.

Together they scrolled to Baca's name.

"Push the green button to call him. Do it now."

When she did and Wally's number appeared on the LED display, a precious smile spread across Liberty's face. Dawn guided her arm so the phone nestled against her ear. Liberty stood with a blank expression, staring at distant cattle.

All at once, she screamed. "Baca! Baca!"

Liberty sprang up on her tiptoes, chattering away to Wally. Dawn couldn't decipher the flurry of singsong words; however, Liberty's ringing laughter sounded the same in any language. The pure joy in her eyes delighted Dawn's heart. She might not be with her Griff, but this was a close second. And she couldn't help thinking that women all over the world were the same—being happiest when talking to their man.

Thoughts of Griff meeting a new woman landed sharply in her heart. Any hopes for their lives intertwining had seemed to vanish like a vapor when he'd told her about the fun time he was having with Claire in Cornwall.

DAWN MARCHED IN A WINDING line, along with a dozen or so young girls dressed in white shifts with pretty ribbons streaming from around their waists. Though sweat rolled down her face, she loved the sounds of boys hooting and beating their homemade drums. Liberty and the other women danced in the dirt at the Sunday service with the light of Heaven shining on their faces. Every villager sang songs to Jesus. Pastor Rick knew a few words of the native tongue and he sang, too.

Reverend Lowery read verses from a small Bible, thanking God for bringing food and asking for rain. "No matter our troubles, God, who created us, sees our needs. Put all your cares on Him and believe in Jesus."

Jeremy translated the Dinka words for Dawn and then snuck away to his airplane, probably to complete the flight check before they left. She was surprised when he returned right away, waving some tins before Dawn's nose.

"My Mum baked shortbread cookies for the children. I might let you try one."

He popped open a lid, letting Dawn inhale the wonderful aroma of butter. Her mouth began salivating.

"These flaky cookies traveled all the way from Australia?"

Jeremy snatched out two, snapping the lid shut just as she reached for one.

"None for me, your trusty co-pilot?" She pretended to weep.

"Did you say rusty?"

At his ribbing, Dawn groaned. "Was I really so bad?"

"You did a fair bit of piloting the plane. I guess you earned *one*." Jeremy laughingly handed her a crispy treat. "Mum lives in Melbourne but she grew up as the daughter of missionary parents in Africa. She knows the needs."

Dawn tasted the delicate cookie, which transported her thoughts to her kitchen. If Brian came home over the summer, Dawn might—she stopped her mind from living for tomorrow. What would be would be. Today, she was a missionary—of sorts—on a mercy trip.

"Just delicious," Dawn said, licking her lips. "If I ever visit Melbourne, I'm looking up your Mum and getting her recipe."

"They'll go nicely with sorghum tea."

Somehow, that sounded more like a native soap. The drumming had stopped and the women were assembling tea near Liberty's tukul. One boy who carried a drum crowded next to Jeremy, inspecting the pretty tins with his roving eyes.

Tea and corn cakes were served. Dawn helped Liberty pass out cookies to all the young children. The two women, who had become friends, sat under an acacia tree, sipping the boiled brew. Dawn found it almost bitter, yet strangely refreshing.

"Baca said most of your family died in the civil war."

"My uncle visits a friend in Kenya."

"I am sorry not to meet him."

"He returns next week. I hope I will see Baca soon."

Dawn lifted her eyebrows. "Oh? Did he say when?"

"After he graduates, he will come to marry me." Liberty leaned forward, her whisper like a hymn. "But do not tell Reverend Lowery yet."

"Your secret's safe. Did you turn off your phone?"

"Yes." Liberty patted the leather case strung around her neck, her eyes sparkling with new life. "Baca is safe."

Dawn understood why Liberty kept asking about Wally's safety. He represented her future.

"Baca is earning the bride price, I think," Liberty said, smiling.

"Does your uncle know all about it?"

From the ethereal look on Liberty's face as she nodded, she was counting the days until her marriage.

"Keep the phone off until you need it. Put in the reserve battery when the first battery wears down," Dawn said. She kept an eye on Jeremy as he talked with Reverend Lowery, who owned a cell phone and would take Liberty to recharge her battery.

The people of Walu loved each other. Their lives were full, despite loss and famine. Being in Walu helped Dawn realize how much Jesus loved people all over the world, no matter their color or shape of their eyes.

One day, every nation would bow down and worship Him. If only Griff could share her joy. In Wally's home village, Dawn silently prayed that Wally's love for Christ would inspire Griff and be a blessing to them both.

24

Dawn said a tearful good-bye to Liberty, wanting to believe she would see her again when she married Wally. Meanwhile, Jeremy examined the plane's tires, fuel, and oil levels.

"Ready, mates? Time to go."

After Rick nestled into the back passenger area, Dawn hopped in, waving to the children. Jeremy started the engine and rolled the airplane down bumpy ruts, all the while gaining speed. Dawn gazed out the window, aware that she'd left behind a piece of her heart in Liberty's remote village.

She watched the ground-speed dial until suddenly, Jeremy pulled back the yoke and the plane sprang into the air. They buzzed over Walu as Dawn memorized the landscape. Liberty looked up, her face luminous. Dawn couldn't wait to share these precious memories with Wally. A movement below caught her eye.

"Jeremy, there's rising dust. We're about to be caught in a sandstorm."

"I don't feel any more turbulence."

He banked slightly for a better look. "No, it's a trading party. Field glasses are under my seat."

Jeremy bent over while holding a steady course and handed her the binoculars. She zoomed into the dust cloud, pressing the powerful glasses against her eyes.

"Looks like horses running. Do wild horses roam in Sudan?"

"None that I know of."

"Are there riders on their backs?" Rick asked, leaning forward.

Dawn strained to see. "Yes, men dressed in white with scarves over their faces. They're carrying rifles! Jeremy, they're heading straight for Walu."

"If they have guns, they'll steal the supplies!" Rick shouted.

"Do something." She grabbed Jeremy's right arm and the Cessna dropped sharply.

"Let's see what happens if we buzz them," he said.

His eyes squinting, Jeremy dipped the plane, flying over the heads of the raiding party. He banked, turning to come back around. Rifle muzzles flashed.

"They almost hit us! I'll call for help." Dawn reached for the radio.

"Out here in the bush, we've few mates to help. But it's worth a try."

Jeremy accelerated, gaining altitude in a flash. Then Dawn tossed him the microphone and he called his base in Nairobi.

"Zulu 4-0, this is Koala. Raiding party near Walu is shooting at us."

The reply came in short bursts amidst strong static. "Roger that, Koala. Take no risks with plane. Return to Bor."

"No! We can't leave them helpless," Dawn objected, the glasses back to her eyes.

"Even if we could get there ahead of the raiders, we have no weapons," Jeremy said, raising a fist. "Besides our hands."

Rick agreed with Dawn. "We should at least warn the villagers."

Jeremy keyed in his radio, telling his base, "Koala on course back to Walu."

No voice replied, but loud static filled the cockpit.

"There are ten on horseback," Dawn said as she finished counting. "No, wait." Her heart plummeted. "There must be at least thirty bandits down there."

"God help us!" Rick cried.

Again, Jeremy tried to reach his base while Rick Nebo prayed aloud. "Lord, you know raiders are about to sweep upon our dear brothers and sisters in Walu. Help them and help us know what to do."

Jeremy dove like a fighter jet, increasing their speed. The riders on horses were drawing closer. Jeremy pulled back the yoke, passing a hundred feet over their heads. The riders looked up in surprise; some horses reared and others stopped. The men on the horses raised their rifles toward the climbing Cessna. Dawn heard a snapping sound as a bullet hit the plane.

Veering sharply to the right, Jeremy yelled, "We've been hit. Hopefully it's not the fuel tank in the wing. I can't risk a dive like that again. Pastor, you keep praying."

Dawn had flash of insight and pulled out the cell phone Jeremy had given her. He continued climbing to avoid bullets.

"You calling your FBI friend?"

She foraged in her pocket, pulled out a small piece of paper, and punched in numbers. "I hope this thing works up here."

"It should," Jeremy said, gripping the yoke.

The phone on the other end rang, but there was no answer. Dawn remembered her final instruction to Liberty to keep the phone turned off except when calling Wally.

"It's no use. She's not picking up my call."

Jeremy climbed out of rifle range, banking for another glimpse of Walu. Raiders descended on their swift horses and villagers fled in panic.

"Oh no!" Dawn wailed.

The horrible scene unfolded before her eyes and she dashed away tears. More gunshots rang out. A loud bang echoed through the plane just as Jeremy turned them for a course back to Bor.

"They've hit us again," he spat. "We're no match for them, but in Bor I can try to get more men."

Dawn lowered the binoculars, and turning toward Rick, she saw his eyes were squeezed shut, his lips moving rapidly. The Cessna roared away from the chaos in Walu and Dawn lifted up silent pleas to God. When she opened her eyes, Rick's head had slumped against the side window and blood oozed on his shirt sleeve.

Dread paralyzed her in the seat. A prompting in her spirit made her throw off her seat belt and squeeze between the seats. She tried rousing him, but Rick didn't respond.

"Give me a towel or your shirt to stem the bleeding," Dawn said.

As Jeremy jostled in the front seat, the plane dropped.

"Hey," Dawn yelled, "do you need me back up there?"

Before she could scramble up front, Jeremy handed over his belt.

"Tie it tightly around his arm. We're on a straight path for Bor." He consulted his watch. "We should get him to the hospital in fifteen minutes. Will he hang on?"

"Only God knows." Her heart aching, Dawn cinched the leather belt above the wound in Rick's arm.

LIBERTY HEARD MEN YELLING and horses coming. Was that a gun firing? Fear jumped on her back and she ran to her friend's tukul, shouting in Dinka, "Nana, raiders are coming! Get your brother."

Nana dropped a bowl of cooked corn, her dark eyes round with terror. Both women flew out of the hut, searching for Nana's little brother, who cared for the cattle. Liberty reached him first, grabbing his flimsy shirt by the neck. His sister hauled him by his arm, not stopping to explain why he had to leave the cattle behind.

Liberty seized the pouch around her neck and thrust it beneath the neckline of her dress. She ran away from Walu as she and Baca had when they were young. But he was not here to help her now. Would these militiamen be satisfied with boxes of soap and food? Or were they coming for her and her people?

She reached the river without Nana or her brother. Liberty looked all around. With the men close behind her, she plunged into the water, raising the leather pouch so her precious cell phone would not get wet. A sharp sting hit against her flesh.

It was not the kind of pain from an insect, but from a whip, a whip biting her back. Liberty struggled against the blows—to stay on her feet, to keep her head above water. With courage that came deep from within, she pushed through the water, staying one breath away from the man on horseback.

He followed her into the river, his whip a long snake trying to snare her. Liberty's dress—the one she had been happy to receive from Reverend Lowery's church—wrapped around her legs, making it impossible to even move against the current. Liberty lifted one leg after another. She had to get away!

Never again did she want to live in a refugee camp. Somehow, she reached the muddy bank, but on the wet sand in her flip-flops, she stumbled and fell. Breathing hard, she waited for fresh stings to strike her back.

Instead, she felt something cool press hard against her arms. It was a man's hand, and he carried no whip. Powerfully built, this one had jumped from his horse to pull her up the slippery bank. A white headdress covered his head and face. She could see his eyes examining her face and her body. She trembled under his intense glare.

"Get on my horse," he ordered in Arabic.

Liberty shrank toward the brush. She didn't want to go with this man holding his horse, but if she ran, he would kill her. To be dead might be better than doing his bidding. The horse lifted its legs and snorted, giving her time to think. From his dress and Arabic language, she knew he came from the north, which meant he held to the Islamic religion. Her people and others in Southern Sudan were mostly Christians. Shockwaves battered her mind.

Would he beat her when he found out she was a Christian? Maybe he would not simply take her life, but cut off her arm, forcing her to serve him as other Arab men had done to women from Walu and surrounding villages. If only God would open a big hole in the earth and swallow him. Smells of smoke burned her nostrils. The raiders must be burning her village!

"I told you to get on my horse!" The man grabbed her arm.

Liberty's heart and eyes fell as one. She had no life to run back to. This man from the north had caught her and, though it was a miracle she was alive and unhurt, tears stung her eyes. Her life was over. She hung her head in submission.

The man hoisted her onto his horse and her heart beat wildly against the leather pouch hanging from her neck. He swung up behind her, spurring his horse away from the river, away from her burning life in Walu. Because his hands rested lightly around her middle, she had one hope—that he would not find her phone. Maybe she could call Baca to send help. Astride the mighty horse, Liberty sought God with her whole heart.

Time passed. The sun scorched her head. Sweat trickled into her eyes, but she wiped it off with her free hands. Beyond some trees, she saw people huddling together, corralled away from goats and cattle. Liberty recognized a woman from Walu on her knees in a striped dress. She looked sad.

Liberty's eyes tore through the crowd. Was Nana among them? In the dirt, a bright swath of green caught her eye. Nana lay on the ground beneath an acacia tree. A small boy was crying over her. It must be her brother. Was Nana alive or dead? Liberty could not help and did not see Reverend Lowery or any men from the village.

Her captor swung off his horse, pulling her down. She landed on her feet and made her back rigid to face what must come. In the refugee camps, she had endured an empty stomach, high fever, and being alone. But Baca had saved her in the river and God had come many times in her dreams, bringing her meat and flowers.

Would she ever see Baca again?

No. As a slave, she would never marry him or dance again. Her future looked dark and bleak. Liberty trailed behind the Arab man to the corral of people, desperate to believe God's power was great enough to save her.

25

Dawn stayed beside Rick, holding the belt tightly against his arm until the Cessna nearly reached Bor. He had not opened his eyes and his strength seemed to be waning.

"I'm about to put her down. Get up here and buckle in."

"We are getting you to the hospital," Dawn told her pastor. "And I'm praying."

She tightened the belt around his arm before scooting to the front right seat. Jeremy dropped them down on the rutted airstrip, applying hard brakes halfway down the runway before stopping and doing a one-eighty. He returned to the dirt tarmac in front of the hangar. He killed the engine before the plane even stopped—proof of his skilled flying in the bush for more than thirty years.

Jeremy and Dawn lifted Rick out of the plane. Jeremy slipped his arms beneath the pastor's arms and knees, carrying the aged man gingerly toward the hospital. After about a quarter mile from the airstrip, Jeremy's legs buckled underneath the weight.

"Put him down under this tree," Dawn ordered. "I'll run ahead for a stretcher."

His breath coming in short spurts, Jeremy carefully laid Rick in the shade before collapsing beside him.

"There's no stretcher," he huffed.

Dawn bustled over to take Rick's pulse. "It's weak, but his heart's still beating."

"Maybe one of the missionary doctors will come help us."

Dawn lurched to her feet, taking off. The first nurse she found spoke no English, so she searched every room until she saw Doc Kidd stitching a man's leg.

"Pastor Nebo is wounded. We need your help."

Doc turned to an Australian nurse who assisted him, telling her to bandage the wound. He grabbed his medical bag and washed his hands with an alcohol-drenched cloth. "How did he get hurt?" he asked.

Dawn told him over her shoulder as they ran how raiders had descended upon Walu and shot at the plane. "If you can stabilize him, Jeremy and I need to gather help to fly back to Walu right away."

"I'll do all I can."

They reached the wounded pastor and the three of them managed to get him to the hospital. A missionary doctor who was spending six months in Bor took over his care; after a quick examination, he announced that the pastor's vital signs were weak, but there was a good chance he would recover.

Meanwhile, Jeremy rounded up the hospital handyman, who owned a rifle. It took about an hour, but finally, he had the plane back in the air. Dawn refused to stay behind, insisting she would be needed to help the women of the village.

JEREMY FLEW THE CESSNA OVER WALU with Dawn watching beneath them through the binoculars. Burnt sticks and smoldering wood made her fear the worst. Had Liberty survived the attack? Was she safe—or even alive?

"The village is burned to the ground!" Dawn cried as she thrust the powerful glasses from her eyes. "Put us down quickly."

"Let's take another look and make sure some rifle-toting militant doesn't fire again."

Jeremy buzzed the surrounding area, flying low.

"I don't see a single person," Dawn whispered, her hand covering her mouth.

She saw no goats or cattle either. But for the burning wood, it was as if Walu had never existed. The plane circled and Jeremy once more threaded the Cessna between the two trees, bumping to an abrupt stop.

Dawn pushed open the door and jumped out, followed by Doc Kidd and the handyman gripping his hunting rifle—only this time, no one ran to greet them. A lone tukul remained standing, wavering in the heat and ready to collapse.

"I never expected to see entire villages burned again. Not since the peace agreement a few years back." Jeremy glanced at Dawn.

She sprinted toward Liberty's burned home, but Jeremy hollered after her, "Hold it, mate! We go together with the bang stick. Sorry, rifle. I am not taking any chances that a wounded militiaman will hurl a barrage at us."

"Right." Dawn pivoted around, her calf muscles taught. "I'll stay behind you."

Their little band of rescuers huddled together, walking as one. Terrible ruin spread before them. Dawn flinched. Gone were the people with whom she'd celebrated Sunday worship services. She nearly stumbled over a dead goat sprawled next to a half-standing tukul; its bloody head had been trampled by a horse. She covered her nose at the smoky stench.

Among the remnants, Dawn spotted a broken string of glass beads, strewn by a tree stump like discarded marbles. She bent down, not touching the round glass. These were Liberty's—the ones she'd worn around her neck. Dawn choked, appalled by the destruction.

Jeremy pushed a pile of ashes with the toe of his boot. A scorpion slithered away.

"Imagine a scorpion surviving this blaze," he said, wiping his eyes with the back of his hand before asking the man with the rifle to circle round the village with him. "Stay close, Dawn. It appears the rest of the villagers have been taken."

"Couldn't some have gotten away?" she asked with a shudder.

"Not likely, with all those rifles and men on horseback."

A charred stick crumbled from the one remaining tukul, giving Dawn an idea.

"Jeremy, we should go look and see if someone's inside there."

With a couple long strides, Jeremy reached the dwelling, which had once housed laughing people. Meanwhile, Dawn peered into the hollowed-out tree stump where the women had crushed their corn. A handful of meal remained. As light as the wind, Jeremy appeared beside her, his voice thick with emotion.

"You were right. I found Reverend Lowery's body in the tukul. We'll load him into the plane and take him back to Bor, where we will give him a Christian burial."

Jeremy's pale lips and cheeks betrayed him. Something horrible must have happened to the kind and loving man. Dawn chose not to ask. While Jeremy and Doc Kidd struggled to get the Reverend's body into the Cessna, Dawn photographed the devastation. The pictures might be useful, but they sure weren't the ministry pictures she'd planned to show her church.

A lump stuck in her throat as she snapped the cap back on her camera lens. She worked with criminals as a federal probation officer and had seen drug overdoses, alcohol stupors, and beatings. But Dawn had never been in a war zone.

Profound sadness at the loss of innocent life hung over her, stabbing her heart as she took a final look at the land that was once Walu. It had been years since Wally had visited the place of his birth and he'd so looked forward to coming here to marry Liberty.

Dawn ran to the plane. She'd flown in it with a light heart that morning, ready to meet Liberty. Now Liberty was gone. How could Dawn ever tell Wally that his intended wife had been captured? She hopped into the plane, covering Lowery's head with an extra shirt. Back outside, the four bowed their heads.

Jeremy prayed aloud. "God, we ask for safety for Liberty and the others who are missing. Bring to justice the ones who have killed and harmed your children. In the name of Jesus we pray. Amen."

Sounds of the morning's march by the children beat against Dawn's mind. *Bong, bong, bong.* She whirled around. Was someone really banging a little boy's drum? But the tike who hours before had made music in honor of Jesus was now missing, and there was no sign of his musical instrument.

Jeremy fired up the engine. Dawn hesitated before climbing in, her hand on the door.

"Wait—I forgot something."

She spun in the dirt and hurried to the tree, picking up scattered glass beads, proof of Liberty's life. Dawn fled back to the plane, securing the beads in her pocket. Jeremy applied power and, in moments, had the Cessna in the air.

Dawn's spirit seemed to have parted company with her body. Her faith in God was seriously shaken. Sweat dripped into her eyes, mingling with her tears. She stared out the front window, performing the tasks Jeremy asked her to do, but she'd stuffed her feelings in a tightly closed box, one she feared opening.

Reverend Lowery's body—not breathing, not living—lay in the back of the plane. His spirit was alive in Heaven. Of that she had no doubt. But a question seeped in. She, Dawn Ahern, sat up front, alive and breathing. Why?

If they hadn't flown off to Bor, Lowery might have lived. A quiet voice in her head whispered, *if you had stayed, you might not be alive either.*

Dawn wrestled with the truth, letting it pull her forward toward grief. Another pastor, Rick Nebo, battled for life in the Bor hospital. That was a lifeline to grab onto.

Jeremy was talking on the radio and Dawn felt compelled to listen.

"All hope of recovering Walu villagers is gone." He paused. "Okay, we're flying along the Nile and will let you know if we spot anything."

Jeremy ended the transmission, turning his head slightly to the back. "Doc Kidd, my wife says the bullet sliced through Rick Nebo's right arm. Because it was folded across his chest as he prayed, his arm protected his heart and lungs."

"Thank God," Dawn sighed. "That's truly a miracle."

"But his advanced age complicates his recovery. He probably won't be cleared for the flight back to Virginia right away."

Dawn slouched back in her seat. She had only four vacation days left.

"Doc, are you planning on staying until the end of June?"

He just stared out the window, and then cried. "Look at that!"

Dawn swiveled her head down to the Nile River, yanking the binoculars from beneath the seat.

"I count two military-type boats along the shoreline. A couple of nervous horses are pawing the ground, tied to a tree."

Jeremy banked left. Dawn glimpsed a man step from behind a tree and saw him lift a rifle to his shoulder.

"Watch out! He's got a gun."

Jeremy must have seen him too, because he rocketed away, crossing the Nile.

"I've seen Sudanese military ships before. They motor down from the north where jihadists have influence in the military. They bring supplies to sympathizers here in Southern Sudan."

Dawn lowered the binoculars. "Do you think they're the rebels who raided Walu and killed Reverend Lowery?"

"I'll swoop over the ships. See who else you spot. Marauders sometimes take prisoners to trade for money and supplies."

Anxiety rose in Dawn's throat. She was afraid to even think what value Liberty would have to the military. Two ships bobbed in the water, ugly scars on the Nile, but no one walked on deck. Jeremy changed course.

"We're heading back to Bor. Many southern Sudanese have become slaves to wealthy people in the north."

An overpowering urge propelled her to get out the cell phone and call Griff. Unworthy thoughts of him and Claire loomed, but Dawn pushed them away like discarded paper. Thankfully, he answered right away.

"Griff, it's me. We're in the air and I may lose you any second."

"What a nice surprise. Grandmother and I are sipping tea, telling stories."

How normal he sounded! His happy voice soothed her, but came only after her own voice echoed against her ears.

"Can you hear me?"

"Sure. Did you fly to Walu and meet Liberty?"

The plane hit a strong thermal current and Dawn's stomach pitched.

"I have terrible news."

"What happened? Are you all right?"

"There's no easy way to say it." Her voice broke and tears stung her eyes. "Raiders on horseback sacked and burned Walu. Liberty is missing and so is most everyone else. I'm praying Liberty fled into the bush."

"Are you safe?" Griff barely whispered these words.

"We've passed the Nile and are making a beeline to Bor. We'd just lifted off when riders descended on the village. We were powerless to help. Griff—" She wiped tears that spilled down her cheeks. "Rick Nebo took a bullet."

"I should have come with you."

Static, then nothing.

Dawn looked at her phone. Had she lost the tower in the air?

"Dawn?"

"Griff, I hear you. Listen, the good news is that Liberty's cell wasn't in the rubble. She may find a way to phone Wally."

Griff's questions popped fast, but she couldn't hear most of them, due to increasing static.

"I'm losing you. Rick won't be able to fly home. I'm calling my boss because I'm going to have to stay longer."

"I know what you're planning. You aren't responsible for finding Liberty!"

He was right—that very thought had lingered in her mind since they'd left the rubble of Walu.

"My pastor needs my help recovering."

"Isn't that doctor there from your church? Let him care for Rick."

"But I've no one else to look out for—"

"It's dangerous. I'm flying home on Tuesday and I planned to meet your flight."

He did? Her emotions soared, knowing he cared, but her heart urged her to stay with Pastor Rick.

"Seems God has a different plan for me."

"Dawn," he said forcefully, "I couldn't bear it if you were hurt. Let me call my contact at the State Department. Bo Rider will know how to track Liberty."

"Be careful telling Wally. I'm not sure he could handle this, especially after his mistreatment in Summit Ridge."

"He'll be as devastated as I am that God let him down again."

Griff's words pierced her to the bone. What he'd been willing to say, Dawn felt. Just then, she sensed Jeremy eyeballing her.

"We're about to land. I miss you," she echoed softly, hoping he could hear.

"Then come home. When will I see you again?"

"I won't know that until after I see how Rick's doing. Take care."

"Wait—are you calling me from your cell phone?"

Jeremy lowered his flaps for landing, then she promised Griff, "Yes, and I'll let you know once I decide."

"Dawn, don't forget me."

He'd hung up. Why did he say that? Anxiety ripped her heart to shreds. Griff and Wally needed her at home, but Rick's life might be in the balance. When Doc Kidd reached from the back seat to pat her shoulder, she jumped. What was wrong with her?

"You should realize Rick may be flown to Nairobi, where the hospitals have more sophisticated equipment."

She hadn't considered that. Should she fly with him to Kenya?

As Jeremy expertly touched down on the airstrip, Dawn searched for answers—which, unlike the plane, didn't descend upon her from above. All she could feel was chaos battering her numb heart.

26

Liberty's captors made sure she could not escape; they tied her hands together at her waist and secured her to a rope. In this way, she was connected in front to an older, tall woman and behind to a shorter and younger girl who wept continuously. An armed soldier led the human chain aboard a Sudanese patrol boat, jabbing his rifle like a stick, poking people in the back.

"Sit and be quiet!"

Liberty understood his harsh-sounding Arabic. The first one in line plunked down on the deck, but when the second one stayed standing, the soldier pointed the gun at her.

"I will shoot."

The woman quickly squatted and so did everyone else. The soldier hurried to the ramp they had walked on and looked toward shore, leaving the people snatched from Walu and other villages to stare at the boat's ugly walls.

The older woman tied to Liberty dropped her head, whispering in Dinka, "They will float us north to Khartoum and sell us as slaves."

"How do you know?"

"Rebels came to the village next to mine. They killed all the men, taking the women and boys north to work. One woman finally escaped. She was made to be a house servant in the day. In the night, her master visited her and—"

The woman frowned, terrifying Liberty. Made a slave? She clenched her fists. If she tried to break the rope and run, the soldier would rain gunfire on her head. But Baca wanted to marry her. No other man could have her. He might find a way to rescue her. She still wore the cell phone around her neck beneath her shift.

Liberty licked her cracked lips, tasting blood. The rebels had guns and would use them. With her hands tied, she could not reach the phone. It was useless.

The boat rocked and Liberty lifted her eyes. A string of her villagers trampled in behind a large soldier wearing a uniform. He shook the arm of a man who was dressed in a white robe with a scarf covering his face. That man must be one of the raiders who had stormed Walu. The soldier aimed his rifle gun between her eyes and Liberty shuddered.

"Stand up," he demanded.

She rose on her tired legs. The robed raider kicked at people in his way, grabbing Liberty's hands and fumbling with the rope. Her ties fell off! Could she run?

Before she could think what to do, the raider began to pull. Stepping on people in his path, he yanked her toward the soldier, who moved forward and put his hand on her shoulders. He turned her in a circle, staring up and down at her body, even lifting her shift up to her knees and peering at her ankles. Then he roughly examined her hands and each one of her fingers. Fear froze her mind and body. What had she done wrong?

The soldier gave currency to the robed raider and pushed Liberty down the metal ramp. He was taking her off the boat—but to where? They stopped near pallets of cargo on the dock as he chattered in Arabic with another soldier.

Liberty hoped someone had made a mistake and she was being returned to her village. Hope rose like a flying bird when he took her to a second boat moored at the dock. She almost asked if she was going to Walu, but as he led her up the second boat's ramp, she grew afraid to speak.

On this boat, many boys were tied to each other, sitting on their haunches. She recognized one from her village—he had banged the drum. The soldier brought her to a huge gun that was mounted to the boat. He shoved her down on the deck, jabbering in Arabic.

Liberty wanted to do what he ordered, but he held her ankles, tying them with a rope. Next, he tied the rope about her waist. She couldn't reach the rope at her feet. He towered over her.

"I will come for you when the boat reaches Khartoum."

Khartoum! It was true what the old woman said. Dozens of boys gaped at her. *They see I am the only woman.* Her heart sank to the bottom like a stone she had thrown in the river. She made her body lie still, glad her hands were free.

Liberty tore her eyes from the boys and, as her head turned, she felt the small leather pouch next to her skin. The cell phone inside connected her to Dawn and to Baca. God had not forgotten. Her body trembled. She wanted to scream, but instead forced herself to close her eyes and rest in the safety of her Father's arms.

FOR DAWN AHERN, DARKNESS LOOMED with the setting sun. Cooler air drifted through the window as she sat in the hospital ward beside Rick, listening to his shallow breathing as he lay on the flimsy cot. Her last conversation with Griff had made her doubt whether she should look after her pastor or return home.

She heard a muffled chirp in her backpack and retrieved the phone Jeremy had given her to use in Sudan. Dawn's heart beat erratically—the screen indicated *Liberty*.

"Liberty, where are you?"

Her soft voice was hard to hear. "Miss Dawn, I am on … river."

"Are you safe? Are you alone?"

"My feet are tied," Liberty croaked. "We are on a boat. A soldier takes me to Khartoum. Now I call Baca."

"We can send a rescue team if we know where you are."

Dawn's mind reeled. Could they really? There was no sound in her ear. Liberty or someone who caught her must have ended the call.

IN THE MISTY TWILIGHT off the southwestern shore of England, Griff stared out at roiling water, concerned about Dawn risking her life in Sudan. He should have gone with the church group. But then, Wally had needed him, too.

Stiff breezes pelted his face with cold ocean spray. About an hour earlier, Claire had driven his grandmother into town. He'd hopped into his rental and sped to Land's End, feeling anything but in control. Dawn prayed about everything, but he prayed for nothing.

He hadn't called Wally to break the awful news that Liberty was missing. Griff was no coward, but he just couldn't tell him. Not yet. As he wiped salt spray from his eyes, he felt his cell phone vibrate in his pocket. The number belonged to Dawn's phone in Sudan. He flipped it open.

"You're on my mind big time."

Sobs sent slivers of fear through Griff's heart.

"It's terrible," Dawn cried in his ear.

She started talking again, but he couldn't understand her.

"Please. Take a breath and tell me again what's so awful."

"Liberty just called. She been taken—" Her voice broke.

"Tell me what happened."

A muffled sound, then, "Liberty's been taken as a slave. She's tied up on a boat. That's all I know. I think she hung up so she wouldn't be discovered with her cell."

Speechless, Griff could not even think. He heard a beep in his ear. He pulled the phone away, glancing at the LED screen. It was Wally.

"Dawn, wait a minute. Wally's calling me."

Griff toggled over to the incoming call.

"Dad, I keep getting calls on my cell. I think it is Liberty. But when I answer, she is not there."

"Son, I just learned she is in trouble."

"She is calling again. I will call you back."

Griff returned to Dawn, telling her of Wally's call from Liberty. "I know Wally will be upset if he speaks to her."

"I'm around the corner from Rick's cot, trying to decide what to do," Dawn sniffled.

"Okay, I promise to call soon."

Griff looked out at the white foam swirling atop crashing waves. Though the D-Day ceremony was scheduled for the following morning and he was bringing Grandma Topping, Griff wished he were anywhere but here. Wally needed him and so did Dawn. He felt helpless standing by the groaning sea, weighing his options, his hand gripping a cell phone. Then it rang.

"Dad, Liberty has been taken!" Wally's voice shook.

"We need to stay calm so we can think. Do you know where she is now?"

"On a boat. Others were sleeping. She whispered softly so I did not hear well."

"Try to recall everything she said. Even the tiniest thing might help us find her."

"She heard a soldier say Port of Sudan. She and some boys were purchased by an Army officer who put her on a different boat. She is afraid they will find the cell phone."

"Son, I will try to book a flight home tomorrow, after the ceremony."

"I have to leave for work, but am afraid for Liberty."

"Stay home while I call Dawn back, okay?"

"Yes, Dad."

Wally sounded so worried that Griff's heart broke. He punched in Dawn's number, sharing what Wally told him about Liberty.

"Dawn, I'm going to call my contact at the State Department and the FBI legal attaché in Khartoum." Griff kicked at the ground.

"What should I do?"

"Fly home. Let me see what our government can do."

"Please stay in touch," she pleaded. "My mind is not working right."

"Mine either. Call me when you know something."

Waves hurtling against the rocks matched the turmoil Griff felt inside. He knew the torments that were in store for rural girls taken against their will to large cities, but there was no way he'd tell that to Wally or Dawn. Griff also knew his call to Bo Rider, the CIA agent, would be a waste of time. While the State Department sometimes launched efforts to save U.S. citizens like Dawn or Griff, they wouldn't search for Wally's Sudanese fiancée, despite the fact he was a U.S. citizen.

But Griff made the call anyway. Reaching Bo's voice mail, he asked Bo to call right away. Griff dashed to his car and spun out of the gravel parking area, the weight of Wally and Liberty's problems on his shoulders.

27

On Monday morning, Bo Rider sat across from Director Kangas, astonished that he was being ordered out of the country again.

"Where to this time, sir?" Bo clenched his fists.

"Rider, you were Army Ranger, weren't you?"

"Yes, sir."

"Good, because I'm sending you into Iraq. We've got to ascertain what Russia is up to. They may be setting us up. You're going in strictly as Army with nothing linking you to the Agency. Do not reveal your plans, not to your wife or Frank Deming."

"How are the Russians setting us up?"

It was as if Kangas hadn't even heard him. "I'm concerned about Bear. Do you trust him?"

"Not completely." Bo folded his arms. The razzing he'd taken from Griff and Eva still stung his pride. "You are aware that Bear helped to divert triggered spark gaps to Iran while he was here meeting with me. Yet he never told me about it."

Kangas slapped his palm against the desk. "Right. And he knows how to reach you, doesn't he?"

"Sir, what does my trip to Iraq have to do with Bear?"

"Rider," Kangas said as he leaned forward, his neck straining against his shirt collar. "Your asset dropped another message to one of our agents in Moscow. He's requesting you meet him in Kirkuk. I suspect he may try to entice you into Iran."

"To gain what?"

"To help Iran embarrass us. Bear is so bold, he waltzes right into Washington one week, and then he's using drops to make contact in Russia the next."

Bo digested Kangas' suspicions. Like an overcooked steak, it didn't sit well.

"Are you saying Bear is working both sides? Is there specific intel that he's a double agent working for Iran?"

"That's what you will determine. Arrive here in the morning as usual. At eight a.m., you'll be driven to Andrews Air Force Base. When you reach your destination, all your calls to me will be encrypted."

"Yes, sir." Bo instinctively stood at attention, as in his former military days, and nearly saluted.

"At ease, Rider."

Kangas handed him a sheet of paper along with an envelope marked *Top Secret*.

"That's the message Bear dropped. Meet with him as he requests, but be wary. You don't want to be the cause of some international crisis. Read and memorize the contents of the envelope, then shred it."

Bo sensed danger crawling up his neck, prickling tiny hairs that grew back there. He gripped the envelope, curious about what was inside.

"I won't disappoint you."

"A given. Have a safe trip."

Bo silently left Kangas' office, his mind reverting to Army Ranger mode. He stalked by Frank without saying a word. Fortunately for Bo, Kangas' assistant was yakking on the phone and didn't seem to notice Bo had left.

He headed straight to his office, tearing into the envelope. The single, typed paragraph was easy to memorize, and Bo knew one thing after reading it—he had to get his affairs in order. The week before, he'd upped the amount of his life insurance in case of accidental death. Now he removed that policy and his will from his safe, penning a note for Julia and then sliding the entire contents into a large, manila envelope.

Only then did he check his cell phone. He had tons of voice mails waiting. The first was from Griff Topping, who sounded panicked. Bo returned his call and Griff answered right away, saying, "I hoped you'd call before I got airborne."

"You sound like you're in a fox hole with rounds flying. What gives?"

"I'm about to catch a flight from Heathrow to Dulles. Yesterday's plane was full and I got bumped. Have a minute?"

"About that."

"You remember Wally from Rob's Deli?"

"Yup, nice guy."

"The woman he plans to marry in Sudan has been kidnapped."

Griff explained to Bo what he knew, but with Bo's upcoming trip revolving in his mind, it took some moments for the grisly details to register. Even then, Bo wasn't sure what he could do.

"You know how things bog down here at State, going through a myriad of channels. I'll make calls—but Griff, I won't be available to follow up."

"I appreciate whatever you can do. You have helped me make up my mind."

"How so?"

"If you're unable to help, I may fly to Sudan myself."

28

It was eight o'clock Wednesday morning when Dawn called Griff, even though it was one o'clock in the morning in Virginia. This was too important to worry about his sleep. The ring—across thousands of miles—echoed in her ear.

"Come on Griff, pick up," she whispered.

Her wish came true, albeit from a somewhat groggy Griff.

"Hmm, yes?" he said.

"Sorry to wake you, but I need your help."

"Okay, Dawn." He paused and she imagined him trying to clear the cobwebs from his mind. "Whatever I can do, you know that."

She pictured his handsome, eager face whenever he performed an act of service, and it made her love him all the more.

"There's a Dutch aid group that Jeremy Bonds works with flying into northern Sudan to buy back slaves. I need to borrow two thousand dollars until I can repay you. If you'd wire it to Bor, I'll use the cash in hopes of finding Liberty."

"Say no more. When do you need it?"

"The group leaves soon," Dawn said, seeing light for the first time in days.

"But I have another idea, one which I swung into action today."

"Really?"

"If you agree, I'll return to the Sudanese embassy tomorrow and find out if they've approved my visa. I want to deliver the money myself."

"Griff, that sounds terrific! When can you get here?"

"I should know by noon. And Dawn, this is my gift. No need to pay me back. You and I are in this together."

FIERCE WINDS PELTED SAND against Bo's face, embedding tiny grains into his eyes as he fought a phantom enemy lurking in the giant dust storm. His vision blurred; the scarf wrapped around his face offered no protection against thousands of stinging particles.

Bullets whizzed by his head and Bo strained to see who had fired. His heart was pounding and adrenaline pulsed through him like a tsunami. He groped for his pistol. No! His holster was empty. Someone had stolen his weapon. The Iranian Revolutionary Guard were after him, seeking to destroy him, just as their homicide bomber had killed more than a dozen of his CIA colleagues the year before.

Sweat and sand blinded his eyes and he fell on his face, bruising his nose and smashing his wrist. Had his end come? He'd never see Julia or his kids again. Bo crouched in the dirt, steeling his body to accept the bullet that would end his life, knowing the fierce sand would be his final cocoon.

"God," he cried, "don't let my children and my wife suffer because of my stupidity."

His words swirled away on the wind, meaning nothing to anyone. But then, without warning, the churning wind ceased. The blowing sand subsided. Bo raised his head, ready to fight whoever pounced on him. He looked up into a great, shining sky devoid of clouds. Everything around him was still—no tanks, humvees, or soldiers.

He rolled to his knees, trying to spot a ditch to lie in, but he saw nowhere to hide from the men who wanted to kill him. Then he heard the sound of rushing wind. A thunderous white cloud swept into the sky above him and he watched it form into a hand; its index finger was a fiery tip. He stared as the finger wrote in the sky, wispy contrails twisting into giant letters, YHWH, which blurred into words: *You must go.*

He squinted, but before he could discern their meaning, the hand turned and pointed its flaming finger at him. He'd finally lost his mind—he'd baked too long in the Iraqi desert.

A bell sounded. Bo forced his mind awake, grappling with his cell phone to stop the ringing. Julia was calling.

"Honey, I don't know where you are. My heart hasn't been easy about you."

"Don't worry, I'm fine," Bo said, trying to steady his voice. "I've got my feet planted up on a desk and I'm issuing orders over the phone. How are the kids?"

"Gregg's upstairs studying. I found a tutor to help him in math. Glenna won a gift card to the camera shop for her photo of the clean-up at Great Falls Park."

Bo yawned, shaking imaginary sand from his burned-out brain.

He managed to say, "Glad to hear it. Has the contractor fixed the hole in the garage roof?"

"He's coming again on Monday. Any idea when you'll be home?"

"As soon as I finish up one or two things here."

Of course, he couldn't say where "here" was. And he didn't tell her anything about the crazy dream he'd just awakened from, even though it still reverberated in his mind.

"Bo, are you listening?"

"Sure, honey. You were telling me about your scrapbook getaway."

He envisioned Julia's toothy smile as she chatted about her upcoming retreat. Bo rolled off the military cot, content to listen to Julia regaling him about events back home. At least he had some connection to his family, even if that tight string seemed ready to snap.

"I have to call in for my messages. Love you, Julia."

Ten minutes later, feeling sore all over, Bo headed over to the communications quadrant, mulling over his upcoming meeting with the Bear. Would the Russian even show? If he did, would Bo believe a word he said?

Bo logged onto the secure computer. Since the military knew him as Captain Skip Pierce from his phony directives, there were no problems getting connected. A new message from Kangas nearly knocked Bo off the chair.

Iran's government killed its opposition leader an hour ago, blaming Israel. It's imperative you find out what Bear knows and reply to me without delay. WK—DNCS

When Kangas had sent Bo to Kirkuk, had he already known the leader had been killed? That was more than twenty-four hours ago, so Bo discarded that as paranoia. He typed a terse reply: *Will advise when I know anything. Meeting Bear tomorrow noon. BR*

Bo bit his lip, tasting blood. What was stirring up between Israel and Iran? And what about his dream of writing in the sky telling him to go? Go where?

29

Bad things happened in the dark. Judah Levitt knew that as surely as he knew the approaching sand storm would turn the city of Kirkuk blacker than night in a few minutes. The bus he followed into town disgorged its passengers and the man Judah had been trailing at a hotel. He thought he had time for a brief meeting before coming back to watch the hotel. He hoped to beat the sandstorm that was about to blacken the city.

Judah swung his long legs from the white sedan, which was much too small for his tall frame. Traveling in the cradle of civilization far from his Jerusalem home had sharpened his instincts. Surviving in the heart of enemy territory, where every day posed a risk to his life, had honed his appetite for justice. And justice he would have.

The Israeli smoothed a gray headdress with its black band low over his forehead and forced his eyes to sweep the busy street. He dropped one sandaled foot and then the other to the dust, being careful not to place either foot on a deadly surprise. He paused before taking a step.

What was that sound? Not the air groaning with the weight of the blowing dust. This was a piercing sound, like a wheel in need of oil. Judah gripped the open door of the car, his heart beating strong in his chest. Could an assassin be lurking in the shadows, ready to prevent Judah from completing his mission?

The storm of sand loomed closer. So did the screeching sounds. As Judah silently closed the car door, caution was his only friend. Above him, the gray sky turned a ghastly yellow. Just then, his eyes snagged a young boy struggling to push a cartload of bricks. In the strong winds, the wisp of a kid was headed straight for trouble.

"Stop! Don't move!"

But the boy didn't heed Judah's warning. He kept stumbling in the dirt, wheeling his cart toward a gate swinging in the wind. An explosion burst in Judah's mind and, forgetting about the improvised explosive devices (IEDs) that threatened him, he raced to the boy.

"Stop!" Judah yanked the boy's arms, shaking him. "Didn't you hear me? If you reach that gate, your life is over."

The boy's black eyes flashed like sharp daggers. Sand from the empty lot whipped up around them, and the boy's fighting words were caught up in the wind. He dashed away from Judah, pushing harder toward the rusted metal gate.

Judah tossed the boy to the ground and shoved the cart with great force. The cart rolled another twenty-five feet and Judah threw himself over the boy. The horrific blast rocked his ears, blowing bricks and pieces of wood into the air.

Beneath him, the child battled hard, squirming to get away, pounding Judah's arm with his balled fists. The Israeli scrambled to his feet while dodging the boy's bruising kicks.

"My cart is gone," he wailed, tears streaming down his dirty face.

The boy collapsed amid the bricks, scooping them up as if protecting precious jewels.

"But it was a land mine! I saved your life. Does that count for nothing?"

"How can I buy food for my mum?"

"Where is your mother?"

The ragged boy ignored his question, piling brick upon brick into his skinny arms. He looked no older than ten. His cheeks were drawn and his legs spindly, as if he ate little food. His mother did not take proper care of him, not by any stretch of the imagination. A painful lump swelled in Judah's throat. His son Eli should be about his age. And his wife would have seen to it …

He refused to relive what had happened to them—not here in front of an angry boy. With the sleeve of his shirt, Judah wicked moisture from his eyes, which were burning more from tears than the blowing sand.

"And your father? Does he not provide for your family?"

The boy jerked his head to look at Judah, dropping part of his load.

"You ask, but do you care?"

"Yes, for I am a father who no longer has his son."

"I am a son with no father. The former dictator killed him before I could walk."

Ah. So Saddam Hussein, the murderous President of Iraq, had been responsible for taking this boy's father. And the current President of Iran was responsible for taking Judah's son; Iran had supplied Hezbollah with the missiles that had killed his young son five years ago. Judah dug into his pocket, peeling away some dinars.

"Are these enough to buy a new wagon to haul your bricks?"

The boy snatched the dinars, stuffing them into a ripped pocket. "Maybe I get a better one."

"You are welcome. Be more careful."

The boy disappeared in the sand, which rose with a fury. It would not be long now before the entire city of Kirkuk, a dangerous place on a normal day, would be completely engulfed by sand. Judah shielded his eyes and hurried back to his sedan, reminding his feet to step carefully.

Kirkuk might be on the road to recovery since the war, but militants still exploded IEDs using cell phones. The devices were secreted in every imaginable place. Here, Kurds and Turkmen fought with Iraqis over ancient claims to the land. Just yesterday, a bomb had taken the lives of a father and his son on their way to a market.

Random violence was senseless, but Judah knew fighting in this region would continue until the Messiah came to bring peace. He gazed first over one shoulder and then the other, as casually as a tourist who was taking in all the sights. He hefted a cloth package tied with string out of the back seat and pushed the package under his shirt, wishing he had twenty more eyes in his head.

With lightning speed, he slammed the car door, locked it, and then escaped the stinging sand by ducking inside Anbar's shop. Judah's large, brown eyes flew about the entire place. A teenaged boy and girl scampered away. Who were they, and where was Anbar?

Judah strode to a rug hanging between two walls and prepared to toss the rug aside, when someone seized his shoulder. He threw out his elbow, jabbing at air. Turning on his heels, he came face-to-face with an enormous man stuffed into a shiny blue suit. With jowls the size of melons, the man's steely eyes flashed a warning to anyone who might cross him.

Unfazed, Judah stuck out his right hand and Anbar grasped it in a bone-crushing grip, the rings on his fat hand digging into Judah's flesh. Despite the pain, Judah would not be the first to break the grip.

"Peace be to you." Anbar hissed the greeting of peace, squeezing even harder.

Through clenched teeth, Judah replied, "And peace unto you."

Anbar's lined face broke out in a lopsided grin.

"I expected you, Desert Rat, two weeks past. How come you delay?"

"My work." Judah easily brushed off Anbar's skeptical tone. "Who ran from me as I entered? I thought whoever it was must have killed you for the Iranian devils."

"You need not be concerned."

Judah hauled the package from beneath his floppy linen shirt, but kept a firm grip on it. "You want what's inside this, you tell me."

Anbar touched a finger to his lips and ambled close to Judah's face.

"My nephew and niece are running an underground church. As you know, we are Christians. Yesterday, militants burned the home of another underground church."

"I am sorry."

Judah handed Anbar the tied package. Christians were not Judah's target; they posed no threat to Israel.

"Here are the satellite phones you ordered. Spread them among your recruits. Time is critical."

"More than you know. Have you heard the opposition leader in Iran was assassinated?"

"No," Judah blinked, stunned by the news.

"The regime blames Israel," Anbar said, lifting his chin. He tore away the string and cloth wrapping on the package and peered inside. "It is good, but the sandstorm could interfere with our plans. Helicopters are grounded."

Judah gazed out the window, seeing nothing but swirling dirt and scraps of junk flying everywhere. Surely an evil force churned up this storm; clear skies had been forecast. His throat felt dry and he smacked his lips.

After storing the parcel underneath a stack of woolen Persian rugs, Anbar held up three fat fingers. Judah calculated. If the Students for Democracy in Iran received the phones Judah gave Anbar in three days, how many more days before they held the rally for freedom? Israel counted on a huge gathering in one final attempt to overthrow the Iranian regime before Iran dropped a nuclear bomb on his homeland.

"Inside the border, coming through the Zagros mountains, I saw a herd of Persian fallow deer," Judah drawled, pressing his back against the rug hanging on the wall.

"Oh? I thought they were supposed to be extinct."

Anbar drew a wad of dinars from beneath the sheath of fabric wrapped around his ample waist. He began counting. Judah secreted the Iraqi currency inside a pocket within a pocket.

"I saw them all the same," he hissed, "along with a hunting contingent carrying shoulder rifles. You don't suppose they were going to slaughter the last of that ancient species?"

Shadows flicked across Anbar's face. "Is not it a perfect time to launch a terror attack, in a raging storm of sand?" he asked, rubbing his full beard.

"Stay safe my friend. We need each other. Let me know if the killing of the students' leader prevents the rally."

With that, Judah whisked out of the shop, walking straight into the sand. He had another job to do.

30

Bo Rider burst into the crowded café, every nerve in his body afire with a sense of constant danger. He rubbed his eyes, which still burned from dust and tiny grains of sand embedded beneath his lids. That real sandstorm had erupted like some twister, coming out of nowhere. Grit covered his tongue, slipped down his throat, and stuck in his hair. Strange how he'd dreamt of it before it happened.

After brushing off his arms, he scanned the tables, assessing the nationality and probable loyalties of everyone seeking refuge inside. He sought a seat away from windows, not wanting to get hit by any intentional or stray bullets—but had to settle for a corner table by a side window.

This café, frequented by locals, held any number of hidden threats. Bo needed to find a safer place for his rendezvous with Bear. He decided to go out and wave him off. Just as he pressed his hands on the table to rise, the owner appeared, dropping a tattered menu to the table. He lifted his chin with a quizzical look.

"I'll have coffee." Bo handed back the menu, all the while scrutinizing every person in the place.

The owner snapped up his limited list of offerings and hustled to the kitchen. Committed to coffee, it was too late for Bo to leave. Even though Iraqi soldiers claimed to maintain security in Iraq, certain perils were even greater.

He appraised the patrons—all men—to gauge if any posed an immediate threat. To a man, each was cloaked with dust, but nothing else seemed unusual until he spotted the somber and clean-shaven face of a man at a rear table. It startled him. The guy stared back at Bo with a knowing look. Why?

Was he someone working with Bear, covering his back? Or could he … Bo shut off the thought as if he were tightening a leaky faucet. He refused to believe he was being followed in Iraq. Still, his years as an Army Ranger and then as a CIA agent had heightened his senses to nuance. Layers of dirt and grime aside, something didn't fit.

A steaming cup of coffee arrived and Bo stirred the thick Turkish brew with a small spoon, analyzing several Iraqis and the few westerners in the small café. With each sweep, his eyes flittered back to the man, who continued to stare at him with those piercing eyes. Through the dusty window, he saw two Hajis walking toward the café, each with an M-16 rifle at the ready, a visual reminder of the present danger.

When Bo had been an Army Ranger, Iraqi soldiers had been a rag-tag bunch carrying AK-47s. Nothing had changed much, except for the type of their guns. While the Haji gave the appearance of protecting the town, they were only as good as the training they'd received from U.S. troops.

He sipped the strong java, forcing his eyes not to glance again at the clean-shaven guy back in the corner. The contact Bo was to meet—the Bear—hadn't arrived. Once again, Bo's Russian asset was late, this time by three minutes. If he didn't appear in another two minutes, Bo would clear out.

Just when he had shifted his knees, ready to declare his asset a no-show, he spotted the Russian clearing the door and swaggering Bo's way. Sounds of a chair scraping against the concrete floor made Bo swivel his head. The curious observer stood and left, passing within an inch of the Bear.

Bo's senses went on the alert. Did the guy just pass something to Bear? Maybe Bo just imagined an exchange.

Bear stalked to a just-vacated table in the back, casting nervous glances around the place. Then he beckoned Bo with a tilt of his head. However, Bo sensed he should wait before declaring he knew Bear. He drank his coffee, letting the owner take Bear's order.

While Bo waited for Bear to get his coffee, he gazed across the street. There was a bearded man holding a cigarette in one hand and wiping off his gray headdress with the other—probably another Iraqi who'd gotten caught in the sandstorm. Believing he was no threat, Bo finally changed tables. He leaned close to Bear, lowering his voice.

"Of all the places in the world, why'd you pick this sandbox?"

That GI nickname for Iraq had taken on a pungent meaning for Bo, since the storm swept dirt everywhere. Bo's tongue searched in his molars for a grain of sand, but it was so small it eluded his tongue.

The Russian looked around the room, muttering, "My employer … what am I saying? I mean my government. After all, you are my employer. They sent me to Iran in support of certain … um … *supplies* we are providing there."

Bo nodded, thinking it best to say nothing that might hinder the giant man's sluggish brain. The café owner arrived with a fresh cup of hot espresso for Bear, who drank his second cup in one gulp, wiping off his mouth with his shirt sleeve.

"When I had to cross through the mountains into Kirkuk, I thought it a good chance to meet you and make sure you keep funding my special account."

Bo bristled at the mention of money. Although cash had been the bait he'd used to entice the Russian to betray his government, Bo distrusted Bear's greed. Moreover, Bear had withheld information about his dual-use research while in D.C.

"I already told you," Bo said, leaning on his elbow, "it's not how frequently we meet or talk, but how good your intel is."

"My record is good. What about the S300 missiles? Have you forgotten so soon?"

"Deposits to your Swiss account have slowed because you failed to tell me about triggered spark gaps being shipped to Liberia. As you know, I had that shipment stopped."

There was no visible sign that Bear even heard what Bo said.

"I wanted the meet because I had information, but I cannot remember what it was," he said. A mischievous twinkle lit up his eyes. "Maybe you buy me some vodka to prime my memory pump."

"Sorry, he doesn't sell vodka." Bo turned, summoning the owner. "Another coffee for my friend."

Bear smiled as he retrieved a flask from his back pocket and took a swig just as his small Turkish coffee arrived. He dropped his voice to a husky whisper. "People in Iran want to buy our TOPOL-M missile."

Bo's heart skipped a beat—this was a game changer. Up to now, the Agency believed Iran lacked the means to deliver a bomb. But Russia's newest, most dangerous intercontinental missile carried a warhead weighing a ton. It had a range of more than 6,200 miles.

"Has Russia already supplied the TOPOLs to Iran?" Bo asked sharply.

Yuri shook his large head. "They said they only want the missile. They do not care about a large payload."

"What are they up to?"

Bo angled his body. Gazing out the dusty window, he saw the smoker toss his cigarette to the ground and crush it with his shoe.

"Something small." Bear's tone made the words sound cryptic, almost sinister. "I need more vodka."

"No, tell me now."

Bear shrugged, pouring the last drop of the clear liquid into the small cup. "My Iranian source says their rocket needs only a payload weight of a monkey, or a dog—like Sputnik."

"Get word to me when you have details of Iran's nuclear intentions."

After draining the small cup, Bear unwound himself from the iron chair, getting to his feet without upsetting the table. "We will meet again. Don't forget to stay in touch with my Swiss friend."

Bear dipped his head and bolted out the door. Bo couldn't help smiling at Bear's final plea for money. He eased back in his seat, watching Bear stroll down the street past a contingent of armed Iraqi soldiers. It was then that Bo glimpsed the man who'd been smoking the cigarette rush to parallel Bear along the opposite side of the street.

Bo quickly settled the bill and crossed the street, striding in the same direction as the man, who was now out of sight. Was Bear's Russian colleague shadowing Bo? At the next corner, the strange man stepped from the side of a building and pointed right at Bo. This close, Bo felt sure he'd seen this man, even prior to watching him smoke a cigarette across the street.

"You are a Christian in Action."

Bo was speechless. "Christian in Action" was slang for CIA. This man, on a side street in Kirkuk, was accusing Bo of being with the Agency. He was obviously Middle-Eastern and wore a heavy beard, trimmed short. Bo's brain scrambled. This man had been out front of the café while Bo had been inside talking with Bear. He was about to weave a plausible story of denial when the man extended his hand.

"I don't remember your name, but we met at the Point. I'm Judah Levitt."

The highly-secret facility at Harvey Point, North Carolina, was where the CIA trained its own agents and foreign intelligence officers. Bo shook his hand, groping for a reply.

"You were my instructor at a class on wet operations," Judah said, keeping his voice low. "It was my only visit to the U.S. and I never got outside the gate. Our plane entered your country, landed on your secret strip and left the same way. I'm with the Institute."

Ah. Judah posed no threat. Bo knew the Hebrew word for Institute was "Mossad," Israel's intelligence agency.

"I'm Bo Rider, known as Captain Skip Pierce here in Iraq. I remember teaching the course and you look familiar to me—but you weren't dressed in flowing attire back then."

"I never thought someday I would meet you in Iraq—after you met with the Russian missile expert I've been following." Judah smiled only with his eyes.

Bo wondered if Bear wore a sign saying "Follow me. I'm a spy." that was visible to everyone but Bo. First he was tailed by Eva Montanna's group, and now by Judah.

"We need to get reacquainted, but not on this street," Bo insisted.

"I agree. Meet at the tomb in thirty minutes."

"Which tomb?"

"Ask any tour guide down by the corner. They'll direct you."

A second later, Judah Levitt, secret agent for Mossad, had disappeared.

31

Bo received directions from the café owner and wound his way to Kirkuk's infamous Citadel, which housed an ancient tomb. He purchased a glass of tea from a street vendor, hoping to wash the remaining grit from his teeth. Against a backdrop of massive stone walls, Bo took his glass over to a bench beneath a shade tree.

He sipped the tea and waited for Judah, Bo's mind barely registering the shocking intel that Bear had just dropped—Iran buying TOPOL missiles from Russia. With such long-range missiles, they could launch a nuclear bomb and destroy Israel overnight.

Judah joined him and, for an awkward second, the two agents simply stared at each other. Finally, Judah broke the ice.

"Good thing I recognized you from the Point. If I had not, you and Colonel Egorov would be in my crosshairs."

It stunned Bo to hear Bear's real name, especially spoken by an officer from another intelligence service. He looked into Judah's riveting, dark eyes.

"Am I right that you trained with the Mossad group I taught in the spring of last year?"

"Your memory is perfect. When I first saw you kibitzing with the colonel, I thought you were Russian."

Judah's thick accent convinced Bo that he was a native Israeli.

"It seems strange discussing this, but when did you tumble onto my identity?"

"The more I watched your face, the more I was convinced I had seen you before. I concentrated and could picture you telling my class about an Iraqi chemist you dealt with when you taught us about wet operations and how you were trained in enemy elimination."

Bo didn't want to talk about his tradecraft so openly with Judah, especially after meeting Bear in a war zone. He shifted on the bench, his eyes landing on a young boy wheeling a cart of junk straight toward them. Did the cart contain a bomb? Bo's pulse quickened.

"I was impressed with what you taught us," Judah said, "but I have discovered your government restricts your use of those same techniques. I am thankful we do not answer to your Congress. If we did, Israel would already have disappeared."

"Do you see what I see?" Bo's gaze never left the ragged boy and his cart of broken things.

Judah jumped off the bench. He turned toward the boy, extending his arms palms-out. The kid, who was younger than Gregg, immediately stopped as if he were a driver responding to a traffic cop. Judah cupped his hands around his mouth, calling across the forty yards in Arabic. The kid called back.

Bo understood enough Arabic to know Judah had agreed to buy some bricks. He also knew the decrepit cart could contain an IED. To Bo's surprise, Judah dug into his pocket and tossed the boy a coin. The lad's eyes followed the coin like a hawk tracking a lizard until he plucked it from the dirt. Pointing to the ground, Judah yelled another command. Selecting two bricks from the cart, the boy placed these on the ground, turned, and shuffled off with his cart.

"I spoke earlier with him when his cart hit a land mine. I am glad to see he has a new one. I buy his bricks to support his widowed mother. He presents no risk, but I was not comfortable with him pushing the cart up to us. Let us see inside the citadel."

"Whose tomb is it anyway?"

"Daniel's," Judah replied, leaning down to pick up his bricks. "Notice the boy still watching over by the corner? I'll leave these here by the gate for him to retrieve. Next time I see him, I will probably buy these same two bricks. I do not think I am supporting a beggar, and he is proud to be working."

Bo shrugged. "I know you're not talking about Boone or Webster, so who's the Daniel buried inside?"

Rather than answer, Judah began walking up the mound with Bo lagging slightly behind. The kid and the cart still had him worried. Inside the Citadel, Bo was surprised to see hundreds of bricks littering the courtyard. A scaffold must have blown over in the sandstorm and several men struggled to put it up alongside the brick tower.

"This is something of a tourist attraction in Kirkuk, so the town is busy restoring the Citadel to its former glory. This stronghold was built nearly three thousand years ago. You see the bare earth inside the walls?

"That sandstorm has piled up a dune along the outside," Bo said as he nudged a brick with the toe of his boot.

"That's how it was before they started digging. Iraq's former dictator razed every house, forcing the Kurds to leave, but the Antiquities law prevented him from destroying the tombs. The Citadel remains a place where three faiths come together, because a Jewish temple was turned into a Christian church, which then became the mosque."

"Your young brick vendor could make a fortune cleaning and selling these bricks."

"And so he does. A seven-year-old man helps his young mother, who is already a widow. My faith tells me to look out for orphans and widows. Ever read the Psalms?"

"Me? No. I'm too busy protecting my country from crazies who mean to kill us."

"A man who faces such enemies needs a powerful protector."

"Thanks for the offer," Bo laughed.

Judah fixed him with such a penetrating look that Bo figured he'd misunderstood. Then Judah led Bo over to a whitewashed building. "The Citadel holds special significance for me," he said.

Bo trailed Judah inside the building, a cool contrast to the remains of broken homes that no longer sheltered life. This interior structure, with its tan, woven rugs and painted walls, was stylish and well cared for. As no one else walked inside, it seemed a good place to talk things over with Judah. Then, Bo's Israeli guide stopped near some outlandish green-jeweled curtains.

"Just beyond my fingertips is the tomb of the prophet Daniel. Darius, the King of Persia, successor to Cyrus the Great, threw him into the lion's den. God protected Daniel from being torn apart by the beasts. That is the protection I referred to."

"My wife and I once watched a movie where followers of Jesus were killed by lions in Rome," Bo said.

Judah's gaze was unwavering. "That was also a time of persecution for my people—but I am speaking of hundreds of years before that time. I come here because I gather strength from Daniel's life. He was a Jew in a Babylonian kingdom, like me."

"I gather your people have been warring in these areas for centuries."

"King Nebuchadnezzar once ruled Babylonia, before the Persians. Iraq's former dictator claimed to be his descendent. Daniel interpreted Nebuchadnezzar's dreams, predicting the rise and fall of the Persian, Greek, and Roman empires—and saving his life in the process."

Bo didn't know how to respond. He'd never opened a Bible and knew nothing of the Jewish faith. He shrugged, saying, "There must be something weird about Kirkuk. If Daniel was still alive, he could interpret the dream I had the first night I arrived."

Judah apprised Bo carefully, as if he were making fun of Daniel. "Do you want to tell me of this dream?"

"It was a bit bizarre, but here goes." Bo looked away and the writing he'd seen came rushing back. "I was trapped, with nowhere to hide. The Revolutionary Guard was after me—in a sandstorm I might add—when I cried out to God. A flaming finger wrote in the sky."

"What did this finger write?" Judah asked, stroking his beard thoughtfully.

"Giant letters in all capitals. First a Y, then an H, followed by W and another H. These words I recognized: 'You must go'."

Judah gaped. "You saw YHWH in your dream?"

"Yeah, so what?"

"Are you Jewish?"

"No," Bo said, shaking his head.

"Your mother or grandmother? It is through the female line that makes one Jewish."

"I said no," Bo snapped. "What difference does it make?"

"You saw the very name for Holy God that is written in our ancient texts. Our rabbis teach that YHWH means Yahweh or Jehovah."

The hairs on Bo's forearms seemed to spring to life. He was ill at ease with the idea of God or Jehovah speaking to him in a dream.

"How do you know Daniel is really buried here?" he asked.

"Some claim Daniel is buried in Susa. Of course, that is in Iran. I choose to believe his body lies in this very tomb," Judah said, before dropping his voice to a mere whisper.

"Daniel was not only a prophet, but a royal prince from the tribe of Judah. My family heritage is of that tribe, and we need such a prophet to fight the evil that blooms all around us like deadly mold."

Bo could grasp that. Israel's great enemy was the Iranian regime, which had publicly ranted they would wipe Israel off the map. Of course, they hated America, too.

"Skip, I know better than to ask about your relationship with the colonel," Judah continued, "but I am relieved to know you are talking to him."

Since Bo knew nothing of Judah Levitt or why he'd been tailing Bear, he opted for extreme caution in his reply.

"The Agency has ways of sharing with the Institute those things of mutual interest. You and I can only get in trouble sharing matters that are far above our pay-grade."

"I do not put you in such an awkward position—but allow me to make an offer."

Bo tilted his head, his alert ears waiting to hear.

"Sometimes an Institute-asset gives me information I am unable to confirm. So I am reluctant to put much confidence in the information."

Bo checked around the dead prophet's tomb for any living ears. Seeing and hearing no one else, he said, "Spell it out, Judah."

"Two weeks ago, I observed your Russian colonel driving out of an S300 missile site. I shouldn't tell you this—he should. If he has not, then your trusting him is dangerous."

Only Bo's nodding head revealed his thoughts.

"I followed him to learn what Iran is doing with those missiles."

"It sounds like you and Mossad already know some of what Russia is up to in Iran," Bo said.

"Only some. Back-check what the colonel tells you. I am satisfied that eventually your agency will share it with mine."

"I'm all for staying in touch," Bo said, keeping things vague.

"Yes, but Iran is now a nuclear state. UN sanctions are worthless in combating the threat. We must act."

"Don't you think that's what the tyrants hope Israel will do?"

Judah pounded his fist into the flesh of his left hand. "So be it."

Bo turned to leave the tomb, but Judah stopped him with a hand on his arm. "God brought me to you this day, I am convinced. I have contact with high-level dissidents in Iran. They tell me an Iranian scientist who works in their nuclear program wants to cooperate, but first he must know he can escape from Iran."

"Why not take the glory for yourself? That would be a major coup."

"He will not defect to Israel." Judah roughly tossed his head. "You and the Agency may be able to meet his needs better than I."

"Have you met this Iranian scientist?"

Bo had to wonder if Judah's defector could be Doctor Cyrus or Doctor Lili Tabriz. No—they worked in microbiology, not physics.

"Suffice it to say, I know who he is," Judah said. "I call him the Termite."

"An apt description. Burrowing within to collapse the structure. I once battled them in my house. Took years of poison to kill their tunnels."

"Just so. Will you consider my proposal?"

Kangas' earlier warning blazed through Bo's mind like fire. Just then, he heard a scratching noise on the other side of the curtain—the side by the grave. Bo clamped one hand on Judah's shoulder, putting the other to his lips.

"I appreciate your giving me this tour of such an important place in Iraq's history. And now, I have another appointment."

Judah nodded as if he, too, had heard the strange noise. He led Bo from the tomb. Out in the heat, beneath a sky that still glowed an eerie shade of yellow because of the sandstorm, Judah gestured to a cab waiting nearby.

"Let's ride together back to the café. I presume you have transport there."

"I do."

Once in the cab, their conversation stayed neutral. The cabbie arrived in town and began a turn in front of a convoy of four trucks driven by Iraqi soldiers.

Judah tapped the driver's shoulder. "Stop. Let them drive ahead of us. Don't get too close."

Bo pulled a business card from his pocket, handing it to Judah. After reading it, Judah smiled.

"United Search Associates is your company. What do you search for?"

"My firm is an employment agency. We're seeking skilled people to place with firms in the U.S."

"Do you find any here?" Judah gestured out the window.

"I talk to U.S. military and Iraqis whose training qualifies them for jobs in the States. By coming to a war zone, I get access to our people before they get back home."

"A captive market, so to speak." Judah gave a knowing smile, pointing out the window at a new school. "With all the foreign assistance, the city begins to rebuild."

Suddenly, the cab stopped. Bo gazed out the front window, noticing the convoy had been held up by a stalled truck in the road.

Judah grabbed the door handle. "We are close enough to walk from here."

Before he could open the door, the windshield exploded. Heat and compressed air tore through the cab. Bo's ears felt the concussion—everything fell silent. Pieces of glass peppered his face and arms. Blood seeped from cuts on Judah's face. Bo wiped his own face with the palm of his hands, spotting bits of blood.

Judah rammed his shoulder against the taxi door, but it wouldn't budge, so he and Bo climbed out the broken door window. Beyond the damaged taxi, Bo spotted the burning remains of the truck that had blocked the intersection. A hulking Iraqi transport was on fire.

Judah's lips were moving, but Bo heard only ringing in his ears. He shook his head, arching his neck to find his way clear. The cab driver bled profusely, much more than either Judah or Bo, and his left arm hung limply as if it were broken. Bo hurried over to help the man.

Once the two agents had pulled the driver through his broken window, they crafted a sling from a shawl in the rear seat of the taxi. After winding it around the driver's arm, Judah yelled to Bo, "We should get out of here!"

Bo managed to make out a few words, and replied, "Yeah, more IEDs could explode."

Judah thrust his business card into Bo's hand before they headed off in different directions, each to his own secret maneuvers.

32

The following day, with Bo's work completed in Kirkuk, he headed to the Sather Air Base to use the secured facility to call Director Kangas. His flight would depart the Baghdad base for Germany in three hours. It was nine in the morning at Company headquarters by the time Bo reached the Director's office. Once Frank Deming was assured the call was on a secured line from Baghdad, Kangas picked up.

"What's up, Rider?"

"Sir, I didn't want to sit too long on this info. I'm flying to Germany in less than two hours, but thought you should know what I've learned."

Kangas said hesitantly, "If you are on a secure line, go ahead and tell me."

"Iran is poised to buy the TOPOL-M missile from Russia."

Silence on the other end, and then Kangas whistled. "That's not good news. This comes from Bear?"

"He was emphatic."

"Then the trip was worth it. Maybe he'll prove his value yet."

Bo considered whether to tell Kangas the rest and decided he'd better. "Perhaps. What's strange is his claim that the Revolutionary Guard does not need a large payload capacity, but one the size of Sputnik."

"That sounds ridiculous … unless they've devised a germ warfare plan."

Why hadn't Bo thought about that gruesome possibility?

"Bear said he doesn't know why. One more thing for you to consider." Out of an abundance of caution, Bo lowered his voice. "I met an agent from another foreign intelligence service who offered me an Iranian nuclear physicist willing to defect."

Another pause. "Be careful, Rider. You could be getting ambushed."

"I didn't commit."

"You mustn't assume we don't already have other sources inside Iran. You could cross wires with another company asset. We'll debrief when you get back here. That's enough for now."

After hearing a click, Bo held a dead receiver.

Back at the departure area, he boarded a C-17 transport plane en route to Germany, where he planned to change into civilian clothes and catch a commercial flight to Dulles. Meanwhile, he maintained his cover as Captain Skip Pierce by remaining in military fatigues. His seat was reserved by the travel orders Kangas had arranged.

Bo settled into an aisle seat for takeoff, his mind brimming with the memo he needed to write. A thought plagued him. Had that IED been meant for him? Bear knew Bo was in Kirkuk; he had lured him there, in fact. But Bear also knew his healthy retirement fund would dissolve if anything happened to Bo.

Or had Bear known about Judah trailing him, making Judah the target? There were no simple answers. After all, Kirkuk was a minefield. Bo turned his thoughts to his previous meet with Bear at the Jefferson Memorial. Kangas had been furious to learn Bear arranged, without telling Bo, for the triggered spark gaps shipment to Iran.

Kangas' comment still irked him: "Maybe you should recruit Eva Montanna. Where would we be without her?"

That stinging rebuke flitted through his mind like a firefly; but in the next second, it disappeared. So did every other thought. It was as if Bo's entire brain had collapsed—all he wanted to do was crash. On that military transport jetting to Germany, sudden waves of cold shook his body from head to toe.

His eyes kept slamming shut. When the military attendant offered him a blanket, Bo grabbed one, drawing it around his neck. His body felt like it had morphed into an ice cube. He hailed the attendant again.

"Bring me another blanket will you? It's freezing in here."

The attendant dropped a second one in Bo's lap, which he burrowed into. When the attendant handed out boxed lunches, Bo cracked open one eye and passed. His stomach started cramping.

"Excuse me," Bo said to a passing attendant. "I'm not well. Got any bicarb?"

He disappeared, returning in moments with another soldier, who wore a baffled look. "I told the flight medic you're sick, and he insists on seeing you."

"Captain Pierce, I understand you're experiencing chills." The corpsman stepped closer to Bo. "Is that right?"

As Bo looked up, intense pain wracked his shoulders and neck.

"Yeah. It's probably fatigue."

The medic touched the back of his hand to Bo's forehead. "You're burning up. Have you been to Kirkuk lately?"

"A few days ago. Why?"

"Follow me please. You'll be isolated in the rear of the plane. A Marine on board also has strange, flu-like symptoms. He was in Kirkuk, too."

Bo struggled to his feet, nearly tripping over the fold of the blankets. The medic seated him in an isolated area across from the sick Marine. Bo shivered beneath two layers of blankets, aware he'd never survive the commercial flight home from Germany. Before he knew it, he fell into a restless sleep.

A man in gleaming white robe hovered above him, beckoning him with a smoldering finger. Bo's body flew toward the man and he reached for the edge of his robe. Before he could touch it, Bo awoke to see an Air Force doctor examining the Marine.

Bo felt a hand drop on his forehead. As he focused his blurry eyes, he nearly gasped. The doctor leaning over Bo with his masked face looked like something out of a space movie.

"Sorry to inform you Captain, but you and this Marine are being transported to Landstuhl for isolation and treatment. Your symptoms suggest a highly contagious form of the flu—one we don't want spreading into the U.S. You are not going home."

Bo closed his eyes, uncertain if he was awake or dreaming. Was he still in the Army or working for the CIA? He wished Julia were here to care for him and to interpret his bewildering dreams.

33

The following Tuesday, Griff Topping folded his large frame in the co-pilot's seat of Jeremy's Cessna. They rolled down the airstrip in Juba, Southern Sudan, heading to Bor. Griff was tired after flying for two days. It had been tricky getting his travel documents, but he'd hung out for an afternoon at the Sudanese embassy in Washington, D.C., begging for a visa.

He glanced at Jeremy, whose forehead glistened. Griff was used to Virginia's intense summer heat, but these one hundred degree temperatures were unbelievable. Jeremy fiddled with his radio frequency.

"I fly a Cessna Sky Hawk," Griff said. "Want me to read your check-list?"

"Thanks mate, but no. I've been doing this so long, I've memorized it."

"She's your baby."

Griff had never known a pilot who didn't visually read through the check-list before takeoff. Instincts told him to be vigilant. He folded his arms across his chest, telegraphing that he was a passenger and not the co-pilot.

Jeremy seemed nice, but Griff didn't like the Aussie pilot's casual approach to flying, especially in a dangerous country that lacked navigational aids. Maybe if he turned his mind to something else, he'd be content to let Jeremy do his thing.

Griff looked around the single engine turbo prop, which seemed roomy enough for fourteen passengers. Flying in this behemoth felt like riding in a station wagon when Griff was used to riding in a sports car. Though he'd flown dozens of international trips for the FBI, Griff could thank Dawn for a couple of firsts: his first flight in a Caravan and his first glimpse of Sudan.

Jeremy got them up quickly and, as they soared in the endless blue sky, Griff hoped Dawn was holding up okay. She had sounded so frightened—yet unwilling to buckle under—the last time they'd spoken.

They had been in the air a few minutes when Jeremy pointed. "Look down yonder."

"Are those elephants?"

"That they are."

Jeremy pointed the nose into a dive. Columns of dust rose below the plane, and thin spires shadowed the impressive beasts ambling on the plain. As Jeremy swept nearer, Griff was amazed how fast elephants could run—toward the river.

"Truly remarkable," Jeremy said, his face erupting in a grin. "Everyone thought elephants had disappeared from this area."

"Years of war probably wiped out lots of animals. But when do we reach the hospital?" Griff asked, more interested in seeing Dawn than ogling wild elephants.

"Twenty minutes or so. Constant war has killed thousands of people, too. You probably know Sudan used to be two countries."

"My adopted son, Wally, has revealed tidbits of his life here, but I didn't have time for research. I'm just glad their embassy approved my travel so quickly."

"I thought Dawn said you weren't here in an official capacity." Jeremy looked askance as he adjusted the throttle, getting them level and back to cruising speed.

"Correct. I'm on vacation using my personal passport."

"Simply great you're here. You're another mate who can handle a gun on the ground when we try to reach agreements with the Arab traders."

"Do you think we stand a chance of recovering Liberty?"

"This is a treacherous place, because the north is Islamic and south is Christian. They've been warring for years."

Jeremy explained how the enmity between the two religious factions had exploded in the eighties when the government had invaded the south from Khartoum. Ever since, the Islamic Northerners attacked the mostly Christian Dinka and Nuer people.

"We'd just left Walu," Jeremy's said, his voice grave, "when raiders plunged into the village, kidnapping Liberty and the others to sell as slaves. Dawn went nuts."

Griff slid his hands over his jeans. "I can hardly imagine how terrible you all felt. When Wally fled the civil war, Liberty had a chance to leave, but she remained in Kenya, returning to Walu a few years ago. Wally found a better life in America. She could have, too."

He said nothing about the farce of a trial Wally faced back in Virginia. It seemed Officer Ryan had testified at the preliminary hearing and Judge Fox had set the case for trial in mid-August. Fortunately, the bond stayed in place, and Wally kept working. Without warning, CJ Huddleston's bloated face loomed before Griff's eyes and he snapped his head toward the horizon.

"Those clouds look ominous, Jeremy. And I'm sensing turbulence."

"Me too."

"Expecting rain?"

Jeremy squinted ahead. "That blew in quickly. When I picked you up in Juba, I anticipated clear flying."

"Can we outrun it?"

"No way. Steady on, mate." Jeremy grasped the yoke with force.

Griff had no experience with African storms, but they couldn't be much different than those in the U.S. Large drops of rain pelted the Caravan, splashing forcefully against the windshield before sliding to the top and disappearing. Winds buffeted the craft, and it lost some altitude, but Jeremy regained level flight.

"There's a vibration in the back! Take over, Griff."

Griff instantly gripped his yoke, placing his feet on the rudder pedals, and Jeremy slid between the seats. As they approached a low cloud, Griff resisted an urge to fly above it. A tremendous boom thundered in his ears and flashes of lightning lit up the plane.

"Wow!" Jeremy shouted from the rear.

"Sure you don't want me to climb? I can get above it."

"Nah, I don't want to do that. We'll be landing shortly," he yelled back to Griff.

Seconds later, Jeremy slid into the left seat. "We'll be all right. These storms usually don't last too long."

As soon as Jeremy placed his hands on the yoke, Griff plunked his on his knees, resisting the urge to grab the yoke again. His eyes locked on the altimeter. Okay, he breathed. It didn't look like Jeremy was going to fly them into the ground. But the plane was still surrounded by total darkness and Griff felt trapped—as if he were stuck in an elevator. His heart began pounding.

In seconds, they broke free of the storm, flying into beautiful sunshine. The last of the raindrops vaporized from the windshield. Jeremy settled into a descent on the final approach to the runway at Bor. He added more flaps, dropping them abruptly halfway down the runway. He nodded toward Griff.

"These runways are in such poor shape, I use as little as necessary."

He braked hard to make the next turn onto the taxiway. Griff felt enormous relief with the ground beneath him. He didn't want to fly with Jeremy, ever again.

AT BOR'S AIRPORT, Dawn languished in the heat behind a low fence, watching a plane do an unusually short landing and quick turn. She narrowed her eyes, spotting the Caravan. Jeremy had treated Griff to one of his signature short-strip landings—but at least Griff should be aboard.

A small measure of gladness welled in her heart, blotting out scenes of death that had paraded through her mind and kept her from sleeping the last few nights. As Jeremy steered the plane toward the fence, Dawn turned to Dirk—a tall, sinewy Dutchman who was leader of a Dutch aid group.

"My friend just landed. You will have your money."

Dirk lifted his clean-shaven face. "I never doubted it. We are not miracle workers, however."

"All I'm asking for is a chance to find her."

"Outsiders cause havoc in these situations. Just do as I say and refrain from acting like cowboys."

Dawn bit back a wry comment. What did Dirk think of Americans, anyway? He and his aid group had been buying back slaves from northern Sudan for several years. Only when Dawn and Jeremy volunteered to charter the flight to Kosti did Dirk begrudgingly agree to allow her and Griff on the next redemption trip.

Dirk leaned against the fence, avoiding Dawn's eyes.

"If your friend and his two thousand dollars aren't on the Cessna, we leave without you Americans."

"So you said this morning. As I said, he *will* have the money."

"We will see. They are already late."

The plane's engine stopped, the propeller halting abruptly. The door banged open and Griff stepped down on the tarmac, his jaw set in determination. Dawn hugged him fiercely and he returned her embrace.

"It seems like months since we've seen each other," he breathed in her ear.

"In the two weeks we've been apart, so much has happened. I didn't realize how much I needed you with me."

Jeremy headed over, interrupting their affectionate moment. "With the rainstorm we flew through, I forgot to ask—did you bring the money?"

"Yup, it's the least I could do for Wally."

"Storm? I didn't hear anything." Dawn angled in between the two men, vying for Griff's attention.

"We were hit without warning. It was the strangest thing I've encountered in Sudan in some time." Jeremy wiped his forehead. "Thunder, lightning, and torrential rain pummeled us. But with Griff's support, we flew right through it. Having Griff aboard was like having a spare tire. God was looking down on us."

"I'm a pilot and I'm used to flying, I guess. Jeremy, are you taking on fuel? I need to make a pit stop."

"Yes and we've time for coffee and breakfast." Jeremy checked his watch. "We leave in, say, forty minutes."

"Griff, you must be hungry," Dawn said. "I couldn't eat a thing."

She meant she wanted time alone with him. He wiped his moustache with his palm, which he always did when thinking.

"Pour me a large cup, Jeremy. We'll be right in."

"Roger that, mate," Jeremy said. But before heading off, he introduced Griff to Dirk and his Dutch team, and added, "He has brought the cash, so we are all on for Liberty."

When Griff patted his cash belt, Dirk's face brightened.

"Good work, Topping. These are desperate times for so many."

Jeremy and the Dutch group made their way to the terminal. Dawn took Griff's hand, leading him to a bench fashioned by the Grace Church mission team. The shade trees were welcome, but she wondered if he felt as happy to see her as she was to see him. They sat close together, knees touching. She folded her hands around his.

"I want to talk about us, but that seems almost ludicrous after the horrible acts I've seen here," Dawn said, squeezing his hand.

"Life is so upside down. Wally's upset he doesn't have his passport and got left behind."

"I hope we find Liberty. Look what I found, Griff. "

Dawn reached into her pocket and gingerly took out Liberty's beads.

"This was all she left behind in Walu," she whispered, her voice strained.

Griff tightened his hands around hers and Dawn leaned her head against his strong shoulder.

"Dawn, this might be the most difficult matter you and I have ever worked on. I've read up on the Sudanese slavery problem. It's entrenched."

"Somehow, I believe God will work this out for the good."

"A good God wouldn't allow such suffering," Griff said, pulling away.

"Come on, you need a break before we get back in the air."

She didn't want to argue with Griff about God's compassion in the middle of a crisis, so she took him by the arm, steering him toward the terminal and his waiting cup of coffee.

"So what's the deal with this money?" Griff asked, fingering his money belt. "The Dutch guys hand it over to the Arab traders, and then what?"

"It's our only hope. Dirk's group has redeemed about fifty thousand slaves."

"Unbelievable," Griff whistled. He stopped at the metal door to the hospital. "Redeemed? I can see ransomed, but redeemed? Maybe it's European."

"Yes, and it's complicated." Dawn sighed. "Arabs living in the border lands between Northern Sudan and Southern Sudan have traded with Dinkas for years. These friendly Arabs act as go-betweens to buy back the slaves, who are then set free."

"Why do militants sell back a slave they've just captured?"

"Each slave is redeemed for forty dollars. Everyone makes a little money that way," Dawn explained.

"It sounds like a new form of trade."

"Just think, when we're sitting at our desks or eating fried eggs and bacon, the people of Sudan are reeling from war and poverty. To heap on the terror of forced slavery boggles my mind."

"I'm so sorry for what you saw," Griff said. He grabbed her hand.

Dawn nodded, gulping back fresh tears. A brown leaf drifted down to his shoulder, and she brushed it away. She ached to locate Liberty so they could buy back her freedom together. It might make all the difference for their future, too.

34

After breakfast and pit stops, Griff and the aid group left Bor, with Jeremy flying north. Though he'd vowed never to fly with the Aussie again, Griff rode as a passenger, willingly letting Dawn act as co-pilot. He sat across from Dirk, plying the Dutch humanitarian with questions about his redemption program.

"Why do slave traders let you pay forty dollars for people they've taken?"

Dirk answered, because Griff saw his lips moving. But with the engine's roar, Dirk's accent, and Griff's bad hearing in one ear, he had trouble making out the fellow's precise words. Griff leaned closer, cupping a hand around his ear.

"Say again?"

"Those who traffic in human beings are the worst sort on earth, greedy and evil," Dirk hollered. "Some slaves are no longer valuable to them, namely the aged or those born while in slavery. Some of the children are part-Arab, being born to female slaves—so the traders sell them back."

At these words, Griff became more concerned for Liberty, not realizing every danger she faced. Maybe Dawn had a clue about what happened to the slave women and that was why she stayed in Sudan.

"I believe Dawn told you we want to use the two thousand dollars I've brought for redeeming Liberty and other female slaves."

"Yes," Dirk nodded, a scowl etched in his fine features. "But in our dealings, we have not told the traders you are looking for Liberty. If they knew we had interest in a certain person, they'd raise the price, which defeats our purpose. We're demanding fifty female slaves for your two thousand. We might get lucky and find her."

"Do you think we will find her?"

"Dinkas are taken as far as Egypt, Saudi Arabia, and even Iran to work in households. Some jealous wives of slave owners push young female slaves out of their house. Liberty might fall in that category."

"Thanks for bringing us along. If we can find her, it will give us great relief. Dawn still hasn't recovered from the brutal acts she saw over Walu."

"Remember, our organization redeems another one hundred. That increases our odds."

Dirk spoke of odds. Griff knew Dawn prayed for Liberty's recovery. Was God up there listening to her, or did it all boil down to chance? In his career, Griff had been protected in some intense circumstances. Had he just lucked out?

He had no answers to these questions, but he knew one thing. He wished Liberty and Wally would be reunited one day. After Dirk's assessment, that seemed unlikely. It would kill Griff to tell Wally that he and Dawn had failed to rescue the woman he loved.

"We land on a dirt strip in a small village near Sodiri," Dirk said as he gestured out the window. "The process goes quickly. Slaves have been waiting for days, brought there by redeemers who've already paid the Arab owners. The redeemers are Arabs, too, only they have traded with Dinka villages for years."

"Dawn warned me about the process. We will allow you to make the trades."

With that, Griff removed the money belt, unzipping its leather liner and removing the cash. He handed to Dirk twenty folded, one hundred dollar bills.

"It's all yours. I trust it does some good."

Griff heard the engine slowing as the plane banked into a dangerously steep descent. About the same time he glimpsed treetops, Jeremy raised the nose before slamming the plane down on the dirt strip. Griff's head jerked forward by the hard braking and he bit his lip.

Dust enveloped the plane. When Jeremy turned the Cessna around and shut down the engine, Griff finally breathed. The Australian guy was truly amazing, the way he landed with no visual aids and no concrete runway.

Dirk plunged out and Griff followed, his legs rubbery from all the sitting he'd done the past few days. The rest of Dirk's team filed out as Griff inhaled deeply, but instead of oxygen clearing his brain, the dry heat nearly melted his lungs.

Dawn and Jeremy both climbed down. Her eyes held a serious glint, but she didn't appear at all traumatized by Jeremy's rugged bush landing.

Dirk strode past the nose of the plane and, with a flick of his hand, he summoned Griff and Dawn to follow. They hiked over to a shady area under a large tree some distance from a collection of men in white robes and skull caps. Griff noted that many of them carried guns. Then he spotted a group of frightened-looking men and women huddled in the shade. He counted close to one hundred and fifty slaves, presumably from Wally's tribe—Dinka.

"Each one will be freed as soon as I pay the Arab redeemers," Dirk said.

"I don't see Liberty." Dawn seized Dirk's elbow. "May I look for her?"

"No. We buy these people in lots, just as one buys cattle, I am sorry to say. We do not inspect them. If you will excuse me, I have business to conduct."

Dirk approached a bevy of Arab redeemers also dressed in white garb, who were standing separately from the Arab guards. Dawn looped her arm through Griff's.

"I'm scared."

"Of what?" He looked at her, feeling compassion.

"That Liberty isn't here, but in some horrible place."

"Let's be patient and not look for trouble."

"And pray."

"A little late for that." Griff grimaced. "These folks assembled here days ago."

Dawn pulled herself closer to him. "Oh, I've been praying for a solid week."

Murmurs rose among the slaves and then a noisier racket filled the air as the entire group rose in unison. They pushed toward the path heading south. Their Arab guards turned, walking in the opposite direction—north.

"Hey, I think they've been freed," Griff said, nudging Dawn's arm.

She wasted no time wading into the throng yelling, "Liberty! Liberty!"

When no one answered, Dawn called, "Atong!"

Griff kept a close eye on her and anyone responding to the name, but Liberty did not run to greet her. Eventually Dawn returned to Griff. She pressed her head against his chest and he had no clue how to comfort her.

"What can we do now?" she sniffled.

"I'm trying to think."

"Your two thousand dollars is gone."

Griff gently took hold of Dawn's shoulders.

"But for a worthy cause. We can only hope these people will make it back to their villages. Maybe we should ask the interpreter to call for Liberty by her Dinka name. Someone might recognize it."

Griff and Dawn ran up to Dirk, who was speaking in English with Nasif, a trader who had facilitated the redemption. Griff interrupted them.

"Can this man inquire if the Dinkas know Atong?"

Nasif stared at him as if not comprehending. But this trader knew English—Griff just heard him. Maybe he needed something to encourage his help. Griff handed him a twenty dollar bill.

That got Nasif shouting, "Atong! Does anyone know Atong?"

An older woman stepped forward, speaking to the trader in a language Griff didn't understand. Nasif told them she knew the name Atong.

Dawn stepped forward. "Atong is my friend, a Dinka woman in her twenties. She is from Walu, though she stayed in a refugee camp for years using the name Liberty."

After the trader interpreted what Dawn had said, the Dinka woman's head immediately started bobbing, her face animated.

"This woman is also from Walu," the interpreter said. "Last week, a newly captured slave from Walu was brought to the home where she was being held."

"Was it Atong?" Dawn stared at Griff, anxiety pinching her lips together.

"No, but this woman talked to that slave, who said Atong was taken along with her from Walu. They went by truck to a boat. There a government soldier bought Atong from her captors, hauling her from the boat."

"Where did the soldier take Liberty?" Griff interjected. "Ah, I mean Atong, if that's the name she knows her by."

After another exchange with the Dinka woman, the interpreter shook his head.

"The boat this woman was on took her to Khartoum, where she was kept as a house servant. She never saw or heard again about Atong."

Griff took Sudanese pounds from his pocket, wrote Dawn's Sudanese cell number on a business card, and handed these to the woman from Liberty's village.

Nodding at the interpreter, he added, "Thank her and tell her to use the money to get back to Walu. If she hears about Atong, she should try to phone us at that number."

"So much money will get her and several of her friends back to Walu." Nasif smiled broadly as he pocketed the twenty Griff had given him.

Dawn headed for the plane and Griff followed, defeat dogging him. He tapped Dawn on the shoulder.

"I'm so sorry. We should tell Wally in person."

"It will crush him to learn she was bought by a Sudanese soldier."

Dawn leaned against the fuselage of the plane, her face downcast. "He has to have some hope."

"I'll call—"

"Ready, mates?" Jeremy strode up to the plane. "Let's beat it before these Arab mercenaries hit us up for more money."

Griff let Dirk's team climb into the rear before he jumped in his seat. He tightened the seatbelt across his lap, realizing his money belt now held a lot less cash. He faced Dirk with a complaint.

"So the Arab traders of misery and suffering are dividing up our money."

"Don't forget, Dinka men and women are walking back to their lives."

"True. That is something."

Griff's eyes riveted on Dawn as she mutely responded to Jeremy's commands. Griff wanted to bring her a measure of peace, and for the rest of the flight, he mulled over what the Dinka woman had said: A Sudanese government official had bought Liberty. That fact sinking into his mind led to an idea.

As soon as Jeremy landed the plane, Griff burst out, telling Dawn, "I'm making a phone call."

He hurried inside the hospital, winding his way through the pseudo-office, which was crammed full of boxes of medicine and bandages. Although he wasn't on a secure phone line, since he wasn't calling about official business, he went ahead and called Bo Rider at the CIA. Bo wasn't in, so Griff left a message, feeling stymied. What were he and Dawn supposed to do? Simply leave Sudan with broken hearts?

35

Griff passed a restless night in a sweltering tent while listening to hoots in the bush and worse—Jeremy's snoring. Kathy bunked with Dawn. Doc Kidd had already returned to Summit Ridge to tell the folks at Grace Church that their pastor was recovering in Nairobi from his bullet wound.

In a side room at the hospital, the four of them shared breakfast together: hot rice and coffee. At this rate, Griff would lose five pounds in no time. Dawn said little and ate less, pushing dabs of rice across her plate. Thankfully, Jeremy regaled them with his flying exploits for the past twenty years, which took Griff's mind from their failure. At length, Griff checked his watch.

"I'm calling Virginia again," he said, hurrying to the office, where he received a nice surprise. Bo had stopped in his office before heading to a meeting.

"I'm in Sudan tracing Wally's future bride."

"What you mean, tracing her?"

Griff told how he and Dawn had gone to redeem the Dinka slaves, and how their hopes of bringing Liberty with them had been dashed to pieces.

"A Sudanese government soldier bought her and may have taken her to the capital city of Khartoum. Bo, do you know anything about Sudanese officials trading slaves? We're at a huge loss trying to figure out where to go next."

"Hmm. No, but I'm not at full speed. What I came down with, you never want."

"Sorry to hear you were sick. What with?"

"This is my first day back working after the worst case of flu you'd ever imagine. Coughed so hard, I thought I broke a rib. Fever so high, I felt like my body was on fire. Spent time in a foreign hospital, can't say where. They pumped me with fluids, antibiotics, the works. My wife says it's a miracle I survived."

That sounded like something Dawn would say.

"You're probably behind. Sure you have time to help me?"

"I'm snowed under, but let me see what I can do. How long ago did this happen?"

"Over a week now," Griff replied. "I've got a few more vacation days, but Dawn's in jeopardy on her job. Neither of us wants to go before we learn something to tell Wally."

"I'll try to let you know within the hour."

Griff hung up, surprised to find Dawn in the ward and deep in a heated discussion with Pastor Nebo.

"You were supposed to fly home from Nairobi. Griff and I can handle things."

"I am fully recovered," Rick insisted. He remained seated on the bed, but stuck out a hand to Griff. "I feel responsible for Wally being arrested on the way to Grace Church. God is prodding me to do something for your young man."

Griff gaped in amazement. This man's simple faith was much like Dawn's. Griff knew nothing about having such trust in a being he couldn't touch.

"That's kind, but—"

Nebo lifted a hand. "No buts in God's kingdom. Wally is one of my sheep. As my body healed on that hospital gurney, all I could think about was finding Liberty, to salvage Wally's life."

"Learn anything on your phone call?" Dawn closed her hand around Griff's.

"Nope."

"Then the best thing you can do, Pastor Rick, is pray to God for wisdom. I'd better call my boss."

"Good luck," Griff said, releasing her hand.

As she strode to the door, Griff admired her strength and courage. Not once had she complained about heat, persistent flies, or lack of water. He eyed Rick, whose cheeks had a healthy glow. Yet Griff had a sense of foreboding about Dawn's call. She'd always been independent, and he knew he couldn't dissuade her from plunging deeper into trouble. She was an amazing woman—but should he take her along to Khartoum?

From everything he'd read, Arab men in Sudan's capital city detested Western women and their free-wheeling ways, viewing them as a threat to their domination over their own wives. Griff toyed with the idea of finding Jeremy and flying out while Dawn made her phone call.

DAWN CALLED HER OFFICE using the hospital phone. She said hello to Stephanie Twining, who was bursting to tell Dawn about her honeymoon.

"I can't wait to hear about your nice time in Hawaii when I get home. But right now, I need to speak with the boss."

"He's on a rant. Watch out."

Rather than understand the dire situation, Melvin Sly demanded Dawn return to Alexandria on the double.

"But sir, the woman has been kidnapped. There's no FBI looking for her."

Dawn said nothing of Griff's arrival, since his travel was unofficial.

"You're absent without leave, Ahern," Sly scolded. "When you called last time begging me to extend your vacation, I told you to get your fanny back here. Your caseload requires your immediate attention. Who's watching your parolees while you sun yourself in Africa? Me."

"This is no lark and you know it."

"Some Sudanese woman isn't your responsibility. The men and women on supervised release in my district are. If you're not behind your desk in two days, I'm taking disciplinary action. You ready to lose your job over this?"

Dawn seethed. How dare he threaten her with losing her job! If only she hadn't transferred from Panama City; her previous boss would have extended the time, no problem. She had almost four weeks of unused vacation time. But it was silly crying over that decision. Rather than argue with Sly, on impulse, she created sounds like static.

"Sorry—connection's fading. I'll call back."

She hung up. She felt guilty for the ruse, but she needed to calm down. Should she stay in Bor with a grim chance of finding Liberty or admit defeat and save her job?

With no immediate solution, she journeyed as far as the shade tree outside, where she lifted up her concerns in prayer. Some time later, Griff found her there with her back pressed against the trunk.

"I've been looking everywhere for you. My high-level contact in D.C. just gave me some news."

Dawn turned to face him, her eyes wet.

"Dawn, I'd like to find Liberty as much as you would."

"It's not that. I did something dumb on the phone with my boss."

"Tell me," Griff implored, drawing her into his arms.

"No," she sniffed, wiping her eyes. "You first."

"I'm going to Khartoum. Jeremy is flying me."

"Then I'm going too," she murmured into his chest, knowing that wherever he went, she wanted to be with him.

He kissed the top of her head and then lifted her chin to look in her eyes.

"I can't let you risk any more danger."

"Which is exactly why you won't leave me behind."

"I'd be happier if you flew home and spent time with Wally."

Dawn's face hardened. "I could say the same about you."

"You're right," he sighed. "I've got a lead on a top-ranking official linked to human trafficking. The Human Rights Commission has named this man in the Sudanese military as the brains behind the slave trade in Sudan."

"Will you arrest him under international law?"

"Dawn, it's such a long shot. Why not stay here with Rick?"

She shook her head. "The Bible says, if God is for us, who can be against us? Let's go ask Pastor Rick. I have a feeling he wants to come, too."

36

Liberty asked God to help her, and He did. She had traveled on the military boat for days and no one laid a hand on her. The soldier who first bought her sold her to another soldier in uniform. This new soldier never spoke a word to her; he just put her in a truck, where she rode in the back for more days.

Though food was scarce and hunger stalked her like a lion, yesterday she had been given figs and almonds. When the soldier had taken her to an airplane full of soldiers, she had drawn back. These soldiers looked fierce; they belonged to another land and had lighter skin and thick, dark hair. As her eyes adjusted to the low lighting, Liberty thought some men sitting behind her were Dinkas. She had to be strong and not show weakness in tears.

The plane flew up in the sky and her stomach rolled. Liberty bent over in the seat; she did not like being in the air with nothing beneath her. Then, suddenly, she imagined Jesus holding a baby goat, soothing it because it could not find its mother.

The sky, the clouds, the wind—hadn't He made them all? Hadn't Jesus calmed a storm with his hands when his disciples were in a boat? So Jesus was holding her and the plane up! Feeling peace, Liberty remembered that Dawn came to Walu in a plane. Only Dawn was not here, and Liberty worried where the soldiers were taking her. The military plane was not Sudanese.

She closed her eyes, imagining her uncle's grief when he returned to Walu to find her gone. What had happened to Nana and her young brother? Words to eternal God filled her mind. *Help them find rest and safety. You delivered me from danger so far. I want to trust You will bring me home, but it is hard.*

Liberty must have gone to sleep, because when the plane landed, it was dark. Her hand flew to her pouch, which still hung around her neck. But something terrible had happened. Her cell phone was gone! She squeezed back tears. Wally was so far away.

She journeyed in a truck to a home where a soldier spoke to a woman in a foreign language, not Arabic. It was hard to see in the dark. A black woman put Liberty in a room and she reached out to feel the walls. They were not made of sticks like her tukul, but something hard like a rock. The air smelled strange, too, as if there were no river nearby.

Fear lodged in her heart—she had no idea where she was. She crouched in the corner. The door creaked open, letting in the first light of day. Liberty cowered further inside, closing her eyes, hoping she would not be seen. She waited to be pulled to her feet.

Instead of being treated roughly, someone's fingertips tapped her arm. Liberty blinked. It was the black woman who had brought her to the room. Her face was wrinkly and a deep scar marred her forehead. Her eyes held pain, but no evil.

"I am Mabel," the woman told her in Arabic. "You will help me care for the child in the home behind the walls."

"I am Liberty. Men took me from my village in Sudan and put me on a boat. *Please* tell me where I am."

Mabel narrowed her eyes. "Are you Dinka?"

Liberty nodded her head up and down. "Yes, I am Dinka. Walu was my home."

"I am Dinka!" Mabel cried. "Raiders sold me here long ago. My son was ten years old and I do not know how old he is or if he is alive."

The two women so far from their home started chattering in their common language. Liberty felt comforted until Mabel told her about the harsh working conditions.

"Where is this place?" Liberty asked.

"Do not question. The people in the home are not friendly. To survive, you must show respect to everything they ask you to do."

Curious about Mabel, Liberty stood, shuffling out of the corner. "What do you do besides clean and watch a boy?"

Mabel shook her head. Her questions would not be answered. "The Lady rules over you, but she speaks no Dinka. You and I will talk when we are alone in this room."

Liberty looked around. The walls were white and only one rug and one pot were in the room. "Mabel, where are we?" she asked again.

"You keep asking, like a small child. I hope you learn to listen. This is a place called Tehran. The lady has one boy. He cries all the time and like a sick cow, he eats almost nothing."

"Where is Tehran in Africa?"

The older woman dipped her head.

"We are a long way from home. In Iran."

Liberty did not know where that was. Even worse, she had lost her cell phone along the journey. If she still had it, she could call Wally and tell him she was in Iran. Maybe he would know where that was and find a way to bring her home.

"Come and meet the young boy who has a sickness. Farvad might not live."

Mabel lifted a black scarf around her head and gave one to Liberty.

"Put this on if you do not want to be kicked in the head. I will show you a room inside. The Lady works behind the door. Do not stop to breathe by it or you will be whipped."

Liberty walked beside Mabel, glad for her new friend, but trembling at what lay before her.

ON THE STREETS of Khartoum, a blast of hot air seared Dawn's lungs. She and her travel companions, Griff and Pastor Rick, left their modern hotel—a glass structure shaped like a giant rocket ready for launch—and set off down busy Nile Street.

Jeremy Bonds had dropped them at a small airfield near Khartoum's international airport; he would return in a few days to pick them up. The trio hadn't walked very far before the back of Dawn's cotton blouse was soaking wet. Her thick boots and long brown skirt only trapped in more heat. She untied a white bandana from her neck, mopping her forehead.

"Whew. My feet are on fire."

"Khartoum is *the* hottest city on the planet," Griff said, wiping the back of his neck. "It's probably 100 degrees already, and it's not even seven a.m."

"My friends live a block from the market on Nile Street, about a quarter mile from here. Can you make it, Dawn?" Rick asked.

"Pastor, I will try," she sighed, her chest heaving as she gasped for air.

"Since we're not at the church, I'd rather you both call me Rick."

He slowed his brisk gait. Dawn forced her legs to cooperate. She was determined not to be a burden, but sorry she hadn't worked out at the gym before venturing to Sudan.

"Okay, Rick," Dawn joked, catching up to him and Griff. "Tell me why your friends live in Khartoum, which is, by all accounts, a hostile place. Two U.S. Embassy employees were murdered here on the streets last year."

Griff gazed at her over his shoulder while Rick explained that Krista and Gary were two farm kids from back home who felt a burden to share their belief in Christ.

"You'll be surprised by how young they are. Krista lost her baby last month, two weeks before she was due. The wee one died in her womb. Her loss is one more reason I asked to tag along."

Dawn shuddered. The risks of living in a place like this were enormous. She'd never met Krista and Gary, though they had once attended Grace. They'd left for Sudan before she ever moved to Summit Ridge.

"Will they stay, after the miscarriage?" Dawn wondered aloud.

"I'm not sure. Krista works at the U.S. Embassy and I want to reach their place before she leaves for work."

"And Gary? What does he do for work here?" Griff asked.

"Engineer by day, and he teaches in his home at night."

"What does he teach?" Griff looked back at Dawn. She seemed to be falling farther behind.

"Go on ahead," she waved. "I'll keep on your heels."

"Let's say no more on the street," Rick said, pressing a finger to his lips. "Gary and Krista live just beyond here."

They had reached the market, a side street where vendors offered spices and vegetables in large, round bowls. Dawn eyed the men selling their produce; she was not surprised there were no women milling about. As she slowed, someone bumped her and she nearly fell, face first, into a bowl of red pepper. Somehow, she managed to regain her footing.

"Dawn, are you all right?" Griff called from up ahead.

She dodged a rug merchant dressed in a bright purple robe who leered at her. She hurried over to Griff, grabbing onto his arm.

"Someone tried to trip me. I didn't see who."

"Dawn, stay close, but don't touch Griff," Rick hissed, motioning for her and Griff to zip through the narrow corridor of vendors. "You're drawing unwanted attention because you're not wearing a head scarf."

She immediately dropped her hand from Griff's arm. She'd known the risks of not wearing a scarf, but she had chosen not to—as an American Christian, wasn't it her right not to? She wouldn't handle snakes if she attended a snake church, either. The way the men looked at her with disgust made her skin crawl. Maybe Griff had been right. She should have stayed in Bor.

They neared a corner as a woman in a burqa slammed Dawn against a cement wall. Pain rocked her back. Her attacker was yelling something in Arabic as Rick and Griff arrived to help.

"Leave the lady alone!" Griff shouted.

The attacker hurried around the corner, springing into a white-washed building.

"She was a man," Dawn cried.

"Krista and Gary live in the first floor apartment across the street. Come on."

Rick waited for a van to whiz by and then ran to their door, knocking loudly. Seconds later, a petite woman wearing a long, blue skirt and white blouse swung open the door. She invited them inside. Dawn felt enormous relief once she was standing behind the door.

"Pastor Rick, Gary and I could hardly believe you were coming to Khartoum," Krista said, a wisp of a smile on her face. "I leave soon for work, but Gary made coffee for you and your friends."

Rick introduced everyone in the narrow hallway, where it wasn't as hot as outside. Still, no breeze cooled Dawn. She ventured a smile at Krista.

"I've been praying for you, ever since I heard of your mission here."

Within seconds, the two women found themselves talking about their shared faith.

"Aren't you afraid? I was just accosted walking through the market." Dawn steadied her voice, feeling safer in the apartment.

Krista drew her to a seating area and perched next to her on a small couch.

"We've lived here for two years. I lost the baby—" Krista dissolved into tears.

"Pastor Rick told me." Dawn patted her hand. "I am so sorry. After my husband died, I found living difficult."

Krista dashed away her tears. "Gary wants to fly home, but I convinced him not to. He's met two friendly men with whom he discusses faith."

"Do you know why we've come to Khartoum?"

"Yes, and I hope you find your friend. My ride will be here any moment. Thanks for listening, Dawn."

Krista retreated to a small room separated from the living room with a hanging cloth. Dawn went over and sat on a rug opposite Rick, wedging in between Griff and Gary. She tried to catch what the men were discussing. Gary gestured toward the barred window, cautioning them to be very careful in Khartoum.

"The government here remains unhappy with the United States' attitude toward Sudan. You may not recall, but in the late nineties, our jets bombed a factory outside Khartoum. It was in response to a terrorist bombing of our embassy in Nairobi."

"I remember that fiasco well," Griff nodded. "Wasn't it an aspirin factory?"

Gary scowled. "It was supposed to be a factory supplying chemicals to Al-Qaeda, but as it turned out, it made baby diapers. Bad intelligence."

"And we've placed trade restrictions against Sudan," Rick interjected.

"Right. Congress decided to punish Sudan for supporting terror and oppressing Christians, so trade is restricted. One exception permits American companies to import gum Arabic from Sudan. It's a substance from the acacia tree that's used in products like pharmaceuticals, soda, and candy."

Dawn wiped her brow. "How do you and Krista live in the midst of such hard feelings toward Americans?"

"With lots of prayer. Some men are open, and that is astounding."

"Gary, you said you might know something that would help us find Liberty," Griff reminded.

"According to my coworker, the home of a Sudanese government official is right across the street from the mosque. That official has what they call guest workers, but they're really Dinka slaves from Southern Sudan. You can see them working on the grounds of his home, even from the mosque."

"How do we get there?" Dawn scrambled to her feet.

"Take care. People are arrested here for minor offenses."

"Right." Griff looked Dawn squarely in the eye. "My contact warned that if we're caught, we'll be treated harshly—as if we're locals. It might mean fifty hard lashes with a cane."

"I'm not afraid," Dawn chimed, heading toward the door. "Maybe one of the Dinkas will know where Liberty is."

Griff rose quickly to join her, but Rick stood so quietly, Dawn wondered what had happened. Was he feeling the aftershocks of his bullet wound?

"Rick, are you all right?"

"Perfectly. Gary and I have some business to discuss, so if you don't mind going without me …"

"If you're adventuresome," Gary said, wearing a ghost of a smile, "hire a tuk-tuk scooter taxi to drive you to the mosque for photos. Did you obtain a permit?"

"For what?" Dawn asked.

"To photograph anything. Be super careful you don't get caught. Dawn, I suggest you wear a hijab. If you don't, people will assault you. Krista will lend you one of her headscarves."

"Tell me about it. I already know." Dawn rubbed her ribs, which were aching from when she'd been slammed against the wall.

"Officials will look for any reason to arrest you," Krista said as she walked in, carrying a royal blue head scarf for Dawn. "Please put this on."

Dawn wrapped the cloth around her head, feeling instantly burdened by the weight of a culture and beliefs not her own. But Liberty's life hung in the balance. Besides, when she left Sudan, she could tear off the head covering and never wear it again. The non-Christian women of Sudan didn't have that luxury; they had to conceal everything except their eyes. When would these millions of women find freedom?

"Dawn, did you hear me?"

Startled by Griff's question, she gathered her wits and her courage.

"No, but I'm ready."

"We must be cautious. If arrested, we're no use to Liberty."

They said their good-byes and, minutes later, Griff and Dawn boarded a brightly painted tuk-tuk, huddling on a small bench seat. The friendly taxi driver up front spoke a smattering of English.

"This heat's unbearable," Dawn whispered, clutching the ties of her blue hijab. Her heart was thudding, trying to cool her down.

"It's worth it if we get a lead about Liberty. I'd love to call Wally with happy news for a change."

Dawn blotted the back of her neck, which was soaking beneath her thick braid and scarf. The closest thing to air conditioning was a hot breeze of air and exhaust fumes from the noisy scooter as it wove through traffic. They reached their destination, and both hopped out onto the dusty street near the mosque.

A motorcycle whizzed by, nearly clipping Dawn's side. She jumped back. Groups of men, some wearing flowing jelabiyas, hurried in all directions. Griff tipped the driver, giving him a few Sudanese pounds and asking him to wait while they toured the area. Griff gazed up at the soaring mosque with no intention of going inside.

"It's gigantic. Give me your hand."

"I'm grateful you're here, Griff, but don't touch me."

"We're definitely not in Virginia," he said, thrusting his hands in his pockets.

"Home seems far away. It must be difficult for Gary and Krista in Khartoum, especially after losing a baby. I hurt for her."

"Hey, look over there at the men repairing the tile walk. They could be Dinka."

Griff nodded diagonally across the street at several dark-skinned men wearing straw hats and laboring in front of a palatial home.

"I'd like my picture taken in front of that mansion."

Dawn adjusted her vibrant hijab, feeling brave. She handed Griff the camera and then dashed into the street, dodging a small bus as she hurried across. She glanced back to see he was following her, all the while focusing the camera. When she turned her head around, her eyes locked onto one of the workers. She waved him over and the man approached most reluctantly.

Would he know anything of Liberty? Dawn had to find out.

37

Griff watched from a distance, concern rippling through him as Dawn held Liberty's picture up to one of the workers. Her voice seemed to snag the attention of a supervisor. The Dinka man shook his head and the supervisor hurried over, his white jelabiyas flapping behind him. He shouted in Arabic, gesturing at Dawn to get away from the Dinka man. Griff snapped photo after photo, unsure if any of them would help.

The white-robed man lunged at Dawn, snatching Liberty's picture. Griff watched horrified as Dawn sprung toward the man, grabbing the picture back. When he clutched her shoulder, twisting her around, Dawn thrust her fist into his prominent nose. He recoiled in shock, but recovering, dove at her again. It all happened so fast.

"Hey!" Griff called, flying to her aid.

The supervisor grasped her hijab, but Dawn ran right out from under it, sprinting to the taxi. Not to be outwitted, the supervisor ran full speed behind her, only to be cut off by another taxi. Griff changed direction, jumping into the waiting tut-tut.

Dawn leapt in and Griff told the driver to go. Looking back, Griff watched the supervisor waving Dawn's bright blue hijab.

"Did you see what he did?" she cried.

"Sure," Griff managed, his heart pounding. "I saw what you did, too. I'll bet his schnoz hasn't been smacked by a woman before."

"The Dinka worker understood English, but he doesn't know Liberty. It's hopeless."

"We can do nothing more here, except get into trouble." He covered her hands with his.

"Fine for you," Dawn said, snatching back her hands. "I won't leave Sudan until I find out what's happened to Liberty."

"You'd even risk losing your job?"

"Griff, you don't understand. Those men on horseback stormed into Liberty's village right before my eyes. I did nothing to save her. I've never felt so helpless."

Tears streamed down her face. Griff wanted to fold her into his arms and comfort her, but not in Khartoum. He also couldn't understand how she could punch a guy one minute and be crying the next.

"What can you accomplish if you stay here with no connections?"

"Jeremy can fly me to Bor and I'll return to Liberty's village." Dawn lifted her head, wiping her eyes. "I can see if her people came back."

Griff refused to allow Dawn to stay in Sudan without him, but did he have any right to insist she go home? He shifted in the fast-moving taxi, seeking her eyes.

"You won't find her there—only death and destruction."

Dawn flashed him a penetrating glare and edged away from him. "I saw that with my own eyes, remember? I'm prepared for the worst."

"Okay, but I'm not. How can I fly home and leave you in a hostile country? Besides, we failed to register as foreigners, which the law requires within three days of arrival. We can't go in and do that now."

"Maybe you can't," Dawn said, glaring at Griff, "but I will."

"That's like begging for disaster. By now, every government official is looking for an American woman with huge hands and a Joe Lewis swagger. You humiliated the man right in front of his slaves."

Dawn was silent, no doubt pondering her scuffle and its potential repercussions.

"Not only that, but Jeffrey Truhart has filed for an evidentiary hearing next week." Griff leaned closer, pressing his shoulder against hers. "Wally needs us."

At his touch, Dawn seemed to freeze. "In my zest to rescue Liberty, somehow I'd forgotten about Wally's legal tangle. What a mess life has become," she sighed, "ever since I moved to Virginia."

"Are you sorry you moved?"

Before she could reply, the taxi jerked to an abrupt stop. The driver started yelling at them to run. A group of robed men, standing shoulder to shoulder, pointed angrily at their heads and then at the taxi. What came next happened so swiftly, Dawn was stunned.

A man dragged the poor driver from his seat. Another one in a flapping robe shouted at the driver in Arabic, pointed at Dawn, and tapped the top of his white skull cap. Griff watched in dismay as the taxi driver was slapped across the face.

Griff poked Dawn with his elbow. "They're upset because your head is uncovered."

"I'm to blame?" she asked, covering her head with her hands.

Suddenly, a third robed man with large hands snatched Dawn, pulling her from the taxi. Griff charged after them.

"Let go of her," he bellowed, raising his fists.

The man kept a firm hold on Dawn. Griff grabbed him at his throat, his momentum bending the man backwards. He released Dawn, falling headlong on a merchant's table of vegetables. He lay sprawled across the onions, holding the palms of his hands toward Griff in submission.

"Get us out of here now!" Griff shouted, seizing Dawn's hand. Together they sprinted to the taxi, where the driver hurried into his seat. Griff may have won one round, but this mob would surely change their minds and come after them with weapons. Once aboard the taxi, the driver shot through an opening in the crowd.

"Maybe that's what the parting of the Red sea looked like," Dawn whispered. "These people are crazy. Can you imagine what they've done to Liberty, a Christian Sudanese from the South?"

Griff shook his head, saying nothing. He would have no words to tell Wally all that had happened here.

As the taxi pulled up to the apartment, Griff paid the driver with a hefty tip for his trouble, clasping his shoulder in thanks. Then he pushed Dawn out.

"I know one thing. There's no way we can register in Sudan."

"Yeah, now they'll be looking for Mrs. Lewis and Joe." She tried to smile.

"Dawn, we've gotta get home. Liberty has grown up here and is smart. If you stay, you'll become a target for their hatred of women."

Dawn narrowed her beautiful black eyes, and Griff wasn't sure what he saw in them. Would she listen or go her own way?

He didn't wait to find out. He practically propelled Dawn into Gary and Krista's apartment and slammed the door. Was the mob right behind them? The taxi driver could have reported back to the mob, divulging where he'd dropped them.

Rick hurried over, his eyes clear and calm.

"Gary is at the Embassy."

"I was accosted again."

Dawn dropped in the first chair she saw.

"She had to defend herself," Griff said, cupping his hand and sliding it over his moustache. "We must leave Khartoum immediately."

A shadow flickered across Rick's face. "Don't delay on my account. I promised Gary that I would wait for his return."

"Why is he at the Embassy? Is Krista—"

"She fainted." Concern flashed across Rick's face, aging him under his white hair.

"That poor girl," Dawn said, trying to catch her breath in the excitement. "She needs medical help."

"Let's pray right now." Rick reached for their hands. "Father God, protect Krista and Gary, who want with their whole hearts to serve you. Guide them with your perfect grace and give me wisdom about coming here in their stead. Amen."

Dawn's eyes few open. "Did I hear you right? You and Laurie are thinking of moving to Khartoum?"

"This is no place for your wife, not after what happened to Dawn." Griff pulled himself up to his full height, outraged at Rick for even considering such a thing.

"At this time of life, rather than seeking safety, my wife and I want to bring the light to men and women living in darkness. Northern Sudan needs believers to show them the way. It's not firm, but Gary and I were talking about it when he took the call about Krista and dashed to the Embassy. He's thinking of taking her to see her mother in Indianapolis."

Shouts outside interrupted Rick and drew Griff's attention. "We'd best head out the back, just in case," he said. He grasped Rick's hand. "You're a special man in my book. Is it all right if we catch a taxi to the airport ahead of you?"

The shouts grew louder and Rick hurried them out the back door. "I think I will take a taxi straight to the Embassy. From there, I'll phone Jeremy for you. Call my cell number if you need me."

Rick walked calmly to the street. Griff navigated Dawn down a narrow alley, not daring to go near the market again. Just then, the skies opened up and rain pelted their faces. The dust became gooey mud beneath their feet. He spotted an overhang.

"Quick, let's wait over there."

They dashed under the tin roof, watching the heavy downpour.

"With Rick thinking of moving to Sudan, I suppose you're convinced it's a sign you should do the same."

"Griff, I didn't get off to a great start, but I hear Liberty calling me to help her."

"Then you believe she's still alive."

"I do."

Dawn wiped her face on her sleeve. "I can't get her face out of my mind. As Jeremy and I were leaving Walu, her eyes flickered with a desire for the same freedom."

After a few minutes more, the heavens had cried themselves dry. Griff was ready to move.

"If I've guessed right, this alley takes us to the main street on the far side of the market. We'll catch a taxi there. Are you with me?"

Dawn took the bandana from around her neck, tying it over her head. "Okay. We'll see what flights we can catch. If the first one goes to Juba, then I'm taking it."

Griff nudged her to begin walking, but he went a few steps ahead, being careful to put his hands in his pockets. He didn't want to argue with Dawn's logic, but he hoped like crazy that the first available flight would take them home to Virginia via London or Amsterdam.

He knew, deep down, that pinpointing Liberty's whereabouts now would be as difficult as spying a diamond in the desert.

38

Dawn did fly home with Griff—they sat in the last two seats on the first plane out of the country, but in separate aisles—landing in Amsterdam, where they faced an unusually long lay over. She seemed distant and cool—or maybe it was his tired mind playing tricks. The found a quiet section in Schipol's terminal.

"The in-flight magazine had an article about a nearby Dutch farm where they make cheese. We could hire a taxi and enjoy the day for a change."

He searched her eyes, but she stared at nothing in particular. She pursed her lips, remaining silent. "You gonna pout all the way home?" He grinned, so she'd know he was teasing, sort of.

"I don't appreciate your criticism," Dawn said, tossing her head. "There's a lot I could say about your behavior, but I won't. Know this, Griff Topping. I won't be getting into a taxi with you anytime soon. You nearly got me killed last time."

Ouch. She'd taken to using his last name. Was she kidding or for real?

"Dawn, I know that, um—"

Griff tripped over his words, unclear how to respond. Dawn's stubborn side had caught him by surprise. But hadn't he always admired her courage?

She stretched her legs and rubbed the back of her neck. "I wish Pastor Rick had gotten a seat on this flight." She sounded tired.

"I take it you're not satisfied with my company."

"Don't take it personally."

His eyes sought hers, but Dawn had closed them, the window to her soul shut tight. Griff did a double take. How could he think of her soul, but not believe in her God? As much as he wanted to, he couldn't fake it. Puzzled over what to do, Griff ran his palm over his moustache. He cared deeply for Dawn. He thought he even loved her. But apparently, his love wasn't enough.

"Dawn, I'm starving. Want a bite to eat?"

Her eyes opened slowly and she shrugged.

"Sure," she said, her voice monotone, as if it was against her principles.

Griff leapt from the hard seat, confused, as Dawn ambled silently alongside. He'd let her down, but he was unsure how. After they ordered burgers and fries at an American chain, she pulled out stools for them at a high table. She finally spoke, her face less tense.

"I'm ashamed that I forgot about Wally's hearing. I was so interested in proving I could discover who had Liberty if I just tried hard enough. As a parole officer, I throw my weight around, and people have to get in line or go to jail. Overseas, no one cares what I do for a living. In fact, most of the people in Sudan hate me."

"That's how I felt in Summit Ridge when Wally got arrested. My being an FBI agent may have actually hurt him."

Dawn's eyes locked onto his and in that look, he caught a glimmer—she was glad to have left Sudan behind. He picked up a French fry and fed it to her.

"We couldn't do that in Khartoum. I can't believe Rick will take his wife there."

Dawn chewed, wiping her lips on a paper napkin. "Maybe you can see how going to the church with Rick and Laurie has made a difference in my life."

"He's remarkable, pledging his house for Wally's bond." Griff shook his head, "At seventy, taking a giant leap and traveling to an Islamic country. I hope I'm that viable when I reach his age."

"You're just as incredible to me, Griff. After all, you flew to Sudan when I needed you. How can I help you and Wally at this upcoming hearing?"

That was more like the Dawn he was growing to love.

"Can we eat and then talk? I'm famished."

"I forgot, you think better on a full stomach."

She sampled her fruit juice and he dove into his burger. They finished their food and returned to the departure area. There, for the next hour, they talked about building a strategy to clear Wally's name. When at last they were called to board their flight, Dawn smiled at him and Griff felt enormous hope. Things between the two of them were going to be okay after all.

THAT NIGHT, LIBERTY curled on a small rug in the whitewashed hut, thinking of Baca. Her dream of marrying him in the village was dead. Walu had burned behind her when the raider caught her.

She wanted to cry, but could not. Her eyes were empty of tears and her heart empty of hope. It was her turn to sleep on the plush wool, but the cloth scratched her skin. Liberty's mind could not rest. So much had happened since she had arrived in this strange place. God seemed far away.

Then she remembered those long days of running with Baca at her side, helping her into a tree and saving her from a hungry lioness. That was a long time ago. He could not come to save her, huddling on the rug alone in the dark. She folded her hands to keep from scratching, trying to think. Had anyone from her village—which she knew had been destroyed by raiders—survived? Why did God keep her alive, only to be made a slave?

She waited and waited on her rug, but He didn't tell her why.

Somehow, Liberty pictured Jesus with small children on his lap. He was teaching them a story of the shepherd who found a lost sheep. Her mind stopped buzzing and she drifted to sleep, but not for long.

Mabel shook her awake, whispering in Dinka, "Get up. Feed the chickens."

"My turn?" Liberty moaned.

"Do not be slow. The lady does not like you to be late."

Liberty rolled from the rug, struggling to her bare feet. Was the sun up yet? Their room had no windows, and behind the thick walls, she could not tell. Mabel opened the door to shake the rug outside and Liberty slipped out into an early gray morning to find her clucking birds, too many to count.

The lady of the house kept the birds behind a fence, behind the white room where Mabel and Liberty lived. No, that was not right, Liberty thought, tossing tiny grains into the cages. The two women slept in the room, working before the sun came up and long after it slipped down.

A scream pierced the air. Liberty dropped the pan of food and ran around the corner. She peered over the wall, horrified to see a slave-woman who lived next door being dragged away by two men dressed in black. Mabel came to look, too.

"Where are they taking her?" Liberty asked.

"To make bombs. Any day, we might be next." Mabel clutched the red rug to her bosom.

Liberty pulled on her arm. "Bombs to be used against Dinka villages?"

"No." Mabel shook her head violently. "They make Dinkas here in Iran build bombs for luggage or vehicles to explode where Muslims battle American soldiers."

Liberty was glad Baca was not a soldier.

"Mabel, tell me where these bombs go. To America?"

"I know they use Dinkas to install a cell phone in the bomb. Sometimes it explodes when wires connect. Many Dinka captives have died."

"Does the Lady in the house build bombs?"

"No. Her husband is an important elder to the chief. He is taken in a vehicle by a driver. The main chief permits the Master and Lady to own slaves, but they have to send us for dangerous jobs. We might attach cell phones to bombs."

Liberty's body began to tremble and her knees to shake. She and Mabel were not safe. Though the screams from the woman had died away, Liberty took Mabel's hand.

"Come inside. You and I will pray to Jesus. He loves us enough to save us."

39

Griff lingered with Dawn in the baggage claim area at Dulles Airport, not eager for the inevitable—going their separate ways.

"I dread telling Wally, but I must," he said, studying her face.

Her eyes seemed laced with sorrow and he wondered what she was thinking and feeling. This trip had been filled with more danger than either of them could have predicted.

"You and Wally are always in my heart. Do you want to give him these?"

She pulled Liberty's beads from her pocket, her lower lip trembling. Griff kissed her, right there in the terminal, not caring a whit who might see. Then he straightened.

"Do you think Wally can handle having her broken necklace?" he asked.

"Take them along and decide when you see him. That's what I'm going to do about my job."

"You shouldn't let Melvin Sly get to you. He's not worth the aggravation."

"You always say the perfect thing to buoy my spirits. The man's arrogance is endless, but I'll keep doing my job until I find another one."

Griff raised an eyebrow. "You're changing jobs? Not moving away …" His words fell off. Was she seriously thinking of returning to Panama City? He didn't dare ask, not right now. He couldn't handle more let down.

Dawn lightly touched his cheek. "We have enough to deal with, so I won't do anything rash. It's just something I'm praying about. Call me later?"

He nodded, helping her roll her big suitcase to her car.

"Dawn, listen. We've been through a lot, and I want you to know I think you are one awesome lady."

Her eyes sparkled for a fleeting moment before she said, "I'm so glad you joined me in Sudan. I don't know …" Her voice broke and she patted his arm. "We'd better get going."

Griff watched her get in her car and then he found his and headed in the opposite direction. He drove straight to Wally's small studio apartment, which was in a building owned by the foster family who had first taken him in. They were nice people who permitted Wally to return to their home whenever he was on school break.

Griff knocked on the door and Wally greeted him with a giant bear hug. Words stuck in Griff's throat as he clasped a hand on Wally's shoulder.

"Son, we did all we could."

Wally dropped his face into his hands, but then he raised it, facing Griff.

"You and Miss Dawn showed great love for me and for Liberty. I will never forget as long as I live your trying to find her."

"Look at it this way. There's still hope, even though she's missing."

Wally stared at Griff, his shoulders slumping. "I guess you are right, Dad."

"Dawn asked me to give you something that is Liberty's. She thought it might help you believe you will see Liberty wearing them one day."

Griff set the glass beads in Wally's large hand. He gaped at the beads and then fled to his bedroom. When he returned, he seemed more composed. "Dad, I leave for Rob's soon. Would you like a cola and toasted bread?"

"Sure thing, son."

Though Griff's body ached and he craved sleep, he relaxed on the sofa, sharing breakfast with Wally. In the quiet setting, Griff shared a few gritty details of their search.

"You wouldn't believe how gutsy Dawn acted in Khartoum. She smacked a man right in the nose," Griff chuckled.

"I would have liked to have seen that." A half-smile appeared before vanishing like a partial rainbow after the rain. "My lawyer has asked the judge for a court hearing. Do you know if I will return to jail?"

"No, no. Mr. Truhart wants the judge to force the prosecutor to turn over evidence in your case. He wants to know what the witnesses told the police. It is routine."

"Are you sure?"

"If you'd feel better, I'll phone your lawyer and you can ask."

Wally shook his head. "I missed you, Dad. Now that you are back, I am not so worried."

Griff's heart filled with concern. Wally relied on him, more than he knew.

"We shall beat this case. A foolish man craving political power made a wrong- headed choice. You were his convenient means. I'm sorry for it, but all is not lost."

"Should I plan to start my last term?" Wally's lower lip drooped.

"Absolutely, son," Griff said. He clapped him on the back. "Did you pick out your classes?"

"Not yet. Will you help me consider the options?"

Griff agreed and they arranged a time to go over his schedule. After embracing Wally in another hug and promising to consult his lawyer about the hearing, Griff wove through heavy Saturday traffic, not at all sure what they'd accomplished in Sudan. He had to force defeat from his mind. He and Jeffrey Truhart had to do a better job with Wally's case.

Griff turned onto his street, vowing not to rest until Wally was declared by a jury, "not guilty."

40

The following Saturday, Griff woke late. Had he really slept until nearly eleven o'clock? After showering and shaving, he went to his favorite local restaurant, unwinding over a platter of fried eggs, crispy bacon, and pancakes slathered with real maple syrup.

The hearty meal restored his drive to get things done. Loads of strong coffee didn't hurt, either. This past week had passed like some car race, with Griff caught on the track, going round and round. He'd worked twelve-hour shifts for days to bring order to his chaotic caseload. Yesterday, Wally's lawyer had told Griff that Judge Fox had set the evidentiary hearing for the following week and CJ Huddleston had filed a voluminous brief to avoid handing over the simplest discovery.

Griff had snapped. "Huddleston's whole approach to Wally's case is ludicrous. What are you doing about it?"

"I'm building my case strategy."

"Maybe you should hire a private investigator and send me the bill. Let me know how I can help."

His mind back in the present—or so he hoped—Griff spread open the *Washington Star* editorial page, scanning the latest twists in Washington politics. When his eyes had consumed the first three paragraphs, he tossed down the paper with no idea what he'd just read.

Wally's confidence was spiraling downward, wearing down his joy in living, and Griff was clueless how to revive it. Maybe if he talked over things with Dawn, that would clarify his thinking. He plunked down his coffee cup and yanked out his cell phone, checking the time. Dawn was probably done with lunch by now, or whatever she had going. Why didn't he know?

Though the extortion case he'd been working on had exploded, that seemed a poor excuse for ignoring Dawn. Was she down at VMI visiting Brian? A creepy feeling assailed him, sending Griff's pulse racing. What if she was out with CJ Huddleston?

Griff punched in her number. With each ring, the distance between them grew. After the fifth ring, he heard, "Hi Griff."

Whew, her tone was inviting. He relaxed.

"I'm at Gus' having my favorite breakfast and missing you."

"Glad to hear it. What's been happening in your week?"

"I've scouted on surveillance all week and have two hours of typing ahead of me. Has your week been good?" he asked. Hearing her voice made him realize how badly he wanted to reconnect.

"Melvin Sly has it in for me since I extended my stay in Sudan. Treats me like I'm a felon. Enough about my problems," Dawn sighed. "It's great to hear from you."

It was? Okay, then. He plunged ahead with the true reason for his call.

"If I drive down, are you interested in going out to dinner?"

When she didn't answer right away, Griff began to sweat.

"Ah, I know it's last-minute, and maybe you have—"

"Griff, I just heard a noise outside and got distracted. Sorry. Dinner together would be nice. Should I make a reservation?"

"How about four thirty? We could drive into Fredericksburg. Let's keep it casual, 'cause I'm behind on my laundry. My jeans are clean, though."

Her warm laugh soothed his ruffled mind. And so did her reply, "I know a perfect spot where we can talk."

Enthused about their outing, Griff signed off, secured his phone, and paid the bill. He'd just stepped out on the sidewalk, the folded newspaper under his arm, when it hit him as hard as the stifling afternoon air.

Dinner together would be "nice" she'd said. And Dawn wanted to talk—but about what?

THE TRIP TO DAWN'S raised more questions in Griff's mind about CJ Huddleston. What were his motives toward Dawn or hers toward him? The creep's attentions toward her perplexed Griff; he wasn't one for lingering doubts, least of all about a woman. Even worse, Huddleston's legal maneuvers made no sense. The guy truly was a menace.

For a split second, Griff tinkered with the idea of running against him when his term expired. Of course, he'd have to earn a law degree first, and that was never going to happen.

He parked in front of Dawn's modest-sized bungalow, admiring the lush flowers she'd planted. Pink roses climbed a white fence beside her tiled walkway. He hiked up the steps, reaching the front door at the exact moment Dawn stepped out, holding a bunch of keys. She pecked him on the cheek.

"I'm hungry, but I want to take a detour, if you don't mind." She hurried on past him, but Griff's feet refused to move.

"What's up?"

"I've been thinking about something and want your opinion. It won't take long. Mind if I drive?"

Griff relented, his curiosity piqued about what she was up to. He slid into the passenger seat of her car, content to let her cruise the streets that were more familiar to her.

"For the record," she said, "a dinner with you on a Saturday evening is better than a whole weekend without you."

He grinned, his tender feelings for her roaring back. They were fine. He had to tear his mind off Huddleston's hostile antics. Dawn's little wave to him at the church that one time rankled, but he would have to accept it and move on.

Dawn pulled onto Main Street while Griff looked out the window at some empty storefronts.

"I started thinking about the Night Owl's surveillance camera being broken," she finally explained. "A traffic control camera might have covered the store."

"I doubt it." Griff frowned. "Those cameras are mostly in big cities with hefty budgets, which gives the contractors who operate them a larger share of revenue from fines."

"Humor me. I won't sleep tonight if I don't confirm my suspicions." She tapped the wheel, and then pointed. "There's the Patriot's Inn where you stayed."

"I'd love to forget that awful day."

Griff scrutinized the area where Officer Ryan had arrested Wally, his eyes examining every utility pole supporting traffic lights.

"I don't see any cameras," he grumbled.

They were passing the Night Owl when Griff suddenly twisted his head. "Whoa. Turn here and go back to the Chevy dealership."

Dawn checked her rearview mirror before swerving into the right lane.

"Did you see a traffic control camera?"

Griff glanced over his shoulder. "Something even better, if I'm right."

Dawn cranked a series of turns, following Griff's orders, before pulling into Witt's Cars and Trucks. Griff threw off his seatbelt.

"Come on, let's take a look."

They bolted over to a light pole, staring skyward. Atop the pole and overlooking dozens of cars in the lot, perched a surveillance camera. It was pointed directly at the Night Owl store, which was across the street. Based on the angle, it was poised to capture folks entering the store.

Griff eyed his watch. It was a few minutes after five. "I wonder if the car lot is still open."

"Let's find out."

Dawn led him to the front door, which she yanked open. They'd barely stepped inside when two sales reps approached, a woman sticking out a manicured hand to Griff.

"I'm Connie."

The guy Connie had beaten to the door skulked back to his cubicle as if discouraged by losing another prospect.

"How can I help you this fine afternoon?" she asked, her lips parting in a glorious smile. "Which new car are you interested in?"

"Please direct us to whoever's in charge of the dealership," Griff said.

"Only two of us stay this late, but I'm happy to show you any new model." On her spiked heels, Connie gestured proudly around the showroom.

Griff was losing his patience, so he whipped out his credentials. The petite sales rep's eyes widened. When she stepped back slightly, he returned his creds to his pocket. Maybe he'd overreacted and should have kept his official ID in his pocket. Griff wasn't used to investigating with a Federal parole officer at his side, especially one in whom he had a romantic interest. He pushed on.

"We need to talk to your boss about a robbery across the street."

"Nathan Witt is the general manager."

Connie turned on her heels. Griff and Dawn trailed behind her down a narrow corridor filled with photos of racing cars, clowns at parades, and a man sitting astride a donkey. They hurried past a break room with a coffee station and large, rectangular window looking out on the corridor. Griff spotted a room directly across the hall, which boasted a monitoring panel with six screens.

He peered more closely. Each monitor was streaming images of the car lots, the showroom, plus the street out front of the dealership. Connie hurried them on to her boss' office.

Nathan Witt sported wire-rimmed glasses and had gray, wispy hair. He sat tipped back in his chair, feet on his desk and sleeves rolled up. When they walked in, he dropped some computer printouts to his desk.

"Nathan, these people are from the FBI."

The manager snapped to his feet while Connie ducked out the door, no doubt in search of a real customer. Griff flipped out his FBI identification.

"I'm Agent Griff Topping and this is Dawn Ahern, a federal parole officer. We have questions about a robbery at the Night Owl."

"When was it?"

"Several weeks ago."

"I heard something about a guy being arrested for robbing the Night Owl."

Griff knew he meant Wally, but he just moved on. "You have a surveillance camera outside on a pole and several monitors in the room down the hall. Have the police or anyone else reviewed your data?"

"No." Nathan crossed his arms, his brow contracting. "Not that it would do them any good. Our cameras don't take in the Night Owl anyway."

"Mind if we take a look?"

Nathan's arms fell, yet he stood still as if debating how to get an FBI agent out of his dealership with as little fuss as possible.

"Alright," he said finally. "Come with me."

He showed Griff and Dawn into the room with the security monitors.

"See? The camera on the front lot covers just our car stock." He stopped, bending close to the far screen. "Wow, it does show the Night Owl across the street."

Griff whistled softly, grinning at Dawn, but she remained noncommittal.

"The camera is angled so our sales staff in the break room can see when a live one ... er, I mean a potential customer, pulls into the lot."

"Is there an archive of last month's images?" Griff could hardly contain himself. They might really be onto some hard evidence to clear Wally.

"We don't have anything that will help the police." Nathan gave a hesitant shrug. "Car sales are in a lull. To cut expenses, I cancelled the contract with—"

"But look!" Griff interrupted. "They're still working."

Witt nodded. "Yeah, but that's because the contractor hasn't removed the equipment. They quit archiving data and the camera feeds aren't being recorded. I haven't pushed them to take down the cameras. Bad guys think they're being watched and my sales people like them."

"When did you cancel the contract?" Dawn asked, her eyes glued to the monitors.

"I'm not sure."

Nathan jangled keys in his pocket before motioning them back to his office, where he thumbed through pages of his desk calendar.

"Here it is, May 11, a Tuesday."

A smile spread beneath Griff's moustache. "Three days *after* the robbery. It's possible you were still taking pictures on the previous Saturday."

"I could call the firm and ask, but they're not open today. First thing Monday, I'll call. They need to get out here anyway and see to their equipment. Want to stop back Monday or Tuesday?"

Griff thought about his extortion case, which might erupt on either day. He hedged. "I don't know, but—" he turned. "Dawn is also working on the case."

She quickly caught on, removing a business card from her purse and handing it to Nathan. "I will meet you and the contractor."

Griff told Nathan to make sure the contractor secured data recorded on May 8th. Nathan stared at Dawn's card before stuffing it in his shirt pocket, his eyebrows raising a fraction.

"Guess it's no ordinary stop and rob. One of your parolees, huh?"

Dawn smiled, her eyes twinkling. "Something like that. Your help could resolve a very difficult case. I'll expect your call."

"Indeed. We at Witt's are good citizens and won't let you down."

Dawn and Griff scooted back to her car, where she started the engine.

"This is the break we so desperately need. I'll sure be praying it is, anyway."

"Say one for me, too."

She nudged the brakes, glancing his way. "Do you mean it?"

Griff shrugged. He wasn't sure what he meant, but Dawn believed in prayer. What could it possibly hurt if she prayed for him?

So she wouldn't get the wrong idea, he added, "And for Wally. He and I talked about Liberty and what happened in Sudan. He's taking it pretty rough. I can tell."

41

Sunday evening, Dawn relaxed out in her yard, enjoying mild summer breezes cooling her skin and rustling the pages of her book about Mary Todd Lincoln. The former First Lady had faced tremendous grief in life, losing two sons and her husband, Abraham, while he served as President.

Her mind flew to Liberty. Where was she? Was she even alive? Not knowing was agony. Her guilt over spending carefree moments eroded her happiness. She closed her book, no longer interested in the past. She'd just stood when her cell phone rang and she scooped it up from the grass.

A honey bee chose that moment to buzz her hand. Dawn swatted, aggravating the bee. It darted up her arm toward her eyes. While she shielded her face and dodged, her phone continued ringing. She managed to duck, grab her phone, and run through the back door.

As soon as she flipped open the phone, she gushed, "Hello?"

"Whew, I thought I'd get switched to your voice-mail. Busy?"

"Battling a bee in the backyard. Griff, did you talk with Wally?"

"He's hanging in there, I guess. I wanted to ask him over for burgers, but I'm stuck on surveillance."

"I can call him."

"Thanks, but don't hang up yet. I just heard from Witt Chevrolet, which has arranged for the security contractor to show you the videos tomorrow at five. Can you see if they reveal the Night Owl robbery?"

"My boss might not let me leave early, even if I ask for personal time," she complained, hurrying into the kitchen and digging in her junk drawer for a pen and pad. "Okay, what am I looking for?"

"Wally shouldn't appear on the video, but if you see him, say nothing. Note the customers coming and going from the Night Owl on May eighth. You might spot the actual robber."

"Any idea of the time frame?"

"Yup. The clerk alerted the police at twenty minutes past three. Under no circumstance take the memory card, or you'll become a witness."

"No problem there, but if Melvin Sly refuses to sign my leave, do we have a back-up plan?"

Griff sighed. "I could ask Chief Dalton, but if there's any chance Wally—"

"He's not on the video, Griff," Dawn interrupted.

"The Summit police force has twisted my thinking. I need to run. Call me, okay?"

"Once I know anything, I promise to call you first."

Dawn closed her phone and immediately called Wally. He didn't answer, so she left a message that she was thinking of him. A sudden idea occurred to her and she called Pastor Rick at home.

"I know it's late, but will you do me a favor?"

"Laurie and I just got through talking with Gary. Remember our host in Khartoum?"

"Of course. How's his wife, Krista?"

"Much better since our visit. She fainted because she is expecting another baby. They will stay in Sudan until closer to her due date and then return to the States."

"Are you still considering taking over their place?"

"No. Laurie and I decided God has placed us in Summit Ridge for a reason. Our time isn't finished here."

"I am one of those reasons. You've both encouraged my faith."

Dawn explained about the video at Witt's and her irate boss.

"If you can't get there in time, I am happy to help, but you know more about the law than I do," Rick said. "I'd be afraid of missing something important."

"Don't worry. I could walk you through it."

"I'd give it a whirl."

Dawn hung up, uncertain what the morning or the next week would bring. If Melvin Sly didn't lighten up, she needed a change. Life was too short to be burdened by people with such a negative view of life.

She had just folded her lawn chair when her cell phone rang again. This time it was Brian who called. A tender smile on her face, Dawn curled up inside on the sofa, where mother and son shared the little things that made up their days. By the time they had finished chatting, she'd regained her bearings about what was important in life.

TO BE ON THE SAFE SIDE, Dawn hurried to the office the next morning at six a.m., arriving way before her boss. She tackled her paperwork. At eight o'clock, she went to find Melvin Sly, learning he had the day off. All administrative matters were being handled by his assistant, Stephanie Twining, who told Dawn with a smile, "You came in an hour early. I saw you. Leave at four and we won't even make a record of your time off."

"Are you positive?"

"Sly's an ogre to you and me both. I hope he's out looking for another job."

"Thanks, Stephanie. Let's have lunch soon. I'm eager to see your photos of Hawaii."

Stephanie answered a call and Dawn returned to her office, where she called Pastor Rick. He was relieved to hear he was off the hook—he needed to visit an elderly man from church who had just been flown by helicopter to a Fredericksburg hospital.

Dawn locked her desk promptly at four, racing from Alexandria with one eye fastened on the digital clock. She drove straight for Summit Ridge, but became snarled in heavy traffic. Things eased, but then a delivery truck slowed in front of her. Dawn jammed the brakes, desperate to get to Witt's by five.

Traffic started moving again. The video at Witt's could reap rewards. If only the camera had picked up *something* to give Wally his life back.

She finally buzzed into the parking lot, scanning for signs of activity. Her heart sank. The place looked deserted. Then a woman swung open the glass door, pushing a baby stroller outside. It was five fifteen and they were still open for business. Dawn shut off the ignition, grabbing her notes.

Her hand rested on the door as she recalled Griff's earlier warning to do nothing even remotely suggesting that she obstructed justice or tampered with evidence. She seized a quick breath. The video could be a sword to defend or to hurt Wally. No matter the result, she refused to believe Wally could do anything violent.

Dawn dashed into the dealership, asking the receptionist to page Nathan Witt. The slender man introduced her to Randy DeBoer, who worked for the contractor and looked no older than Dawn's nineteen-year-old son. Randy brought her to the room across from the customer lounge and asked her to sit at a desk with a computer monitor.

"Mr. Witt told me to access from two to four o'clock on May eighth. I froze the video here at two. Click this mouse to start or stop. You can even reverse or pause it."

Randy showed her the fast-forward and slow buttons.

"Thanks. This might take some time, you know."

"No problem. I've got equipment to remove."

He left her alone. The grainy video began running and she zoomed in, focusing on the Night Owl entrance. She fast-forwarded through the first hour, seeing no evidence of Wally.

Randy popped in. "Any problems? When you're done, I have to take the monitors, so I'm heading for a burger."

"I've another hour to zip through. Sorry to keep you here."

"It's my job," Randy said with a shrug. "Want anything?"

"You are a full service contractor." Dawn dug a few bucks from her wallet. "Hot coffee and one of those chicken wraps would be great."

Randy left Dawn to her video. So far, the Night Owl customers seemed legitimate, paying for gas or buying beverages. Then, at ten minutes after three on the time indicator, Dawn saw something important—a man entered the store wearing a sweatshirt with the hood trailing down the back. Her pulse quickened. She leaned in close.

If he was African-American, he had light complexion, whereas Wally's skin was very dark. Two Hispanic-looking women rushed in after this man.

"Come on," Dawn muttered, tapping the pen on her pad and waiting for Mr. Hooded Sweatshirt to emerge.

That took all of four minutes. She watched, transfixed, as the Night Owl door burst open and out flew the man in the sweatshirt carrying a paper bag. His hood was still hanging down his back. He had short, dark hair, but was clearly *not* Wally. And his sweatshirt had no Washington Redskins emblazoned across the front, as Griff's did.

"Here's your lunch, ma'am, with ten cents change," Randy said. "Hope you don't mind, but I bought you a biggie coffee and a burger with pickles. It's what I like."

Dawn pressed pause while Randy rattled the two small bags, placing them next to the monitor. The dime he set in her palm.

"I'm eating mine in the lunchroom cross the hall." His eyes jerked toward the video monitor. "Find what you're looking for?"

"I'm almost through. Thanks for the large coffee. I need it."

Randy disappeared out the door and Dawn hit play. Over the next fourteen minutes, three males and the two Hispanic-looking women left the Night Owl. Still no Wally, thankfully.

Suddenly, as she watched the small monitor, she saw a Summit Ridge police car jerk to a halt at the Night Owl's front door. A uniformed officer sped into the store, probably in response to the 911 call. Dawn had not seen Wally nor observed any black man or even a man with a hood *over* his head.

She played the video to the end, sipping the hot java. Griff's instincts were correct. Dawn couldn't wait to tell him the clerk had lied. She found the lunchroom, but Randy wasn't in it. She dashed to the receptionist.

"I need Randy, but he's not in the break room."

"That's because he left to buy batteries for his radio."

Great. She *must* secure the video before the dealership destroyed it.

"Is Nathan Witt available?"

"Nope," the receptionist said as she shook her head, soft curls trembling from the force. "He left." Then she snapped on her headset again.

Dawn ran to her car, where she called Griff's number and punched send. The call went to his voice mail. She left him a message to call her ASAP. Okay, she had to think. Dawn folded her phone and was about to attach it to the holder, when it buzzed. A look at the LED screen told her nothing. It was a restricted call.

She opened her phone, saying tentatively, "Dawn Ahern speaking."

The voice sounded tired. "I'm flying as the spotter on surveillance. We're three thousand feet above I-66. Between the road maps on my lap, binoculars hangin' round my neck, I couldn't get to the phone. Hold on a sec."

Squelch from a police radio blasted her ears. Dawn yanked the phone away. She'd sure called Griff at a bad time.

"Careful, 907. Target is slowing down and entering right lane. Looks like he may be exiting at James Madison highway."

Dawn ignored more squelch.

"Okay, he's northbound on Madison. Sorry, Dawn, we're tailing an extortion victim who's dropping money in the Manassas Battlefield, making sure he's not being followed. What's urgent?"

She gathered her thoughts. "I watched what was taped from two to four o'clock. Guess what? Wally *never* appears. There's a man in a hoodie, but he's not Wally. His skin is blotched, like it's sunburned."

"I knew it! Tell the contractor to secure the optical discs so Wally's lawyer can subpoena them. Okay, he's straight north on Madison."

"Do you want to call me back? I have a problem."

"Hold on."

She waited, wondering why demands of their jobs always kept them at arm's length from one another.

"Okay, but things are getting dicey. I may hang up."

"Neither the contractor nor Nathan Witt are here to preserve the media. I could call CJ and ask him to come over."

"No way! Wait! The victim is turning right into a school lot, not the Battlefield. "

Griff's shout startled her. He didn't trust her to call the Common-wealth's attorney? Dawn cleared her throat, but rather than razz Griff when he was in the middle of a case, she posed a safe alternative.

"How about Chief Dalton?"

"I trust him with the memory card a hundred more times than CJ. If he could—"

He spoke to someone else and then said to her, "Get Dalton to watch that video now! I've gotta go. Our victim is confused about where to go. Call me back and if I don't answer, leave a message."

Griff was gone. Her heart pounded in her ears as she scrolled to the chief's number—as a federal probation officer, she'd dealt with him a few times—and hit enter.

42

Thirty minutes passed and Griff watched as the extortion victim dropped the money under a foot bridge in Manassas Battlefield. During the wait for the pick-up, the encrypted FBI radios fell silent, giving Griff plenty of time to think. Had Dawn called CJ?

The pilot flew a pattern at six thousand feet and Griff focused his eagle eye onto the bridge, ready to call out orders to surveillance cars hidden in the area if a vehicle or person on foot suddenly appeared.

He'd been working for more than forty hours straight, having snatched four hours of sleep on a chair the night before. That airport, where the FBI kept its surveillance plane, was a dingy place. He and the team had been ready to launch back into the sky, but hoping they wouldn't have to, because aerial surveillance at night was almost impossible.

Griff had stayed on high alert most of Monday, when the call finally came for the victim to take the money to the battlefield. That had happened a couple of hours earlier. He lowered his binoculars now feeling flat-out tired. His cell phone buzzed in his pocket and he yanked it out, recognizing Dawn's cell number.

"What did Dalton say?"

"Claims he can't get here for some time. I'm in Witt's parking lot."

Her voice shook with strain.

"Can't you wait?"

"Yes, but I'm afraid they'll close before Chief Dalton arrives. I'll have to change an appointment."

A fleeting thought burst into his mind, but Griff refused to believe her appointment involved CJ Huddleston.

"Give me Dalton's number."

After memorizing the number, he punched it in, reaching Dalton's voice-mail. After the beep, Griff swung into action.

"Chief, it's FBI agent Griff Topping. I just finished typing a civil rights violation report for an FBI agent from Richmond to investigate injuries to Wally Manja. A witness saw Ryan kick him while his hands were cuffed. Ryan's career is finished. He might even do time. Your career could also be in the toilet."

The plane banked sharply and Griff clutched his map before adding, "Witt's surveillance video shows *no* black man entering or leaving the Night Owl. I'll hold off e-mailing my report if, in the next ten minutes, you hustle over to Witt's and watch the video yourself. My money says the clerk who called 911 stole the cash and made up the robbery story. I'll confer with Dawn Ahern in ten minutes."

That should get Dalton moving. A few minutes passed and Griff angled his binoculars on a SUV stopped a quarter mile from the foot bridge. He watched a person get out and then keyed his microphone.

"Woman exiting SUV with dog on leash. Will advise if she walks to the money."

The phone in his pocket vibrated and he answered. Dawn sounded light, happy even. "Thought you'd want the latest," she quipped.

Regretting how terse he'd sounded last time, Griff asked evenly, "Heard from the chief, have you?"

She chirped a laugh in his ear. "What did you say to him? He's meeting me in five minutes."

Ready to boast of his bluff, he thought better of it; she might not approve. After all, he'd already flashed his credentials at the dealership, and Wally's case wasn't official.

"I just left a message suggesting he meet you right away."

"You are my hero. His cruiser's pulling into the lot right now." Her smile reached him over the phone.

"Great. Did you change your appointment?"

Dawn must not have heard, because she ended the call. Griff cleared his head, focusing his binoculars and watching the woman trotting in the Battlefield with her dog. He picked up his mic to alert the other agents. "Stand by. Dog walker's heading to the bridge."

Griff motioned for the pilot to bank the plane, and then bellowed, "She has the package and is hustling to her car."

He watched as the woman thrust her dog into her SUV and scrambled in after it.

"Okay, she's in her vehicle and may count the money first."

The plane continued its squared-off pattern. Griff held his microphone and watched the SUV's brake lights and then back-up lights go on. As she rolled the vehicle out of its parking spot, heading toward the park's entrance, Griff barked into the mic, "Suspect is on the move."

FBI surveillance cars on the ground along James Madison Street approached the stone gate. Griff's transmission—"She's getting to Madison now, but is still in the park"—was followed by the supervisor's order, "Stop her before she leaves!"

In a flash, two FBI cars careened in front of the large, black SUV, which jumped the curb. FBI agents rammed behind it so the driver couldn't back up or make a run for it.

Griff breathed easier. "Head to the airport," he told the pilot. "We're done for the day."

The plane looped for the airport, allowing Griff's mind to travel to Summit Ridge and Witt Chevrolet. It was Dawn who'd thought of looking for the traffic cameras. Griff's anger against CJ Huddleston had so clouded his mind that he hadn't been able to think straight.

They landed and Griff drove the short way home, hoping to hear from Dawn. She didn't call. He crashed on his bed without eating dinner; his last thought was that he should advance things with her, but he fell asleep before he figured out how.

A ring punctured his dreamless sleep. He groped and answered the phone with a gruff, "Yup."

"It's late."

"Uh-huh." What time was it anyway? He struggled to clear his mind in the dark room.

"Griff?"

Okay, he recognized her voice. "Ah, I fell asleep. Has Dalton come around to our way of thinking? Are they dropping the case?"

"Yes and no."

"What do you mean?"

Griff lumbered off the bed. No lights blazed in the house. He needed to get his bearings. He stood, his head feeling woozy.

"It means Dalton went to CJ Huddleston, but Huddleston insists on a trial."

"The dirty snake! Where's the evidence? I will file a civil rights complaint against him. See if I don't."

"It's unbelievable. Want to hear what happened?"

Griff was on fire. "I just see him protecting his non-existent case against Wally, threatening Dalton. That's what he did, isn't it?"

"Listen, he came by a little while ago trying to talk me out of sticking up for Wally. We may need to get the Department—"

"Whoa. He stopped by your house?"

"I didn't invite him. He just appeared at my door. I felt I should talk to him."

"Oh, really? You could have referred him to me."

"Oh, right. Look where that got us in the first place," Dawn cried, her voice rising.

Griff hurtled down the hallway and into the kitchen, where he flipped on the switch, the garish light nearly blinding his eyes.

"I see how it is. All along, you've thought I was to blame."

"Griff, no. I didn't mean—"

"Hey, I'm beat. Let's forget it until I've had some sleep."

He hung up the phone, pity and foreboding pumping through him. He couldn't believe it, but Dawn had made the giant leap and gone over to the other side.

43

The next day, Bo Rider stood ogling the contents of the fridge. A fresh apple pie on the top shelf tempted him. His mouth watered. Alright—his increasing appetite must be a good sign. Though he'd returned from Landstuhl's Army hospital more than two weeks earlier, after surviving the worst flu ever to ravage his body, he hadn't regained his strength. Of course, he'd been worn out to begin with.

So Bo had left work and come home early. He had just reached for the pie when his cell phone vibrated. He stared at the screen. Julia was out shopping for scrapbook stuff after dropping the kids at a local church for vacation Bible school, so she probably wasn't calling.

Though it said "private," Bo answered anyway, closing the fridge. Robert Shank, his immediate boss, didn't bother asking about Bo's health.

"Director Kangas wants you in his office."

"Did he say what he wants?"

"He never tells me, Rider."

"Okay, but do I need any files?"

"Get here by four. You shouldn't have gone home."

Shank hung up with a clatter. Bo's mind jumped to Yuri. Had something happened? He perched on a stool near the counter, trying to figure where Yuri was supposed to be. Since Bo had returned to work after his illness, time had stolen away.

He plunked a raisin bagel in the toaster and, when it was golden brown, spread it with peanut butter. Bo consumed the snack in a few bites, wondering if his Russian asset had dropped another stealth message in Moscow.

He should get to the Agency and check his computer for any new messages. After downing a glass of milk, he slid his stocking feet back into his loafers and scribbled off a hurried note for Julia— he'd be back home in time for dinner.

He grabbed his keys, slamming the back door behind him. Once inside his car, he turned the radio to light jazz, enjoying being alive. What a bizarre whirlwind he'd just survived! Did Kangas mean to toss him back into one? Bo gripped the wheel. Julia might really lose her mind this time if he had to leave again so soon, especially after he'd dropped out of sight at Landstuhl.

Bo hurried to his office, but had no urgent messages waiting. He grabbed a blank pad and rode the elevator to the suite for the Director of National Clandestine Service. Kangas' executive assistant, Frank Deming, smiled broadly. His face rarely reflected his pain.

Bo was one of the few in the Agency who knew Frank's wife had been kidnapped in Pakistan. So far, she hadn't been found. Frank had been ordered state-side for his own safety. Bo never brought up the sensitive topic unless Frank mentioned it.

"Hey Frank, how's things around here?"

"You look pretty good for a guy who could've died in Iraq."

Bo bristled, always paranoid about secrecy. "Frank, even Shank doesn't know where I was. How does it happen that you do?"

"Easy, man," Frank said, lifting his palms toward Bo. "Shank put you on sick leave, which Mr. Kangas cancelled because he knew your illness was service-related."

"So?" Bo refused to back down.

"So? Do you think Mr. Kangas fills out the paperwork to reinstate your sick leave balance? No, he relies on me to do it."

Bo raised his hand, as if he had another question for the teacher. "What do you mean, my sickness was service-related?"

Frank picked up his phone and jerked his thumb toward Kangas' office. "He's waiting. Ask him."

Bo had arrived ten minutes before four o'clock, but Kangas was already waiting? How he knew Bo was on the floor when Frank hadn't called was a mystery. Bo stepped cautiously into the large office, feeling unprepared for this meeting.

Kangas sat with his back turned, typing on a computer at his credenza. Bo simply waited as the office door closed with a loud click. No doubt it was done with a remote switch, as always, but this time it made him jump. Whew, his nerves were edgy.

Kangas swung around, gesturing toward a chair. "Rider, Landstuhl told us you've survived a severe bout of the flu. How are you feeling?"

"I'm okay, but there were times I thought I might not make it."

Bo got comfortable in a leather wing-chair across from the desk, but figured that wouldn't be for long. Kangas cut right to the point.

"What is Bear up to?"

"Sir," Bo crossed his legs. "As you recall from my earlier report, he ordered oscilloscopes through a circuitous route. They were dual-use products for shipment to Iran."

"Yes, and he intentionally didn't tell you about the … ah," Kangas said, looking at his notes. "Here it is. Triggered spark gaps. It's a good thing—" He glanced down again. "It's a good thing Agent Montanna at ICE has a more reliable source than Bear, or Iran might be installing those spark gaps into a nuclear bomb."

Bo started to melt in the hot seat under Kangas' intense glare. He had to wonder what else Kangas knew about Yuri. Otherwise, why would he have sent for Bo?

"I have no explanation, but I am convinced Bear arranged for the triggered spark gaps, too. Has he dropped another message?"

"No. Thanks for getting out your report while you recuperated at Landstuhl."

Bo wondered if the meeting was over. Nothing had really been discussed. Then Kangas snapped forward, placing his elbows on the desk.

"What are we to make of Bear's assertion that Iran wants the TOPOL-M rocket for a Sputnik-sized payload? What does Iran intend to do with something that small?"

"Bear didn't elaborate." Bo shrugged. "He said he'd be in touch."

"He must think we're a bunch of idiots." Kangas seized his notes and began stuffing them into a shredder under his desk, talking over sounds of paper crunching.

"I'm stopping payments to his numbered bank account. Remain in contact with him, but he doesn't get another cent until you figure out what he's doing."

Bo had something else he wanted Kangas to know. "Sir—"

"What is it, Rider?"

"I told you when I called from Baghdad that I'd met a Mossad agent in Kirkuk who was tailing the Bear."

"Right. How did you happen to meet the Israeli agent?"

"He recognized me from a class I taught to Mossad agents at the Point. He walked up to me on the street, accusing me of being a 'Christian in Action'."

"That must have been a shock."

"There's more that I didn't put in my report, because I was unsure how it would be received. I'd just left my meet with Bear and Judah Levitt observed it. We exchanged e-mail addresses."

"Be circumspect in e-mails," Kangas ordered, narrowing his eyes.

"Yes, sir. We're using generic addresses and will use them carefully."

"Did this agent enlighten you about Bear?"

"He was aware of Bear's involvement in assisting Iran on behalf of Russia."

"I'm sure Mossad is all over Iranian shipments. Your Mossad agent mentioned a scientist interested in defecting?" Kangas scowled.

"Yes, his code name is Termite. He won't cooperate with Mossad because he refuses to live in Israel. Mossad offered to work a deal with us."

Kangas drummed his fingers on his desk. "That's intriguing, but I need to know the Termite's particulars."

"He's in the Iranian nuclear program. I know that much."

"Don't forget everything *official* goes to Mossad through channels."

"Yes, sir. I will attempt a contact with the agent. Oh, and Frank said you changed my sick leave because it was service-related. I don't understand."

"Shank put you on sick leave. If you hadn't been in Kirkuk on assignment, you wouldn't have picked up swine flu. I changed it to a service-related illness."

"The doctors never said I had *swine* flu." Bo used a hankie to blot his forehead, which had gotten clammy that fast—just from thinking about how sick he'd been.

"Well, that's over. Forget it. I'm off to the State Department. Our satellite picked up provocative actions by Iran across the Iraqi border."

Bo nodded, slipping out of Kangas' office before he received any more orders to head back to that mine-filled quagmire. Did Kangas say, "Be on stand by" as Bo left—or was it his vivid imagination?

44

Liberty woke early to feed the chickens. Her head felt light from not eating. Mabel found her inside the fenced area and waved at her to step out.

"Shhh. I bring you a rice cake."

Hunger gnawed at Liberty's insides. She dropped the pan. Grabbing the cake, she ate it swiftly, licking her fingers. It hardly filled her hollow places.

"It is good. Thank you."

Mabel smiled, opening her palm to reveal a purple ball.

"The boy did not eat this. He is very sick. You eat half and I will eat half."

"What is it?"

"A fruit called a plum. Quickly, before the Lady catches us."

Liberty bit into the fruit's flesh, its sweet taste bringing hope to her meager existence. The chickens raised a fuss for more grain. Liberty thrust the plum into Mabel's hands, returning to her chickens before their clucking brought out the masters.

Later, Mabel came over and told Liberty, "I hid the fruit seed inside the hut. We will plant it behind the wall and see if it grows." Then she laid a hand on Liberty's shoulder. "I heard the Lady speaking on the telephone."

"Did you listen by the forbidden door?"

"No, she spoke on a small phone that she carries and was in her son's room. She talked to a doctor."

"What did she say?" Liberty asked in a whisper.

"She wants to get him the best medicine in Tehran, no matter the cost."

"Where are we, Mabel? Where is Tehran?"

Suddenly, the Lady inside the big house banged opened the back door calling, "Mabel, come inside at once. I need you."

Liberty dropped her eyes toward the birds, wondering what it all meant. After giving all the grain to the noisy chickens, Liberty remembered to thank God for the good plum and for her friend, Mabel. She and Mabel had been many days together, with the sun coming up and going down. Liberty weeded the garden, tended chickens, and washed laundry in a tub next to the hut. She ate only bits of food, always brought by Mabel.

The warm morning passed, becoming a hot day. Mabel never returned. That night, Liberty crept onto the rug with no more food and no water. Rest did not come because strange sounds kept her awake. Was that crying she heard in the big house?

Worried for Mabel, Liberty turned onto her side, thinking of happier times. She remembered meeting Dawn and celebrating the Lord's Day with her. She thought of Baca and his caring eyes, or talking with him on the cell phone. She closed her eyes and could almost see his face smiling at her. Liberty did not feel so alone.

She awoke with a start. Mabel was bending down over her, shaking her shoulder.

"Get up and scrub this rug. Here is liquid and a brush."

Liberty rubbed her eyes and sat up. "Are you all right? I heard crying and you never came."

"The boy will not eat. He cried all night and I brought him tea. After the rug, you help me clean the big house."

"Mabel, do you have any food?"

"No," she said as she shook her head sadly. "After we clean, I will shop for food at the market. It is the first time I can leave the big house in many days."

Liberty grabbed her arm. "Maybe you can escape!"

"No! I have no papers. I would be killed."

"Do I have to go inside?" Liberty wished to remain with the chickens.

"You must help me or the Lady will hit me. I will show you everything, but be careful. The lady is mean, even to her husband. She is not from Iran. We should be glad she is angry."

"Why should we be happy if she is angry?"

Mabel glanced over her shoulder. "Iranian men use slave women for their needs. Not this man. Each day, he leaves to do his work. A black vehicle picks him up. He acts afraid of his wife, so we must fear her, too."

Liberty had more questions, but Mabel pointed at the rug. "Clean it. She will beat us if she thinks we do not work."

After Liberty washed the rug with a brush, Mabel brought her into the big house of their masters. She had never been in such a cool and beautiful place. Maybe she should not be afraid of it. Bright rugs were spread on shiny floors and chairs the color of the sky had cushions.

But in seconds, Liberty changed her mind. She felt darkness sweep over her as if a rain storm were about to fall. Her arms felt prickly, as if bugs were walking on them. Mabel was right—something was wrong with the house and the people who lived in it.

Mabel brought her to the kitchen and a white platform for a cooking fire. Mabel turned a knob and blue fire appeared.

"Oh!" Liberty jumped back.

"Watch me."

Mabel slid her hand above the heat and then quickly pulled it away. "Now you feel it."

Liberty did so, cautiously. "It is much hotter than the village cooking fire."

"This is where I cook their food. The remains I bring outside for us."

"Do you want me to cook over the flame?"

"Not today. Clean the house and the child's room." Mabel pointed to a closed door leading from kitchen. "Remember, that is where the Lady works. First clean the kitchen and then her room, touching nothing."

"Who are the people in this house? What do I call them?"

Mabel looked over her shoulder before whispering, "Lady Tabriz is the mother. Master Tabriz is the father."

"What does Lady Tabriz do behind the door in the room I will clean?"

"Do not ask questions. Here is your rag."

She showed Liberty how to put soap in a bucket of water. Liberty bent on her hands and knees, scrubbing the rag on the kitchen floor, trying to be strong. She needed food, but knew she had to wait.

After cleaning every corner, she stood, hoping Mabel would give her a rice cake. But she did not. Mabel carried bedding and clothing to wash. Liberty pointed to the kitchen floor, which was sparkling clean and dried.

In Dinka, she asked, "May I eat?"

Mabel stuck out her bottom lip and whispered in Dinka, "Do not speak our language in the big house or in front of Lady Tabriz. I take you to her work place. She might want you to have medicine first."

"Medicine?"

Liberty had heard Baca and her uncle speak of such things, but she had never taken any. She feared the unknown and being in the house made her shiver, even in the heat.

"Do whatever she says, even if she asks you to make the bomb."

Mabel knocked on the door and Lady Tabriz opened the door. She did not let Liberty in her room. Instead, she stepped into the kitchen, closing the door behind her. She glared at Liberty with blue eyes that flashed like lightning behind black rimmed glasses. She wore her dark hair piled on her head like a jar of water.

Lady Tabriz spoke in Arabic to Mabel, but Liberty understood what she said.

"The girl does not clean my laboratory during the day time. She should come back tonight."

Then she snatched Liberty's arm and led her behind the thick door inside the laboratory. Mabel followed. The large room was tidy, like the home, and Liberty did not know what the machines and lighted screens were for.

At the one end sat a cage with furry mice. The smell in the room was strong and bad. Why did Lady Tabriz catch mice for the cage? Liberty did not ask, deciding it was because she was afraid to kill them and throw them outside. Lady Tabriz opened the door to a small cupboard and white air escaped; Liberty felt cold air rush against her skin.

Lady Tabriz took out a little bottle, the size of a stone. She jabbed a small spear into it. Before Liberty knew what was happening, the Lady lunged at her with a soft white ball rubbing something cold on her upper arm. Then she aimed the sharp spear at the spot.

Mabel nodded it was okay, but Liberty felt threatened. But what could she do in the strange place? Quickly, Lady Tabriz thrust the small spear into her arm on the cold spot. Pain jabbed Liberty's arm until the spear came out. It must be the medicine Mabel told her about.

Liberty bit her lip, looking around the room. Her eyes landed upon a cell phone sitting on a wooden table. It was just like the one Dawn had given her. Liberty still had the leather pouch on a string around her neck, but only Baca's picture and phone number on a paper were in it now. She did not touch the pouch while she was in the room.

Lady Tabriz pointed at the walls and floor. "I want those scrubbed clean," she said in Arabic.

On the tile floor, Liberty saw a paper sticking out from under the table and leaned over to pick it up for Lady Tabriz. As she touched the paper, Lady Tabriz stomped on her hand.

"Do not touch my things!"

She stepped so hard, Liberty screamed in pain. Still, the Lady pressed down her foot, her piercing blue eyes glaring down at Liberty, who knelt on the floor.

"Do you understand, girl?"

Liberty could only sob in pain. The pressure continued and the woman screamed, "Do you understand?"

Liberty looked up, nodding repeatedly. Finally, the woman removed her shoe from Liberty's hand, motioning with her hands.

"Get out of here."

Liberty slunk away without looking at Mabel or the Lady. She crept outside to her chickens, holding her right hand but refusing to cry. In her heart, she knew Lady Tabriz was not more powerful than God. He would heal her hand and all her hurting places.

45

Days went by. Liberty's hand no longer hurt and she became used to doing hard work and existing on small scraps of food, a rice cake or piece of cheese Mabel hid in her robe. Each day, Liberty cared for the chickens, killing and plucking them for Lady Tabriz's dinner. Sometimes she scrubbed floors or cleaned up vomit and bed things for the sickly boy.

On this day, Liberty went into the laboratory to feed the mice and clean the cages. Lady Tabriz was doing something on a machine when there came a knock on the door.

"Go away," Lady Tabriz ordered.

"This is Mabel. Come quickly, your son does not breathe."

Lady Tabriz abruptly left the room and her laboratory machines. Liberty kept cleaning until some time later when Mabel came in.

"I go with the Lady to the hospital."

"If you escape, do not forget me!" Liberty felt her heart pounding.

"You will see me again," Mabel promised.

She touched Liberty's hand and she was gone. Liberty darted to the table. Was it there? Yes! The cell phone she had seen before was left behind. If she tried calling Baca, would it work?

She carefully removed the pouch from around her neck. She slid out Baca's picture with his number on it and reached for the cell phone. Her hand stopped, her brain remembering the last time when Lady Tabriz crushed her hand for touching a paper. She quickly shoved the paper back in the pouch.

On tip-toe, Liberty walked into the residence, making sure she was alone. All seemed quiet. She held her breath and ran back to the laboratory, where she picked up the phone, her legs and arms shaking. She took Baca's picture from the pouch and turned it over. There was his American number.

She walked back to the door, and watching, dialed Baca. The phone rang several times before Liberty heard his strong voice.

"This is Wally. Sorry I missed your call. Please leave a message and number."

Her heart started leaping in her chest. What should she say to the phone? She trembled by the window, afraid Lady Tabriz would return from the hospital.

"Wally, it is Atong, I mean Liberty," she said. "I am not allowed to use this phone, so will call one time. I am in Tehran, forced to work in the home of an important person.

"They make Dinkas connect cell phones to bombs against American soldiers. I may have to do this, too. Mabel is an older Christian Dinka woman and is the only one who leaves the house for market. I wanted to marry you, but now it will not be. I go now before I get caught or beaten again. I pray God protects us both."

Liberty carefully put the phone right where she found it. She threw the extra paper from the mice cages in a bin. She crept to the hut, wondering how Wally would react when he heard her message. He would graduate from college and build his life in America. He was free. She would be a slave forever to Lady Tabriz, a woman who did not know respect or love.

Mabel stayed away and Liberty's stomach hurt. She ignored her hunger pains as she collapsed on the rug, stroking the soft wool. Finally, she fell asleep.

IN THE MORNING, Liberty stepped outside, the hot sun already scorching her skin. Mabel scurried from the house toward their hut. Two large men followed, pulling her by the arms back inside. Mabel's eyes were large with fear.

Terror seized Liberty and she quickly folded her hands so her friend could see she was praying. The door closed. Would Lady Tabriz use the sharp spear against Mabel?

How could Liberty think about work? What had they done to Mabel? The Dinka woman had shown her such kindness. If only God would take Liberty out of Tehran in a fiery chariot from the sky like He did to Elijah. She looked up. Only gray clouds drifted over her head.

Suddenly, a man appeared by the chickens and her heart thumped in surprise. She grabbed the fence, her fingers digging into the wire. He smiled, handing her a bucket with gray liquid, the same color as the sky.

"My wife wants you to paint the wall behind our house."

He moved his arms up and down with the brush and she thought she understood his lilting Arabic. She nodded. He gave her a brush and turned away. He must be Master Tabriz. She looked down at the bucket and brush. If she did not do as he asked, what would he do?

Lady Tabriz was mean. Her husband, a tall man, was probably even stronger. Liberty trembled, dipped brush in the liquid, and then smeared paint on the wall, hoping Master Tabriz would not come back.

Only when the sun started slipping down in the sky, did she set down her brush, her hands and arms aching. She sat on her rug and closed her eyes until she heard a rustling sound. Her eyes flew open. Mabel stood before her in a new robe. Liberty blinked. Was she real?

"Mabel, are you all right?"

"The Lady wants to see you. First I tell you what she wants."

Did Lady Tabriz find out she had made a call on her cell phone? Liberty shuddered, worrying about what she would do. Mabel crouched beside her.

"You saw the men take me away."

"Yes, and I was afraid."

"They drove me to a factory," Mabel sighed. "All day, I connected cell phones to bombs made by others. Anyone who has a slave must donate us for a day to wire cell phones. It is dangerous because the bomb might explode when I attach the phone. We have no value to them."

Liberty held Mabel's hand. "But you are my friend. I prayed you would be safe."

"Thank you, daughter." A tear trickled down Mabel's cheek. "The Lady says you go tomorrow to the factory. She will see you now."

Liberty jumped to her feet and fled toward the wall. It was too tall for her to jump, but she wanted to run. Mabel grabbed her arm.

"It is my turn to pray God will protect you."

Was she being sent to make bombs because she had called Baca?

Mabel looked into her eyes. "Please, you know the Lady is waiting."

Liberty closed her eyes for a moment, trying to be strong. The bombs could blow up, Mabel told her. But Liberty swallowed her fear and went to the laboratory, where Lady Tabriz was putting something into a machine.

When Liberty and Mabel walked in, she looked up from her work. This time she did not look angry, just sad. Her eyes were red and swollen.

"Mabel, you may leave us."

When Mabel obeyed, Lady Tabriz eyes flashed. She said in Arabic, "Tell no one." Then she pulled open a drawer, taking out something small that looked like a clear stick.

"Tonight, hide this vial and keep it secret. See this piece of foam tape?"

Lady Tabriz moved it with her finger and Liberty nodded. She saw it.

"This vial is closed on both ends. At the factory, when you connect the cell phones, peel off this tape," she pointed, "and press this vial to the underside of one of the phones. Do you understand?"

Lady Tabriz picked up her own cell phone, the one Liberty had used. Would she hit her for making a phone call? No, she showed Liberty how to attach the vial to the phone.

"Yes, my Lady," Liberty replied.

She stared into Liberty's eyes before patting her hand, the one she had stomped on. "I believe you do. You are a good girl. If you return to me, you will receive a new robe, as Mabel did today. Isn't it pretty?"

"Yes, my Lady. Is your son any better?"

The Lady's face looked as if Liberty had hit her with a stick. "He died this morning, and I no longer care. It is time for me to act. You go and mind everything I told you."

Liberty clutched the vial in her right hand, returning to the hut. Mabel held a large bowl, her face happy. "Look! Tonight we eat as much lamb and rice as we want."

"The boy died," Liberty said. She wanted to show Mabel the vial, but she had been warned not to.

"I am sorry. He cries no more."

"Master Tabriz smiled and brought me paint. Did he care for his son?"

"I think so, but he is always working."

"Maybe he is glad the boy is no longer sick."

"Did the Lady promise you a new robe?" Mabel wondered.

"Yes, but I do not want to do what Lady Tabriz asked."

"What did she say?"

"I am hungry and want to eat. Then I may tell you."

They both dipped the fingers of their left hand in the bowl. To Liberty, the rice and meat tasted delicious. She kept the vial hidden in the palm of her other hand. Between the two women, the food did not last long. After they finished their lamb and all was quiet, Liberty showed Mabel the vial.

"She told me to put this on a cell phone at the factory."

"She did not give me one," Mabel said, touching it with her fingertip. "What is inside?"

"I do not know."

"Well, the Lady will not know if you attach the vile."

"I thought of that. I want to ask God what to do."

ANOTHER MORNING AND LIBERTY tossed more grain to the chickens, her only companions. Mabel cooked breakfast over the fire in the big house, but Liberty had eaten none yet. Just as she set down the pan of chicken food, two men wearing black came for her. Liberty wanted to run, but she knew it was useless.

She raised her chin and, dressed in her faded dress and bare feet, gathered every bit of courage as she walked with them to a car. The vial Lady Tabriz gave to Liberty rested in the pouch hanging around her neck.

The men shoved her into the back seat. The car door was smooth, with no way to get out. Liberty tried not to let her heart collapse in fear.

The night before, an angel had come, telling her in a dream what to do with the vial. She had not told Mabel because her friend had left the hut before Liberty awoke.

They drove for a long time. Liberty looked out the window at passing trees, many big houses, and fast-moving cars. After they stopped, the men grabbed her arms and pushed her into a large building. People, not Africans, worked behind rows and rows of tables.

On the first table sat many parts. Next to the table sat a line of small wagons with things inside. Were these the bombs Mabel had told her about?

Liberty's scalp tingled as she watched a worker place what must be the bomb on a wagon. A boy pulled the wagon to the next table, where another worker added more parts to the bomb. Attached to the wagon was a leather strap reaching the ground. At the end of the building, a large overhead door was open to the sunny outdoors.

Liberty was taken to the last table, where she met a stooped woman wearing a ragged red shift. Though her face had many tiny bumps, this woman's eyes reminded Liberty of her mother's. The two women stared at each other, the older one showing Liberty a cell phone with two wires sticking out the back.

"Are you Dinka?" she asked in Arabic.

Liberty nodded, but her lips formed no words in this place where people worked so men and women would die. Maybe Americans—maybe Wally!

Liberty gazed into the woman's eyes as she held the phone. They were as dark as mud.

"I am Dinka," she whispered to Liberty in their tribal language. "I have seen many of our people killed by the bombs."

"God will save me. He told me."

"That is good. Now listen and watch."

She pointed at two wires sticking out of the phone, telling Liberty how to attach a metal connecter on each end. "You connect these to the wires on the bomb."

The Dinka woman pinched the ends with a metal tool and then made Liberty connect practice wires. She led Liberty to the open door, where several wagons sat.

"Each holds a bomb. Take the cell phone and connect it to the bomb as I showed you. But this you do outside."

Liberty watched a slim girl wearing a torn green dress pull her wagon outside to one side of a large field. The Dinka woman grabbed Liberty's hand and together they pulled the wagon to the opposite end of the field, far from the girl who worked over her wagon. They reached the stubby grass and the woman again showed Liberty how to connect the wires.

"Wait for me to go into the building," she instructed Liberty. "Connect the wires and pull your wagon back inside, where you will take another wagon."

"I understand everything."

As she stood in the bright sun, Liberty waited for the older woman to hurry inside. Behind her, the little Dinka girl pulled her wagon to the building. Liberty took her tool, but before she connected the wires and the phone, she talked to God.

"Father of everything, You see me. Protect me from the bomb and the people who are near this bomb, wherever it goes."

She told her fingers not to shake. Fear breathed down her neck as Liberty crimped the first wires. She waited. All remained safe. Holding her breath, she crimped the second wires. Nothing happened, and thankfulness rushed into her heart.

She took her wagon back to the warehouse, giving it to the Dinka woman, who pointed to the connected bomb.

"It explodes when someone calls this cell phone. The only person who knows the number to call is the bomber."

Liberty hoped no one called the phone while she was near it.

"There is your next wagon."

Liberty had to make another bomb! This time, she walked more slowly with her little wagon. She had survived one time. Would she again?

LIBERTY MADE THE TREK back out to the field, placing one foot after another. When she had reached the far end, she gazed up into the great sky. Just then, a bird hovered over her head. In that moment, she knew she was not alone. The bird soared away and Liberty leaned down to attach the wires, feeling less afraid.

The morning wore on. The sun beat against her head and her back as she labored in the field, trying to keep her fingers from shaking or connecting the wrong wires. Liberty finished one more cell phone and returned her wagon with another armed bomb.

She saw the younger Dinka girl from the field, who was tiny compared to Liberty and had scars climbing her bare arm like steps of a ladder. Liberty smiled, but the girl's lips curved down. Mabel had told Liberty that some men scarred girls who resisted their advances. Liberty changed wagons and kept toiling in the heat, her nimble fingers working on wires.

She had not attached the vial given her by Lady Tabriz. It stayed in her pouch, just as the angel told her. Better there than hurting someone else when a bomb exploded.

She shuffled back toward the building with one more finished bomb, her eyes glimpsing the other Dinka girl bending over her wagon. Suddenly, Liberty was knocked to the ground by a powerful explosion that left her ears hurting. She rolled over, stunned. At the other end of the field there was a cloud of smoke and the girl was gone. So was her wagon.

No scrap of green fabric remained to show where the other Dinka girl had been. She had ceased to exist. No one came to help, and Liberty started to weep. She crouched on the dusty ground, sobbing until she felt a warm touch on her cheek. The Dinka woman from inside took Liberty's hand.

"You must get up or we will have trouble."

Somehow, Liberty stood on her feet and stumbled to the building, tears clouding her eyes. Inside, she found many more wagons at her table. Were they from the little girl in green? Her stomach convulsed. Just then, a man dressed in black walked in and started yelling for her and the others to work harder.

"If you do not go faster, no food will be given."

That mattered nothing to Liberty. How could she be any hungrier?

Still she took hold of another handle, pulling the wagon out into the heat, not wanting the other Dinka slave to be beaten. As Liberty trudged to her end of the field, she gazed across at emptiness where the little girl had been.

No one cared besides Liberty. Some important Iranian had just lost a slave. Although the tube remained in her pouch, she resisted the evil inside the vial with every breath she took.

46

Monday afternoon at one o'clock, Bo left his office for Rob's Deli, absorbed with how tense Griff Topping had sounded when he phoned.

"Bo, something's come up. Can we meet?"

"Is it about our mutual Russian friend?" Bo had asked testily.

"No, Wally and his Sudanese fiancée. I wouldn't bother you if it wasn't critical."

"Fortunately for you, I'd enjoy another Birdie."

Bo had squeezed in time for Griff, although his work load was jam packed. So was the restaurant. Bo went to an empty table in back, just as he had last time, only this time he had arrived first—for once. Wally tended a table of three giggling ladies. Bo would eat, hear what Griff had to say, and then roar back to Langley, with no time for fun. Not even one second.

His eye ran over the specials written on a blackboard. Griff pulled out a chair and sat next to him.

"How's everything at the State Department?"

Bo grinned back, continuing the ruse even though he knew Griff knew differently. "My appetite's finally back after the flu. I found out I had H1N1."

"Yikes, swine flu? Sure you're not contagious?"

"I'm not, or so the Army docs claim. There were times when I thought I would die and times when I wished I would."

"That bad, huh?"

"Worse."

Wally brought an Arnie Palmer for Bo and a steaming cup of coffee for Griff.

"Hi, Dad. Do you both want your usual?"

Bo nodded, sensing a deepening connection to Wally, knowing the heartache he endured behind his smile.

"Bring me a Birdie," Griff said.

Wally's lips lifted in surprise, but he hurried to the kitchen, head held high.

"He handles it with such strength," Bo remarked.

"You have no idea what he's been through. He's why I need your help."

Griff jerked his chair closer to the table, sliding a business card to Bo. "Liberty phoned Wally from the number written on this card.

Wally wrote it down from his cell phone. Her message said she's working in Iran as a slave to some important person."

Bo arched his eyebrows, attuned to what else Griff might have for him about Iran.

"Can you want to find out who owns the cell phone?"

"I wasn't surprised to learn that a Sudanese Army officer trafficked in Dinka and Neur slaves," Bo said as he sampled his drink, "But this is the first I've heard of them slaving for the ruling class in Iran."

"Wally can better describe Liberty's message."

"As a State Department employee, right?" Bo lobbed a concerned look.

"That's where you work, right?"

Bo pushed away his drink, not enjoying the tart lemonade and tea combo, a sign that his system was still not running on all cylinders.

"Griff, thanks for the heads-up after the incident at the Jefferson Memorial. I've been in touch with Eva and she saved my bacon recently."

"Mine too, more than once," Griff laughed.

"Through her, I learned my asset didn't provide me with everything he knew."

Wally placed their crab cake sandwiches and crispy fries on the table. When he turned to go, Griff reached out a hand.

"Wally, my friend works at the U.S. State Department. When you have time, tell him about Liberty's call."

"Now is good," Wally said. He knelt on one knee.

"Try to recall precisely what she said," Bo urged. "I understand she's been kidnapped in Sudan. Maybe I can help to locate her."

"I gave Dad the number. Liberty called from Tehran, where she is a slave to some important people. She and other Dinkas are required to connect cell phones to bombs."

"Does she have a phone that works in Iran?" Bo asked.

"No. She risked using one without permission. She said another slave named Mabel, who lives with her, goes shopping at the local market alone."

"Anything else?"

Wally paused, his face crumpling with pain. "She thinks we'll never see each other again or get married."

"I'm sorry. My associates might investigate the phone number you wrote down. That was quick thinking on her part and yours."

Wally ambled to his feet, bowing slightly. "You give me belief all is not lost. I should retrieve another order."

Bo and Griff ate in silence until Bo tossed a crumpled napkin in the basket.

"Nothing tastes right. I have backchannel ways to ID the owner of the cell phone number."

"Just what I thought. Even if you find out, that might not help us free Liberty from Iran. That regime controls its people tighter than a drum."

"Withhold judging just yet." Bo tapped a finger to his temple. "I'll think on it. What Wally just told me has intelligence value."

"How so?"

"We've known that some Iranians, with or without the regime's permission, are building improvised explosive devices (IEDs), which they conceal in vehicles or disguise by other means and ship to Iraq and Afghanistan. Insurgents use them against the troops and civilians, trying to destabilize the region."

"So Liberty's message verifies they *are* building IEDs in Iran?"

"Yes. It sounds like the most dangerous part, connecting the cell phone detonators, is being done by Sudanese slaves."

"I know how these work," Griff said, pursing his lips. "The bomb is secreted on the side of the road under garbage or a dead animal. Someone nearby watches for a military convoy to near the bomb and then dials the phone connected to the bomb. With the push of a single button, the bomb explodes, killing whoever's close by."

"It's a miracle one didn't wipe me out," Bo said. He didn't elaborate, but his comment was enough to raise a question in Griff mind. Before he could get clarification, Wally returned with their checks. Griff grabbed both, handing Wally the cash.

"Keep the change, Son. I'll let you know what we learn."

"And I'll stay right on my people at the State Department," Bo promised.

Wally simply bobbed his head and dashed toward the kitchen.

Bo gripped Griff's shoulder. "This could be huge. Be on the ready for my call."

BO POWERED ON HIS office computer, reflecting on his good fortune. In his intelligence-gathering world, he scratched around for months, sometimes for a sliver that turned out to be nothing. Wally had dropped not just a nugget but an entire goldmine into Bo's lap. The Agency suspected Iran was aiding insurgents in the region, and now Liberty had given him evidence that the regime assembled IEDs for Iraq and Afghanistan.

Respect and slight awe swept over him as he recalled past dealings with two diligent federal agents, Griff Topping and Eva Montanna. Whenever he worked with them, his fortunes improved. Was it some kind of uncanny karma, or something more?

He shook his head free of the unknowable and toggled down to the site he needed. Uncovering the cell phone's owner could be the weapon to pierce Iran's secrets. That should please Kangas. But it would be foolish to gloat before he had the info in hand. He still had to find out whose number Liberty had called from.

Bo racked his brain. Then, like a camera flash, a possible solution exploded into his mind. He logged onto his Hotmail account and typed a message to the Mossad agent, careful to use Judah's alias.

Greetings. Hope you're okay. After our last meeting, I got rocked by a terrible case of swine flu. Here's a dilemma for you to help me solve. Recently when I was in Tehran for business, I lost my cell phone. Have you any friends there who can help me find it?

Bo typed in the phone number off Griff's business card, sending the e-mail on its way. He secured his computer and locked his desk before heading home. He was unsure when or if Judah would even see the message.

47

Bo checked his Hotmail account for the next three days expecting a reply to his e-mail, but each time got the same disappointing results. He heard nothing from his colleague in Israel's intelligence service.

Bo had promised Wally he'd do something, so he sped down to Nanette Bing, the intelligence analyst.

"Run this number for me as soon as you can."

The petite Asian woman placed her hands on her hips. "Looking for what?"

"See if we've documented this number at all. I need the account holder's name."

"Okay, wait while I enter it. My mom's in intensive care, so I'm leaving early."

Bo bit back a retort that he had a life too and watched Nanette load the number. Although her computer held millions of pieces of data, he didn't hit the jackpot.

"Sorry, no entries. If you want me to check anything else—" she said. But Bo just shook his head.

He zipped back to his office in time to grab the ringing phone. It was Griff, hoping for an update. "Sorry, Griff. My source let me down."

"It's not your fault."

"International data collection isn't as smooth as what you do domestically. Everything takes longer." Bo struggled for breath. "But, I have an inquiry out there and I figure I'll hear soon."

"I'm not piling on the pressure. Wally just called asking me."

"How's he holding up?"

"You don't know this," Griff sighed, "but a rookie cop in Summit Ridge arrested him. I went to Sudan while Wally's lawyer was gearing up for an evidentiary hearing, and the prosecutor was granted a postponement. It's a real circus down there. "

"Why was he arrested?"

"He went with me to Dawn's town for a wedding. Wally was going to speak to her church team about Sudan. Mission trips are all new to me."

"Me, I don't go to church, but my wife has been lately. I keep putting her off. So what he's accused of?"

"Robbing a local convenience store. Wally happened to loosely fit the description of the suspect. They picked him up as he was leaving the hotel to walk to church."

"He's such a nice guy. Anyone can see he's not a stick-up type. Are the cops down there amateurs?"

"The chief is a decent sort, but the Commonwealth attorney might be trying to prove something to me as an FBI agent."

"Wish I had pull there, but I don't know a soul in Summit Ridge."

"Lucky for you. But we're not going down without a fight. Stay in touch."

"Will do."

The first thing Bo did after he hung up was to log on to his Hotmail account. Bingo! Judah had sent a reply.

You're not the only one with swine flu. My friend, I had a potent strain and nearly died. You must have left your phone at your friend's beautiful, large home. Surely you remember visiting Lili Tabriz? We should get together again soon. Regards.

Not Lili Tabriz again! Bo stared at the black letters on his monitor, Judah's answer shocking him to the core. She was the scientist who nearly exposed Bo in London. Had Liberty really called from her phone, or was this Judah's sick humor? How did he even know Bo had tangled with Tabriz? Had he been following Bo after all and not Yuri?

He accessed his archive while he stewed over these questions. He swiftly pulled up his report of the London conference, his mind humming like a finely tuned engine. Did the wife of Dr. Cyrus Tabriz, Director of Iran's Institute for Scientific Advances, own slaves to foster terrorism against Americans? But a second question burned—how in the world did Liberty get her hands on Lili Tabriz' cell phone?

Then a control number, for a report written *after* his, flashed on his screen. The compilation by a CIA intelligence analyst—not Nanette Bing—summarized the publicly-available data about Lili Tabriz. Because data had been collected without asking questions in the field, no suspicions would have been raised in Lili Tabriz' home or her peculiar mind.

Why hadn't Bo thought to check for updates? More disturbing was why Nanette didn't tell him she'd handed the task off to another analyst. But there was no time for second guessing. Bo plunged in:

Lili Tabriz is the married name of Lovisa Sorenson. She grew up in Brooklyn, became a member of the National Honor Society in high school, and graduated from Harvard with a degree in biology. Lili studied at Oxford, earning a PhD in microbiology.

In the early nineties, she met at Oxford an Iranian—Cyrus Tabriz—who taught microbiology. After marrying Cyrus in Tehran, Lovisa changed her name to Lili Tabriz. She made network news: Dr. Cyrus Tabriz applied for a visa to enter the U.S. and was denied a visa and entry. Lili appealed, claiming they wanted to live in New York. He sought U.S. citizenship based on his marriage to Lili, a U.S. citizen. All attempts failed.

Lili Tabriz, the former Lovisa Sorenson, held a press conference on the steps of the U.S. Courthouse in Manhattan where she denounced her U.S. citizenship, tearing up her birth certificate, but not her U.S. passport. She used that passport to return to Brooklyn for her father's funeral. His obituary mentions another daughter, Ingeborg Sorenson. Her mother died two years later, but there is no evidence Lili attended her funeral.

All Bo's earlier suspicions of Lili Tabriz congealed. She was from New York, as he had guessed. He now focused on her past, trying to fathom how Liberty's enslavement could help him get justice against Dr. Lili Tabriz.

Judah had made a slam dunk—producing the phone number—while Nanette Bing couldn't even hit the backboard! Bo seethed, itching to pen a caustic note to her boss. But taking action against Nanette's negligence would have to wait.

He had a potent enemy to tackle first. With every passing hour, Lili Tabriz was developing into a more despicable character. What else had she been hiding in that leather valise in London? Those drawings Bo had stumbled on might relate to making IEDs.

Liberty had said in her message that she was being forced to connect cell phones to bombs. As Bo's fingers flew over the keyboard, he began to believe it was all a coincidence. Judah knew nothing about Bo's London trip, yet he'd nailed Tabriz' hide to the wall. Bo dashed off a revised intelligence report and called Frank Deming.

"Get me in to the Director ASAP. I've got something hot."

"Since when do you dictate to me?"

"Frank, I'll buy your lunch and say I'm sorry for running over your job, but this can't wait. Who's our greatest enemy?"

"North Korea?"

"Strike one."

"Iran."

"Home run, now get me in."

"We're both in luck. Director Kangas returns at one thirty. I've entered you onto his calendar. He always checks it on his cell phone. You have time to buy my lunch."

Bo slammed down the phone, locked the report in his safe, and tore upstairs to confront Frank.

"Is Kangas in his office? If he is and you're jerking me around, I won't forget it."

"Rider, he happens to be in session at the National Institutes of Health. I have some news about my wife I wanted to share with you," Frank said in a raspy voice, his face pale and lower lip trembling.

Bo gulped, fumbling for an apt reply. "Let's go down and I'll buy you a cola. I'm not up to eating much."

"Me either."

Downstairs at the CIA's bustling cafeteria, in the midst of dozens of men and women taking a break from the pressures of keeping America safe, the two men sat at a far table, both breaking soda crackers into bowls of hot chicken soup.

"Is there anything I can do to help, Frank?"

Frank hung his head but then raised it, gazing at Bo.

"I doubt it. Some Taliban fighter our guys in Pakistan took into custody admitted—" Frank's voice broke. "It's over. I'll never see her again."

As Frank choked back tears, Bo couldn't help thinking what he'd do if Julia was ever snatched. It was too gruesome to contemplate.

"Listen, go home and split the Agency for a while. I can meet with Director Kangas in the morning."

"Nope," Frank grunted. "Work keeps me sane."

"I am sorry." Bo clasped Frank's shoulder.

"Thanks for lunch," Frank muttered as he pushed back from the table, plunking his bowl onto a tray.

The world seemed to be lurching out of control all around him. On impulse, Bo called Julia. He had fifteen minutes before his appointment with Kangas. When she answered, relief overwhelmed him.

"Honey, just calling to say hello. Things are pretty slow around here. I should make Gregg's tee-ball game, no problem."

"You have made my day," she said, laughing. "I just finished my book and I'm taking the kids for pizza before the game. Glenna is home from her sleepover and bored."

"It's a date. See you guys at five-thirty."

Bo folded the phone, his spirits somewhat higher after speaking with Julia. He zoomed straight to his office, where he retrieved his

newest report from his safe and locked things up again. He anticipated what questions Kangas might ask about Lili Tabriz as he rode
the elevator upstairs.

FRANK WAS ON THE PHONE, conducting business as usual, but
Bo knew he was grieving. He simply motioned Bo to Kangas' door,
mouthing, "Go in."

Bo walked inside the spacious office and the door clicked shut.
Okay, Frank probably controlled the electronic door closer. Kangas
was hunched over his conference table, writing on paper scattered
among some baseball cards. Bo leaned over and could tell the cards
were old by their yellowish cast. He spotted an autographed card—
Sandy Koufax, the famous pitcher.

"Sir, who do you like for the World Series?"

Kangas snapped his head up. "Bah, I can't stand baseball. Too
slow for me."

Bo took a step back wondering about all the baseball cards.

"Rider, you wanted to see me on urgent business. I'll be right with
you."

"Didn't think it could wait, sir."

Kangas wrote on a greeting card before stuffing it into an envelope, licking it shut. "I trust you're ready for the next step."

Next step? Bo hedged, "I'm improving every day."

"Heard from Bear?"

"Not a roar since you stopped his funding, which is surprising. I
have an update on Dr. Lili Tabriz, the scientist in London who … ah
… I spoke with. It's a long story."

"Give me highlights only. What I've just learned at NIH requires
my immediate attention."

"She has strong anti-American feelings."

From there, Bo wove the intricate story of an American turned
Iranian epidemiologist who married an important Iranian scientist
and who used slave labor for arming IEDs.

"Sir, I've just learned the Israeli Mossad agent I met in Kirkuk also
contracted swine flu." Bo leaned across the table. "That happened
following detonation of an IED we experienced, which I never mentioned to—"

"You what?" Kangas bellowed. He hit the table with his elbow and
a few baseball cards flew to the floor.

Bo retrieved the cards, handing them to Kangas. "It was no big
deal. We rode in a taxi behind an Iraqi convoy that got blown up

by an IED. Neither the Mossad agent nor I were injured. Anyway, the important thing is, we both came down with a type of H1N1. Now I've found out Lili Tabriz compels Sudanese slaves to arm IEDs. Combine that with what Bear told—"

"That Iran is buying Russian TOPOL missiles," Kangas interjected.

"Yes," Bo said as he punched his fist into the palm of his hand. "With payloads too small for nuclear warheads. I wanted you to know this right away. It's possible Iran—and maybe Dr. Lili Tabriz—are developing a flu strain that could kill more people than a nuclear bomb."

Kangas' mouth hung open before he muttered, "A deadly germ bomb." He leapt from his chair and snatched a piece of paper from his credenza before rushing back.

"I don't know if you're lucky or a blessed man, but you have a way of stumbling onto the truth."

That compliment hit Bo as strange. He hadn't a clue what was on that paper.

"Sir, can you explain?"

"This report is from Health and Human Services." Kangas jabbed the sheet with his finger. "Seems they got a slide from the Army hospital in Germany of the flu you had. They've analyzed it."

"Swine flu, right?"

"Yes and no. It's no garden variety of H1N1. Rider, you had a highly-virulent stain of flu *similar* to swine flu but closer to what scientists call 'Armageddon flu.'"

"For days, I doubted I'd live. Judah Levitt told me something similar."

Sweat began pooling under Bo's arms just from recalling his illness.

"No wonder. With the avian or bird flu, *sixty percent* of the people who catch it die. Rider, you had a combo of not only swine flu, but bird flu as well. Surely the Israeli agent had the same thing."

Bo had known it the second he'd laid eyes on the raving woman: Lili Tabriz was the worst sort of maniacal fiend.

Kangas fluttered the report. "H5N1 combined with H1N1 is a lethal weapon. From every indication, Iran has perfected the mutation. Our health types are up in arms. They insist this strain is worse than the plague or even the 1918 flu pandemic. Eighteen million Americans died from that outbreak. Armageddon flu will cause many more deaths."

The numbers were staggering. Bo's pulse skyrocketed. He and Kangas had to think fast and act faster.

"Sir, Iran probably has Dr. Tabriz developing an influenza germ to wipe out every single Israeli. But how can they launch it without killing their own people? Anyone can catch the flu."

"True, but perhaps she's developed a vaccine to protect their own people. You're onto something, as usual."

"We have to stop her—but how? I had her in my crosshairs in London," Bo muttered. He got up and started pacing.

Kangas was already shaking his head. "Not the way you mean. We won't be doing those types of missions for a while. Washington has no stomach for strength."

"May I share with Mossad what you've just told me?"

Kangas shuffled his baseball cards. "Rider, here's what I'm willing to do. Use our system to tell the Mossad agent your theory. Take no action without my express permission."

"I understand." Bo shifted his feet. "I won't get us into WWIII without telling you first."

Bo retreated to his office and prepared a message for Judah Levitt to be routed to the U.S. embassy in Tel-Aviv and hand delivered to Mossad. *Judah, you unearthed the Holy Grail when you sent me that Hotmail message. Dr. Lili Tabriz is most likely responsible for nearly killing you and me twice—first by the roadside bomb in Kirkuk and secondly with a deadly form of the flu.*

Bo detailed why he'd asked for the phone number and how Liberty and another Sudanese slave worked in her home and on IEDs. *One named Mabel is permitted to go to shop in the nearby market. Your response is urgent. Skip.*

48

Monday morning brought Bo more quandaries to solve. He'd been sequestered in his office since seven a.m. reading unclassified reports about Russia's TOPOL-M missiles that Iran wanted to buy, when the sound of his desk phone burst his concentration. It was Frank, Kangas' assistant.

"Bo, what've you done now?"

"What does that mean Frank?"

"You started a ruckus. There are people in 'the man's' office from NIH. He wants you up here."

"We're not holding a blood drive?" Bo quipped, trying to make sense of it all.

"That's the Red Cross."

"What's up then?"

"I have no idea, which is why I ask, what've you done?"

"I'll be right up."

Bo banged down the receiver and considered his business-casual attire. With the door closed, he removed the sport coat, dress shirt, and tie that hung on the back of his office door for emergencies and changed clothes. Jacket in hand, he sprinted to the elevator.

Frank cleared Bo right in. He opened the door and, after closing it silently behind him, slid into an empty chair at the end of Kangas' conference table. No baseball cards were in sight.

Kangas abruptly nodded at Bo. A man and woman wearing dark blue suits tossed furtive glances at each other. They must be from the National Institutes of Health. The woman continued talking.

"We assumed, because the Agency sent the sample vial to our lab, that the virus originated from outside the U. S. We stress how important it is to locate and contain this influenza strain. It's a potential weapon of the greatest magnitude."

She paused, staring at Bo as if he were an unwanted interloper. But Kangas waved away her concerns.

"He's one of my agents and is responsible for the sample arriving at your lab. He'll be involved in *all* efforts to contain this lethal virus."

The woman faced Bo. "Before you arrived, I told Mr. Kangas this is the most virulent and dangerous strain of influenza we've seen in modern times. The 1918 flu outbreak is considered the 'mother' of all pandemics, and the current strain of H1N1 is derived from that viral strain. It's highly contagious. The distantly related H5N1 is highly pathogenic; six out of ten victims die. Mix the two, and we face a virus that could cause substantially more than one hundred million deaths worldwide."

She paused to breathe. Kangas somehow took her doomsday prediction in stride, gesturing at Bo. "He's in our clandestine operations division, which is why I won't introduce him. I wanted him to hear your conclusions, but I'm the one you have to convince."

When she turned again in her seat, speaking to Kangas, Bo felt as if he were watching a tennis match. However, what they were discussing was no sport, but life and death. He clamped his jaw, leaning forward so he wouldn't miss a single word.

"The Army recently sent NIH samples collected from soldiers and civilians who developed flu in Kirkuk, Iraq, after an IED explosion there," she explained. We believe that bomb released the Armageddon virus. Analysis shows it is a mutated form of H1N1 and H5N1."

Bo swallowed, thinking the obvious. The lethal strain the NIH lady was so afraid of had nearly killed him.

"We're familiar with that incident," Kangas said with a frown. "Move along."

"Did you know twelve Iraqi soldiers died in that *incident*?" she glowered.

Bo watched Kangas' face muscles twitch, but the Director said nothing. Neither did Bo. At that precise moment, he simply felt thrilled to be alive. He gripped his moist hands beneath the table, his mind devising methods to stop Dr. Lili Tabriz. But the NIH woman was still talking, so Bo forced himself to listen.

"Do you see the potential threat this virus has as a weapon of mass destruction? If whoever developed this sample duplicates it, he or she could eliminate the entire population of the world."

"What do they accomplish by destroying themselves?" Kangas asked. He raised both hands.

"Sir," the NIH man jumped in, "suppose this is a foreign government and they've produced a vaccine. They could inoculate their population and be the only country on earth to survive. Forget nuclear weapons. These germs will get us all."

A foreboding silence filled the room, sucking out the oxygen. It weighed on Bo and presumably everyone else in the room. Not one to stay mired in the probable, Kangas rose at the end of the table and started barking orders.

"Get to work and find out which Dr. Frankenstein created this deadly virus."

Both NIH officials glared at Bo as if he already knew, but Kangas lobbed another question.

"How long to develop a vaccine?"

"We know from creating the vaccine against the swine flu that one can be developed, but for this strain—" she shrugged, crinkling her nose. "Of course, we go through a testing phase. How long it would take to inoculate an entire population depends on the country."

"What makes it so devastating is that our enemies don't need a strong army or even a missile system capable of reaching around the world," Kangas said. He forced a sigh. "This Armageddon virus spreads itself."

While Kangas escorted the visitors from his office, Bo digested the information from the horrific briefing. He heard Kangas telling the officials, "We appreciate your heads-up and will devote every waking moment to combating this WMD. We'll call on your expertise as we proceed."

He turned the visitors over to Frank to be escorted from the building and closed his door with a click, stalking back to the conference table.

"Sorry to bring you in so late, Rider. Apparently, your friend in Mossad had sent a message and sample vial through channels, requesting you be notified. That didn't happen. Instead, the sample arrived at NIH and you just heard their report."

"I wondered why I didn't hear back. I even worried he might have died from complications."

"Nothing so drastic, just a miscue. I have the Mossad agent's report for you."

Kangas sorted through a sheaf of papers and found what he was looking for. "He's working with a group of dissidents in Iran who already made contact in the local market with a slave named Mabel. She told the dissidents she works in the home of Master and Lady Tabriz, who operate a lab in their home."

Kangas handed Bo the report, which he tore through. He learned that the dissidents had verified Dr. Cyrus Tabriz was the Director of the Institute for Scientific Advances and his wife, Dr. Lili Tabriz was an Iranian epidemiologist working in a sophisticated laboratory in her home.

Bo raised his eyes. "I told Judah Levitt about Mabel and Lili Tabriz. I never met her husband at the conference. She is one sick woman with a heart of vengeance against the U.S."

He still chose not to admit that Lili Tabriz was a tough adversary who had practically run Bo out of London. Then again, maybe Kangas already knew. Still, Bo's mind turned in circles—he strove to devise an operational plan and listen to Kangas.

"Judah Levitt's relationship with the dissidents might get them or us into the doctor's home lab to neutralize her operation of annihilation. Work up an Ops plan. Make it a priority—but remember, our politicians are all trying to get re-elected."

"What if I concoct something for Israel?"

"Perfect. We'll sell them on the plan. They've been waiting to strike."

Bo stood to leave just as Kangas tossed him a curve ball. "Have your Ops plan ready for my approval close of business tomorrow. We'll dub it Operation Enigma."

One day to stop a germ-wielding psycho American who'd jumped to the dark side? Bo hardly believed he could do it. He paced toward the door, halting in the middle of the room.

"Sir, I'll work all day and night. Believe me, I know she must be stopped."

He'd almost reached the door when Kangas called, "Rider, one more thing."

Bo turned slowly on his heels, expecting another ax to land on his head.

"Agent Odessa's wife gave birth to twin boys, yesterday. Guess what they've named one of them?"

"Wilt, after you, sir?"

"Nope." Kangas wore a wide grin. "Pierce, after your undercover name. Odessa appreciates you going to London for him."

"And I have him to thank for sticking me with the toughest case I've ever handled."

"You're the man for it, Rider. Don't let me or the country down on this one."

Bo strode out past Frank, who didn't look up but kept his face glued to his computer screen. Poor guy. Bo felt for him. Maybe he and Julia should invite him over sometime and grill steaks.

He waited for the elevator, glad for Kangas' belief that he was up to the task. But after the near misses in London and Eva and Griff tailing him, was he? The biggest operation of his life was about to begin. Would it be his last?

BO SOUGHT SOLACE in his windowless office behind a locked door, feeling the heavy burden Kangas had dumped on him. He had twenty-four hours to come up with a plan. If only he could talk to Judah.

Well, he couldn't, and going through channels had seriously backfired, so he turned to the next best thing. Bo logged onto his computer and sent Judah an e-mail—*Buddy, we need to talk pronto. Call on the private line from your house to mine*—certain Judah would understand and call Bo on a highly secured phone system between their HQ offices.

He leaned back in his chair, consumed with a burning desire to outwit Lili Tabriz and destroy her lethal plan. Bo penciled a few over-the-top ideas on a pad. But he immediately scratched a line through each; the risk of failure was too great.

He figured enough time had passed for Judah to respond. Wrong again. A quick flick to his Hotmail account showed nothing. Bo sidled down to the cafeteria, buying a tall coffee and a gooey doughnut. He was glad not to see Frank Deming. Bo was in no mood for any distractions. He ate the sugary snack at his desk and, by afternoon's end, he'd concocted a few options to mull over during the night.

Bo locked up, deciding to open his Hotmail account one last time. At last, he had a message from Judah.

Be by the phone nine a.m. your time. I have more news. I'll call your house.

Rats, he couldn't talk to Judah before morning. Well, he had no choice. Bo secured his office with a firm plan to hit Com Center early and swiped his badge through the secured exit, his mind abuzz with doubts. How would Judah react to Bo's plan for Mossad—and what did Judah have for him?

49

At nine sharp Tuesday morning, Bo hovered in the Com Center, waiting for Judah's call. He'd already been in his office a good two hours; he'd only been able to sleep the previous night for about an hour. Even Julia had poked him and said that he was too restless, sleepily suggesting he crash downstairs on the couch.

He'd brewed coffee instead, drinking the whole pot while he arranged the final touches for his Ops plan, like an artist finishing his masterpiece. When a Com Center technician turned to wave at Bo, he knew it was his turn up to bat.

"Sir, I have the Israeli intelligence service on this line asking for you. Take the call in Booth Number Two."

Bo opened the metal door to a small booth with acoustical tiled walls. But he was no music lover entering a listening booth picking out a favorite CD. He gripped the hand set, ready to get his plan moving.

"This is Bo Rider."

"Judah here. Do I call you Bo or Skip?"

The clear connection had a slight delay. Bo laughed.

"I'm Captain Skip Pierce only when traveling undercover, even within the U.S. Army."

"Good to talk with you, Bo. Medics here in Israel isolated me like I had the plague."

"We probably had the closest thing to the plague. Thanks to you, we know where it came from."

Judah's response came on the heels of a pause. "How did I help?"

The encryption delay hindered dialogue, so Bo launched into a lengthy account.

"You linked the phone number to Dr. Lili Tabriz. I've since learned she's an epidemiologist working on what's called 'Armageddon influenza.' Our labs analyzed the sample Mabel delivered to your dissidents in Tehran. It can kill *several hundred million* people once the virus becomes weaponized and delivered in the most rudimentary missiles or IEDs."

"Wow," Judah shot back.

"There's more. We're assuming she's making an anti-viral serum to inoculate those the Iranian regime will allow to live. It's Adolph Hitler all over again. Israel and the U.S. are most likely first on their target list."

"We all know what a monster Hitler turned out to be. Iran's germ warfare poses a grave danger to the civilized world. I'd better brief my superiors with no delay."

"An official report is ready for your superiors, but I've been tasked with creating an Ops plan to neutralize the threat. Judah, don't you think you're in the best position to execute it, as you have many feet on the ground there?"

Silence, and then, "We should prepare the Ops together, provided we both have deniability."

"I agree."

"I have other news I thought would be earthshaking, but I think you've—oh, what's the term?—upstaged me. You know I have friendly types in Lili's town. To be blunt, the nuclear scientist is willing to defect, but have you thought of being nice and offering him asylum?"

After the pause, Bo jumped in. "I discussed that with my boss. I need a proffer of his cooperation. My plan's due to my boss by five. Think about how we can join our two missions and call me again tomorrow, same time, with those details."

"Will do."

The connection ended. Bo remained in the booth, thinking over what Judah had just shared. He respected the Israeli intelligence agent, but did Bo dare trust Judah's Iranian sources, including the supposed defector?

AFTER A DAY of coordinating Operation Enigma with Judah and Kangas, Bo sat at his kitchen table enjoying homemade sausage pizza. Now that Bo had his sights on sinking Lili Tabriz, his appetite had returned.

"Pass the salad, Glenna."

He grabbed the bowl of crisp veggies before asking, "How was day camp?"

"Long. I'm really tired, Dad."

"She got a ribbon for being the most accurate archer," Julia said, praising her with a smile.

"I loved archery at camp, too," Bo said. He gave her a high-five. "And Gregg, how's the transformer you're building with Legos?"

"Sweet, Dad."

"Bo, here's the book I read by Dr. Hendrik Van Horn." Julia slid a hardback book near his elbow. "I was intrigued by his stories of Jesus' life in Israel. My ladies' group is planning a trip there next year."

Bo eyed the long-haired man on the cover holding a piece of wood. The book's title, *Jesus was a Jewish Carpenter*, might interest Judah Levitt, but not Bo. For one thing, he had no time to read.

"Sounds great, honey. How about putting another slice of pizza on my plate?"

"My friend, Janice, asked if I'd think about going on the trip."

"To Israel?" Bo was incredulous. Julia loved to travel, but to the Middle East?

She smiled and patted his hand. "We can talk about it later, maybe after you finish Dr. Van Horn's book. I couldn't believe how he made the people from the first century come to life. Maybe we should all go."

"Yeah, why not," he quipped. "This is the best pizza I've tasted in a long time."

The more Bo stared at the book cover, the more that man's face reminded him of Judah without a beard. His mind immediately replayed that crazy fiery finger writing in the sky from his dream in Kirkuk. Should he even tell Julia?

"Dad, I want more pizza," Gregg said.

Bo reached over and handed his son a slice. His family life was coming together as he wished his Ops plan would. Bo finished a second helping of salad and had just grabbed a third slice of pizza when the phone rang. Glenna's head collapsed on her arm.

"Let it ring. Bridget wants to practice clarinets but I'm beat."

"It's rude to ignore people. Tell her yourself." Julia grabbed the receiver and handed it to Glenna.

She announced, "Bridget, I don't want to practice … Oh, yeah sure. Hold on."

Glenna crossed her eyes, thrusting the phone to Bo.

"It's for you, Daddy," she croaked, running from the table.

Bo's mind grew suspicious and Julia cast him a funny look. He received few calls on his home phone.

"Hello?" he said tentatively.

"Rider, I hope you're not too comfortable at home."

"Ah … sir, we are eating dinner."

"Your vacation plan sounds good and I'm signing off on your leave."

That meant only one thing. He leapt from the chair, hurried into the downstairs bathroom, and slammed the door.

"You mean my overseas travel?"

"Yes, pack your bags. You leave at eight a.m. Follow the itinerary you gave me. I'll have one of our couriers bring your tickets to you tonight. That's all."

Before he could pose a single question, Kangas hung up. Of course he hadn't been on a secured line, so what could Bo have asked? Anyway, Operation Enigma was a go.

He leaned against the vanity, his mind hurtling back to the restroom stall in London when he'd searched Cyrus Tabriz's leather valise and discovered his passport. It all had revolved full circle, and here he was heading to Iraq again. Julia knocked softly on the door, interrupting his mental travels.

"Honey, are you all right?"

He pulled open the door. "Director Kangas is sending me out of town. Routine intelligence stuff and nothing to worry about."

"When do you leave?"

"Early morning, before the kids get up."

"You said it wasn't urgent." Julia's eyes were welling with tears.

"Now honey," Bo said as he drew her into his arms, "I promise it's not dangerous."

"Look what happened last time you went away. You got awfully sick."

"I'm all better and that won't happen again."

Her head flopped against his chest and he enclosed her safely in his arms. He could not predict the outcome of Operation Enigma, but this might be the last time he ever held her.

"Julia," he whispered as he stroked her hair. "Never forget how much I love you."

She pushed back, raising her face. A somber look in her eyes told him that she knew—he was about to risk everything.

"I love you, too," Julia whispered, her voice wavering. "You just go and collect what you need to collect, like when we used to do on Easter egg hunts with the kids. I'll be here waiting for you to come back home."

Her bravery meant a lot. Bo cupped his hand under her chin, lightly touching her lips with his.

"Sounds good. What's for dessert?"

Her smile quivered, but she grabbed his hand and together they strode into the kitchen. Gregg had arranged toy soldiers all across the kitchen counter.

"Who are you fighting, buddy?" Bo asked.

"Bad guys," Gregg said, a cowlick sticking up on his head.

He paraded a tiny plastic soldier armed with a rifle, aiming it at Bo, and shouted, "Pow, pow."

"Hey, I'm not the enemy." Bo ruffled Gregg's hair. "And don't ever point your gun at a person unless you are fighting for our country. How about ice cream?"

"Okay, Daddy."

"Then go find your sister."

Gregg dashed upstairs, gripping his toy soldier. Glenna came down. She still looked embarrassed over the way she'd handled the phone call from Bo's boss. He put an arm around her thin shoulders. "Not to worry. My boss is one cool guy."

"Want to come to my dance recital? It's tomorrow at three."

"Ah, we'll see. How many scoops do you want?"

Julia displayed the fixings and Bo scooped heaping bowls of chocolate chip ice cream, letting the kids drizzle on their own hot fudge. He enjoyed the sundaes, aware the lighthearted banter with his family was about to end.

A courier arrived and Bo signed for his packet out on the front porch, saying nothing to his kids. Then he climbed the stairs to pack. Julia joined him upstairs in time for him to kiss the children goodnight. Glenna was reading a mystery story about a spooky house. Julia went to turn out Gregg's light.

"I have to miss your dance. That was why my boss called. I'm flying on an airplane, but will be back before you finish that story," Bo said. As he tapped her book, he believed he would return home.

She shut her book, her eyes searching his. "Daddy, it's more fun when you're home. Mom gets sad alone. Hurry, okay?"

"For sure."

He reached down to hug her, hiding the tears stinging his eyes. After adjusting her lamp shades, he snapped off the light and hurried into the master bedroom, glad Julia wasn't in it. He pulled a manila envelope from the top drawer of his dresser; it contained his will and other papers. After what Glenna had just told him about Julia, he didn't want to keep the legal stuff around the house.

A sudden idea pulsed in his mind. He whipped the cell phone off his dresser and called Griff.

"Glad you answered, buddy. It's Bo. Do me a favor?"

"Depends. Will I have to schmooze State Department types?"

"Nothing like that," Bo forced a laugh. "It's personal."

"You name it, I'll do it."

Bo quickly explained about his will and other insurance papers. "I'm leaving, and I don't know when I'll be back. There's no one else I feel comfortable leaving these papers with. Mind meeting me on the way to the airport?"

Ever the gentleman, Griff agreed. They arranged to connect at a bakery that opened at the crack of dawn and was a few blocks from where Bo could hop on the freeway for Dulles.

"I'm happy to check on things while you're away, too."

"Great. I'll give Julia your cell number. I feel her panic, though she tries not to show it."

"You probably won't say, but this sounds pretty serious."

"You could say freedom is at stake—but it's nothing I can't handle."

"Stay safe out there. When Dawn went to Sudan, I never dreamed what she'd be up against."

Bo pulled the cell phone away from his ear, hearing Julia's light tread coming down the hall. "I gotta go. See you about six."

He stowed the envelope and legal documents in the front pocket of his suitcase and headed downstairs to lock up, passing Julia in the hall.

"I'll be right back up, honey. I'm making sure everything is locked up tight so we get a peaceful night's sleep."

50

It was Bo Rider who arrived on a commercial flight into Baghdad, but Captain Skip Pierce, wearing fatigues, who boarded the Air Force transport headed for Kirkuk. The heavy plane lumbered into the air, streaking over dry terrain mottled brown. Bo mulled over Kangas' final instructions.

"Let your Mossad agent take all risks. This is to appear in every respect like their Op. Rider, do not step foot in Iran. The last thing I need is for Iran to capture one of my agents. But do whatever's necessary to stop the Armageddon flu threat."

Bo had his orders, but they didn't sit easy. Though he carried in his mind the secret details to implement Operation Enigma, he was on his own and could expect no support if things went awry. He shifted in his seat as Julia's tearful good-bye paraded before his eyes. How long could he keep plunging into risky operations before he'd fail to return home?

He and Judah Levitt hadn't spoken of family. Did the diehard Mossad agent share the same concerns? Bo looked around at the military crew, wanting to believe that, in a few short days, he'd be flying with them back to Baghdad.

The transport landed before Bo was ready. He steeled himself for the unexpected and snatched his suitcase. The thing was crammed with ordinance that he'd procured from the military in Baghdad and directions for Judah on how they could be used. A speeding, gum-chewing Army private drove him in an armored humvee to the hotel, tires squealing.

"Happy landings, Captain. I'm heading home in the morning."

"Where's that, soldier?" Bo asked.

"Fremont, Michigan. Ever hear of it?"

"Can't say I have."

"We're known for baby food. My grandpa has a farm with a swimming hole, and I'm can't wait to kick back in the cool water."

"I wish you luck."

Bo hefted his bags up the steps, glad that at least someone was getting the chance to return to the States. He walked into the hotel and noticed the interior was a bit run-down. Because most military officers camped out here while in transit, Bo settled in without much complaint.

He tried to rest, but he couldn't. The idea of stumbling onto an IED kept him awake. Bo swung his feet to the floor, changed into khakis and a white cotton shirt, and hired a taxi to drive him to Daniel's tomb. Traffic seemed as congested as if he'd been circling the beltway back home. At the Citadel, he spent thirty minutes in the idling cab before even glimpsing another person.

Suddenly, an Iraqi man garbed in a traditional, flowing robe perched on the stone wall surrounding the Citadel. Bo squinted in the fading light. The man's facial features resembled Judah, but was it a trick?

He paid the driver, but to be safe, he told him to wait. Bo strode past the robed-man and Judah flashed a knowing smile. Bo waved off his taxi and entered Daniel's tomb where he immediately began perusing the ancient stone walls.

"How convenient. No one else is here."

Bo whirled and faced Judah. The Mossad agent looked every bit an Iraqi in his dark beard and flowing robe.

"I dread meeting you here again," Bo quipped. "When I think of this place, it reminds me of wrapping my arms around a toilet."

"Me too, but Jehovah chose to spare my life," Judah replied with a shake of his head. "I wish I knew why. My wife and child are already dead."

Bo flinched. That gave him some insight into why Judah had taken up camp in Iraq. On closer inspection, Judah's face appeared haggard. Bo clasped the agent's hand.

"Sorry. I didn't know."

"Of course not. That story is for another time. The tomb is a convenient place to meet since many international people visit here."

Bo led the way to an unpainted bench on the mostly-deserted grounds of the tomb. "We've nuances to discuss—far too many for encrypted e-mails."

Judah edged toward Bo, showing him an Arabic pamphlet about the tomb as if they were discussing the contents but speaking in low tones.

"After a briefing from my sources in the Iranian underground, I have adjusted the plan. My superiors approve. Before I describe the changes, I will brief you on what I learned based on the phone number you gave me."

"It was a stroke of luck Liberty even phoned Wally."

"My friend, it is more than a stroke of luck. Jehovah himself has intervened to protect my country. Let me tell you why. Some you know."

"Yes, I know all about Lili Tabriz. Did you know she is an American married to Cyrus Tabriz, director of the Institute for Scientific Advances?"

"Of course, Mir's people—I mean, my source's people—followed a slave lady working in the Tabriz home. They met Mabel in the market and she was most cooperative after hearing promises of freedom. You know about the vial she smuggled to my underground contacts?"

"My NIH analyzed the contents and the frightening result is *one* reason I'm here. Judah, is Mir your man in the underground? His name is safe with me. I won't document his identity."

Judah smiled sheepishly. "Mir leads the underground opposition to the Iranian regime. He is a vital spark, commanding hundreds of courageous volunteers who seek liberty for their own lives. So you see it is no accident the woman named Liberty provided us with the key clue."

"I suppose so, but what else have you discovered about Dr. Tabriz?" Bo wasn't as ready to give religious significance to coincidence.

"They learned from Mabel that Lili Tabriz works night and day in a laboratory behind the kitchen. They live in a compound, complete with chickens and caged mice for her experiments. She has inoculated the slaves in her home, and she injects other Sudanese slaves who toil elsewhere. Some of those have died. Her own young son died recently. Mabel believes his death resulted from a bad injection."

"Unfortunate for the boy, but what a life he would have had. She is a hateful woman. The boy deserved better."

"Mir's people have followed Lili Tabriz on several occasions to a secure military installation. Of course, they cannot go inside."

"And their conclusions?"

"Based on the analysis of the vial's content, it seems her plan is to wipe out all of Israel, while protecting her whole country. That is why the highest levels at the Institute give consent to neutralize her threat."

Bo shuddered at the thought. "What makes you think the regime will stop with Israel? They can wipe out everyone, except any inoculated Iranians."

Just then, three men wearing robes sauntered in, all speaking in Arabic. Judah instantly stood.

"So you see how important Daniel was to the Babylonian empire. King Nebuchadnezzar elevated him to a high position after the prophet interpreted his dreams. Come outside and I will share more with you."

The two agents quietly left the Citadel, with Bo checking over his shoulder to see if any of the robed men followed. They didn't, so he figured they were probably tourists. Bo told Judah where he was staying.

Judah waved down a taxi, whispering, "My friend, take this cab to your hotel. I will catch another taxi and come to your room shortly."

They reviewed Operation Enigma for more than an hour in Bo's hotel room. Bo was astonished by how deeply the Iranian opposition was connected to Mossad. The group was able to move Judah around within the country right under the nose of the Iranian Revolutionary Guard.

"I envy your close relationship with the democracy movement in Iran. We Americans are not as welcome."

"To the Iranian regime, both our countries are enemies. But to the dissidents," Judah said, pursing his lips, "we help their cause. The Revolutionary Guard's invasion of the U.S. Embassy was a dark period for your country."

"I wasn't with the Agency then, of course, but I'll never forget how my Dad cheered when the Iranian's released the U.S. hostages on January 20, 1981, the day of Ronald Reagan's inauguration. They greatly feared the newly elected president."

"We all miss Reagan—a strong supporter of my country." Judah's smile flashed and then vanished. Had Bo really seen it?

"Yeah. These days, sometimes I feel like I'm fighting alone," Bo replied.

Judah folded his hands, his penetrating gaze capturing Bo's attention. "The Institute has authorized me to work directly with you. I am more at ease working with the one the CIA trusts to teach wet operations to my class from Mossad than simply relying on Iranian dissidents for support."

"Because I taught your group about conducting enemy assassinations, you want me with you on this gig? Does that mean you intend to eliminate Dr. Lili Tabriz?"

Judah unfolded his hands, spreading them wide. "How else can I prevent her from starting a new batch of H5N1 and H1N1? I do not *intend* to assassinate her, but I will not guarantee she will survive."

Action against a U.S. citizen? Even though Lili Tabriz claimed she had denounced her citizenship, Bo and others in the CIA still considered her a citizen.

"I need to think this over. There's some bottled water on the window sill and my wife tucked some nut bars in my suitcase. I don't mind one myself."

They broke open the water and the bars as Bo consulted his conscience. Kangas had told him to support Mossad in anyway possible, as long as there was plausible deniability. Bo weighed Kangas's precise words: "Don't go into Iran." But then in the next breath he'd added, "Do what's necessary to eliminate the flu threat."

Everything Bo had heard from Judah convinced him that Mossad would "neutralize" the threat from Tabriz, but the Institute's plan didn't include freeing Mabel or Liberty. Obviously, Mossad considered them expendable.

Bo made up his mind. "My orders are to support you, but also to ensure no U.S. citizen gets arrested in Iran. I'm uncertain how I can help."

Judah started rummaging through a canvas bag. "I thought that might be a problem, so I will guarantee no U.S. citizen is caught in Iran."

The deadly serious Israeli agent held up a packet of theatrical black hair dye and an Iranian passport, lacking a photo. "The same group that smuggles me in and out of Iran will get us both in and back out again. I already have an Iranian passport."

"But if we're stopped, I can't utter a single word of Farsi."

Judah winked. "I know a little, enough that I've done this several times. We go by truck. All trucks, except petroleum tankers, are unloaded at the border. That is how I travel."

"You pose as a truck driver?"

"No. The freedom fighters have truck drivers with special tankers. The front compartment has never contained any petro. It is used solely for smuggling. It's lined with insulation and has air vents. I drop inside from a porthole at the top."

"Whew, sounds claustrophobic."

"It is a long and stifling ride," Judah admitted. "You can travel with me and actually lose weight. It's like twenty hours in a sauna."

Bo smirked "Sounds like just another day at the office. When do we go?"

"You can't look so American when we arrive in Tehran." Judah shook the hair dye and smiled. "Should we make you look more like an Iranian?"

"Fine, but there is one more glitch."

When Bo told Judah what he had in mind, Judah didn't even flinch. He simply answered, "No problem."

51

As he watched the sun hovering at the western horizon, Bo couldn't believe he'd survived sneaking into Iran. He and Judah had ridden forever in that cylindrical compartment of the gasoline truck with bottled water, power bars, and several portable urinals.

Bo stretched his cramped legs in the rear seat of an SUV as they rolled silently along the streets of Tehran, driven by Mir. The Iranian dissident allowed no music on the radio and absolutely no conversation. Bo studied Mir's profile as the leader of brave intellectuals—including many educated abroad—eased around a corner.

Twilight gave Bo sufficient light to glimpse a passing neighborhood, which looked similar to an upscale American city with stucco-walled yards, although his view was somewhat dimmed by the SUV's heavily tinted windows. Bo slid over on the seat to examine his face in the rearview mirror.

The man reflecting back startled him. Judah had dyed Bo's hair and eyebrows jet-black and had taken him to a barber. When finished, Bo's former brown curls sprinkled the floor and his hair was parted and combed to make him look like an Iranian. Bo's fake Iranian passport, the work of a master forger, rested in his pocket. An Israeli-issued Beretta model seventy pistol was stuffed in his waistband. He sure hoped he wouldn't have to use either.

Judah had agreed with Bo that neither would be captured alive—a corpse couldn't be pressured to admit its citizenship—and both would do whatever was necessary to fight their way back to Kirkuk. Before going to bed the night before he left home, Bo had written a letter to his wife and children. He reflected on what he'd said:

My dear family: Hopefully you will never see this letter. If you do, it means I was killed in Iran and FBI agent Griff Topping has met with you. I love each of you more than I can explain. I go on this dangerous assignment to keep Iran from doing something terrible to you, to Americans and other innocent people around the world. I hope each of you finds happiness in life. I won't be in a position to miss you and I trust you will get over the pain of missing me. All my love, Bo and Dad.

He'd sealed his letter along with his will, giving the manila envelope to Griff. Bo trusted that, if he were killed in the Middle East, Griff would eventually hear of it and would deliver the envelope to

Julia. But for now, he shook off those gloomy thoughts. As a spy in-side of Iran, he had to be strong in body and mind.

The night wore on, heavy silence and blackness enveloping Bo as they passed along the darkened streets. By two o'clock in the morn-ing, he'd yet to speak to a soul. Judah knew enough Farsi to converse with the dissidents, but so far he had avoided talking, too.

Bo leaned close to Judah, whispering directly in his ear: "Mir waits nearby until we get Mabel and Liberty over the wall and into the SUV, right?"

"Yes," Judah hissed. "Then he withdraws until he returns for us."

Operation Enigma had several levels. Any number of details could blow up in their faces. He tried to breathe easy. Bo's elbow pressed reassuringly against the Beretta tucked under his black silk shirt, which was hanging over his black slacks, but he couldn't remember ever being so detached from U.S. support.

Between his feet nestled a backpack stuffed with explosives, duct tape, and other supplies. As blue light streaked across the car's in-terior, his heart leapt. Flashes of pulsating blue light followed. Mir's eyes locked onto the rearview mirror. He spoke quickly in Farsi. Ju-dah tapped Bo's leg.

"Police are behind us. Do not look back."

Bo slowly reached down, resting his hand on the zipper of the backpack. Could it end so quickly, before they even arrived at the Tabriz home? He would not be taken alive!

Judah tersely ordered Mir down a side street. As he turned, the flashing lights disappeared as the police vehicle continued down the street they'd been on.

"That was too close," Judah muttered.

He plunked the backpack, which he'd lifted to his lap, back down on the floor. Minutes later, the Mercedes SUV pulled over, stopping across the street from an intersecting alley.

"This is it," Judah said. "He will park here at the end of the alley and wait for us to reappear."

Bo and Judah emerged from the SUV, their backpacks hanging from their shoulders. The duo stepped into the alley, blending into the black night. When they reached the fourth house, they set their packs on the ground. Judah boosted Bo to the top of the wall and then handed him the two packs. Bo pulled Judah's arms and he scaled the wall with no trouble, both agents dropping silently into the rear yard. Everything was just as Mabel had reported when she'd spoken to the dissidents.

Bo and Judah crouched, moving as one toward the open door of the small building attached to the main house. They stepped inside the hut, shining their light, which fell upon two dark shapes—two Africans asleep on the floor.

Following their Ops plan, they each approached a slave. Bo bent over, tapping the shoulder of the one he figured was Liberty. Knowing she'd learned English at the refugee camp, he told her, "Liberty, Wally sent me to save you."

She turned and with her fists, struck Bo in the head. He stumbled backward, bumping into Judah, who was grappling with Mabel. Suddenly, a powerful hand squeezed Bo's throat and shoved him against a cement wall. In the fog of battle, he realized he wasn't fighting Liberty.

This was a strong man, one determined to kill him. Bo clasped his hands at his waist, thrusting them straight up above his head, the resulting wedge forcing the hands from his throat. Bo slugged the guy in the head, which sent him hurtling through the dark room. He seized his attacker from behind, locking his neck in a tight hold.

The moment he had the advantage, Bo got knocked down by Judah and the other man tussling. Bo managed to keep a grip until his assailant went limp and then Bo flipped around. Judah was sprawled flat on his back, with the other African bending over him.

Mustering his remaining strength, Bo drove his fist into the man's head. As he collapsed to the floor, Judah scurried to his feet.

"He is not Mabel, but I do not see anyone else."

Bo removed a roll of duct tape from his pack and began wrapping his assailant's arms behind his back.

"Have we been ambushed?"

By now, Judah was wrapping the feet and legs of his quarry, a man who was obviously Sudanese. "Wrap their mouths and arms. I understand most residents in this area own Sudanese slaves."

Bo assessed their situation. It was fortunate the slaves, now wrapped in tape, had not screamed out; the silent struggle apparently had failed to awaken anyone else in the house.

"We can't leave these men here and risk they'll alert their masters."

Judah agreed. "We take them back over the wall."

Bo and Judah carried the thin African men to the wall, their light weight making it easier for Bo and Judah to push and pull them to the other side. Minutes later, Judah shined his flashlight down the alley toward the SUV.

It didn't take long for the bound men to be placed like rolled rugs into the rear of the Mercedes. Judah briefed Mir, who then resumed his post on the side street.

Judah joined Bo at the base of the wall. "Mir believes we climbed into the wrong yard. Mabel and Liberty's hut is not attached to the Tabriz house. Chickens live outside. He said to try the next house on the left."

"We've lost valuable time. If we wake those birds ..." Bo's words fell away as he thrust the pack over his shoulder.

After Bo and Judah had hoisted themselves over the neighboring wall, they scooted through the rear yard. Bo spied some hutches containing chickens beneath a pitched roof, against the rear of the stucco house.

He flicked his light about the yard and in a flash spotted a cement-walled room with an open door. They entered the dark room. Bo saw two dark, skinny shapes huddled on the ground, one in the dirt, one on a rug. A bucket was propped in the corner.

This time Bo proceeded more cautiously. He aimed his light on one head, confirming young feminine features, and then whispered, "Liberty, I was sent by Wally. You are going to America."

The girl sat up quickly, blinking in his light.

"Tell Mabel. We take you both. Be quiet, but hurry. Are people in the house?"

Liberty nodded, her eyes round and huge. "One man and one woman. The boy died of sickness."

Pleased at Liberty's command of English, he asked, "Does the Tabriz woman work inside the house?"

She bobbed her head again as she struggled to her feet. Bo heard Judah whispering to Mabel, but couldn't tell if he was making any headway.

"Liberty, will you show me her lab?"

She recoiled, fear paralyzing her face. She shook her head.

"Do you know where the lab is?"

This time Liberty just stared, as if deathly afraid.

Bo whispered, "If you show me, I will be at your side, protecting you from Dr. Tabriz. Do you believe me?"

Suddenly, Mabel began talking to Liberty in a language Bo didn't understand. Both women were animated, looking very frightened.

Finally Liberty faced Bo. "I will show you."

"Tell Mabel to wait outside near the back wall. The three of us will join her soon."

The ladies whispered to each other. Mabel lifted the rug and began walking to the far wall. Bo and Judah carried their packs, following Liberty into the rear of the Tabriz house. Liberty opened a door so slowly, as if whatever was in there would attack her. Bo instantly recognized the room as Lili Tabriz' lab.

While Judah kept watch in the doorway leading to the living quarters, Bo flashed his light around—the room was outfitted as completely as any university laboratory, only this place smacked of death. He saw safes, scales, computers, and refrigerators. Bo's eyes landed on a machine and his mind rushed back to London, where he'd picked up a brochure on the PCR technique for analyzing disease.

This must be the cycling machine where Lili Tabriz tinkered with her deadly experiments. Before he could inform Judah, Liberty moved through the darkness like a vapor, opening a smaller compartment in the refrigerator. She showed him some vials and then pointing at her arm, made a motion like an injection. Bo grabbed three glass tubes, stuffing them into an empty slot of his pack.

Liberty opened still another refrigerator, revealing more vials. This time she placed her hands under her armpits, flapping her arms like a chicken. Again using her hand like a syringe, she pulled back her thumb as if extracting something from a chicken. Dr. Tabriz must have used the chickens as hosts for her freakish experiments. Bo swiped three of these vials, stashing them in a different pocket.

Without warning, Judah flashed his light once at Bo and Liberty. All three froze. Bo heard footsteps—someone was walking through the house. Steps came closer and then stopped. Bo stood motionless. He heard sounds of water running in the living quarters. He barely breathed.

If Lili Tabriz dared enter the laboratory, there was no telling what Judah would do to her. The footsteps came closer, only to grow quiet. Bo exhaled, motioning Liberty toward the door. Someone must have returned to the bedroom from the bathroom.

Bo removed a flash drive from his pack and inserted it into Lili Tabriz' computer. In what seemed like forever, he downloaded files from her hard drive. As he pulled the drive from the USB port, a noise behind him made him jump. He turned his flashlight toward the noise. A mouse scratched in its cage.

He scrambled over to Judah, telling Liberty, "Go outside and wait by Mabel. We'll be along soon."

She glided out on bare feet saying nothing.

"Let's do our thing and split," Bo growled.

He reached into his backpack, digging out a RDX explosive grenade, which he stuck beneath that PCR cycling machine. He placed another grenade in a refrigerator at the far end of the lab.

Judah seized an explosive device from his pack. "Okay, we arm these and get out of here."

As Judah stalked out of the lab and toward the residence, Bo pulled the pin on the delayed fuse of the grenade in the refrigerator. Like a bullet, he shot to the PCR machine, yanking up the ring on that grenade.

Both agents scrammed toward the rear door of the house, closing it quietly behind them. They sped to the wall, where Bo boosted Judah to the top. Using his flashlight, Judah signaled Mir at the street at the end of alley.

Next, Bo cupped his hands to form a stirrup, first boosting a slender Liberty and then the older—but equally light—Mabel to the top of the wall. Judah leaned down, fetching Bo up and over the wall. The SUV drove up, its headlights still off. Judah and Bo jumped down from the wall; a moment later, they caught Liberty and Mabel safely.

Judah lifted the vehicle's rear hatch, motioning Liberty inside, but she jumped back at the sight of the two African men wrapped in duct tape.

"Liberty, it is all right. Get in beside them and tell the men they will be released and can go back home."

She did. The men nodded and seemed to relax. Mabel crawled in. Judah shut the hatch quietly, and then Bo and he dove into the back seat with their much lighter backpacks. The SUV slipped down the alley and onto an adjacent street. The delayed fuses gave them enough time to leave the area before the explosions would rip through the Tabriz home.

Bo took a cell phone from his pack and toggled down to Lili Tabriz' cell phone number. It rang three times before a woman answered in a sleepy voice.

"Dr. Tabriz, this is the American spy you met in London. I've sent an American drone to your house. You have thirty seconds to get out. Don't forget to take your husband's valise with you."

Bo hit the end button and smiled at Judah, although in the dark, he probably couldn't see his smile. It wasn't payback that exhilarated Bo; it was justice, pure and simple. Lili Tabriz sought the death of millions. If her death saved all those people, then so be it.

Mir eased onto the main highway. For all of five minutes, their ride was uneventful. Bo began to sweat it: had the grenades even activated? Then suddenly a Tehran police car swerved around the corner, driving straight at the Mercedes SUV, its blue lights whirling and sirens blaring. Bo gulped. They had four undocumented Dinkas back there.

The police car veered in front of them, blocking the intersection. An officer jumped out of the car, looking directly at Mir. Holding one palm toward them, he motioned with the other hand, summoning another speeding police car, which careened into the intersection from the right.

Bo screamed, "Go! Go! Try to out run them."

He grasped his Beretta. He wouldn't be caught in Tehran!

Judah was shaking his head, yelling in Farsi. The speeding car from the right passed between the SUV and the officer. Behind it barreled two fire engines with lights blazing and sirens screaming, whizzing by in the direction of the Tabriz home.

"My friend," Judah said as he jammed an elbow into Bo's side, "it seems our plan worked. Jehovah has protected me once again."

Bo breathed easier. The grenades must have detonated. The question was: had Lili or Cyrus Tabriz gotten out alive?

52

Bo and Judah settled Liberty, Mabel, and the two Dinka men into a well-lit warehouse, where the dissidents would provide food and water. Bo told Liberty, "We will return and take you from Tehran to Sudan if you want. After the men agree not to make trouble, the tape will be removed from their mouths."

Liberty translated for the men, who seemed happy at the idea of returning to Sudan.

All was ready for Phase Two of Operation Enigma—only this part hadn't been approved by Kangas or Mossad. The ad hoc operation was a scheme created by Bo and Judah, who now climbed into the rear seat of the SUV, leaving Mir behind the wheel. The doors to the warehouse swung open and they drove into the darkness. Bo and Judah stayed quiet in their thoughts.

It wasn't until after he met Judah in Kirkuk that Bo had learned the extent of Mir's relationship with Kia Aliabad, the preeminent nuclear physicist for Iran's Ministry of Energy. Even now, Bo considered Kangas' worry—that Kia's claimed defection wasn't real—despite what he had claimed to the dissidents.

Kia might be the bait the Revolutionary Guard was using to entice Israeli or American intelligence officers into Iran. Once Bo and Judah made contact with Kia, the Guard might very well surround them, showcasing to the whole world that they were spies from evil empires.

Bo turned to Judah. "It's best we swoop on Kia like an eagle, giving him no chance to set us up. If he comes peacefully and spills what he knows of Iran's nuclear ambitions, we'll take him with us back to Iraq."

Judah exhaled loudly. "Right. And if he rejects your offer of asylum, then this day he breathes his last."

Bo did not sanction taking the man's life. Mossad had their ways, and he would have no part in it. From then on, they rode in silence through the mostly empty and dark streets of Iran. Bo realized that tonight he had worked with a new partner and, between them, they'd managed one successful joint operation—rescuing Liberty.

In minutes, they would commence a plan they'd cobbled together on a paper placemat. They both carried backpacks of supplies; however, this time there was no insider like Liberty to let them into the target house. Kia had been educated in Tehran and London before working his way through the Natanz nuclear facility to his senior position at Iran's Ministry of Energy in Tehran. Bo knew it would be a major blow against Iran's nuclear ambitions to flip this scientist.

Fortunately, the nuclear physicist was divorced and lived alone, so there'd be no collateral damage if he failed to cooperate. Surveillance by dissidents of his home had revealed that he used no security guards or equipment.

Mir turned down a different alley, dimming the lights. Bo, with Judah at his side, jumped out, scaled a six-foot wall, and crossed the rear courtyard. Bo hardly breathed, fearing they might encounter a barking dog or other obstacle. But they reached Kia's residence in total quiet.

"Sure this is the right place?" Bo whispered.

Judah nodded, shining his penlight on the door. Two locks to break. Bo removed a leather pouch from his pack and took out a slender lock pick and a tiny, L-shaped, metal pry bar. He inserted this bar at the bottom of the first lock and inserted the pick. Bo had spent hours of his spare time practicing on every imaginable lock.

Tonight, within sixty seconds, it paid off. The tumblers moved against the slightest of pressure and he finally felt the tool turn. The dead bolt slid open.

Bo grinned at Judah, flashing a thumbs-up; however, the second lock proved more difficult. Sweat began pooling under his arms. If the sun rose before they were even inside, both he and Judah would be toast. Bo stroked the tumblers—first slowly and then quickly—raking his pick across them with no success.

Sweat dripped in eyes and he wiped it off on his shirt sleeve. Again, ever so slowly, he gently tapped each tumbler, feeling the barrel respond. Yet one tumbler refused to give. Judah tapped his shoulder.

"Let me try," he whispered.

Judah had his own set of tools. He inserted his pick, working ever so quietly. Seconds ticked by without results. Judah wiggled his pick and Bo dried his forehead, hoping like crazy that Judah could get them in. If not, Operation Enigma might end to the sounds of crashing wood and screams.

Seconds passed. Bo heard the faintest click. Judah silently turned the handle and pushed the door open, but left it slightly ajar as he returned the picks to his pocket. Bo tiptoed behind Judah into the pitch-dark house in total silence, their pen lights checking their path periodically.

The sparsely furnished house smelled musty, lacking a woman's touch. They checked one small room that appeared to be an office. No bed and no one inside. They crept to the other end of the hallway and entered a doorway—there, on a twin bed, lay Kia Aliabad ... if they were in the right house.

Judah strode to one side of the bed and Bo to the opposite side, ready to grab Kia. Judah shone his flashlight in the man's face. Bo raised his hand to cover Kia's mouth, if necessary. Judah said the name "Kia" in Farsi.

The man's eyes popped open. He looked frightened and sat up, but Judah and Bo forced him back down. Kia did speak English, having studied in London.

"Mir says you want to leave Tehran. My friend next to you is an American. We are here to take you to the U.S."

As Kia's eyes flashed from Judah to Bo, Judah quickly aimed his light on Bo's face. Bo reached toward Kia with a strip of duct tape.

"To be safe, I am placing this tape over your mouth."

Bo did so gingerly and Kia didn't struggle or resist. Maybe he was legit and really did mean to defect. Judah helped Kia into a sitting position and then swung his feet over the side of his bed.

"We're taking you away, so gather clothes and whatever else you need," Bo said. "But we do not have much time."

He led the slightly built Iranian to the bathroom, certain Kia would have no trouble squeezing into the tanker truck. After Kia refreshed himself, Bo and Judah helped him dress and collect his passport and wallet. Bo was astounded by his willing compliance. He seemed to have no interest in escaping—unless it was a ruse and he'd pushed some hidden alarm in the bathroom.

Bo would take no risks, although he hadn't heard an alarm go off when they'd opened the door to the house.

"Kia, we're binding your hands behind you and when we reach the car, your feet. Is there anything else you need?"

The Iranian pointed down the hall. Judah followed as Bo took Kia to his office, where the defector nodded toward a laptop computer and then indicated a drawer in his desk. Bo started thumbing through hanging files. Suddenly Kia started mumbling and pointing.

"He might want the address book," Judah suggested. "Be quick about it."

Bo snatched some kind of address list and Kia bobbed his head in approval. Bo shoved the little book and Kia's computer into his backpack, hissing, "Let's go."

Near the rear wall of the courtyard, Kia allowed Bo to wrap his feet with duct tape. This was going too well. Bo believed that any second, a Revolutionary Guard would respond. With his eyes searching and ears straining to hear, Bo boosted Judah to the top of the wall. Judah flashed his light toward Mir at the end of the alley and then grasped Kia's hands. Bo heaved another bound man to the top of a wall. Judah extended a hand, and Bo climbed the wall. But from the top, he saw no SUV.

"Where's our ride?" he snarled.

Judah flashed his light again at the street, but the SUV was gone. Hair on Bo's neck prickled. Had Mir been discovered and arrested? Bo dropped to the alley, his eyes probing for some clue.

His ears heard it first—the quiet approach of the SUV coming from the opposite direction. Total relief! Bo caught Kia as Judah lowered him down. Judah descended, and then they half-rolled Kia into the back seat of the SUV, where Mir started encouraging him in Farsi.

Bo scooted in next to Kia, unable to discern his mumblings. He leaned over, stressing, "Once Mir assures us that you truly intend to defect, we'll remove the tape. Not before."

Bo's nerves were on fire all the way to the warehouse. What would Kangas say if he saw him stealing an Iranian physicist out of Iran? He might find out, but only if they made it out—and he knew anything could still go wrong.

As they pulled into the warehouse, Bo relented and allowed his mind to rejoice. Phase Two of Operation Enigma was nearly complete. If Kia Aliabad had intended to deliver them to the Revolutionary Guard, he'd failed.

Of course, they still had to make it out of Iran unscathed.

53

Judah and his team of Iranian dissidents stuffed Liberty, Mabel, the two Dinka men, Kia Aliabad, and Bo into the crowded tanker compartment, before Judah wiggled in. The drive across Iran and through the Zagros mountains into Iraq turned out to be stifling and long.

Bo arrived back in Kirkuk at midnight. The tanker pulled into a warehouse and the hatch flew open. Bo climbed out, gasping for fresh air, his arms and legs severely cramping. As he stood, he ignored shooting pains to help pull out their five guests. At last, Judah emerged through the port, his face smeared with grease.

Anbar, the rug merchant who was Judah's Iraqi friend, provided them with dates, almonds, and water, plus the clothing Bo and Judah had left behind before sneaking into Iran. Anbar then handed over something even more precious to Bo—his cell phone. He'd had to relinquish it so he couldn't be traced by Iranian security forces.

Bo immediately placed a call to his Defense Intelligence Agency (DIA) contact in Baghdad. Within the hour, an Air Force transport would zoom to Kirkuk and fly all seven of them to Baghdad—quite a motley crew. Bo caught a nap and, although he'd managed a shower, the earthy smells of the petro tanker clung to his nostrils.

It wasn't until they all were safely in the rear of a U.S. transport streaking toward Baghdad that Liberty opened up to Bo, telling of the horrors of connecting cell phones to bombs for Lady Tabriz.

"Thank you for rescuing us. You are part of a miracle."

He was? Bo stretched out his legs, knowing nothing of miracles. He felt compassion for these women and men who'd been ripped from their homes to further the greed of others. It all seemed so unfair.

"Liberty, you are welcome. I am sorry you suffered under the hands of a former American. She can't hurt you anymore." Bo kept mum about the fate of Cyrus and Lili Tabriz, who had both perished in the explosion. Liberty had endured enough heartache.

"The Dinka men want to find their family members in Southern Sudan," she said.

"What about you and Mabel? Have you both decided to head for America?"

The two women whispered with their heads close together until Liberty finally announced, "She and I are family. We go as one."

"That works—but I have arrangements to make first, so I need to know where you're going."

"We will tell you later," Liberty answered, her dark eyes somber.

Touchdown in Baghdad happened smoothly. Bo took Judah aside, offering a hand. "We made it. I feel like I've been to the lion's den with you and Daniel," he said.

"My friend, you are one tenacious partner. I believe our circuitous paths will cross again."

Neither agent felt the need to say more. Bo rushed away to find the United Nation's attaché assigned to the base. The attaché, a grizzled diplomat from the seventies, argued with Bo for a good hour, not caving until Bo bluffed that he'd elevate the crisis to his boss, the Secretary of State.

Then the attaché raised both hands. "No need. I will return the men to Juba, in Southern Sudan. The women are your responsibility. But how four Dinkas managed to sneak from Tehran into Iraq is beyond me."

Bo shrugged, hating to admit that either he or Judah had been involved.

The greatest challenge remained. Bo found Liberty at the end of a long table in the commander's side office, dressed in camouflage pants and shirt. She rested her head on her folded arms. Bo rapped lightly on the table.

"Liberty, are you sleeping?"

"No," she said, lifting her head and blinking her eyes.

"I will help reunite you with Wally, but first I must know. Is that what you want? If I send you to the States, you can never return to Sudan, because you will be a refugee."

"Mister Pierce," Liberty said, her eyes glistening, "I must think of Mabel."

"Will you allow me to look into your going to America? It will take time."

"Yes, but I am not promising to go."

BO CHECKED HIS WATCH. Chances were good that federal agent Eva Montanna would be in her office, so he left Liberty, Mabel, and Kia Aliabad under guard at Intel HQ and hiked to the Com Center to find a secure phone line.

Their past dealings had taught him the ICE agent was just as hard-nosed as any guy he'd met in the CIA or the military, or any cop. As an enforcer of immigration laws, she was the go-to person for him to call. Besides, Eva was one of a select few in Washington, D.C. who knew he worked for the CIA.

He held his cell phone in one hand to retrieve her office number from his contact list, but he called her on the secure line. After four rings, Bo was ready to leave a voice mail message when he heard, "Sorry I got delayed. I've just got in. Traffic was a mess."

Bo had never heard such a voice mail announcement. "Hey Eva, it's Bo Rider and I'm calling—"

"I'm sorry," she chuckled. "Now we're even—I thought you were my Miami phone conference on the line. Can I buzz you later?"

"I'm calling from Kirkuk, Iraq."

"No kidding! You sure get around. Okay, what do you need?"

Bo closed his cell phone, organizing his thoughts. "Did you know that Liberty, Wally's bride-to-be, was kidnapped in Southern Sudan?"

"Griff told me. I like Wally. Between those two, I'm not sure who's the saddest."

"Liberty was sold into slavery in Iran, of all places."

"Oh dear. That'll be the end for her. She'll never get out."

"Wrong," he quipped and couldn't help smiling. "She escaped from Iran and is in Iraq with me."

A scream pierced his ear. Bo yanked the receiver away, not touching it to her ear until Eva said, "Shame on you for leading me on! How did she escape?"

"Ah, that is—"

"Never mind. It can't be a coincidence you're there. Let me just say, you're a hero."

"Thanks, but here's how you can help. If I bring her back with me, you know what a hassle that will be. She's a Christian kidnapped by Arab raiders, so she qualifies for refugee status on political and religious grounds. But the routine takes years. She escaped with an older Sudanese woman who'd also been sold into slavery."

He heard a pause before Eva replied, "I'll start working on it as soon as I'm free."

"Eva, I have my own idea. The Agency keeps a secret base on the East Coast—"

"Not so secret," she interjected. "We federal agents know about the Point."

Bo wouldn't confirm the obvious. "Anyway, if I fly the ladies there without having to clear Customs and Immigration, can you get them processed?"

"Bo, here's an idea. Have the Agency fly all of you to Harvey Point," Eva laughed. "How soon do you and Liberty arrive in North Carolina?"

"Uncertain. If she goes, Mabel comes, too. I will get the Company to send a plane for us. Oh, and Eva?"

"They're beeping me for my conference."

"Let me tell Griff the news."

"Fine. We'll connect later," Eva said, ending the call.

Bo scrolled down for Griff's number, eager to share a few details of his successful mission.

54

Most Tuesdays at seven-thirty in the morning, Griff would be edging his bureau car into the parking lot at the FBI office in Manassas. But this morning, he happily made a detour, fulfilling a long-awaited desire.

The night before, Bo Rider had phoned Griff from Iraq with unbelievable news. Liberty had been freed! There was one unexpected twist. Griff had immediately called Wally, arranging to meet early. Griff hadn't shared the reason, wanting to break it to him eye to eye.

He trudged up the steps, relieved that Liberty was safe. Griff raised his hand, about to tap on the door, when Wally opened it. He was dressed in one of Rob's shirts, which had crossed golf clubs sewn on the pocket. Something smelled burnt. Griff wrinkled his nose.

"Trying to burn the place down?"

Wally flashed his bright-white smile. "I forgot my toast. Want some?"

"No thanks," Griff said, walking to the kitchen counter. "How about coffee?"

"This is not Rob's Deli, you know. I have cola, but it is not decaf."

"I forgot young guys like you don't drink coffee."

"Why did you want to come see me so early?" Wally asked, pouring a glass of orange juice, which he set before Griff.

"I'm expecting my friend to call any minute. He has someone who wants to talk with you. In fact, I gave him your phone number."

"Is it about my court case?"

"He's calling from Iraq."

"For me? I do not understand."

"Liberty has been found," Griff beamed.

Instead of smiling, Wally's frown deepened. "You are serious?"

"Wally, I would never tease you. She has escaped from Iran. Don't ask me how, but she is with U.S. Army personnel in Iraq."

"The Lord be praised! I knew He would find her," Wally cried, jumping up and down.

He stopped, suddenly overcome with tears. Griff clasped him in a giant bear hug.

"It's true, you'll see. But," Griff added, "Liberty may return to her village. She is looking after an older woman named Mabel."

Wally wiped his eyes. "She is safe. That is what counts, no matter when we see each other."

Apparently, Liberty hadn't decided to come to America, which meant Wally wouldn't see her anytime soon. He still had no passport—all because of CJ Huddleston. Griff ground his teeth, saying nothing about his fear that in Sudan, Liberty could easily be kidnapped again and sold back into slavery. Whether she wanted to stay was her choice—that's what the spirit of freedom meant.

Wally slapped his leg, digging desperately into his pocket.

"What's the matter son?"

"My phone!"

He retrieved his vibrating cell phone, flipped it open, and pressed it to his ear.

"Hello?" He paused. "Liberty, it is you!"

Griff couldn't contain his smile. Tears rolled down Wally's cheeks.

"You wonder what?"

Wally listened, and then erupted, "Yes, come right away. Bring your friend. Mabel is welcome in our home. I will talk to my dad."

Like a switch had been flipped, Wally changed to Dinka dialect. Griff guzzled his orange juice, sliding a thumb near his ear and little finger near his mouth. He waved goodbye to Wally, whispering, "Call me later."

He shut the door, his spirits soaring at the melodious conversation of extreme joy behind it. Griff sauntered to his car, where he called Dawn.

"Are you already at work?"

"Running to get inside by eight. I had an early meeting in town."

"Let me make your day with fabulous news. Liberty has been found."

"Wonderful! I'm so happy," she squealed in delight. However in the next second, Dawn began weeping. "She's really safe?"

"She is. I hope those are tears of joy and that you're not upset," Griff said.

"I'm stunned, but want to hear every detail."

"How about lunch on Saturday?"

"I planned a shopping day, but could cancel," she managed a laugh, adding, "for you."

"We'll pick up turkey subs for a picnic. Dawn, I need to ask something."

"Before you ask, I saw CJ. That was my appointment this morning."

"Is it serious?"

"Yes. Life-changing."

Oh great. CJ had wormed his way back in, big time.

"I'll see you Saturday," Griff sighed. "Will noon work?"

"Perfectly. I bought fresh peaches and will brew iced tea."

"Jeffrey Truhart hasn't returned my call about the video you watched."

"He has all the new evidence. I hope by Saturday we'll know more. My boss is roving this way. I've gotta go."

"See ya."

Griff hung up, mystified. Just when he thought life with Dawn was on a roll, she whammed him. The rest of his day, he typed boring reports about his extortion case, feeling like he'd been punched in the gut. Saturday seemed years off.

AS SOON AS GRIFF opened his door, he headed for the bedroom to change into running gear. Then he huffed out the backyard for a long jaunt through Nottoway Park. The blazing sun near the ball fields drained his energy, and he darted beneath the lush shade of towering maples and oaks.

Yet the coolness didn't relieve his angst over Dawn's chat with CJ. At least two things had gone right. Wally had reconnected with Liberty, and the extortionist had been indicted as a result of true FBI professionalism—a stark contrast to the keystone cops at Summit Ridge.

Griff dodged a low-hanging branch, perplexed at how Chief Dalton—by all accounts, a stand-up guy—could allow Wally's case to be so badly mishandled. After all, Dawn had found evidence that proved they'd made a baseless arrest. With new vigor and resolve to beat CJ in court, Griff passed a jogger, leaving the chubby guy behind.

His feet pounded the wood chips with force. The trail eventually ended, but Griff's questions about Dawn did not. If she "preferred him," why did she continue seeing CJ Huddleston, the power-hungry attorney responsible for ruining Wally's life? Why wouldn't she tell the guy to take a hike?

He jogged slowly home. His future looked pretty bleak as he gazed at the sculpted white lilies. Those happy flowers, planted years earlier by Sue before cancer took her, still bloomed beautifully. Their existence was orderly and peaceful, unlike Griff's work-saturated life.

What would Sue think of what he'd become? Would she approve of his sputtering relationship with Dawn? He picked a white flower, its fragrance reminding him of the great love that once lived inside of him for Sue. It seemed she was speaking to him. He had to believe that she would want him to find joy.

He'd poured his life into Wally, which was bearing fruit. Ever since Dawn had moved to Virginia, he'd begun to believe she could fill the void in his heart. Yet, he'd observed on their recent time in Sudan, that he didn't share Dawn's deep spiritual convictions.

He slumped into a lawn chair, perplexed about which way to go. The lily felt light and smooth against his skin, so much like Dawn. She cared for people and believed God did, too. He guessed that Eva Montanna, his occasional task force partner, held the same beliefs. He respected both Eva and her husband Scott. But, as a guy, was Scott religious? They did take their kids to church with them.

Though Sue had never focused on God the way Dawn and Eva did, maybe it was strictly a female thing. But then, how to explain Scott? What about other guys he knew? It must be that women had genes men didn't, which made them sensitive to spiritual things. That explained the obstacle between him and Dawn. A vague understanding flitted through his mind.

One thing he knew: he should clean up and eat dinner. With little appetite and less enthusiasm, Griff wandered indoors. Before taking a cool shower, he plunged the flower into a glass of water.

Later, in fresh shorts and shirt, he heated the grill and tossed on a couple of brats, his mind reflecting on his theory about women needing religion. He mentally checked off guys he knew who didn't go to church. There were plenty. He wasn't genetically flawed. All was well—until he remembered his partner, Sal Domingo. Sal was an active member at a local church, always helping the poor. And how about Trenton Nash, son of legendary FBI agent Duke Nash?

Trenton had been a deputy sheriff once, assigned with Griff to Eva's task force. Against Griff's better judgment, she'd made him the senior partner to Trenton. The rookie deputy had proved every bit as driven as Griff and not easily influenced. Trenton's determination had caused him to cross an ethical line, a situation that ended in disgrace and imprisonment.

That was years ago. Since his release, Trenton had married and finished college and seminary, becoming a pastor at a church not too far from Griff's house. Go figure. Griff tapped the tongs against the grill. He'd always thought he and Trenton were wired the same—except Griff stayed within legal bounds.

Griff smiled. Dawn had met Griff's colleagues at a task force reunion party Eva hosted in her yard. Trenton had come with his wife,

Hannah. As Griff flipped the cooking brats, it occurred to him that Trenton might even remember Dawn. On a whim, he turned down the flame and went inside to grab the phone book. He flipped to the yellow pages, found the number to Trenton's church, and dialed.

Prompts led Griff to Trenton's voice mail and he said, "You and I haven't touched base in a while. I'd appreciate time to see you." Griff left his cell number, wondering if Trenton would bother calling back, or if he'd much rather leave his past behind him.

55

G riff took Trenton's call bright and early on his way to the FBI office the following morning. They arranged to meet at noon. Griff's morning was slammed with phone calls, typing requests for subpoenas, and answering e-mails. In spite of the hectic pace, his mind was stuck on the bomb Dawn had dropped about CJ. Suddenly, he looked down and saw that he'd typed the same sentence twice on his report. Brother, he needed a change!

Griff headed for his car at eleven-thirty, entering the pastor's suite exactly at noon. A stout woman with waves of gray hair greeted him.

"You must be Griff Topping."

"That's me," Griff nodded. "I used to work with Trenton."

"Please take a seat." She nodded at an upholstered chair. "Reverend Nash just received a call from the board chair, but he should be right along."

Griff looked around, feeling a tad uncomfortable in this outer office adorned with Bibles and icons of faith. His prior memories were of Trenton wearing a gun, digging to get incriminating evidence before Griff could find it. The intervening years must have made a huge difference for Trenton—but what about for Griff?

The pastor's door flung open and there stood Trenton in a beige suit and green tie, grinning broadly at Griff. He thrust out his hand.

"Sure is a pleasure to see you again, Griff. Come right in."

Griff followed the younger man into his office, glimpsing no trappings from Trenton's law enforcement years. Trenton's hair had splashes of gray at the temples, giving him an air of maturity. At least Griff had won on that score. His hair was still a rich brown.

"Your digs are much nicer than we had at the task force," Griff said in jest. "You've come up in the world."

"In those days, I never considered the ministry. How much has your life changed?"

Griff shrugged, slumping into a leather chair.

"Are you still single?" Trenton asked as he angled behind his desk. "Seems when I last saw you at Eva's, you had a pretty lady with you."

Odd that Trenton should blurt that out. Griff shifted in his seat. "That's one of the reasons I'm here. Sure you have time?"

"For you, plenty," Trenton replied, still wearing his smile.

"I am seeing only Dawn Ahern. She moved here about a year ago from Florida. Her son's a cadet at VMI."

"What's the trouble? I see it in your eyes."

Griff blinked, but he shouldn't have. He had come for advice. Why hide the reason?

"I really like her, but we've run into some bumps in the road."

"My seminary degree's in theology, not counseling. But you're an honorable man, and I'll help if I can. What's the stumbling block? Your jobs?"

"In a way, I guess. Most of us in law enforcement deal with people in society as right or wrong, black or white, but not gray."

"That was my experience, yes. And Dawn, she is—"

"A federal probation officer. I always saw her more like a cop than most social workers, who rescue anyone running afoul of the law or down and out."

Trenton nodded, saying nothing.

"Our values are similar, yet recently she acts in ways I can't predict."

"How so?"

"She's emotional, showing more patience with people I find obnoxious. Is it because, as a woman, she's used to helping parolees? Or is it because she's religious? I can't decipher it."

"What do you mean, she's religious? You imply you aren't." A shadow of a smile graced Trenton's lips. "Yet you've come to me."

"Right." Griff considered the paradox. It made no sense to him, either.

"I'm attracted to her. She's a widow, doing a great job raising a son and she's not a loose woman, if you catch my drift. That's fine by me. I think she's the way she is because of her religion. She attends church on Sundays and helps others."

"So she is a Christian?"

Griff nodded. "Yeah, that's how she describes herself."

"Are you a Christian, Griff?"

"Not like Dawn. I'm not a Buddhist or an atheist. A higher power is up there somewhere, but I don't rely on God for help."

"That's exactly how I would've answered when we served on the task force, back when we were kicking in doors and taking names. I gave no thought to Holy God." Trenton paused, lifting his eyebrows. "I came to the end of myself, however. It wasn't going to prison that got me considering the truth about God. It was Hannah, the Christian woman I met just prior to my troubles. You met my wife at Eva's event. By the way, she's also emotional. It sounds like she has lots in common with Dawn."

Griff wondered if marrying Dawn meant he, too, would become a minister. Not likely. "You're saying God is feminine?"

"Jesus described God as our Father and His, so no. I think women are created with more emotions than men. Some might be offended by my opinion, but God designed us differently, each bearing some of His characteristics. Women can be nurturing mothers and men strong fathers. Think about it, Griff. Your mom probably met your daily needs more than your dad."

"No doubt," Griff said, nodding.

"Secondly, I believe many women feel more vulnerable. For these two reasons, they sense a need for God before we men do. Independent guys like us don't require God in our lives until we've exhausted everything else. Interested in a quick primer?"

"I'm not sure I'll understand it, but shoot."

Trenton pulled out a Bible, but held it in his hands respectfully, as if it were a precious treasure. Griff heard his explanation—God made all things, creating humans to have a relationship with him. Mankind became sinful, losing the special relationship with God.

"God came as a human to bridge the gap. Jesus Christ was born on earth so people alive back then could see and know him. Jesus died as a sacrifice, so we all can become acceptable again to God. Through Jesus, we can enjoy the relationship God intended."

"I see," Griff muttered, understanding none of it.

"Jesus is God's gift to mankind, which we each personally must accept. Based on what you've told me, I think Dawn has such a relationship with God."

"So God is for the emotional or the needy."

Trenton turned his thumbs toward his chest. "Am I needy and emotional?"

"Not hardly." Griff switched topics. "I was telling a CIA agent about you recently. Remember when we raided a townhouse looking for terrorists? Eva had a guy sitting on his sofa who lied through his teeth. You strode in the front door and called him Farouk, assuring him that you had sat beside him on a flight from London days before. You had him nodding, admitting the truth. Eva just stood there with her mouth hanging open."

"Yeah," Trenton said, and he burst out laughing. "Eva knew I wasn't on the flight. We had great times back then."

"And accomplished much good."

"Let me tell you about one who is purely good—Jesus. When on earth, He revealed Himself to twelve disciples, a group of real men who, over a period of three years, came to understand and believe He was who He claimed to be. Some were fishermen, one was a tax collector."

"Like Earl Simmons, the IRS agent."

"Yes. After Christ's ascension to Heaven, religious leaders pressured the disciples to deny that Jesus was the Son of God or the physical form of God. Despite threats and bribes, they refused to do so. Another follower, Stephen, stood his ground, defending Jesus. They killed him with rocks. That's a real man, Griff."

A shudder rippled through Griff. "So they put their lives on the line for God?"

"Like you do as an Agent, only in a different way. One religious leader present during Stephen's stoning was Paul, a lawyer. Ever hear of him?"

"Not really."

"Christ appeared to Paul on the road to Damascus, demanding to know why Paul persecuted Christians. Paul later accepted God's gift and traveled ancient roads, telling everyone he met that Jesus and God were one and the same. The religious leaders were furious and set about to silence him."

"Happens all the time these days." Griff felt his eyes narrowing. "What happened to Paul?"

"He sailed to Greece, where he was arrested and imprisoned in Rome for his beliefs. He could have been freed if he'd recanted, but Paul stayed true, dying in prison. Griff, wouldn't these guys have been great to work with on a task force? How many times have you seen their names on churches, Saint Stephen and Saint Paul?

"You've given me plenty to think about."

"Here's the perfect help." Trenton slid the Bible across his desk. "Inside, I inserted a thin booklet at the beginning of John. He was also a disciple who traveled with Jesus. After reading John, you should have a better understanding of Dawn's faith. In the booklet, there's even a sample prayer for anyone who wants to accept Jesus, God's gift."

Griff picked up Trenton's gift carefully; he'd never really handled a Bible before. "Thanks. I rely on myself, and I haven't seen the need for God. I've heard of the Ten Commandments and all, but I never killed anyone."

Trenton asked smiling. "You've never gone off the deep end like I did. Do me a favor, Griff, and read the words of Jesus?"

"I'm not sure why I came to see you, but I will look over this John portion and let you know if I gain any insights."

The two men shook hands. Trenton offered to meet with him again, maybe for lunch. His hand lingered on Griff's shoulder.

"Give thought to the times you've been saved from what seemed like an impossible situation. Maybe God was behind you, pushing you out of danger."

That touched a nerve with Griff. He could tick off many such dilemmas—Sudan, Kazakhstan, Florida … even that extortion case he'd done surveillance for. And Liberty being found in Iran? Surely her freedom hadn't come about by mere human hands.

THE FOLLOWING NIGHT crept up on Griff. He'd been working pretty much non-stop since he'd met with Trenton. The previous evening, he'd read a portion of John before his eyes slammed shut.

Griff kicked off his shoes, shoved on flip-flops, and fired up the grill. The hefty burger, topped with onions and cheese, hit the spot. He downed two glasses of iced tea, the caffeine stirring his nerves. He kept picking up the Bible and setting it down again.

He flopped down on the sofa to watch the nightly news. Flooding in Pakistan, a bombing in Kirkuk killing fifty people in one fell swoop. People dying all over the globe. Griff snapped off the TV and got up, holding a photo of him and Dawn taken at the recent wedding. She looked so beautiful, even making the guy she was with look happy.

And Griff had cherished the time with her. As he gazed into her smiling eyes now, it was as if she were there with him in the living room, leading him back to the sofa. He picked up the leather-bound Bible. Some of the words were written in red and Griff tried to understand the parables, but his eyelids grew heavy. He closed the windows, retiring for the night. But then he wasn't tired, so he flipped open the Bible again.

He'd read about one-half of John, stopping at a verse where Jesus said, "I am the way and the truth and the life." Griff considered what Trenton had said. Griff had arrived at this point in life without learning of God. Why?

After another thirty minutes of his mind slowly absorbing the truth, he turned to Luke, where he read that Jesus was crucified on a wooden cross he'd carried on his own back. Griff flipped open the booklet Trenton said contained a prayer. He read this several times, processing the full meaning. He fell asleep with the Bible on the bed, and it was right where he'd left it when he awoke again at four a.m.

He rose, trotting to the kitchen to brew coffee. His eyes half-open, he started whistling. He threw open the kitchen window, drinking in the beauty of the white lily on the windowsill. All the strain from the past few weeks seemed to have evaporated. Griff had spent a restless night, but he knew he'd never be the same.

He called a number, expecting to reach voice mail. After two rings, Trenton answered, "Pastor Nash. How can I help?"

"It's Griff and I intended to leave a message."

"My hours vary, just as they did when we served on the Task Force. I'm going over sermon notes a final time."

Griff's thoughts tumbled in his mind. "Last night I read in John and thought I understood it. Then I turned back some pages and read about Jesus in Luke."

"I am pleased. Any new insights?"

"For one, I don't think much of their system of justice in Bible days. They killed Jesus because they didn't want to accept that He and God were the same. What's worse, they hung him between two thieves. Of course, we wouldn't have crime here in the U.S. if we crucified thieves."

"I never really thought of it that way, Griff," Trenton chuckled. "What do you make of Jesus' claim that He and God are the same?"

Griff started speaking, but the words caught in his throat. He swallowed.

"Trenton, I was insulted when I read that a dirt-bag thief mocked Jesus, telling him to come off the cross and save them all."

"But the other thief seemed to understand who Jesus really was."

"Yeah. I liked how that other crook told off the dirt-bag on the other side." Griff choked up again. "What's so amazing is that Jesus, despite what he suffered, forgave the dirt-bag and all of us. That blew me away, and I felt His presence personally."

"Sounds like you had a breakthrough, Griff. Let me mention one more thing to think about. The thief who defended Jesus also prayed for Jesus to remember him in Heaven. Recall what Jesus told him?"

"That's a little hazy."

"Jesus promised that the thief who believed would be with Him in Heaven that very same day."

"Hey, Trenton," Griff said, smiling into the phone. "I called to tell you that I prayed the prayer in your booklet. I now understand what being a Christian is."

"You should tell Dawn! You two have a new dimension to share with each other. Let's have lunch, because I have some reading suggestions for your faith journey."

Griff ended the call. His heart and mind were truly opened, as if he'd raised the sheer curtains on the windows and doors of his soul, and rays of sun shone in every room. Excitement bubbled within him. He wanted to do just what Trenton suggested and call Dawn. Then he put down the phone. Wouldn't it be more satisfying to watch her gorgeous eyes when he told her on Saturday?

56

Griff raced north along I-95 on Saturday afternoon, but he had lost his zest for talking, content to feel Dawn next to him. His eyes focused on the highway, his hands gripping the wheel. She hummed a tune as she gazed out the window.

"You're too quiet. Taking me someplace secret?"

"How does Paris sound?" He glanced her way.

"Maybe someday," she giggled. "Griff, watch out. Traffic's stopping."

"You're right, and I'm ditching this gridlock."

After braking hard, he veered off at the next exit. Once on the county road, as they passed quaint farms and fruit stands, his spirits began to lift.

"You look like the cat that ate the canary," Dawn said.

"Who, me? I've never owned a cat."

"Where are we going?"

"If not Paris, how about the beach?"

"Wonderful!"

Dawn's humming carried them to a quiet beach town along the Potomac.

"It's not the ocean, but I didn't want to be driving all day," he said. "The weather's fine for our picnic. Blue sky above and great company here on earth."

"Say, picnics bring out the poet in you," she chuckled.

He turned the car into a spot next to another couple who were shoving lawn chairs into their trunk before they sped off. Super— looked like he and Dawn would have the park to themselves, which was just what he'd planned.

They unpacked the car and spread a blanket on the upper slope, which gave them a stunning view of the river. Dawn poured iced tea, handing a plastic cup to Griff. They sipped their tea to sounds of chirping birds.

Griff slid over next to her, setting their drinks in the grass. After reading his Bible the previous night, he'd finally vanquished all doubts involving CJ Huddleston. Griff decided to just tell Dawn what he had to say.

"Thanks for bringing me here. The view is lovely," she said.

So was her smile, but Griff forced his mind into gear. "Dawn, I'm not great with words, but here goes."

"You're acting kinda strange, but I'm intrigued why you brought me all the way out here. We can talk anywhere, you know."

"I wanted a beautiful setting to tell a beautiful woman how much I love her."

Her eyes glistened and her cheeks glowed with a faint pink blush. He reached for her hands, taking them in his. Her touch sent his heart pounding.

"Things have happened. Rick Nebo put up his house for Wally's bond, though he was virtually a stranger. You flew to Sudan so Wally could call Liberty. She gets kidnapped; you stay to find her, risking your job and your life. You don't find her, and call me to help. Your call changed my life."

"It did?" She squeezed his hand. "But when are you going to tell me about Liberty?"

"I'm getting to that. You showed great courage in a dangerous place. I was wrong to try to keep you out of Sudan, but right to urge you home."

"I followed my heart, and God gave me the courage," she said. "You are right—because we came home when we did, we discovered the video to clear Wally."

"A lot of good that did," Griff said bitterly. He dropped her hands, the morose feeling washing over him again. CJ Huddleston was a complete jerk.

"But that's what I wanted to tell you!" Dawn cried, sitting up on her knees. "Pastor Rick went with me to talk to CJ. He's dropping the case."

"That's why you met with CJ? To pressure him about Wally's case?"

She nodded, a stunning smile on her lips. "You should've seen pastor put the squeeze on CJ. I just happened to be in the room."

"Finally," Griff said, shaking his head. "Has he notified Judge Fox?"

"He will on Monday."

"So CJ saw the video and caved."

"Yes, in part. After Chief Dalton showed the video to CJ, he told him the clerk had admitted to stealing the money to pay off a drug debt. Pastor Rick told CJ that to continue prosecuting Wally would not only result in a miscarriage of justice, but it would plague his heart forever. I won't forget the startled look on CJ's face when he heard that."

"Good for Rick."

"I think he really meant CJ couldn't get elected governor if he pushed forward. We may never know, but CJ has agreed to dismiss it. I asked him to call Wally's lawyer and he did, right then and there."

"Is that what you meant about life-changing? For Wally?"

Dawn's eyes held his and he forced himself to look away, sipping more tea.

"You're a rascal, worrying me like that."

"I'm sorry," she laughed. "Forgive me?"

Her lovely black eyes smote Griff's heart. He returned her gaze, trusting she wouldn't mistake his meaning.

"Forgive and forget is my new motto. Wally's getting his life back and that's an answer to my prayer."

"Really?" Her eyes widened.

"That's what I've been trying to tell you. When Rick mentioned he might return to Sudan with his wife so the people there could hear about Jesus, a part of me began to change. I grew curious about God."

"Griff, that's terrific!"

"Then, after we returned home and you stumbled on that video at Witt Chevrolet, I met with Trenton Nash, another pastor. You met him at Eva's task force reunion."

"I remember. And he made a difference?"

"Sure did. Now that I've studied the book of John, I understand that God's plan is for everyone to know Him. You see before you a new Christian."

Dawn smiled through her tears, a rainbow shining through raindrops.

"That's an answer to so many prayers of mine. We should celebrate." She reached for their glasses.

"Wait. There's more."

Dawn froze.

"I got the call, but didn't want to tell you on the phone."

"Griff, has something else happened to Wally?"

"Liberty escaped from Iran."

"Where is she? How do you know she's alive? Does Wally—"

"Shhh."

Griff slid her hands into his, drawing her to him. He pressed his lips gently against hers. When they drew breath, he told her the rest.

"Liberty will be flying to North Carolina. Eva is helping her and her friend Mabel come to the States."

"Oh Griff!"

Dawn broke down, sobbing in his arms. He held her, and with his fingers dried fresh tears clinging to her cheeks.

"Shhh. There's more."

She shook her head. "No. Not until I get myself in check. Just a minute."

Dawn practically flew to the nearby ladies' room, her face in her hands. Had he blown it again? He guzzled his tea, pouring more in his glass, which wavered in the grass. Suddenly, cold fingers wrapped around his neck. He caught the hand, spinning around. Dawn grinned down at him.

Griff bounded to his feet, folding her into his arms.

"Better?"

"Much," she murmured into his chest. "This has been quite a day. My head's spinning. I'd love to talk with Wally and Liberty as soon as possible."

He titled her chin, pushing a stray lock of hair out of her eyes. "I have something else to tell you."

She pushed back, looking around. "Are they coming here?"

He pulled her back close to him.

"Dawn, I want to marry you. Do you feel like you could build a life with me?"

"I do and I will! I've been hoping—"

Their kiss lasted for some time. When their lips parted, Griff grinned.

"What do you say to a double wedding?"

57

Aweek after Dr. Lili Tabriz and her Iranian husband died in the fire that consumed their home in Tehran, Lili's sister, Ingeborg Sorenson, spoke to a small gathering about her memories of Lili.

She concluded her eulogy by saying, "My sister was a wonderful scientist on the precipice of an amazing discovery. With her life cut short, we will never know her full potential."

Ingeborg wiped a small tear from her eye before plunking down in the front row. This memorial for her sister was nothing like her family's earlier funerals in the chapel at Swanson's Funeral Home in Brooklyn. Ingeborg sighed, feeling alone—she had no living relatives. Her father and mother were long gone. And now, Lili was, too.

Instead of hundreds, a mere handful had assembled to pay tribute to Lili's life. Ingeborg saw the minister keep wiping his glasses on a wrinkled handkerchief. She'd paid him to officiate; at least he could appear concerned. Organ music played over the sound system, echoing around the tiny room. The minister thrust the hankie into his pocket.

"Does anyone else want to say a few words?"

Ingeborg turned from her front row seat, staring at the six people present. One she recognized from her youth in Brooklyn. The others must be people Lili knew from high school or college, as she'd spent most of her adult life studying in England or living in Iran with her late husband, Cyrus, and Farvad, her late son.

She glimpsed a nice-looking couple who arrived late and calmly sat in the back row. No one rose to share memories of Lili. Then Mrs. Berglund, their former neighbor, hobbled to the podium, passing by the low table on which sat the urn containing Lili's remains. Although Mrs. Berglund had attended services for both of Ingeborg's parents, today she was more bent-over and feeble than Ingeborg remembered.

"I express my sympathy to Ingeborg," Mrs. Berglund said, her voice quivering. "Both she and Lovisa were my neighbors. What nice girls they were. While others in the neighborhood pursued boys and folly, both Ingeborg and Lovisa were studying."

Ingeborg noted that Mrs. Berglund referred to Lili by her given name, Lovisa. She probably didn't know the heartache Lili had endured, changing her name and moving to Iran. If only Cyrus could have received a visa to enter the U.S., everything might have turned out beautifully.

"Lili was especially fond of my cat, Skittles," Mrs. Berglund said softly. "She would come as a child to pet him. When my husband— God rest his soul—and I traveled to visit our children, Lili cared for Skittles. God bless you, my dear."

Mrs. Berglund crinkled a smile at Ingeborg and shuffled back to her seat. After a short pause, prerecorded music played an old Swedish hymn. Ingeborg listened silently, consumed with sadness for Lili. The music abruptly ended and the minister pronounced a benediction before scurrying away.

Some elderly man walked up to express his sympathy; Ingeborg was surprised to learn he had taught Lili biology in high school. Then all the visitors left, leaving Ingeborg to clutch the urn under her arm. She had never found out the identity of the couple that came in late.

When she headed to the office to pay their services, she spotted the couple. They were heading her way, no doubt to give their condolences. How did they know Lili?

The man spoke first. "Excuse me, Ms. Sorenson." He snapped a folder from his suit coat pocket. Affixed to it was a gold badge. "I am FBI Special Agent Griffin Topping."

He nodded to the lady. "This is Special Agent Eva Montanna from Customs Immigration Enforcement."

Because the lady agent was tall, she gazed down at Ingeborg as she whisked a similar folder from her purse. It also contained a gold badge.

"Are you the same Ingeborg Sorenson who is a supervisory microbiologist at the National Institutes of Health in Washington, D.C.?"

Ingeborg's confusion turned to stark fear. She stuttered, "I … ah … yes."

The FBI agent took Lili's urn and at the same time, Agent Montanna took handcuffs from her purse, dangling them before Ingeborg's eyes. "We have a warrant for your arrest."

She reached for Ingeborg's hand, twisting her around. Then she clasped one cuff on her wrist before pulling her other wrist behind her back. When the second cuff clicked on, Ingeborg panicked, not knowing what to do.

"You are charged with conspiracy to commit bio-terrorism and interstate travel in furtherance of that conspiracy," Agent Topping said. His tone conveyed his contempt for her. "You have a right to remain silent and to ask for an attorney. If you cannot afford an attorney, one will be appointed for you by the court." The agent looked her straight in the eye. "Understand?"

Ingeborg stood there in total shock, barely jerking her head up and down.

"You have to do more than nod, Ms. Sorenson. Do you understand what I just told you? Yes or no."

"Yes," she squeaked.

"1 will leave this urn here with the proprietor. You can retrieve it later, whenever you are released."

This couple, whom Ingeborg thought loved her sister, led her from the funeral parlor and put her in the rear seat of a car with handcuffs digging into her wrists. This was terrible and so wrong. If only Lili was still alive—she'd tell the world her sister, Ingeborg, was no bioterrorist.

58

A few nights later, when neighbors of the secret CIA facility in North Carolina were most certainly asleep, Bo Rider sat aboard the stealth flight with his contingent of refugees. Although the good folks who lived nearby were used to low-flying jet aircraft gliding over their homes and landing inside the fenced perimeter, they'd never know the debt they owed to those on board this plane.

The whine of slowing jet engines broke the dark quiet and the special CIA aircraft landed at Harvey Point. Bo disembarked and got busy assigning Liberty, Mabel, and Kia into guest quarters where, over the next week, they'd be interviewed. Arrangements for their futures would eventually be made.

Bo and Judah Levitt, having returned to the place where they'd first met, unwound in the commissary over sandwiches.

"I find it incredible that you recognized me in Kirkuk," Bo chided, finishing his burger.

"Ah, good friend, God blesses me with a photographic memory."

"Well, mine's razor sharp, but you beat me there."

Bo lifted a coffee cup to his lips when a staffer approached, handing him a sealed note. He ripped open the envelope, his eyes consuming the few lines.

Bo, the Director arrives first thing in the morning to meet you and your guests, bringing some guests of his own. It's critical you phone me on a secure line before he sees you. Frank Deming

Concern hit Bo squarely between the eyes. Now what? He had no option but to get Frank on the phone. He folded the note into his shirt pocket.

Judah nodded toward Bo's pocket. "Receive bad news?"

"I'm not sure. My Director's flying here to see me in the morning."

"Would you like me to be scarce, so he can ask me nothing of our overseas endeavor?"

"That sounds about right. On the other hand, you may need to vouch for me, so don't fly the coop just yet. I'll be back."

Bo went to find a phone, hoping Frank Deming would be at his office.

"I'm glad it's you," Frank said when he answered the call. "I hear congratulations are in order, Bo. Good job."

Bo was uncomfortable with how much Frank always knew, but he tried to adapt to that and move on.

"I'm not sure how much credit I deserve. I'm thinking it was more serendipity."

"You can believe that, but I don't. Neither does the man. He's pretty excited about this latest *coup d'état*. That's why I sent you the message."

Something struck Bo as odd. Frank was usually nonplussed as was Kangas.

"Okay, what don't I know that I should?"

"He's coming down bringing nuclear physics analysts and an Iranian specialist."

"Frank, I already knew that. Why the urgency to call you?"

"Bo," Frank lowered his voice, "I don't know if he will admit this to you, but Kia's defection created one whale of a stir around here. Did you know that both Lili Tabriz and her husband, Cyrus, died when their home was blown up?"

"I do know that they were warned to get out," Bo replied.

"Well Mr. Kangas is catching flack from DST."

"From who?"

"Our Directorate of Science and Technology."

"Okay, so the scientist and engineers who help us look smart are peeved. Big deal. Are they like people for the ethical treatment of other country's scientists?"

Frank laughed hoarsely. "Even worse. Remember when you were denied access to Cyrus Tabriz' files up here and I had to let you in for limited background?"

Bo tried to anticipate where Frank was going with this. "Sure, but why?"

"That file was the initial debriefing of Cyrus Tabriz when he became an Agency asset. I can tell you, heads will roll."

Bo was stunned. He and Judah had wiped out a valuable CIA asset. Panic raged through him like a swollen river.

"So Kangas is coming here to fire me? Is that what you're telling me?"

"No! In fact your stock with him is sky high. But there are some in DST who want somebody fired. I guess Tabriz was poised to be huge. One of our DST microbiologists had debriefed Cyrus in London, probably trying to impress his boss with his clandestine ways."

Bo's mind was so rattled, he could hardly think straight. "The same London conference where I had my run-in with Lili Tabriz?"

"Right. You saw the registration list—three other Americans were there. Ingeborg Sorenson, Lili Tabriz's sister from NIH. Another was Sylvester Teatree, the alias for our CIA microbiologist."

"No way! Did Kangas know he was there?"

"Absolutely not. It was one of those left hand didn't know what the right hand was doing fiascos. I guess DST sends their scientist and engineers to these conventions to learn what's new in the field. But, they're not supposed to be developing assets."

Calm settled over Bo. "So you think my job is safe."

"Sure. Director Kangas may not mention it, but he spent most of yesterday screaming at the head of DST, who was hot because some American agent off'd Cyrus Tabriz. They were being protective of the only asset they weren't supposed to have."

"Frank, could you be wrong? Could Kangas be out for my hide?"

"Director Kangas assured DST it was Mossad's doings. You weren't there, right?"

"Exactly."

"Bo, I sent you the note because I didn't want you ambushed."

"Thanks for watching my back. Hey, Frank, Julia and I want to have you out to the house. We'll grill steaks."

"I'd like to meet your wife and kids."

Bo hung up realizing he and Frank had become friends—as close as they could be, in their own secret worlds.

59

Bo and Judah strolled along a wooded path beside the Sound in the early morning haze. Seabirds called overhead and dense fog burned off as the sun edged above the tree line. Bo had taught at Harvey Point several times, including training Judah Levitt and other foreign intelligence agents. Yet walking here and discussing what they'd survived bordered on surreal.

Judah had shaved off his beard and, in street clothes, no longer looked like an Iranian or an Iraqi.

"So the sister of Lili Tabriz also was steeped in diabolical terror," he sighed, clasping his hands behind his back. "Some bevy of venomous snakes we stirred up."

"Mind blowing. No matter how many scientists we uncover, more are waiting to take their place." Bo felt enormous pressure to get back out there and do it all over again.

"We can gloat for a day of our achievements."

Bo came to a halt, facing Judah. "How about our first debriefing of Kia? Eighteen hours inside that hot and stinky tank-truck compartment."

"A debriefing with only one common language, English. And four Dinkas eavesdropping."

"At least we confirmed Kia intended to defect," Bo replied. He divulged nothing about Cyrus Tabriz having been a CIA asset. And he never would.

"Will Kia be safe here? Has Iran made overtures to your country about his defection?" Judah wondered aloud.

"He stays at the Point while our nuclear experts turn his brain inside out. After that," Bo shrugged, "who knows?"

Judah clapped Bo on the back. "Then, my friend, let's head to breakfast. My orders are to remain as long as I'm needed on either the nuclear or the flu plot before returning to Israel."

"I guess I could eat," Bo said, wondering about the true reason for Kangas' trip to the Point. This might be his last day working for the Agency.

BO WALKED INTO BUILDING A without Judah, recalling the anxiety he'd felt the first time, years earlier, when Kangas had called him in. He'd felt like a kid being hauled to the principal's office. Only this was no spit ball he'd thrown at Sammy Piper.

If Kangas chose this moment to kick Bo out, well, so be it. Why else would the Director fly to North Carolina? Otherwise, Bo could have briefed him over a secure line, as he had a dozen times before.

Bo held his head high. Since his early years at the Agency, he'd achieved one goal: he'd ripened into the kind of CIA agent he once longed to be. Now he was ready to meet daunting challenges with humor and grit. He summoned those qualities into his mind, ready to explain everything. But how much of what had occurred in Iran was good fortune, and how much could he claim flowed from his hard work?

Of course, there were some things he wouldn't take credit for—but had the rest been more than just dumb luck? He swung open the door.

"Rider, I've been waiting," Kangas barked across from a metal behemoth, some Navy surplus hulk.

"Sorry, sir, I had to catch up with the Mossad agent."

"Fair enough. Take a seat."

Bo eased in a firm metal chair across from the outdated desk. Kangas minimized a computer screen and turned to Bo, his eyes reflecting a haggard glare.

"There's been an astonishing development. It turns out Ingeborg Sorenson was the evil genius behind the Armageddon flu plot. She hates this country for snatching her sister, Lili, away from her, leaving her a hermit. I've also heard a rumor some NIH folks are shook up."

"I'll admit, I'm pleased how things have worked out," Bo said as he cracked a grin.

"And so far, we've done it all without a whisper that the Company is even involved." Kangas beamed a rare smile, his gaunt look disappearing. "Are you aware that the Tabriz home in Iran blew up and the Iranian regime is blaming dissidents?"

"No." Bo shifted in his seat, adding, "I'm sorry if the People's Mujahideen become more of a target."

"The Iranian regime claims it was the dissidents who released a deadly influenza strain near the Tabriz home."

"They'd never do such a thing."

"Pretty sure of that, are you, Rider?"

Bo refused to confess under Kangas' steely glare.

"When you sent me recruiting to the science conference, I felt like a shark out of water. Then I snagged a roster of attendees and found that leather case like some gift from above. Minutes later, I locked horns with Lili Tabriz, who claimed I'd stolen her husband's valise."

"I presume she was the scientist you referred to in your report who would *not* be a possible asset?"

"Yes," Bo admitted. "What I kept from my report was that I was ready to copy the contents when she found me with it and accused me of being a spy. You simply called me back from London."

"Rider, it seems we misjudged Bear," Kangas intoned.

"I bumped into Judah Levitt just after Bear insisted Iran wanted to buy TOPOL-M missiles with a small payload—far too small for a nuclear bomb."

"And I wrongly assumed that, because he hadn't told you of the triggered spark gaps, he might be hedging on that intel, too. I've started money flowing into his fund, with a significant raise."

"Then I'll probably be hearing from him soon."

"We'll see. I want to know what else you've uncovered about Ingeborg, in case the President corners me in a meeting."

"After I survived the IED attack and the resulting flu, I heard from FBI agent Griff Topping, who I've worked with in the past. He was in Sudan trying to redeem a woman named Liberty, who'd been kidnapped by Arab traders and sold into Iran."

"What?" Kangas launched out of his chair. "How come I never heard of that?"

Bo shrugged. He wanted to reply that he didn't know Kangas cared, but opted for facts. "It caused Griff great anxiety, because she's engaged to marry his adopted Sudanese son."

"Okay." Kangas waved, returning to his seat. "Get on with it."

"It's complex." Bo explained how Griff gave Bo a cell phone number in Iran, which Judah linked to Lili Tabriz. "Iranian dissidents met up with Mabel, a Sudanese slave working with Liberty in the Tabriz household."

"What's the nexus to Ingeborg Sorenson? I was out of the office last week with my own health issue."

Bo stared.

"No, I'm not back on chemo," Kangas growled. "I threw out my back."

"Okay, then. Mabel gave the People's Mujahideen a vial from Lili Tabriz's home lab. Mabel confided Tabriz had ordered Liberty to attach the vial to an IED."

"The three vials your Mossad agent swiped from the Tabriz lab all contained Armageddon flu virus. The two others he secreted held the vaccine for Iranians."

"Thankfully, he smuggled them out without any accidents."

Kangas lifted an eyebrow. "So Bear's intel that Iran wanted a small payload for its rockets takes on a sinister meaning."

"Sir, I'm not volunteering, but we must find out if other Iranian scientists are working on the highly pathogenic flu. They could wipe out all of humanity."

"Even though Tabriz experimented on a vaccine, we don't know if it works. Iran would be crazy to release such a virus," Kangas argued.

"Here's the interesting part." Bo slid to the edge of the chair. "The Mossad agent informs me that Liberty and Mabel were inoculated by Tabriz."

Kangas leaned back in his chair, cupping his hands behind his head. "Rider, I appreciate Mossad doing all of this without our help. It might have created a huge international incident if we had *any* people in Iran. More than Washington has the stomach for."

Did Kangas know Bo had snuck into Iran to ensure Operation Enigma's success? If so, he wasn't letting on yet. So Bo was careful to convey no hints.

"Understood, sir. I'll pass that along."

"NIH will want a blood serum sample from the two women to see if they have developed antibodies to Lili Tabriz' vaccine. I will personally thank Liberty and Mabel for their heroism. Through my discretionary funds, Liberty can receive a scholarship to a college of her choice—within reason, of course."

"Outstanding, sir."

When the phone buzzed and Kangas turned to pick it up, Bo rose, thinking he'd scoot before Kangas pinned him down about his Op inside enemy territory.

Kangas snarled into the phone, "Tell him to have a seat and cool his heals. I'm not through here!" Then he banged down the receiver. At the same time, Bo eased himself back down into a chair.

"Rider, I want to know what led to Ingeborg Sorenson's arrest."

Bo gave details about how he had tasked an analyst to investigate Lili Tabriz. "Lili, who was born Lovisa Sorenson, denounced her U.S. citizenship. The analyst found Lili's sister, Ingeborg Sorenson. That name stuck in my craw. Then I recalled the roster from the London conference. Ingeborg Sorenson attended for NIH."

Kangas spread both elbows on the desk, staring at Bo. "What did you do?"

"To minimize our involvement, I contacted Griff and ICE agent Eva Montanna. Griff briefed NIH. They investigated Ingeborg's activities prior to the London trip."

"How did they confirm her activities? A home-grown terrorist using our nation's resources so she could kill Americans stings, I'll tell you. Where was the FBI?"

Bo folded his arms. "Griff and Eva scrutinized entry and exit records at NIH, discovering Ingeborg entering the lab late one night just prior to flying to London. NIH has hidden surveillance cameras, which only their security people know about."

"What did they catch her doing?" Kangas asked, his eyes rounding.

"Video showed Ingeborg removing a tiny fragment from a classified sample of influenza A from 1918. She placed it in a vial, which she inserted into a ballpoint pen."

"An enemy spy in our midst. Disgusting."

"Imagine my shock, sir. Inside the valise I'd examined were a bunch of pens. I probably held the flu vial in my hands without knowing it."

"Rider, well done. Your efforts led to her arrest."

Bo shrugged off the credit. He was almost golden—and Kangas hadn't pressed him about his own involvement in Iran.

"Sir, the important thing is that NIH compared the data on the virus from Tabriz's laboratory with their own. They're convinced that Lili's Armageddon flu was derived from the sample Ingeborg delivered to her sister in London."

"Proves my point. You made the case."

"In fact, Ingeborg doesn't deny bringing the sample to Lili, but insists her motives were pure. Her defense is that Lili requested the virus so she could develop an antidote, giving Cyrus Tabriz the credit. Ingeborg hoped the U.S would then invite him back and her sister could return."

"Pure baloney. The Bureau's not buying that, are they?"

"It doesn't matter. Ingeborg may believe it, but I know for a fact that wasn't Lili's intent. Ingeborg violated the law and will be convicted of bio-terrorism."

"Other CIA analysts are here to debrief Liberty and Mabel. I know you weren't in Iran, but these two women assert that some nice American helped free them."

Bo remained still and sought to divert Kangas' attention.

"The Mossad agent told me the good news. Kia is providing evidence against Iran's nuclear intentions. Can he shed light on their bio-weapons program?"

"Already has. He dropped a huge bomb last night, which is another reason I flew in. He says he inherited two nuclear physicists and Cyrus had inherited three microbiologists from Saddam Hussein's Iraqi program, all of whom were smuggled through Syria before the war."

"No kidding!" Adrenaline surged through Bo's veins. "I always believed Saddam's military repositioned their WMD labs in Syria. This could be huge."

"Politicians might like to know of Iraq's WMD research, but they won't find out from us. We're keeping it as a bargaining chip. Oh, and Rider—guess what else Kia said."

"No idea, sir."

"He also claims an American helped smuggle him out of Iran."

"Keep in mind, sir, a number of American Jews have immigrated to Israel and entered the military. Mossad must have hired one of them."

Kangas glared at Bo for a moment and then smiled. "That must be it, since we have no agents in Iran. Anyway, Rider, one more thing: I'm assigning you to our embassy in Tel Aviv."

Bo sat back, dazed. His tongue and brain refused to cooperate.

"Don't look so shocked. You and this Mossad friend of yours have hit it off. I want you over there keeping close tabs on this pending peace process. See what the Israelis are secretly planning to counter Iran. You'll have full diplomatic cover within the State Department for your temporary assignment. Your family might enjoy living there."

Kangas had just dumped cold water on Bo's visions of success. Julia and the kids going to Israel, and liking it? He couldn't even fathom Julia's reaction.

"That's the thanks I get? You're demoting me, ripping me from the field."

"Not so! I want you to stop risking your life and give it rest for a few months. You've earned it."

Bo's mind galloped at a fierce pace. He had to uncover Kangas' true reason behind this latest move.

"Sir, what if those Sudanese women and that Iranian scientist were wrong and no American helped them? Would I still be going to Tel Aviv?"

"Rider, this isn't punishment," Kangas said, folding his arms. "Over the next few months, Israel will move certain chess pieces in the Middle East. It's so classified, I can't tell you, but I want my best agent over there. You will be my eyes and ears. On your way out, send in Colonel Hurt. He's waiting to see me. That's all."

Bo wished he could leave without shoving his foot in his mouth. He inhaled deeply, and let it rip.

"I'm not sure my family will love the idea as you do. You may need to explain to my wife how this is a good thing, but you can count on me. As always."

Bo turned on his heels and stalked out, telling the Colonel, "Go on in. He's in a rare mood today."

His mind reeling, Bo banged out of Building A and leaned against the railing. Julia's meltdown was a specter that haunted his every thought. A hand clamped down his shoulder and Bo craned his neck to see whatever phantom had sprung up behind him.

"Well, Skip or Bo, or whoever you are, you look glum. Missing Iran already?"

"Judah, you wouldn't believe it if I told you," Bo griped, shaking his head. "How do you like working with Mossad?"

"Ah, my friend, Mossad never sleeps. I could ask for no better assignment than to keep my country alive and breathing." Judah pointed skyward.

"Okay, fill me in on Tel Aviv. Seems I'm heading your way and I need some positive angle to sell my wife. I have a sneaking suspicion she won't want to come."

"Then I cannot wait to introduce you to the rest of my team!" Judah's smile was infectious. "Here is what you tell your wife. That she will visit an ancient land where Jehovah watches over His people."

"Oh yeah, and she'll understand my dream about seeing those letters in the sky, the letters you claim were written by God." Bo shoved clammy hands in his pockets. "Even to my ears, it sounds unbelievable."

"Try it. Women have a sense of spiritual things. My wife did."

Wait a minute. Hadn't Julia mentioned before he left for Iran that her ladies' bunch was planning a trip to Israel and she wanted to go? How weird was that?

Bo and Judah plunged down the steps, heading for places unknown. Then Bo stopped cold.

"Just who's on your team? Anyone else I trained here at Harvey Point?"

After Judah told him, Bo felt a burst of danger. But there was no way Julia would be as excited about going to Israel as he was.

"Judah, I'm going to call my wife. Wish me luck."

"Ah, my friend. I believe luck has nothing to do with it." Judah smiled and headed off to his barracks.

Bo's heart thumped in his chest as he pulled out his cell phone and punched in his home number. Julia picked up after one ring. He told her he was coming home soon.

"Great," she chuckled. "The kids just asked me that this morning. When?"

"I'm not exactly sure. But I have news I hope you'll like."

"You're buying us a new van?"

"Nah, think bigger." He hated to just spill where they were going.

"Um, your boss is giving you a vacation and you're taking us to the beach."

"We are going away, together as a family. Can you believe it?"

"Finally, we'll have you to ourselves," she sighed.

"It's not the beach. It's Israel."

"Bo!" she screamed in his ear. "What a wonderful surprise. We're going on the trip with my church group."

"Honey, we're being relocated to Tel Aviv. You can spend all the time you want learning with the kids about their customs. Some folks have agreed to show us around."

"After Gregg and Glenna watched a movie about Jesus last Sunday, they said if I go to Israel, they're coming too. Now you have to read *Jesus was a Jewish Carpenter.*"

"Sure thing." Bo couldn't believe this was happening. All his angst about Julia being upset and here she was happy as a clam to be moving to Israel.

"Bo, you might think this is peculiar," she lowered her voice to a whisper, "but I was reading Dr. Van Horn's book while you were gone on your last trip. I dreamed I was walking around the city of Jerusalem. Now I'm going to Israel. It's incredible."

Bo blew out a breath. She had been dreaming too?

"Honey, we have lots to talk over and plan for. This move won't be easy, but I'm glad you're okay with it. Kiss the kids and I'll see you soon."

Bo pocketed his phone. Maybe Kangas and Judah had it right. Even Julia thought so. Heading back to the Middle East sounded like a wild ride—just the type Bo had always craved.

60

Dawn couldn't have dreamed of a more perfect day for her September wedding, with the sky painted azure blue and the sun reflecting the light of her love for Griff. Pure white clouds lingered lazily over the Jefferson Memorial as if each one had the entire day to float over the white dome, a majestic symbol of freedom.

Dawn held Griff's hand as they mingled with a small group of family and friends, waiting for Reverend Nash to arrive. Wally clasped his hands nervously beside Liberty, who wore Dawn's mother's lace wedding dress, which had been altered to fit. Blue glass beads—the very ones Dawn found in Walu—sparkled around her neck. Mabel looked dazed, a pink carnation pinned to her new dress.

For herself, Dawn had selected a simple, pale yellow linen dress. White orchids adorned her black hair, which she wore long and free. Her son, Brian, was telling Pastor Rick all about his hopes for this next term at VMI. Dawn had called him the Sunday after Griff proposed, and over the phone Brian had shouted one giant, "Whoopee!" She'd thankfully accepted his approval.

Grandma Topping, looking sprightly in a mauve print dress, hobbled over, using a cane. Dawn pecked her warm cheek, just beneath gold-rimmed glasses.

"Mrs. Topping, your coming all the way from Cornwall is special. You've made our wedding day one to remember for always."

"Call me Grandma," ordered the ninety-year-old woman, patting Dawn's hand with her brown speckled one. "I wouldn't have missed it, even though the flight was a little long. But I can nap anytime, and will only see my grandson get married once."

"I've been urging her to visit and it took my marriage for her to fly across the Atlantic for the first time in her life," Griff said, a smile fixed permanently beneath his groomed moustache.

Eva, wearing a silk blouse and skirt, pulled Dawn aside. "You and Griff are perfect for each other. I've thought so ever since he introduced you at my backyard party. So did my husband, Scott."

Dawn gazed upon Griff's radiant face as he hugged his brother, who'd just arrived. "Eva, I almost can't believe my marriage to Griff is real. There were times in the past year when I felt my life spinning out of control. Yet, here I am, enormously happy."

"It's sure wonderful for you both. Sounds like you have a few changes ahead."

"My house is for sale and I hope it won't take too long to sell in this market. How could I have known when I moved there what heartache it would cause Griff and Wally?"

"But all turned out well." Eva squeezed her hand. "Oh, Scott's waving me over."

She dashed off to find out what he wanted. Dawn savored the moment alone, joy lifting her heart. She'd come through the terrible times—Wally's arrest for a crime he didn't commit and Liberty's enslavement—with her faith, bruised and battered, but intact. And now her deepest desire—marrying Griff—was about to come true.

Wally tapped Dawn's shoulder. He grasped Liberty's fingers with his other hand and his black eyes brimmed with love.

"Miss Dawn, are you sure you do not mind sharing your wedding with us?"

"For all of us to be married together is truly a gift," she assured them. "Liberty, I only wish my mother were here to see you wearing her dress. You are a beautiful bride."

Liberty smiled shyly. Just then, Reverend Nash hurried up. Hannah quickly adjusted his crooked tie with deft fingers. Dawn and Griff joined hands, as did Wally and Liberty, and their friends surrounded them in a loose circle.

"We gather in the sight of God to join Griff and Dawn," Trenton said, grinning at them, "and to join Wally and Liberty in holy matrimony."

Dawn's heart soared as she and Griff exchanged vows, promising to love and care for each other the rest of their lives. He slid the diamond ring onto her finger and she pushed a knotted gold and silver ring on his. After pronouncing their vows in English, Liberty and Wally gazed at one another, tears shining in their eyes.

With no warning, Liberty switched to Dinka. Dawn understood a word or two. The happy look on Wally's face confirmed that, whatever she said, he found marvelous.

Pastor Rick asked the two couples to hold hands for a closing prayer.

"Almighty God, protect these precious souls who have come before you in a sacred ceremony pledging their lives. Thank you for your miraculous intervention, Father. Bless all their days in the name of Jesus, our gracious Redeemer."

Griff sealed his troth to Dawn with a kiss. After hugs all around as family and friends wished them well, Griff gently tugged Dawn over to the Jefferson Memorial.

"I can't wait to see you sign your name, Dawn Topping," he snickered.

"Mr. Topping," she said as she lifted her chin, "I already have a complaint against you."

"Ach, the honeymoon's over before it began."

"Exactly. You refuse to tell me where we're going on our honeymoon. You promised me Paris, once."

"Confession is good for the soul." Griff winked. "How about Khartoum? I've booked an early morning flight."

She didn't want to blister him with all their guests watching, so tossed him a keen look, replying with a firm, "No."

"Okay, I see your point. How about a casual drive along the Blue Ridge? You don't have much time off work, so we're staying at a secluded country inn, nestled beside a private lake. We'll swing by Walton's Mountain and tour the museum from your favorite TV show."

"Sounds like fun for me, but how about you?"

"I'm showing you Gettysburg and Antietam Battlefields. And for dessert, we're flying to Sudan."

Dawn caught her breath. Did he mean it?

"When?"

"As soon as Wally graduates from college. He's returning with Liberty to spend time with her uncle, and we're taking them. By then, Mabel will be settled in with Rick and Laurie Nebo."

"It's great how they've become like family."

"It's not surprising, though. Anyway," Griff said as he looped her arm tenderly in his. "Jeremy Bonds put Wally in touch with the hospital in Bor where Wally will assist them. He told me he wants to go to medical school and eventually serve his people there."

Dawn didn't know if she felt like laughing or weeping or both. With God redeeming Liberty, Dawn and Griff were ready to build a new life together. So were Wally and Liberty. What a miracle.

FACT VS. FICTION—A NOTE FROM THE AUTHORS

Our novels are "factional fiction" because sometimes we include real-life facts and events, or weave in events from cases we worked on in our justice system careers. *Redeeming Liberty* is the inspirational story based in part on our relationship with several young men and women who came to America as refugees after wandering thousands of miles in Sudan, Ethiopia, and Kenya to avoid civil war in Sudan.

Griff Topping's "son" Wally and Liberty are fictional characters. Wally is a composite of thousands of "Lost Boys from Sudan" and Liberty represents the lesser number of girls who fled the terrors of war. After working multiple jobs and attending college here in the U.S., some "Lost Children" have completed seminary training and are preparing to return to Sudan to minister to their people. In fact, some of these young men have saved enough money to buy cows for the bride price for women they will marry upon returning to Sudan.

Raids into Southern Sudan have resulted in thousands being taken as slaves. Humanitarian aid groups do raise funds and travel to the north to redeem slaves for about forty dollars each. Thousand have been redeemed using this method.

Iran has purchased from Russia S300 surface-to-air missiles, which are superior to defenses aboard all U.S. fighter aircraft except the F-22. As of the publishing of this novel, the U.S. government had cancelled contracts to produce more F-22s.

Christian theologians agree on a "sinner's prayer" similar to the one Griff Topping prayed. The brief prayer by one seeking a relationship with Holy God goes something like this: *Lord Jesus, I need You. I open the door of my life and receive You as my Savior and Lord. Thank you for forgiving my sins. Take control of my life. Make me the kind of person You want me to be.*

May God hear your prayers and bless your life and the reading of our books.

D & D

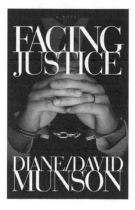

ISBN-13: 978-0982535509
352 pages, trade paper
Fiction / Mystery and Suspense
14.99

Facing Justice

First in the Justice series, Diane and David Munson draw on their true-life experiences in this suspense novel about Special Agent Eva Montanna, whose twin sister died at the Pentagon on 9/11. Eva dedicates her career to avenge her death while investigating Emile Jubayl, a member of Eva's church and CEO of Helpers International, who is accused of using his aid organization to funnel money to El Samoud, head of the Armed Revolutionary Cause, and successor to Al Qaeda. Family relationships are tested in this fast-paced, true-to-life legal thriller about the men and women who are racing to defuse the ticking time bomb of international terrorism.

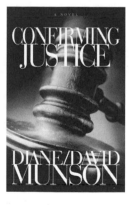

ISBN-13: 978-0982535516
352 pages, trade paper
Fiction / Mystery and Suspense
14.99

Confirming Justice

In *Confirming Justice*, all eyes are on Federal Judge Dwight Pendergast, secretly in line for nomination to the Supreme Court, who is presiding over a bribery case involving a cabinet secretary's son. When the key prosecution witness disappears, FBI agent Griff Topping risks everything to save the case while Pendergast's enemies seek to embroil the judge in a web of corruption and deceit. The whole world watches as events threaten the powerful position and those who covet it. Diane and David Munson masterfully create plot twists, legal intrigue and fast-paced suspense, in their realistic portrayal of what transpires behind the scenes at the center of power.

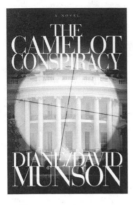

The Camelot Conspiracy

The Camelot Conspiracy rocks with a sinister plot even more menacing than the headlines. Former D.C. insiders Diane and David Munson feature a brash TV reporter, Kat Kowicki, who receives an ominous email that throws her into the high stakes conspiracy of John F. Kennedy's assassination. When Kat uncovers evidence Lee Harvey Oswald did not act alone, she turns for help to Federal Special Agents Eva Montanna and Griff Topping who uncover the chilling truth: A shadow government threatens to tear down the very foundations of the American justice system.

ISBN-13: 978-0982535523
352 pages, trade paper
Fiction / Mystery and Suspense
14.99

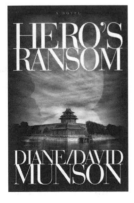

Hero's Ransom

CIA Agent Bo Rider (*The Camelot Conspiracy*) and Federal Agents Eva Montanna and Griff Topping (*Facing Justice, Confirming Justice, The Camelot Conspiracy*) return in *Hero's Ransom*, the Munsons' fourth family-friendly adventure. When archeologist Amber Worthing uncovers a two-thousand-year-old mummy and witnesses a secret rocket launch at a Chinese missile base, she is arrested for espionage. Her imprisonment sparks a custody battle between grandparents over her young son, Lucas. Caught between sinister world powers, Amber's faith is tested in ways she never dreamed possible. Danger escalates as Bo races to stop China's killer satellite from destroying America and, with Eva and Griff's help, to rescue Amber using an unexpected ransom.

ISBN-13: 978-0982535530
320 pages, trade paper
Fiction / Mystery and Suspense
14.99